DREAMLAND.
BITING BACK.

D1013536

DREAMLAND
DUTY ROSTER

LT. COLONEL TECUMSEH "DOG" BASTIAN

Once one of the country's elite fighter jocks, now Dog is whipping Dreamland into shape the only way he knows how—with blood, sweat, and tears—and proving that his bite is just as bad as his bark . . .

CAPTAIN BREANNA BASTIAN STOCKARD

Like father, like daughter. Breanna is brash, quick-witted, and one of the best test pilots at Dreamland. But she wasn't prepared for the biggest test of her life: a crash that grounded her husband in more ways than one . . .

MAJOR JEFFREY "ZEN" STOCKARD

A top fighter pilot until a runway crash at Dreamland left him paraplegic. Now, Zen is at the helm of the ambitious Flighthawk program, piloting the hypersonic remote-controlled aircraft from the seat of his wheelchair—and watching what's left of his marriage crash and burn . . .

MAJOR MACK "THE KNIFE" SMITH

A top gun with an attitude to match. Knife has a MiG kill in the Gulf War—and won't let anyone forget it. Though resentful that his campaign to head Dreamland stalled, Knife's the guy you want on your wing when the bogies start biting . . .

MAJOR NANCY CHESHIRE

A woman in a man's world, Cheshire has more than proven herself as the Megafortress's senior project officer. But when Dog comes to town, Cheshire must stake out her territory once again—or watch the Megafortress project go down in flames . . .

CAPTAIN DANNY FREAH

Freah made a name for himself by heading a daring rescue of a U-2 pilot in Iraq. Now, at the ripe old age of twenty-three, Freah's constantly under fire, as commander of the top-secret "Whiplash" rescue and support team—and Dog's right-hand man . . .

continued . . .

NIGHT OF THE HAWK
The exciting final flight of the "Old Dog"—a shattering mission into Lithuania, where the Soviets' past could launch a terrifying future . . .

"[A] gripping conclusion . . . masterful mix of high technology and *human* courage."
—W.E.B. Griffin

SKY MASTERS
The incredible story of America's newest B-2 bomber, engaged in a blistering battle of oil, honor, and global power . . .

"*Sky Masters* is a knockout."
—Clive Cussler

HAMMERHEADS
The U.S. government creates an all-new drug-defense agency, armed with the ultimate high-tech weaponry. The war against drugs will never be the same . . .

"Whiz-bang technology and muscular, damn-the-torpedoes strategy."
—*Kirkus Reviews*

DAY OF THE CHEETAH
The shattering story of a Soviet hijacking of America's most advanced fighter plane— and the greatest high-tech chase of all-time . . .

"Quite a ride . . . Terrific. Authentic and gripping."
—*The New York Times*

SILVER TOWER
A Soviet invasion of the Middle East sparks a grueling counter-attack from America's newest laser defense system . . .

"Riveting, action-packed . . . a fast-paced thriller that is impossible to put down."
—UPI

FLIGHT OF THE OLD DOG
Dale Brown's riveting debut novel. A battle-scarred bomber is renovated with modern hardware to fight the Soviets' devastating new technology . . .

"A superbly crafted adventure . . . Exciting."
—W.E.B. Griffin

DALE BROWN'S

DREAMLAND

piranha

Written by
Dale Brown and Jim DeFelice

JOVE BOOKS, NEW YORK

DALE BROWN'S DREAMLAND: PIRANHA

A Jove Book / published by arrangement with the authors

PRINTING HISTORY
Jove edition / August 2003

Copyright © 2003 by Dale Brown
Cover design by Steven Ferlauto

ISBN: 0-515-13581-X

A JOVE BOOK®
Jove Books are published by The Berkley Publishing Group,
a division of Penguin Group (USA) Inc.,
375 Hudson Street, New York, New York 10014.
JOVE and the "J" design
are trademarks belonging to Penguin Group (USA) Inc.

PRINTED IN THE UNITED STATES OF AMERICA

10 9 8 7 6 5 4 3 2 1

I
Piranha

THE OCEAN SAT BEFORE HIM LIKE AN AZURE MIRROR, its surface gleaming with a light haze of silky heat. His small sloop glided forward slowly, as if too much movement would disturb the tranquility. There was no wind for the sail and he had just cut the engine, content to drift into the calm of the open sea. A man could count on one hand the number of days he might encounter such perfect peace, and as Mark Stoner gripped the rail of his boat, the *Samsara*, a sensation of great ease came over him, a taste of the nirvana his Zen Buddhist teachers promised would come when he managed to shed worldly desires. The moment lingered around him, vanquishing time in its perfection. As the thick muscles of his neck and shoulders loosened, the rest of his body seemed to float upward, assimilating into the universe.

But all was not as it appeared.

A geyser broke three hundred yards off *Samsara*'s port bow, the water erupting as if a volcano had tossed a fireball into the sky. The blue water furled green and black as a thick spear crashed upwards, rising quickly from the ocean's surface. It stuttered momentarily, as if it were a

fish shocked at the sudden loss of water flowing over its
gills. Then it steadied and began picking up speed, rocketing north by northeast at something over five hundred
miles an hour.

"Shit," said Stoner aloud, though he was the only one
on the boat. "Holy shit."

Then he ran back to the cabin to make sure the recording devices were working.

Aboard EB-52, "Iowa," west of Hawaii
August 16, 1400 local time

LIEUTENANT COLONEL TECUMSEH "DOG" BASTIAN
slipped the throttle forward, continuing to pick up speed
as they approached the approximate location of Task
Force Nirvana. The Megafortress's forward airspeed
pushed up past five hundred knots as the big plane shot
no more than twenty feet over the ocean swells. Dog hated
flying over the ocean, especially at low altitude; he somehow couldn't shake the feeling that a massive tsunami
lurked just ahead, ready to rise up and engulf him. Even
at high altitude, he had a landlubber's paranoia about going down in the water. Something about the idea of struggling to inflate and then board a tiny rubber raft filled him
with irrational dread. It didn't help that any time he
thought about it, his mind supplied a posse of circling
sharks to supervise the operation.

"Should be able to see the test area buoys in sixty seconds," said Bastian's copilot, Chris Ferris. "We'll have
the feed off the Flighthawk."

"Roger that," replied the colonel. "Zen, how are we
looking?" he asked over the Dreamland com circuit.

"Ocean's clean," replied Major Jeff "Zen" Stockard.
Stockard was flying two U/MF-3's or Unmanned Fighters,
nicknamed Flighthawks, from Raven, the second EB-52
in the flight. The two robot planes, roughly the size of
Miata sports cars, acted as forward scouts for Bastian's
three-Megafortress flight. Two other U/MF's, flown by

Captain Kevin "Curly" Fentress in Galatica, were flying above the EB-52's as a combat air patrol. The Megafortresses were spread across the water at roughly half-mile intervals, flying what would have looked like an offset V from above. Though all shared the basic Megafortress chassis, each craft was outfitted differently.

Galatica, on the left wing, had a radar suite comparable to an E-3 AWACS. Since the powerful radar would alert their quarry, it was currently in passive mode—for all intents and purposes turned off.

Raven, at the right of the formation, featured a suite of electronic listening devices that would rival any Rivet Joint RC-135 spy plane. A myriad of antennas picked up both voice and telemetry transmission all across the radio spectrum; the computer gear stuffed into the rear compartments provided the onboard operator with real-time decoding of all but the most advanced encryptions. A second operator commanded a suite of gear similar to that found in Wild Weasel and Spark Vark aircraft; he could both detect and jam active radar units at roughly two hundred miles. The rotating dispenser in the bomb bay included four Tacit-Plus antiradiation missiles. Launched from just inside one hundred miles, they could either fly straight to a known radar site or orbit a suspect area until the radar activated. A thick, eighteen-inch section had been added to the weapons behind their warhead. This new section had been designed specifically for the sea mission. The gear inside the area allowed the missile to use its active radar on its final leg if the target switched its own radar off. Though relatively weak and short-ranged, it was hard to detect and also difficult to jam. Once fully operational, the missile promised to make aircraft essentially invulnerable to surface ships—at least until enough missiles were used so that an enemy could figure a way around them.

The payload aboard Iowa, Bastian's plane, was the reason the three Megafortresses were here.

Stuffed into Iowa's forward bomb bay were a half-dozen fiberglass and steel containers that looked like the old-fashioned milk containers once used to gather milk from cows on the copilot's family farm. A thick ring that sat about where the handles would have been contained just enough air to properly orient the container's "head" and counter the weight in the bottom, helping the buoy float a few meters below the surface of the water. Above the ring was a triangular web of thin wires that, once deployed, would extend precisely 13.4 meters. The wires were attached to a line-of-sight radio transmitter that generated a short-range signal across a wide range of bands. These signals could be received and processed by a specially modified version of the antennas and gear used by the Megafortresses while directing Flighthawks.

The bottom portion of the buoy contained three different arrays. The first was designed to broadcast audible signals that sounded like a cross between the clicks of a dolphin and the beeps of a telephone network. The second picked up similar audible transmissions in a very narrow range. The third transmitted and listened for long and extremely-low-frequency (or ELF) radio waves. These devices were actually relatively simple and while not inexpensive, were considered expendable—which was why the buoyant ring was equipped with small charges that would blow it off the buoy, sending them to the bottom of the ocean.

In essence, the milk cans were simply sophisticated transmitting stations for "Piranha," the larger device strapped to Iowa's belly. Piranha looked like an oversized torpedo with extra sets of fins on the front and rear. Once in the water, the conical cover on its nose fell off to reveal a cluster of oval and circular sensors that fed temperature, current, and optical information back to a small computer located in the body of the device. Between these sensors and the computer was a ball-shaped container that held a passive sonar; this too fed information to the computer, which in turn transmitted it, whole or in part, back to the buoy. The rear two thirds of Piranha contained its hydrogen-cell engine. Pellets made primarily of sodium hydride were fed into a reaction chamber where they mixed with salt water, creating hydrogen. This part of the engine was based on the hydrogen-powered, long-endurance, low-emission motor that powered an ultra-light UAV being tested at Dreamland. The sea application presented both major advantages—the availability of water allowed the compressed, pelletized fuel to be substituted for a gas system—and great challenges—the fact that it was salt water greatly complicated what was otherwise a fairly simple chemical process.

Rather than turning a propeller as it did in the ultra-light, Piranha's engine was used to heat and cool a series of alloy connectors that ran through the outer shell of the vessel. Similar to a keychain or a child's toy, the outer shell was connected in sections, allowing it to slip and slither from side to side. Using a technique first pioneered at Texas A&M, the expansion and contraction of the alloy strands moved the outer hull like a snake through water. The process was essentially wakeless, impossible to detect on the surface and almost impossible below. While there was still work to be done, the propulsion system was nearly as fast as it was quiet—Piranha could reach speeds close to fifty knots, with an endurance of just under eighteen hours at a more modest average pace of thirty-six knots.

Piranha had been developed by a joint Navy and Dreamland team; it represented the next generation of unmanned probes or UUVs (unmanned underwater vehicles) designed for launch from Seawolf submarines. Current UUVs used active forward- and side-looking sonars and had an overall range of approximately 120 nautical miles. They moved slowly, and could cover about fifty square miles of search area a day. They were fantastic weapons, intimately connected to the Seawolf and Virginia-class boats, and were perfectly suited for the inherently hazardous missions they had been designed for, such as searching for mines in littoral or shallow coastal waters.

Unlike those probes, Piranha could be operated from aircraft, thanks to the buoy system. Like the buoys, the probe itself was disposable, or would be in the future. For now, a low-power battery mode took it back to a specific GPS point and depth for recovery by submarine or surface ship up to 150 miles from rundown.

The data transmitted back to the buoys—and from them to a controlling airplane or vessel ship—was considerably greater than that possible in the current-generation UUVs, thanks largely to compression techniques that had been pioneered for the Flighthawks. These "rich" signals were difficult to decode and had a short range, which limited the ability of an enemy to detect and track them. In the stealth mode, which used only the intermittent audible mode to communicate, the operator received enough information to identify size, course, and bearing of an enemy target out to seventy-five miles, depending on the water conditions. In "full como," or communications mode, the signal fed a synthetic sonar system. This sonar was passive, and thus completely undetectable. It painted a three-dimensional sound picture on an operator's screen; the computer's ability to interpret and translate the sounds into pictures of the objects that created them not only meant that combat decisions could be made quickly, but the operators required considerably less training than traditional sonar experts. Just as the improvements in sensor gear and computers allowed the copilot on a Megafortress to perform the duties of several B-52 crew members, the synthetic sonar would allow a back-seater in a Navy Tomcat to handle Nirvana while taking negative G's.

In theory anyway.

Today, Colonel Bastian and his people were going to find out if the impressive results in static and shallow-water tests could be duplicated in the middle of the ocean, against some of the best people the Seventh Fleet could muster. The *Kitty Hawk,* steaming out toward Japan after a brief respite at Pearl, was the target.

If you're going to test a new weapon system, might as well go against the best, thought Dog.

"Piranha Buoy in ten seconds," said Ferris.

"Ten seconds," said Dog. "Piranha Team, you ready?" he added, speaking over the interphone circuit to the Piranha specialists, Lieutenant Commander Tommy Delaford and Ensign Gloria English. They were sitting downstairs in what ordinarily was the Flighthawk deck on the Dreamland Megafortresses.

"Ready," replied Delaford, the project leader for Piranha. Delaford worked directly for the Chief of Naval Operations, Warfare Division; his handpicked Navy team included people from N77 (the submarine warfare division), N775 (science and technology), and the Space and Naval Warfare Systems Command.

"I have Task Force Charlie," said Captain Derek Teijen, piloting Galatica. "Tapping in coordinates—they're a bit closer than they're supposed to be, Colonel. Lead ship is barely one hundred miles away. Have it ID'd as a DDG. Carrier is sending two F-14's toward us."

"Roger that," replied Dog. He'd expected the Navy to jump the gun; in a way, it was surprising that the task force had waited so long. The new Seventh Fleet commander, Admiral Jonathon "Tex" Woods, had boarded the aircraft carrier to personally oversee the tests. While his military record was sufficiently impressive for him to be known even in Air Force circles, he was said to carry a healthy grudge for the Air Force—and hated to be shown up in combined-forces exercises.

Which, in a way, this was.

"Zen, those Tomcats are yours if they get close enough," Dog said. "Curly, stand by for launch of Piranha system. Chris, open bay doors."

The Megafortress shook slightly as the large doors of the bomb bay cranked open. The sophisticated flight computer system compensated for the plane's altered aerodynamics so swiftly Dog hardly noticed. He pulled back gently on the stick, pushing the plane exactly onto the dotted red line the computer put on his screen.

"Three, two, one—" said Ferris.

There was a loud rumble from the rear as the buoy fell into the water.

"Device launch in twenty seconds," said Ferris.

"We concur," said Delaford. "Counting down."

Dog pitched the big plane's nose toward the waves; the optimum launch angle was a fairly steep forty-three degrees.

"Tomcats are looking for us," reported Ferris. "Ten seconds to launch—we need more angle, Colonel."

"Got it," said Bastian, hitting his mark. The weapons section of the flight computer that helped manage the Megafortress projected the launch countdown in his HUD. "Launch device," he said as the numbers drained to zero.

"We're off," said Ferris. "Over the river and through the woods, to Grandmother's house she goes."

Dog ignored Ferris's attempt at comic relief and began to pull the plane upward. He'd had to drop fairly low to the waves for the launch, and the vision of sharks circling his dinghy returned. As they climbed, the Piranha team went through the shakedown procedure, establishing contact with the probe. They immediately began steering it toward the target task force. Traveling at just over forty knots, Piranha had already identified the ships in the group for the operators. She dove to four hundred meters, completely undetected by the screening vessels and the two ASW helicopters, which had set up a picket of sonar buoys. The operators detected a submarine operating a towed array—probably the *Connecticut*, a killer in the ultramodern Seawolf class, though they were too far away for a real ID or even an accurate range. Meanwhile, the stealthy profiles of the Megafortresses made it possible for them to elude the Tomcats for close to half an hour, even though opening the bay doors to drop the buoy had alerted their airborne radar plane to their presence. Dog began to think they'd manage to complete the exercise scot-free.

His copilot brought him back to reality.

"Tomcats are on us, changing course," said Ferris. "At bearing—shit—they're launching weapons!" yelled Ferris, as usual far more agitated than the situation called for.

"Evasive maneuvers. Hang on. Zen, those Navy birds are yours."

"Engaging," replied Major Stockard. His voice, although relayed through a satellite system in orbit several kilometers above the Megafortress, sounded like he was in the next seat over.

Aboard EB-52, "Raven," west of Hawaii
August 16, 1440

THE F-14's HAD SLOWED TO FIRE THEIR LONG-RANGE Phoenix AIM-54's, but they were still closing on the Megafortresses at over five hundred miles an hour. It was clear from the way they were flying their radar hadn't picked up the Flighthawks, which were now heading into a bank of clouds just over the attackers' flight path. Raven began blanketing the air with a thick fog of countermeasures, confusing not just the Tomcats' radars, but the Grumman E-2 Hawkeye feeding them data more than a hundred miles to the north. The Navy interceptors were now limited to what their Mark-1 eyeballs could feed them; which meant they had to close to visual distance. In another sixty seconds, they'd be able to nail the Megafortresses with short-range heat-seekers or cannons.

Simulated, of course.

Zen didn't intend to let that happen. The U/MFs had several disadvantages fighting the sort of long-range combat the Tomcats preferred; they were equipped only with cannons and their mobility was limited by the need to stay within ten miles of their mother ship. But in a close-quarters knife-fight, they were hard to top. Hawk One broke from the cloud bank she was sitting in as close to the canopy of the lead F-14 as he could manage, flashing across its bow like a meteor shot from the heavens.

Or an air-to-air missile launched by an undetected fighter.

The slashing dive had the desired effect—the lead F-14 pilot jinked madly as he unleashed a parcel of flares and chaff, not quite sure what was coming at him. The decoys would have been more than enough to clear an enemy missile from his back—but Zen wasn't an enemy missile. He curled Hawk One upward, angling toward the dark shadow of the Navy aircraft. The Tomcat's variable-geometry wings had flipped outward to increase aerodynamic lift, a sure sign to Zen the plane was caught flat-footed. He pressed his attack into the Tomcat's belly even as its upgraded GE F110's spit red fire, the massive turbines winding to push the plane away.

Had this been a "real" encounter, the Navy pilot might have escaped—an ol' big block Pontiac Goat could beat a slammed Civic off the line any day of the week, and Zen at best could have gotten only a half-dozen shots into the belly of the accelerating beast—not nearly enough to bring her down, barring ridiculous luck. But the computers keeping score took the U/MF's chronically optimistic targeting gear at its word. According to its calculations, something over a hundred 20mm shells raked the Navy plane's fuselage and wings, turning it into a mass of flame and metal.

"Score one for the AF," said the event moderator blandly, circling above in a P-3 Orion. "Nirvana Tomcat One splashed."

Zen had already jumped into the cockpit of Hawk Two. He had the other F-14 on his left wing, cutting back toward its original course. C^3, the sophisticated control-and-tactical-assistance computer that helped fly the Flighthawks, suggested a high-speed attack at the rear quarter of the F-14. Zen recognized it immediately as a long shot; even with the computers keeping score, such an attack would have an extremely low kill-probability.

Deciding that was better than nothing, Zen told C^3 to implement the attack plan, then jumped back into Hawk

One, changing the view screens and control selections via a verbal command to the computer of "One" and "Two," then pulling around, trying to set up an ambush on the Tomcat. A call from Raven's radar operator changed his priorities.

"Bogies at one hundred miles—make that a four-group of F-18's, angels twenty."

"Hawk leader," acknowledged Zen. Even as the information about the bandits' course and speed was downloaded into his computer, Zen had decided he would pass off the Tomcat and concentrate on the Hornets.

"Yo, Curly—you see the Tomcat gunning for the flight?"

"On him," said the other pilot.

Aboard EB-52, "Galatica," west of Hawaii
August 16, 1449

UNLIKE ZEN, CAPTAIN KEVIN "CURLY" FENTRESS HAD never flown in real combat; nor was he a fully qualified jet pilot. He'd only racked up ten hours so far in Dreamland's T-38 jet trainer, every minute among the longest of his life. Curly had come into the Flighthawk program after helping develop early-model unmanned aircraft including the Predator and Global Hawk. While a very good remote pilot, he lacked both the experience and instincts of a first-rate combat jock.

But he was learning.

The Tomcat packed a pair of all-aspect heat-seekers. While Fentress had to be respectful of the missiles, they were considerably less dangerous than AMRAAMS. It was also to his advantage that the Tomcat was gunning for the Megafortresses and probably had only a vague notion of the Flighthawks' location. Fentress's two robot planes were running roughly half a mile apart, separated by five hundred feet at thirty-one thousand and 31,500 feet. His game plan was relatively straightforward—he'd engage the F-14 with one plane in a diving attack, and at the same time have the computer arc the second Flight-hawk so it could grab the Tomcat's tail for the kill. It was a classic strategy, basically the same double attack per-fected by Army Air Force Captains John Godfrey and Don Gentile against Me-109's during World War II—mi-nus the missiles, radars, and very high speeds the planes were using.

The Navy jock wasn't flying a Messerschmitt. Rather than engaging the small fighter as it dove in front of his F-14, he lit the burners and blew past both the U/MF and the approaching Megafortresses. Fentress gave a few blinks from the gun of Hawk Four, but the smaller engines couldn't drive the Hawk close enough to the muscular Navy plane to record a hit.

"We can take him with a Scorpion," said Captain Tom Dolan, the copilot in Raven.

"No, he's mine," said Fentress tightly. "You're going to need that Scorpion later."

He knew better than to try to run the F-14 down. Fen-tress held back as the Tomcat started tracking north, wait-ing for the plane to single out its quarry and start to close.

Though it had a much easier angle on Raven, it seemed to be picking out Iowa.

Coincidence? Or had he been briefed beyond the ac-cepted rules?

No matter. The F-14 began picking up steam as it pressed toward the Megafortress's tail. Fentress had a good intercept plotted—the target indicator on Hawk Three began blinking yellow, indicating he was almost in range. Just as it went red, the F-14 pilot belatedly spotted the robot and abruptly nosed downward. Fentress once more found he couldn't stay with the Tomcat, but ac-cording to C^3, did manage to put six shells into its wing.

The event moderator called it "light damage." Under the rules of the game, the F-14 should have broken off and gone home. But instead, the Navy jock lit the burners and jerked his nose up, pulling a good seven or eight Gs. He recovered from his evasive maneuver and bullied his plane toward a firing solution a bare five miles off the EB-52's vulnerable V-shaped tail.

Iowa
August 16, 1452

Dog shook his head as his copilot reported that the F-14 was getting ready to launch AIM-9's.

"Flares."

"Flares. Stinger ready," said Ferris. "They're cheating," he added bitterly. "Bastards."

"Fire when you have him," answered Dog calmly. "Don't hit the Flighthawk. Crew, hold on for evasive maneuvers."

Dog jerked the stick hard, pushing the big plane to the left, then back again, jinking the massive bomber as if she were an F-16. Adrenaline shot through his veins, and he realized he was laughing. It was times like this that reminded him why he'd joined the Air Force.

Galatica
August 16, 1454

Fentress slapped Hawk Four toward the F-14's tail as it closed on the Megafortress. The magnified screen showed the bomber's tail stinger tracking back and forth, obviously taking aim at the aggressor—its air mines were fatal at 2.5 miles, which was just inside the fatal range of the Sidewinders. Undoubtedly the Navy pilot wasn't concerned about "surviving" the conflict; he'd get close enough to launch the Sidewinders even if it meant he got slammed himself.

Fentress pushed his nose down, moving his pipper dead into the canopy of the Tomcat's two-man cockpit. He waited a second after the red bar flashed, remembering Zen's admonitions regarding the Flighthawk control computer's unyielding optimism.

Fentress then fired a long, concentrated blast that, had

this been the real thing, would have reamed a large hole in the Navy jet.

The next second, he got a warning that the EB-52 was getting ready to fire its Stinger. Fentress had to jerk off quickly to avoid getting nailed by an air mine. As he did, another warning buzz sounded—the F-14 had just launched its Sidewinders.

Iowa
August 16, 1500

"ONE SIMULATED MISSILE HIT ON ENGINE FOUR, ONE miss," reported Ferris, Dog's copilot. "He cheated big-time," added Ferris. "The Flighthawk nailed him."

"We'll send it to the Rules Committee," stated Dog. "Wing damage?"

"Negligible." Ferris began reading through the damage-control reports; the simulated hit wasn't bad enough to keep them from completing their mission. But unlike the Tomcat, Iowa's flight computer was plugged into the game and trimmed the plane as if it had really been hit—within reason, of course.

"How you doing down there, Delaford?" Dog asked the Navy Piranha specialist.

"Still no contact. We should be about thirty seconds away."

"Too bad it's not a torpedo," said Dog.

"Believe me, Colonel, if this were the real thing, the target would be dead meat as soon as we see it. Now under Option Four, carrying the double warhead—"

"We're a little busy," said Dog. "You just have fun down there."

"Oh, I will, sir. It's not every day you get to blow up an aircraft carrier."

Raven
August 16, 1500

WHILE THE HORNETS THUMBED THROUGH THEIR RADAR scans trying to sort out the Megafortresses behind all the electronic noise, Zen brought the Flighthawks around, positioning himself for a diving, rear-quarter attack. Once his attack had begun, Galatica would launch Scorpions at the remaining planes. Another wave of fighters was sure to follow; hopefully, they'd be ready to saddle up and get away by then.

The Hornets were in double two-ship elements separated by over a mile. Zen launched his attack against the plane at the point closest to the Megafortresses; it was on his left as he angled Hawk One downward, Hawk Two holding above. The attack went ridiculously well—he could see the white globe of the pilot's hard hat dead on in his pipper. Two squeezes on the trigger and the Hornet was gone; by the time the event observer called out the kill, Zen had jumped into Hawk Two and slashed another dozen slugs through the tail of the first plane's wingman. This Hornet tried to tuck into a turn, hoping to throw the Flighthawk in front of him. It would have been a fine strategy against nearly any other plane in the world, but the U/MF could turn far tighter than an F/A-18. Zen could have driven his plane right through the Hornet—a fact that made him more than a little annoyed when the referee failed to call the hit. He turned back and stuffed another long fusillade of simulated shells into the Hornet's twin tailpipe.

"Yo," he said.

"Cougar Two splashed," said the event moderator with obvious disappointment.

The delay kept Zen from pressing an attack on the second element. In his absence, the flight computer had managed to set Hawk One up for a reasonably good front-quarter run at one of the Hornets. Zen jumped in the cockpit, but then decided to let C^3 finish the job. The computer obliged by tossing two dozen slugs into the Hornet's belly and another dozen into the canopy area.

That left one plane. Zen had lost track of it in the swirl. He had to select the sitrep screen—a God's-eye view of the battle area piped into his console courtesy of Galatica's powerful radar. C^3 highlighted the Hornet, which was shooting back toward its carrier group.

Running away?

No, decoying him, as had the other F/A-18's.

"We have bogies south," said Galatica's radar operator tersely. "In range for Phoenix launch in thirty seconds."

"Clever bastards."

**Iowa
August 16, 1505**

COLONEL BASTIAN CHECKED THE OVERALL POSITION ON the sitrep screen in the lower left-hand corner of his dashboard. Piranha, still undetected, was now closing on the *Kitty Hawk*.

He wished he could say that Iowa was also still undetected.

"Eight Tomcats, positively ID'd," Ferris said. "They'll launch any second."

"Not a problem," said Dog.

"Got it," said Delaford.

"Yes!" added Ensign Gloria English. "We are within five miles of the aircraft carrier. Closing. We're not detected."

"If this were Option Four, they'd be dead. We could download to a sub now—boom, boom, boom!" sang Delaford.

"Tomcats are launching missiles!" shouted Ferris, so loud he could've been heard back on the tail.

"Evasive maneuvers," said Dog. "If we're in, we're going to break, Tom," he told Delaford. They were already at the extreme range for the Piranha system, and would have to close off contact to duck their attackers.

"Colonel, if we can hold contact for another sixty seconds, I can have Piranha pop up across from the *Kitty Hawk*'s bridge. Kind of put an exclamation mark on the demonstration," Delaford said.

"Missiles are tracking," said Ferris.

"Can we break them if we stay here?"

"Trying. The Tomcats are still coming. They want our blood."

"We'll hold our position as long as we can," Dog told Delaford. "Hopefully, we won't get nailed in the process."

"It'll be worth it," said Delaford, whose project had faced considerable skepticism from the Navy brass.

Dog told the other Megafortresses they could break off.

"Sixty seconds," said Delaford. "Right under the admiral's nose."

"Colonel, one of those Navy logs won't quit."

"Tinsel," said Dog, giving the order to dispense electronic chaff designed to confuse the radar guiding the long-range missile.

"Fifty seconds," said Delaford.

"Missile impact in twenty," warned Ferris.

"Hang on, everybody," said Dog. He pulled the Megafortress hard right, then back left, accelerating north briefly but then pulling back west, trying to stay within range of the Piranha buoy.

"Must've graduated from Annapolis," said Ferris. "That missile isn't quitting."

Dog decided to do something he'd never be able to manage in a stock B-52—he twisted the massive plane through an invert and accelerated directly toward the AIM-54. Against a "live" missile, the strategy would have been dubious, since the proximity fuse would have lit the warhead as he approached. But the gear in the nose used to record a hit was a few beats slower than the real McCoy, and Dog just managed to clear the AIM-54 before it "exploded."

"Shit, I lost the connection," said Delaford as Dog recovered.

"Can you get it back?"

"Trying." Dog could hear Delaford and English tapping furiously on the keyboards that helped them control the remote devices.

"We can drop another buoy," suggested English.

"We should," said Delaford. "But this one is closer. You know Colonel, I think they're trying to jam us."

"They have two jammers aloft," said Ferris.

"Give me a course," said Dog. "Delaford, is there any way to make Piranha spit in the admiral's eye when it comes to the surface?"

"Working on it, sir."

Galatica
August 16, 1507

UNLIKE THE EARLIER ATTACKER, THESE TOMCATS NOT only knew Fentress's Flighthawks were there, but considered them enough of a threat to target them with their Phoenix missiles. Ducking the long-range homers wasn't that difficult—Fentress had done so in about a dozen simulations over the past two weeks—but it did take time. It also cost him position—he lost control of Hawk Four as his Megafortress jinked out of the ECM-shortened communications range to avoid another volley of missiles. The onboard computer took over the robot, turning it toward the EB-52 in default return mode.

Fentress pulled Hawk Three higher, hoping to get into position to break the next wave of attack, which he expected to be a close-in dash to fire heat-seekers. But the Tomcats had something else in mind: AMRAAM-pluses, fired from just over forty miles away.

A red-hot wire snaked around his chest. Not one but two of the Scorpions locked on his plane. These were considerably more difficult to avoid. Even in simulations, he'd never gotten away from a pair. Galatica, with its performance significantly hampered by the revolving radar dome in its upper body, would have an even more difficult time, regardless of the countermeasures it spewed.

Fentress reconciled himself to his job; he'd do his best to obstruct the attack until he was nailed. He threw tinsel and jinked in the direction of the lead Tomcat, which was already homing in on Galatica. To catch the Navy pilot's attention, he winked his cannon. Though several miles out of range, the F-14 diverted just long enough to launch a pair of Scorpions at him.

Two more missiles that can't target Gal, Fentress thought to himself. He threw the Flighthawk downward, then cut diagonally, hoping against hope to beam the missiles.

He did. As he started to recover from the dive, he realized he had also gotten away from the missiles launched earlier. But all his jinking and jiving had left himself open to another F-14, which screamed toward him, gun blazing. Fentress started to turn, confident he could get out of the Tomcat's gunsights. His screen showed a simulated run of bullets trotting past the canopy—and then everything buzzed red and a large "2" filled the control screen. He'd been nailed by a Sidewinder he'd never seen.

Hawk Four, flown by the computer, had already suffered the same fate. Shorn of its defenders, the overmatched EB-52 found itself sandwiched between a pair of Navy Top Guns, whose M61's made confetti of the wings.

"We're hit," said the Megafortress pilot, Captain Teijen. "Performance degrading. Prepare for ejection."

"Aw, shit," grumbled the copilot.

Still, the EB-52 was a tough airframe. Teijen held her up, swooping left and right, and managed to take out one of the Navy fighters who apparently didn't believe the brief on the potency of the Stinger tail weapon. There was no shaking the Tomcat flight leader, however, who came in close and winked his cannon, then rubbed their noses in it a bit by putting his plane directly over Gal's tail.

"You be sunk," said the pilot with a laugh.

The computer and the event moderator concurred.

"Yeah?" said Teijen. "We'll see how loud you laugh when your carrier goes down."

Raven
August 16, 1507

ZEN'S FINGER STRAINED AGAINST THE SLIDER ON THE back of his combined stick-throttle. He had the engine nailed on the redline, trying to hustle the Flighthawks back to help Fentress fend off the rear-end attack. The Navy attackers had done an excellent job against the Dreamland planes, overcoming their technological disadvantage with shrewd tactics and kick-butt flying. They didn't call these guys Top Guns for nothing.

Not, of course, that Zen would admit that in mixed company—mixed company meaning anyone who showed an affinity for bell bottoms and pea coats. Naval aviators might have proven in combat they were every bit as good as Air Force jocks, but no red-blooded USAF zippersuit would say so—except under extreme duress.

And maybe not even then.

Zen calculated a good merge on two planes coming in on his left figuring to turn and then let the Tomcats' superior speed bring them into his gunsights. That worked fine for one of the planes, but the other wingman simply accelerated out of range as Zen brought Hawk Two to bear. He twisted off and gave the robot to the computer, telling it to target a new knot of Tomcats aiming for Iowa from the west. The computer handled it fairly well, but with four Scorpion AMRAAMs in the air, and its need to engage the enemy at close range, it was soon overmatched, taken down by a simulated explosion about fifty feet off its wingtip.

In the meantime, two Tomcats closed on Iowa for Sidewinder shots. As Zen tried to dive on them, his seat spun wildly, moving in the opposite direction—Raven's pilot, Major Alou, was jerking madly to avoid a fresh missile attack. The movements disoriented Zen, who had an image in his screen more than four miles away. He had to break off his attack after pumping a dozen shells at the F-14, doing some damage but not enough to splash it.

The air was thick with flares, electronic fuzz, and dummy weapons. Zen rolled around and found himself approaching Raven. Making the best of the situation, he slid Hawk One into a gradual turn, figuring to try and catch the planes that were closing on his mother ship. At the same time, he got a warning tone from the computer that his fuel stores were getting low.

The Navy fliers stayed just out of reach of Raven's Stinger as they kicked off their missiles. All but one of the Sidewinders missed their mark; the one that did explode caused "fifty-percent damage" to the right wing control surfaces and some minor damage to the power plants. Enough, claimed the moderator, to rule the Megafortress down.

"Down?" said Alou. "Down? No way."

The other crew members' reactions were considerably less polite. Zen had one of the Tomcats fat in his pipper—he laid on the trigger, then whipped across the air like a stone skipped on a pond to nail the second.

Except that, under the engagement rules, he was dead once the Megafortress was.

The Tomcat jocks were laughing. Zen had considerable trouble restraining himself from riding Hawk One over their canopies.

"Navy referees," muttered Alou.

Iowa
August 16, 1507

DOG COULD FEEL A CURTAIN OF SWEAT DESCENDING down the front of his undershirt, as if he were coming toward the kick lap of a great workout. And in a way, he was—jinking and jiving as a pair of Tomcats, now out of missiles, tried to get close enough to use their guns. He fended them left and right, riding up and down, all the while waiting for Delaford to tell him when they could launch the buoy. They'd temporarily lost contact with Piranha, though its operator was confident it was close to the aircraft carrier.

"We're going to lose speed as soon as we open the bay doors," said Chris Ferris. The copilot had a habit of worrying out loud. In Dog's opinion, not a particularly endearing trait.

"I'm counting on it," replied the colonel, flashing left as one of the Tomcats began firing again. The Navy planes couldn't position themselves effectively because of the air mines spitting out from the back of the plane, but that advantage would soon be lost—the computer warned they were below a hundred rounds.

Worse, another quartet of fighters were coming from the north.

"Okay," said Delaford.

"Chris, turn off the Stinger as if we've run out of shells," Dog told his copilot. "Then open the bay doors and launch. Everybody hang tough," added Dog. "This will feel like we've hit a brick wall."

The Tomcats, seeing the Stinger had stopped firing midburst, closed in tentatively, expecting a trick. Meanwhile, Ferris gave Dog a five count. When he reached one, the colonel did everything but throw the plane into reverse—and he might have tried that had he thought of it. The Megafortress dropped literally straight down in the sky, an elevator whose control cables had suddenly snapped.

The Tomcats shot overhead.

"Piranha Buoy Two launched," reported Ferris, immediately closing up the doors to clear the Megafortress's sleek belly. Dog banked so close to the water, its right wingtip might have grazed a dolphin.

"They're coming back, and they're mad," said Ferris. "Whipping around—rear-quarter shot." He started laughing. "Suckers—Stinger on and firing."

Their anger and fatigue took its toll. One of the Navy

fliers was mauled; the other backed off—then declared a fuel-emergency and broke off.

"Four bandits still coming at us. In AMRAAM range," warned Ferris.

"How we doing down there, Delaford?" asked Dog, cutting back north to stay near the buoy, though this meant closing the gap on the approaching F-14's.

"Got it! Ten seconds to surface!"

Dog jinked back, hit chaff as one of the Tomcats launched from long range.

"Where did they get the Scorpion missile codes?" asked Ferris. "They're only supposed to use operational missiles."

"Take them over," said Dog.

"Huh?"

"Override their guidance. Use our circuits."

"I don't know if I can, Colonel. And even if I could, that would be cheating."

"Weren't you just complaining about them using missiles that aren't in their armament lockers?" inquired Dog. "Issue the universal self-destruct. See what happens."

The Scorpion—still some months from production—had been designed at Dreamland. The test missiles contained what the programmers called off-line paragraphs—telemetry code useful for testing but not intended for the final product. Among them were instructions allowing the testbed aircraft to override onboard guidance and detonate the missiles—useful in case one veered off course. Dog wasn't sure the code had been included in the simulated version, but it was worth a try.

Ferris dutifully hit the commands, and got an extra bonus—not only did the two dummies "explode," but so did the four simulated ones that hadn't been launched yet.

Fortunately for the Naval aviators carrying them, the self-destruct merely killed the programming.

Ferris laughed so hard and loud he drowned out Delaford's report that they were spitting at the carrier's bridge.

"Almost," said Delaford. "We're twelve feet off their starboard side, bobbing up and down. I hope some of those sailors have cameras."

"Gentlemen, and Miss English, job well done," said Dog, who, despite his best effort to sound professional, was chuckling a bit as well. "Let's go home."

South China Sea
August 17, 1997, 1900 local (August 17, 0100 Hawaii)

STONER STEADIED HIMSELF AGAINST THE RAIL OF HIS boat as he drifted toward the piece of torn gray fabric. A bulky piece of flotsam bobbed a few yards beyond it; Stoner suspected it was the tip of something large enough to damage his boat. But he wanted the fabric, and decided the approach was worth the risk. There were words on the cloth, or at least something that looked like words.

He reached out with his long pole, sticking it in the middle of the material. Like a jellyfish prodded from above, it slipped downward and drifted away. Stoner reached again, nearly losing his balance before grabbing the cloth.

He pulled the stick up quickly. The characters were definitely Chinese, though he couldn't make them out. He'd have to use his digital camera to take a picture, then transmit the image back.

Enough to go on.

Stoner looked back at the water. The flotsam was only a few feet away. It was smaller than he thought, and not connected to anything. Even so, he put his pole out, trying to fend it off.

It rolled upward, revealing a face and torso. There were no legs, and only half-stumps where the arms had been.

In his career, Stoner had seen many unpretty things. He went back over the rail and reached down to a fabric-covered pocket at the top of the hull. Opening the compartment, he took out his camera, examining it quickly to make sure the settings were correct before slipping the thick strap over his neck. He went back and photographed the dead man's face, recording it in case it might prove useful in the future. Then he put the long stick in the body's chest and pushed it away, leaving it for the sharks.

Back at the helm, Stoner took the engines out of neutral, and steered the boat eastward. As he started below, he heard the drone of an aircraft in the distance.

The transmission would have to wait. He continued forward past the paneled lounge area to the compartment at the bow. He threw the camera and media card inside, then stepped back and slammed the hatch shut. He struggled with the three long bolts at either side of the wall until his fingers were raw, finally taking off his sneaker to push at the end of the last bolt. By then, the aircraft was overhead.

He waited until he heard it pass, then pushed his head up to look. He knew, of course, that it would be a Chinese patrol plane, though there was always hope he'd be wrong.

He wasn't. And now a pair of delta-shaped blurs approached from the west—Shenyang F-811Ms, long-distance attack jets.

While he knew enough about the Chinese military to identify the planes' units and air bases if he cared to, Stoner was much too busy to do so. With an immense leap, he threw himself overboard and into the water, just as the aircraft began firing.

It took approximately ten minutes for *Samsara* to sink. It would have taken considerably longer had Stoner not begun flooding it by removing the bolts. He spent much of the time well below the surface of the water; what he lacked in negative buoyancy, he more than made up for in motivation.

When the aircraft were gone, Stoner bobbed to the surface, floating with as little effort as possible. It was at least an hour before sunset; if he were to survive the night he had to conserve his energy. And of course he knew he would survive. It was his job. It was what he always did.

Samsara's life raft had been shot to pieces by the attack. Nothing else came off the boat after it went down—a matter of design, not accident. And so it was inevitable that Stoner resorted to the wreckage of the Chinese freighter—or what he strongly suspected was a Chinese freighter—to stay afloat. It was inevitable that the half-man he had poked before would float toward him. Stoner wrapped his arm's around the torso without emotion. He kicked slowly, just enough to stay afloat and awake. Despite the warm day, the water cramped his muscles with its cold, and made his teeth chatter.

The sun turned the sky pink as it set. Stoner waited in the water with his dead companion. Night crept up with an immense, bright moon. In the distance, he thought he saw the shadow of a shark's fin. The wreckage of the freighter was drifting closer; paper with Chinese characters drifted near his nose. He moved to grab it, but found his arms frozen in place. He let go of the man's head and sunk down in the water, trying to shake his limbs back to flexibility. When he reached the surface, the paper was gone and so was the head.

For the next hour he treaded slowly, faceup in the brine, cold and salt sandpapering his lips and nose. Then, suddenly, the water began to churn. He felt it coming for him now, the shark, drawn by his fatigue like a radio beacon in the night. It broke water fifty yards to his right, a massive thing of blackness.

Stoner waited. He had no weapon.

There was a sound behind him, an eerie cry not unlike the death rattle of a man at the end.

"Here!" Stoner yelled. "Here!"

A searchlight played across the surface of the water. Two SEALs in diving gear paddled a rubber boat toward him.

"Here!" he yelled again.

"Mr. Stoner?" said one of the men.

"You're not expecting someone else, I hope," said Stoner as the raft crept up. His muscles were so stiff he had to be helped into the boat. But he managed to climb onto the deck of the waiting submarine and go below without further assistance.

"Stoner, I'm Captain Waldum," said the skipper. "Glad we found you. Your signal's getting weak."

"Yeah," said Stoner. "Let's retrieve the bow pod from my boat and get back. About a dozen people are going to have their underwear in knots about now."

II
An excellent coffin

CAPTAIN BREANNA STOCKARD SHIFTED HER LEFT LEG for the five hundredth time since getting into the cockpit, trying to make herself comfortable. Her seat, which canted back at a twenty-degree angle, had ostensibly been form-fitted to her anatomy and designed for maximum comfort on a long mission. Its inventor joked it would be so comfortable the pilot would be in constant danger of falling asleep; Breanna thought that a remote possibility at best. While the chair adjusted in several dimensions, it was impossible to find a setting that didn't put a kink in her back—or somewhere else.

Captain Stockard was surrounded by four large panels, one in front, one overhead, and one on each side. Constructed of a plasma "film," each panel provided, at her command, a full instrument suite, optical views from all four compass points, or synthesized views composed from radar or infrared sensors. The stick at the side of her seat and the pedals at her feet did not actually move, instead sensing the pressure exerted on them and translating it as commands to the flight computer that took care of the actual details involved in trimming the large craft. The throttle was the closest to a "normal" airplane control in the cockpit—assuming, of course, such a control could select a standard turbofan, a scramjet, and a restartable rocket motor or some combination of all three depending on the flight regime. All of the controls could be discarded if Breanna preferred; the computer stood ready to translate her words into commands as quickly as she could utter them into the small microphone at the end of her headset.

That, Breanna felt, was a big part of the problem. The aircraft had been designed to be flown entirely by the computer; the cockpit was really just an afterthought, which explained why it was so stinking uncomfortable. Had it actually been in the plane, however, it would have been even worse. There, it would have had to squeeze into a thick, double-layer ceramic-titanium airfoil whose sinewy, weblike skin slid back from a needle nose into a shape described by its designers as an "aerodynamic triangle." Its midsection looked something like a stretched B-1 bomber with engine inlets top and bottom, and wings capable of canting about ten degrees up and down as well as swinging out and in. It had a shallow tailfin on both the top and bottom of the fuselage. In order to keep the tailfin clear when landing or taking off, it sat on a set of landing gear that undoubtedly broke all previous records for height. Even so, when the aircraft was fully loaded, less than eighteen inches separated the wingtips from the runway, making it necessary to physically sweep the runway clean before take off so any mishap might be avoided.

This tedious process added considerably to the pilot's consternation as she waited for clearance to begin her test flight.

Known as the UMB—Unmanned Bomber Platform—or B-5, the plane was among Dreamland's most ambitious projects to date. Once fully operational, it would fly at somewhere over six times the speed of sound, yet have the turning radius at Mach 3 of an F/A-18 just pushing five hundred knots. The UMB was designed to fly in near-earth orbit for extended deployments; there it could serve as an observation platform and launch-point for a suite of smart weapons still under study. Its engines, which were powered by hydrogen fuel, were not yet ready for such lofty flights, though today's test would take it to a very respectable 200,000 feet. Similarly, the configurable leading and trailing portions of the wings—inflated by pressurized hydrogen to microcontrol the airfoil—had not yet replaced the more conventional leading- and trailing-edge control surfaces, thus limiting its maneuverability to a more conventional range.

Assuming taking ten Gs could be called conventional.

"Ground is clear. How are we looking, Captain?" asked Sam Fichera, who led the team developing the controls and was today's mission boss.

"I think we're ready to rock," Bree answered.

"Ready for an engine start. Everything by the book."

"Ready when you are." Breanna looked at the left corner of her front screen, where the engine data had been preprogrammed to appear. "Computer. Takeoff engine start. Proceed."

"Computer. Takeoff engine start," acknowledged the electronic copilot.

The two GE-built turbofans used for takeoff and low-speed flight regimes whipped to life. A detailed checklist appeared at the right side of Breanna's screen, laid over the endless vista of the cleared runway and the surrounding dry lake beds that encircled Dreamland. Breanna and the computer moved through the long checklist slowly, making sure everything was good to go. The computer could facilitate quick takeoffs by color-coding the items—those it knew were "in the green" or good to go were shown in green letters, problems were in red. No caution (yellow) was permitted on takeoff; the items would be marked red instead, and the takeoff held until the trouble was corrected.

With the systems checked and rechecked, everything from fuel flow to air temperature recorded, parsed, and fretted over, Breanna glanced at the static camera from the runway to make sure her path was clean. Cleared, she loosened the brakes and took a long, slow breath.

And then she was off. The B-5's engines cycled up to takeoff power and she trundled down the runway, speed building slowly. Relatively heavy for its airfoil even with the wings horizontal, the plane needed more distance than a B-52 to get airborne. That would change with the new wings. Even then, the rocket engine would probably be selected for a brief burn to make the takeoff easier, and more comfortable for Breanna.

Though she'd flown it several times now, Breanna's feel for the UMB remained distorted and distant. As her indicated speed climbed above one hundred knots, the plane began to lift on its own. She held the stick a second too long, but came off the ground smoothly. The slight hitch bothered her; she was still slightly disoriented as her altitude began to climb.

Maybe if they added some sound feedback, she thought, making a mental note to bring it up at the post-flight briefing.

Captain Breanna Stockard had headed the UMB project for three weeks now. It was supposed to be a permanent job; the previous UMB director had been posted to the Pentagon months before. But Breanna had stubbornly insisted the duty be officially "temporary," so she could decide if she really wanted the assignment.

Of course she did—it was potentially the most important job in the Air Force. Even if the UMB never won approval as the follow-on to the B-2, the technology it tested would undoubtedly serve the military for the next two or three decades. But it meant leaving the Megafortress, and flying, behind.

Breanna's husband, Jeff "Zen" Stockard, had flown the aircraft on its first two flights. His overall take on flying the plane could be summed up in one word: "boring." He complained it was even more reliant on its native or on-board computer than the Flighthawks, and probably didn't

need a real pilot at all. Unlike the U/MFs, which needed
to be fairly close to their command plane, the UMB was
designed to be flown entirely from the ground at vast dis-
tances using hooks in the Dreamland secure satellite system.

Boring? Maybe if you were a pilot used to taking six
or seven Gs with your morning donut.

"Dreamland B-5 UMB is airborne and passing marker
three-seven," reported Breanna as they reached the airspace for the morning tests. "We have green indicators all
around. I did ask for salsa music in the background, however, and it's not coming through."

"Preempted by baseball," shot back Lieutenant Art
McCourt, who was flying chase in an old but reliable
F-5. "I'll give you play-by-play if you want, Major. My
Dodgers are ahead."

It was far too early in the day for a game, or McCourt
might *really* be listening to baseball; the test pilot had a
reputation for using his engineering prowess in uncon-
ventional ways. Supposedly, he had found a way to pres-
surize a Mr. Coffee and enjoyed hot, zero-gravity coffee
breaks.

The UMB continued to climb at a leisurely pace, reaching ten thousand feet as the structural-integrity tests began. Breanna pushed her stick left and let the plane turn
into a fairly steep bank. Small sensors similar to the devices used to measure earthquakes recorded the effect of
the turn on the wings and superstructure; one of the
ground people monitoring the numbers gave an approving
whistle as she came through the turn.

"Looking for a date, Jacky?" Bree shot back.

"Sorry, ma'am. Structure is looking very solid."

"That's what I figured you meant," she said, continuing
through the set of turns. Test complete, and passed, she
began spiraling upwards, looking at the ground through
the belly cam as she climbed.

Dreamland sprawled over a defunct lake in the desert
wilderness north of Las Vegas. Its existence was so secret

it appeared on no list of facilities or bases. No one was ever assigned here; instead, they were given "cover" jobs or assignments, usually though not always at Edwards Air Force Base.

Until recently the heart of the Air Force High Technology Aerospace Weapons Center, Dreamland had evolved a great deal over the past two years, more rapidly in the past few months. The command had lost some of its best military people and projects to the newly designated Brad Elliott Air Force Base, named in honor of the former general who had lost his life in the China conflict only a few months before. Nearby at Groom Lake, Elliott AFB was a high-profile and prestigious command, which, though structured along traditional lines, was to be tasked primarily with introducing new weapons into the Air Force mainstream. Meanwhile, Dreamland and its high-tech facilities would remain a cutting edge facility with a much more experimental bent—as well as its own combat team named "Whiplash," which operated directly at the President's command. In charge of Dreamland was a scrappy, forty-something lieutenant colonel who everyone outside of Dreamland knew was in way over his head—and everyone inside of Dreamland knew was about as can-do as any ten other officers in the service combined.

Breanna was just slightly prejudiced in favor of Dreamland's director. She happened to be his daughter.

Her left leg began to cramp, and then spasmed. Trying to loosen the cramp, she knocked her knee against the lower edge of the front panel.

"Perfect coffin," she grumbled.

Unlike everything else connected with the plane, the computer could not adjust the seat; it had to be fiddled with manually, a procedure that had at least as high a chance of making things worse as better.

Breanna tried flexing her leg as she rose toward twenty thousand feet, stifling a curse as the muscles in her other leg started feeling sympathy pains. She banked again, then asked the computer for the environmental panel, deciding she felt cold.

The computer claimed the temperature in her coffin was a balmy seventy-two.

"My ass," she told it.

"Captain?" said Fichera.

"Relax, Sam. I'm getting all sorts of leg cramps, that's all."

"Too hot in there?" asked Fichera.

"Negative. I doubt it's really seventy-two, by the way. All right, I should be at angels twenty in one more turn."

"We copy that," answered the engineer.

Both the climb and the cramps continued in silence. Though much larger at about 170 feet in length, the aircraft handled a lot like an F-111 to about Mach 1.5, if the F-111 was being flown by remote control.

"You're looking really great," said Fichera as the UMB hit into the orbit over Glass Mountain just a nudge under 25,000 feet.

"Looks good from here," said McCourt from the chase plane. He was flying off her right wing, separated by about a half mile in the open sky.

"All right. Telemetry test ready?" Bree asked.

"Roger that," said Fichera.

"Computer, begin scheduled test B-5-6A: photographic data flow. Smile for the cameras, Dreamland."

"Begin scheduled test B-5-6A," acknowledged the computer.

A panel in the fuselage slid open, permitting a camera array from a mini-KH satellite to see the earth. The camera sent a rapid succession of detailed photos back to Dreamland.

"Hey, Major, this stuff going to show up in the *Sports Illustrated* swimsuit edition?" asked McCourt.

"Hell, Art, we're going straight to *Playgirl*. The photos I took of you in the shower last week with the spy cam cinched it."

"I thought I felt a draft."

"Data flow under way," said Breanna, her tone once again serious. The test was a fairly simple affair, sending back high-resolution optical photos to the ground. As the system was essentially the same used in Dreamland's mini-KH-12 tactical satellites, it should pass without much difficulty.

Which it did. Breanna continued a long, lazy orbit around the Dreamland test ranges, slowly building her altitude until she was at 35,000 feet. The next series of tests were the meat of the day's mission.

"Ready to test engine five," Breanna told her team. Engine five was the restartable rocket motor.

"Roger that," said Fichera. "We're hot to start."

"Three-second burn programmed," she said, reading off the program screen. "Counting down."

There was a slight hitch as the rocket ignited; the plane's nose stuttered downward for a microsecond before the massive increase in thrust translated into upward momentum. This was a by-product of a glitch in the trimming program, which the team was still trying to fine-tune. Otherwise, the burn and plane worked perfectly; Breanna rode the B-5 up through fifty thousand feet. A soft tone in her helmet accompanied the visual cue that they had reached their intended altitude; she leveled off, then started a gentle bank. At the end of a complete circuit she nosed down, gathering momentum. As the plane hit Mach 2, she prepared for the next test sequence.

"Ready to test engines three and four," she said, referring to the scramjets. "Counting down."

The hydrogen-fueled scramjets lit as the plane touched Mach 2.3. By the end of the test sequence, Breanna was at Mach 3.4 and had climbed through 85,000 feet. She continued to climb, powered now only by the scramjets.

"Ready for engine five," she told her team, leveling off for the next test sequence.

"Good. Temp in four slightly high."

"Acknowledged." She took a quick glance at the screen, making sure the temp was still in the green—it was by about five degrees—then told the computer to light the rocket motor.

"Looking good," she said as the speed built quickly.

"Aye, Captain," Fichera said, giving his best impression of Scotty, the engineering officer on the Starship *Enterprise*, "the dilithium crystals are shining bright."

"Har-har," said Breanna, whose leg began acting up again.

They touched Mach 5, but then began to slow inexplicably.

"Problem?" asked Fichera.

"Not sure," said Breanna. The thrust on all three engines was steady, yet according to the instruments she was slowing.

Now if she'd been in the plane, she would have known exactly what the problem was. She'd've felt it.

Really? Could you feel the difference at eighty-something-thousand feet and four or five times the speed of sound, with things rushing by? Or would you have to rely on the instruments anyway? How far would you be removed from the actual sensation of flight, lying in a specially canted seat wrapped in a special high-G suit?

Breanna pushed forward. Unencumbered by restraints or even a simple seat belt, she put her face nearly on the large glass panel as she had the computer run her through the vital signs on all the power plants. The speed had leveled off at Mach 4.3. They had reached the end of test sequence.

"Computer, cut engine five," she said, referring to the hydro.

"Cut engine five."

"I feel like I should be punching buttons at least," added Bree.

"Repeat command," said the computer.

"I thought it wasn't supposed to try to interpret anything without the word 'computer' in front of it," Bree barked to Fichera.

"The computer expects you to either follow the original

flight plan called for, or prepare a new course. Since you're doing neither, it is confused."

The snotty voice belonged to Ray Rubeo, Dreamland's head scientist.

"Hey, Ray," she retorted, "I didn't realize you were sitting in."

"I wasn't," said Rubeo.

"We can adjust that if it's annoying," said Fichera. "Can we proceed with the rest of the tests?"

"Roger that," said Breanna, belatedly nosing the plane onto the planned course for a second battery of telemetry downloads.

They worked through the rest of the morning's agenda without incident. Running ahead of schedule, Breanna suggested a few touch-and-go's to practice landing technique.

"If that's okay with you, Ray," she added.

"Dr. Rubeo has left," said Fichera.

"Yeah, I thought you guys sounded more relaxed."

"You shouldn't have called him Ray," said Fichera. "He looked like he swallowed a lemon."

"Oh, if I really wanted to tick him off I'd've called him Doctor Ray," said Breanna.

There was no arguing Rubeo was a genius, though his social skills needed considerable work. He was especially prickly concerning the B-5 project, not only because he had personally done much of the work on the computers, but because it had been conceived as an entirely computer-flown aircraft. Rubeo's contention that its tests be controlled by scientists using simple verbal commands had been overruled by Colonel Bastian.

"Stand by, Dreamland B-5," said the airfield flight controller as Bree lined up for her first approach. "We have a VIP arrival via Runway One."

Ordinarily, non-Dreamland aircraft, even those belonging to VIPs, did not use Dreamland's runways; they came into Edwards and their passengers were ferried via a special helicopter. Breanna selected her video feed to watch as the aircraft, an unmarked 757, came in through restricted airspace. It banked over Taj—the low-slung administrative building, most of which was buried several stories below ground—and the rest of the main area of the base, as if to give its passengers a good view of Dreamland. Even though it had permission to land, two Razor antiaircraft lasers turned their directors on the Boeing, while an older Hawk missile battery leveled its missiles for delivery. If the plane deviated even a few yards from its permitted flight plan, it would be incinerated and then blown up for good measure.

"Whose jalopy?" asked McCourt from the chase plane.

"Got me," said Bree, taking a circuit before starting her touch-and-go's.

Wrestling her foot cramp into submission was more difficult than the practice landings. After three go-arounds, she was ready for the real thing.

"You're going to have to hold off your landing," said the controller again. "VIP jet taking off from Runway One in thirty seconds."

"Must've tasted the food," quipped McCourt.

Dreamland "Taj" building
1000

COLONEL BASTIAN PUT HIS SIGNATURE ON THE LAST PAPER in his chief master sergeant's hand, rolling out the last letters of his name with a noticeable flourish as the elevator stopped at the ground level.

"Admiral'll be wanting lunch," said Terrence "Ax" Gibbs. "Should I call over to the Starlight Room?"

"Rustle up a peanut butter and jelly sandwich," said Dog as the doors opened.

"More flies are trapped with honey than vinegar. Goes triple with four-boat admirals."

"Four-boat?"

"Stars, braids, whatever the sailors call those things on his shoulders that make him think he's important."

Ax followed Dog into the lobby of the Taj. A member of Danny Freah's security team stood by the door—Technical Sergeant Perse Talcom, better known as Powder, waiting to drive the colonel over to Hangar D, where the Piranha system was headquartered.

"We'll see about lunch," Dog told Ax. "Anything else?"

"No, sir. I hear the salmon's especially good down in the Red Room."

"What salmon?"

"Flown in yesterday," said Ax. "Allen's favorite. I'll make sure they put some aside."

There was no way—absolutely no way—the fish had been special-ordered for Admiral Allen, since his arrival hadn't been expected.

Then again . . .

"Hangar D," Dog told Powder, walking over to the black SUV near the entrance.

"Yes, sir." Powder slammed the Jimmy into gear and left considerable rubber on the pavement.

"I'd like to get there in one piece," Dog said, grabbing at the door to keep his balance.

"Good one, sir." Powder nearly tipped the truck over as he veered onto the access ramp that led to the hangar area. He zipped past a Hummer and a fuel truck, then beelined for the hangar area. The security detail posted in front of Hangar D snapped to attention as they approached—then took up safer positions behind a set of obstructions.

Powder whipped the Jimmy around in a tight three-pointer near the head of the detail, rolling his window down as he spun to a stop.

"Hey, Nursy, got the Big Guy aboard. Looking for the admiral."

Sergeant Lee "Nurse" Liu, another Whiplash team member, blinked several times, then saluted Dog.

"Carry on," managed Dog as he got out of the vehicle and went into the building. The upper floor housed two heavily modified C-17 transports designated as MC-17/Ws, intended as prototypes for a new hostile-area infiltrate/exfiltrate aircraft, roughly along the lines of the venerable and battle-proven MC-130H Combat Talon II. One of the MC-17's had already seen action during Whiplash's last deployment. The techies were now working on a number of improvements, including an as-yet-untested version of the Fulton Surface-to-Air Recovery (STAR) system. Dog headed to the ramp leading to the first level down. Wide enough for a tractor-trailer, the cement ramp led to a secure elevator, which opened only after scanning his retinas. Once you were inside, the elevator could be operated only by voice, and then only if the computer decided the vocal pattern matched its records.

"Fourth," said Dog as the doors snapped closed. He folded his arms and waited.

And waited.

"Fourth," he repeated clearly.

Still nothing.

"God damn it—"

Either finally recognizing the voice or the threat, the elevator snapped into action. Dog stepped off impatiently at his destination, and was immediately greeted by a familiar if not exactly affectionate hiss.

"Colonel, why is the admiral here and why weren't we notified he was coming?" The thin lips of the senior scientist at Dreamland, Ray Rubeo, pursed into a funnel. "These scientists aren't military people. They get nervous. It's like dealing with a hotel full of prima donnas. There'll be a run on Prozac tomorrow. We'll be three weeks getting back on schedule. And Piranha is hardly the most important project here. Frankly, if it were up to me, it would be turned back to Naval Weapons, which is not only competent but is used to dealing with oversized Pentagon egos."

"I wasn't told either," said Dog, continuing toward the project area. "And I believe Admiral Allen's headquarters are in Hawaii."

Dog passed into the main project development room, an open lab area dominated by low-slung workbenches and enough computer and electronics gear to outfit fifty Radio Shacks. Lieutenant Commander Delaford, the project specialist, was holding forth for the admiral and a small group of aides near the center of the room. His laser pointer danced over a Piranha chassis, highlighting the propulsion sections. This wasn't a mockup—it was a live, though unfueled, unit. Delaford was talking about one of his favorite topics—the applicability of the unit's hydrogen propulsion system to civilian applications such as cars. It was a noncontroversial selling point sure to win a few votes in Congress, though the admiral's overly furled brow showed he wasn't particularly impressed.

"Turning now to the program," said Delaford, nodding at Dog, "our next phase of study adds autonomous modes and more stealthy communications techniques, useful for submarine applications. And, of course, the warhead launching modes. We're confident we could put a fully suitable version, based on the test article, into production immediately. Using this propulsion system and the communications-link technologies Dreamland has developed, the production model would be controllable from fifty to seventy-five miles, either by airplane as we've demonstrated, or small surface craft. The submarine version is a little further behind, due to the detectability issues. We're confident, though, of eighteen-month viability. That's a year and a half from the word 'go.' "

"Budget line," said the admiral.

Delaford, who was unpracticed in the art of winning funds, hesitated and then lost his way, trying to argue for the project rather than simply giving Allen a number.

"Well, as a whole, compared to previous projects, say the probes for the Seawolf, the UUVs, it—"

"How much?"

"That would depend on the configuration, sir. And in, um, perspective—"

"What I think Commander Delaford is trying to point

out," said Dog, who thought the program was worthwhile even though it belonged to the Navy, "is that you have to compare the costs to an entire weapons system. The fact that it's intended to be expendable means the low per-unit cost ups the overall budget. Still, in a combat situation, the cost per engagement would be very low, since it would, by definition, be replaced."

"Is it worth two nuclear submarines?" asked Allen.

"Well, that's your call, Admiral," said Dog.

"It's not my call," said the admiral. "But if it were, I'd take the submarines."

"Actually, sir, at three hundred and forty million for the whole project," said Delaford, regaining his balance, "it's considerably less than a submarine. And tactically, it can do the job of a submarine without the exposure of, uh, risk, as the tests off Hawaii show."

"I'm well aware of the results of the tests," said the admiral.

Danny Freah, standing behind the admiral, suppressed a smile. Colonel Bastian belatedly realized what the visit was all about.

"Yes, the results were impressive," continued Allen. "But once countermeasures are employed, the device will be easily countered."

"Hardly," said Rubeo, characteristically choosing the most undiplomatic moment to butt in. "Face it, Admiral, large ships are obsolete."

Allen snorted. "That's been said since galleys ruled the ocean. Colonel—I'd like some lunch."

"I'm told it's ready when you are," said Dog.

"Yes," said Allen. "I'm sorry, the colonel and I are meeting alone," he added, as if Delaford and the others had actually volunteered to accompany them. "I'll be back."

"We'll wait," said Rubeo.

Fortunately for the scientist, Allen either didn't hear what he said, or had a tin ear when it came to acerbic irony. Dog led Allen back to the elevator, Captain Freah trailing behind him.

"Do we need a shadow?" the admiral asked as they got inside the car.

"I'm afraid close security is the order of the day here," said Dog. "All visitors, no matter how high their rank."

"Even a theater commander."

"Yes, sir," said Dog. He could have told Danny to make himself scarce; the orders to shadow Allen were his own. But he was a bit ticked at the surprise visit, and even more so now that he suspected Allen had come to lobby him on the report. Allen seemed to mellow ever so slightly, and in fact his mood visibly improved fifteen minutes later in Cafeteria Two, a private dining area known as the Red Room because of the decor, when the airman serving them told him that Thai-infused salmon headed the menu.

"I don't want sushi," said the admiral.

"No, sir, of course not, sir. It can be cooked to your specification."

"Medium then, but still moist."

"To drink?" said the airman, with the precise intonation of a waiter in a high-class restaurant.

A true achievement, since the man was a bomb ordie on special assignment. Dog marked him down mentally for a weekend pass.

"Water," said the admiral.

"Evian, or perhaps Dolmechi?"

"Dolmechi?" said the admiral. "The Italian mineral water?"

"Yes, sir."

"Very good," said Allen. "I haven't had that since I visited Naples."

The waiter—who had obviously been heavily briefed by Ax—turned toward the colonel.

"I'll have a burger," said Dog. "And a Coke."

"Yes, sir. Captain?"

Danny glanced at Dog. "I was thinking I might catch

up on some items," said Freah. "Since we're not in a secure area."

"Very good, Danny."

"Admiral." Danny nodded, getting up to go.

"Just a second." Allen rose and stuck out his hand. "Some of my Marines made sure I heard about what you did in Iran for them. Good work, son."

"Thank you, sir," said Danny.

"You ever think of switching commands, remember the Pacific," said Allen.

Danny smiled and nodded, then left.

"An impressive officer," said Allen.

"One of the best," said Dog. "That's why he's here."

"And you're wondering why I am, aren't you?" said Allen. He smiled, showing signs that somewhere beneath the weight of command he did have a sense of self-deprecating humor.

Maybe.

"Actually, Admiral, what I'm wondering is why you didn't give us a heads-up that you were coming," said Dog.

"That's not the way I do things," he said abruptly.

The colonel looked over at the airman approaching with their drinks. He didn't intend on getting into a pissing match with Allen, who as commander in chief of the Pacific Command (USCINCPAC) was one of the most powerful people in the military. The admiral commanded all forces in the Pacific, including Air Force and Army units as well as Navy. He also had considerable input at the Pentagon and, more important, the White House.

On the other hand, Dog wasn't going to roll over for anyone. Allen had no more real business here than Dog did on the flight deck of one of his carriers.

Admiral Allen took a small, almost dainty sip from his mineral water as the waiter retreated. "Colonel. Tecumseh—can I call you that?"

"My friends call me Dog."

Allen smiled indulgently. "Dog. How'd you earn that?"

"It's God spelled backwards," said the colonel, who didn't mind telling the story on himself. "I was a flight leader with a bit too much of an attitude, and some people thought it fit. They were probably right."

Allen laughed. "This was before you shot down the MiGs in the Gulf, or after?"

"My kills were unconfirmed," said Dog, though there was little doubt he had indeed splashed the enemy planes.

Another indulgent smile from Allen. "Let's cut to the chase," said the admiral. "The Piranha report—what's it going to say?"

"I would imagine it will say something along the lines of what Commander Delaford said—the system is ready to be implemented, and it's ready for the next phase of tests, if that's approved."

"Specifically, concerning the test."

Allen was undoubtedly worried about the details of the test engagement, which would show his Navy commanders—Woods especially—in a somewhat embarrassing light. With the proper emphasis, Admiral Woods—and, by extension, Admiral Allen—could be seen not only as enemies of the program, but as going overboard to scuttle it. In a politically charged atmosphere, such nuances could be deadly.

Or not. It was a game Dog had long ago decided not to play.

"Writing the report itself is not generally regarded as one of my duties," said the colonel.

"You'll sign off on it, though."

"As I see my job, Admiral, it's to develop weapons, not worry about egos that might be bruised because test results make them look bad. If you have a specific worry, maybe you ought to lay it out."

"Steady there, Colonel. Steady."

They were once more interrupted by the waiter, who brought out two dishes of fancy salad. Dog now regretted letting Danny leave; courtesy demanded someone keep the admiral company, and he didn't feel like hanging around to be harangued on what he considered a minor matter. He was somewhat surprised that Allen himself changed the conversation, turning to a totally neutral topic—the Megafortress.

Allen claimed to have long admired the big bombers, and was impressed by their showing during the recent showdown with China. Politely, Dog offered to put him in a copilot's seat on an orientation flight.

"Can't do it, unfortunately," said the admiral. "Ever since the flare-up, we've been going nonstop. I guess you heard the press is calling it the Fatal Terrain affair. Makes good headlines for them, I guess." He smiled wryly, but then added, "I was sorry about General Elliott."

"Yes," said Dog. In a brief but brutal encounter between America and China known to some as the "Fatal Terrain" affair, Elliott had given his life. He'd died successfully preventing an all-out nuclear war between the U.S. and China. He was a bonafide war hero—at least to Colonel Bastian. Others saw it somewhat differently; some people even criticized the maverick general. They didn't realize how close the Communists had come to running over Taiwan—and starting World War III.

"Things are still hot there. Touchy. We've got a lot of assets along the coast."

"You're probably stretched thin," said Dog.

"Absolutely," said Allen. "And contrary to all the talking heads, there's still no guarantee war won't break out. I don't trust the Chinese as far as I can spit, even with our carriers along their coast. And, hell, even the Indians seem to be spoiling for a fight."

"India?"

"Oh, yes," said Allen. "Minor incidents so far. Saber-rattling. Frankly, I don't take them too seriously. But all South Asia's boiling."

Dog nodded.

"Admiral Woods is an excellent man," said Allen. "A little competitive sometimes. Especially if he thinks the

Air Force is trying to get ahead of him. Very competitive."

"How about yourself?" asked Dog.

"Never play tennis with me."

"I meant, do you think the Air Force is trying to get ahead of you?"

"Piranha is a Navy project, Colonel."

The accent on *Colonel* was sharp enough to fillet a salmon. Having to negotiate with someone so far down in rank obviously pricked at the admiral. The fact that Dog essentially answered to no one in the military undoubtedly irked him as well.

Their lunch arrived. The conversation once more tacked toward more friendly waters. Allen compared the salmon favorably to several dinners he'd had recently in Washington, D.C.—a not too subtle hint that the admiral could muster considerable political muscle if displeased.

"Extend my compliments to the chef," said Allen as the waiter cleared the plates.

"Thank you, sir."

"Dog, if you run the rest of your ship as well as you run the mess, you'll do well," the admiral added.

"I can't take the credit," said Dog. "Brad Elliott staffed the kitchen."

Displeasure or sorrow—it was impossible to tell which—flickered over Allen's face. "I'd like a copy of the draft report," he said.

"That can be arranged." In truth, Colonel Bastian would have forwarded him one as a matter of course, since his command had been involved in the testing and had personnel involved in the development. Had Dog not taken such a dislike to Allen, he might also have noted, for the record, that Dreamland reports focused on the system under study. Personalities, and what orders they might or might not have issued during test exercises, were never included.

But the colonel didn't see much reason for adding that.

"You have a nice little operation here, Colonel. No reason for us to be enemies," said Allen as they walked back to the SUV that would take the admiral to his plane, which had returned after being refueled at Edwards.

"I didn't realize we were."

Allen only smiled.

ZEN PULLED HIS WHEELCHAIR TOWARD HANGAR A, where the UMB's control unit was housed. Bree had promised to meet him there for lunch. He was running his standard ten minutes late—the only place he was punctual was in the air—so it was somewhat surprising when she was not standing impatiently outside the door.

Zen breathed a reassuring sigh, since she was sure to get on him for being late. Instead of justifying his tardiness, her absence presented a perfect opportunity for turning the tables on the notoriously punctual captain; he could claim he'd been here the whole time, waiting outside. He stopped a few feet from the doorway and pulled his paperback from the corner of his seat, starting to position himself as if he'd been reading in the shade.

"More Roosevelt!" said Bree behind him.

"More Roosevelt," he said, closing the biography of the President. "Where you been?"

"I was necking with Chief Parsons around the corner," she said. Chief Master Sergeant "Greasy Hands" Parsons was in charge of the maintenance team and old enough to be her father—or grandfather.

"I've been waiting," he said.

"Oh, baloney. I saw you come up."

"Musta been some other gimp in a wheelchair." Zen smiled at her.

"So which book is this?"

Bree reached down and picked it up; Zen saw the opening and snuck in a kiss.

"Heavy reading," she said. The book was Geoffrey Ward's *A First Class Temperament*. "Whatever happened to *Sports Illustrated*?"

"I only get it for the swimsuit issue," said Zen. His

interest in Roosevelt had started by accident during his
flight home from Turkey, and now he was truly fascinated by the only man to have been elected President
four times—all the time confined to a wheelchair. He'd
worked through several FDR volumes, and was now eyeing Kenneth Davis's five books, the definitive tome on
Roosevelt's life. While he joked that he wanted to see
how a "fellow gimp made good," what truly fascinated
Zen was Roosevelt's ability to get along with so many
people.

His charm certainly was innate. As Undersecretary of
the Navy, well before being crippled, Roosevelt had practically started a war with Mexico—against the Administration's wishes and the country's interests. Still, his boss
had treated him like a son.

How did he manage to get on with so many people
after polio took his legs? Wasn't he bitter? Why didn't
bitterness come out in his relationships, which seemed to
show no trace of anger or frustration? Zen didn't fool
himself that his own relationships were on nearly so lofty
a plain; at least privately, he railed about his condition
every day.

"Ready for lunch?" Bree asked.

"Starving."

"Red Room?"

"Nah, Admiral Allen's there, and Ax says stay away."

"Allen? Is that who landed on my runway?"

Zen gave her the gossip he'd heard from Chief Gibbs:
Apparently the admiral was on a tear because his people
had gotten their fannies waxed during the Piranha exercises. One of Allen's favorite commanders, Admiral
Woods, had pulled some strings to alter the parameters of
the test in his favor—and still lost. There was justice in
the world, Zen concluded. The Navy being so damned
concerned about their little egos being crushed that a top
admiral had to come and personally try to soothe things
over gave Zen immense satisfaction.

It wasn't until they were at their table with full trays

of food that Zen realized Bree was distracted. He made a
joke about her choice—salad with a side of yogurt—then
one about his—a double helping of homemade meat loaf,
with extra gravy. She hardly snickered.

"Bad flight?" he asked.

She shrugged.

"Something up?"

"You miss flying?"

"I fly every day," he said.

"You know what I mean. Flying a robot. It's not the
same thing."

"Yeah," he said. He missed a lot more than flying.

"I don't know if I can do it, Jeff," she said.

"You don't have to," he told her.

"It's a promotion. It's important."

Zen slid back a little in his seat, looking at her face.
Breanna was not, by any definition, a worrier. Her eyes
were fraught with it now.

"Hey." He paused, not really sure what to say. After
an awkward silence, he stumbled on. "There're plenty of
different projects out there. You don't have to take something you don't want. But if you do take it, I know you
can do it," he added quickly. Her lips had pursed—a bad
sign. "I mean, you're beyond capable of it. I mean, that's
why you got it."

"The Megafortresses."

A sore subject, he knew, since she had hoped to inherit
Major Nancy Cheshire's place when she left. But Merce
Alou, who outranked her, had been tagged.

"To be honest with you, Bree, the EB-52, not that it's
a dead end or anything, but it's now, uh, mature." Zen
hated using the bureaucratese, but it did essentially de-
scribe the program. The EB-52 was now a production aircraft; the advances were sure to be incremental. "The
UMB. Hell, that's the future. Or something that comes
out of it. Ask anybody. But if it's not what you want to
do, don't worry about it."

"It's a big adjustment, that's all," she said, poking her

salad. She frowned, but this time at him. "You're not going to eat all of that, are you? It's pure fat."

He laughed and reached for his soda—then yawped with pain.

"Problem?" she asked.

"Tooth. Geez."

"Are you going to get it fixed or what?"

"This afternoon." The cold soda had shot through the nerve into every cell in his skull, and his head reverberated with pain. He put down the glass and rubbed the back of his jaw on both sides, hoping to ease it somehow.

"Not going to cancel this time?"

"I didn't cancel on purpose," he mumbled.

Bree's manner had brightened; in fact, she seemed to be suppressing a giggle.

"I'm glad my misery is entertaining," he told her.

"Don't be a sissy."

"You filled it with extra ice," he said. "You knew I had the appointment."

"Just a coincidence," said his wife.

FREED FROM HIS ONEROUS ESCORT DUTY, DANNY Freah took a tour of his perimeter, checking on the security posts. His body still felt the lingering effects of his "visit" to Turkey, Iraq, and Iran a few months before; he'd been injured in a mission that recovered data and parts from an Iranian antiaircraft laser facility. His legs were especially bothersome—Danny had stretched and partially torn ligaments in his right knee.

Not that he'd taken any time off to mend. You had to break something for that. Like your neck.

Danny eyed the fence along the road, looking at the video cameras posted at irregular intervals. The entire base was constantly watched. Not just by human eyes, but computer programs, which searched for spatial anomalies, as the programmers stubbornly referred to intruders. Additional sensors were buried in the perimeter area. Mines and remote-controlled ground defenses—basically old M2HB machine guns with massive belts of ammunition in modified fifty-gallon drums—were webbed around the fences. A generation ago, it might have taken the better part of an Army regiment to provide as secure a perimeter; Dreamland could, at least in theory, be secured with only six men, though Danny's security squadron was considerably larger and growing every day.

He turned off the perimeter road, driving up a short hill toward a bunker halfway between the underground hangars and the main gate. A brown slant of cement marked the entrance to the hardened security monitoring station. Lieutenant William McNally and two airmen were inside, reviewing the security feeds and drinking coffee, not necessarily in that order.

"Hey, Boss," said McNally as Danny came through the doors. "How's the admiral?"

"Looked like he was searching for a boat."

"Can we shoot down his plane next time? Razor guys say they had it nailed at twenty miles."

Danny grunted. He checked through the logs, then told McNally he was going over to the weapons lab to check on his gear. His smart helmet and body armor had been damaged in Iran; its custom-fitted replacement was due for a final fitting.

McNally stopped him, saying a message had come for him while he was with the admiral.

"Just leave it in my cue," Danny told him.

"Actually, it was a voice message, uh, your wife," said McNally. "She decided to talk to me."

"And?"

"Says she'll be out here this afternoon. Said something about a hotel."

"Okay," Danny told him. Jemma knew exactly what Danny did, and had gone through her own security check before Danny was allowed to take his post. Technically, she could come to Dreamland and stay at his quarters on the base. However, the procedures were elaborate, and it was much easier all around to put her up in a nice hotel for a few days.

Put himself up too.

"Surprise that she's coming?" McNally asked.

"Not a surprise, no," Danny said. "You have a handle on things?"

"Boss, you can take off for the next few months as far as I'm concerned. You earned it."

"Thanks, Billy." He tapped his radio and then his beeper, wordlessly telling his lieutenant to call if needed, then headed toward the handheld-weapons lab.

Annie Klondike sat hunched over a desk, staring at a small, liver-shaped piece of metal. Her thin white hair had been pulled back into a tight ball, enhancing her school-marm look.

"Hey, Annie, whatcha got going?" asked Danny.

"Hmmmpphhhh," she said without looking up.

Danny bent over and inspected the metal. "New explosive?"

"Hardly." She pushed herself up from the chair. "You'll want your helmet, I suppose."

"If it's convenient."

"Convenient? Captain, you've added a new word to your vocabulary."

"I even used it in a sentence," said Freah.

"I'd be curious as to your definition," she said, beginning her shuffle toward one of the back areas. "We took the liberty of adding upgrades," said Annie, opening the door to a storage closet. "Try the vest first."

The carbon-boron vest that Danny pulled over his chest was no thicker than a good-quality goose-down ski vest, and weighed nearly the same. The side that nestled against his ribs had a crinkly feel; pressing it against his side felt a little like squishing the Styrofoam of a packing peanut.

"What's the cushion?"

"Styrated aluminum," said Klondike. "Actually a carbonized alloy, but mostly aluminum."

"Aluminum?"

"It bears only a passing resemblance to the material used in soda cans, Captain, not to worry," said Annie. "I'm told a bullet from an M60E1 at five yards won't leave a bruise, though I haven't found a volunteer willing to demonstrate."

"Does the next upgrade come with a built-in nurse?"

"Your helmet is this way," said the weapons expert tartly. "Have I ever told you you have a big head?"

"All the time."

Danny's smart helmet and its connected Combat Information Visor included a display shield with video, low-light, infrared, and radiation-detection modes. When plugged into its com modules—these were generally carried in a small pack on the wearer's back or belt—it could tie into Dreamland's secure satellite communications system. But that system required coordination back at Dreamland, as well as being in line of sight of the satellite—fine in some situations, not in others. Team members on the ground communicated through a discrete-mode unit that was also line-of-sight—again, fine in some situations but not in others.

"We have bowed to popular demand and added a standard radio link," announced Annie. "I would caution you: The encryption is merely based on a 128-byte key on a random skip; it can be broken easily."

"By anyone outside of the NSA and Dreamland?"

Annie smiled—slightly. "A simple beacon detector could be used to locate the transmissions, which, as requested, have a range of five miles. We are looking at a complementary-wave transmitter that would interfere with the transmissions beyond an operator-specified range, but alas, it remains to be perfected."

"This'll do," said Danny. "It beats having to stand up under fire."

"I imagine it would."

Danny took the new helmet and fit it onto his head. It felt just like the old one—way too tight and far too heavy.

"Yes, I know," said Klondike, sighing though Danny

hadn't said anything. "We balance function and utility. We are scientists of the possible, Captain. If we could shave off another pound while not giving up protection or functionality, we gladly would."

"You'll get it right, Annie," he said.

"Hmmmph. The shape-recognition program is finally operational and so we have added it. It defaults to 'on.' I find it annoying myself, though the weapons detector is useful."

"If we can trust it," said Danny.

"Yes. Well, Captain, you've seen the tests yourself." The device used pattern recognition to check shapes in the screen against a library of weapons and "suspicious polygons." It was excellent against the obvious—like tanks and artillery pieces—but tended to be overly suspicious about things like bulges in pants pockets. On IR mode, however, it could tell the difference between a toy gun and the real thing, which was potentially valuable in certain situations.

"Let's go test the targeting screen," said Annie. There was almost a suppressed cackle in her voice as she said that, and Danny knew he'd find a surprise in the weapons locker at the firing range. Sure enough, the weapons scientist presented him with a new gun.

"Silenced MP-5," he said admiringly, taking it from her hands.

"Hardly," said Annie. "Try it."

Danny studied the stubby wire at the end. On the other systems that worked with the visor targeting system, a thin wire ran from the gun to his helmet.

"No, there's no connection. Just point it at the target and shoot," insisted Annie.

As Danny pointed the business end of the German submachine gun down the alley, crosshairs appeared in the middle of his visor.

"Please, I have work to do," said Annie.

As Danny pressed the trigger, he unconsciously raised his shoulder to brace against the recoil. For a submachine gun, the MP-5 was famously easy to handle; unlike many predecessors that justly earned the moniker "spray guns," this was a precision weapon in the hands of a trained and experienced professional. It was, however, still a submachine gun, and all the brilliant engineering in the world could not completely remove the barrel's tendency under automatic fire to kick a bit.

Or could it? For the gun in Danny's hands was not only exceedingly quiet—quieter by far than even the silenced versions of the MP-5 he'd used—but it spit through its fifteen-bullet magazine with less recoil than a water pistol.

And continued to do so. Though it appeared no larger than the standard box, somehow the magazine contained twenty bullets.

"Heh," said Annie. She took another clip from her lab coat and gave it to him. Danny realized it was slightly longer and just a hair fatter than the standard box. The addition of five bullets didn't sound like much—until you had to use them.

"You might try aiming this time," added Annie.

"I hit the target square on, bull's-eye."

"You should have put all the bullets through the same hole."

"You want to try?"

He'd been set up. She took the gun with a smile and pressed the button on the wall to send the paper target back another fifty feet. Without bothering to take his visor, she blew a rather narrow and perfectly round hole through the "100" at the center of the head area.

"It's the bullets. Primarily," she said. "Though I must say our German friends were quite ingenious with the improvements they suggested to the gun. We're still working on them, of course. But we should have enough to outfit your entire team in a month."

"That long?"

"My best advice, Captain, is not to let them try the weapon until then. That boy Powder especially; he'll never give it up. Want to take another crack at the target?

Best two out of three. You can use your visor if you want."

Aboard the trawler _Gui_, South China Sea
August 22, 1997, 0600 local (August 21, 1997, 100
Dreamland)

KNOW WHITE. BE BLACK.

Chen Lo Fann held the ideograms in his head as he scanned the horizon. The thick brush strokes and their stark ideas contrasted with the haze of the horizon, the fickle world flowing in its chaos. The words from the twenty-fifth chapter of the Tao Te Ching draped themselves across his consciousness, the old master's voice as real in his thoughts as the shadows of the ships in the distance.

Know white, be black. Be the empire's model.

There was no more perfect statement of his mission, nor his desire in life.

Chen focused his binoculars on the closest shadow, a mere speck even at highest magnification. It was a destroyer, an escort for the largest ship in the squadron just over the horizon, the aircraft carrier _Shangi-Ti._ Named for an ancient creator god, the carrier was considerably smaller than the _Mao,_ the pride of the Chinese Mainland Navy. But though half _Mao_'s size, _Shangi-Ti_ and her sister ship, _T'ien,_ were nonetheless potent crafts, similar in many ways to the British Invincible class. Displacing about twenty thousand tons, _Shangi-Ti_ and _T'ien_ held four Dauphin multirole helicopters and a dozen Chinese versions of the Sukhoi Su-33.

The Su-33's were launched with the help of a special catapult system on a ramped deck, then recovered with the help of arrestor gear. It was an awkward system in some respects, still in need of refinement; even with the ramp, the heavy Sukhois dipped low over the bow on takeoff, and botched landings were particularly unforgiving. The maritime versions of the planes were fairly short-ranged, and the Dauphins' ASW gear somewhat old. But the crews were well trained and dedicated.

And unlike the *Mao*, which had originally been built by Russia, the two pocket carriers were an all-Chinese design—not counting, of course, certain useful items of technology that had originated abroad and found their way surreptitiously to Asia.

Know white, be black.

Fann's thoughts and gaze turned southward, in roughly the direction of the Spratly Islands. Another task force was making its way northward there, this one also centered around an aircraft carrier—the Indian *Vikrant.* Just out of dry dock where she had received new avionics and a ramped deck, the ship was roughly the same size as the *Shangi-Ti,* though its basic layout harked back to World War II. Originally built by the English and refurbished several times, she boasted eighteen Harrier II jump jets, along with four or five helicopters and one rather limited radar plane.

Ostensibly, both forces were sailing into the South China Sea to protect ships bound for their home ports. The reality was more complicated—and less so. On their present courses, it would take only a few days for them to meet.

Everything Chen did aimed at that moment of intersection.

He himself commanded five ships. To the naked eye, all were noncombatants, weak and vulnerable sisters that had no business near the caldron of battle. Four were similar to the small freighter on whose bridge he stood. They looked innocent, but their simple superstructures and wide hulls were crammed with spying gear, and their sophisticated communications devices kept them in constant touch though they were spread across several thousand square miles of ocean.

The fifth vessel, still far to the north, was unlike them in many ways. To the naked eye from one hundred yards, it looked only like a decrepit oil tanker. But it held Chen's greatest tool—robot planes the scientists called Dragons. They would not be available for several days. Even then, it was doubtful what the aircraft could accomplish; they were still experimental.

They would extend his eyesight, which was enough. His more conventional tools were sufficient to his larger purpose.

Know white, be black. Be a model for the empire.

Chen satisfied, put down his glasses and went to have his morning tea.

New Lebanon, Nevada (near Las Vegas)
August 21, 1997, 1530 local

JEFFREY "ZEN" STOCKARD HAD FACED CONSIDERABLE danger and hardship during his Air Force career; he had gunned down MiGs, nailed enemy antiaircraft sites, and lost the use of his legs in a horrific accident while testing robot fighters. He'd dealt with enemies ranging from poorly trained Libyan pilots to highly polished government bureaucrats, vanquishing all. His confinement to a wheelchair had not prevented him from deftly directing one of the most important programs at Dreamland. If any man might truly earn the title "courageous," it was Zen Stockard. If he was not fearless—no man in full possession of his wits is completely devoid of some sliver of fear—he was so much a master of fear as to be without peer in military service.

There was one thing, however, that turned his resolute will into a quivering mass of jelly:

The whine of a dentist's drill.

Zen took a last, sharp breath as the dentist closed in, aiming at a molar deep in his mouth. The way had been prepared with a heavy dose of Novocain, and in truth Zen couldn't feel much of anything as the drill bit touched the tooth.

But he could hear its nerve-wracking, cell-tingling howl, a shriek of devastation so violent it reverberated in the suddenly hollow ventricles of his heart. Pain, incredible pain, pulsed through every vein, every artery, every capillary, coursing through his body like hot electricity. The world went black.

And then, thankfully, the storm broke. Pain and fear retreated. The viper had stopped his hiss.

Only to gather strength for a curdling scream five octaves higher as it tore through the vulnerable enamel and weakened dentin of the defenseless back tooth.

"Got to get it all," growled the dentist, as if Zen had somehow hidden part of the cavity to spite him.

The worst thing was, the sadist enjoyed it all. When he finally stopped, he smiled and held the drill triumphantly in one hand, waving it like a victory flag.

"See—that wasn't bad at all, right?"

"Awgrhfkhllmk," said Zen. It was the most coherent sound he could manage with his mouth full of dentist tools.

"Geez, you'd think I was an *Air Force* dentist." Dr. Gideon—Ken to friends and victims alike—poked fun at the Air Force whenever possible. His discharge papers from the Navy were prominently displayed in the hallway.

Sure they discharged him. He was a dentist.

"Awgrh," said Zen.

"Maybe I'll break for coffee," teased Gideon.

"Awgrh-agrh." Zen tried to make the mumble sound threatening, but there was only so much you could do with a sucker clawing at your gum. Gideon picked up another tool and shot cold air into the hole he had just created.

The pain nearly knocked Zen unconscious.

"You know, Jeff, I really have to compliment you. You've become a much better patient over the past year. Must be your wife's influence."

"Awrgr-kerl-wushump."

"Yeah, Breanna is a perfect patient. Never a word of pain. I don't think she needs Novocain at all. Wonderful woman. You're lucky to have her. You guys should think about kids."

"Awrgr-kerl-wushump."

Gideon took Zen's garbled protest as an invitation to expound on the joys of fatherhood. He had three children, all between the ages of five and ten. They all loved to play dentist—more proof that evil is hereditary.

"Due for their checkups soon," added Gideon. "We started 'em young."

"I thought child abuse was illegal in this state," said Zen. With the Novocain and dental equipment, the sentence came out sounding like "thickel giggle hissss."

"Yeah, they're cute, all right. You ought to think about having some. Seriously."

Gideon prolonged Zen's agony by polishing down the filling and then using what looked and tasted like old carbon paper to perfect the bite. By the time he was done, Zen suspected the dentist could see himself in the surface.

"Very good," said Gideon, standing back as if to take a bow. "Want to grab coffee? I'm free for the rest of the day."

"You just want to see me with coffee dribbling down my face," said Zen.

The actual sound was more like: "Yuwwa see muf fee dippling dowt mek fack."

"What language you speaking, Jeff?"

"Novocain."

"See you in six months."

"Not if I can help it."

The Nevada Desert
1600

MARK STONER SHIFTED HIS EYES FROM THE HIGHWAY to the bluffs in the distance and then back, scanning every possible place an ambush might be launched from. It was the sort of thing he couldn't turn off; ten years as a covert CIA officer on top of six years as a SEAL rewired your brain.

Not that he or Jed Barclay, the man driving the car,

were in any danger of being ambushed. Coming from Washington on a scheduled flight offered expediency, but led Stoner to insist on a number of precautions, most of which caused Barclay to roll his eyes: dummy reservations, Agency-supplied false documents, even an elaborate cover story designed to be overheard—all routine precautions for Stoner. The fact they were traveling to a top-secret, ultrasecure facility changed nothing.

Stoner had never dealt with Whiplash before, and knew only vaguely about Dreamland. He tended to be agnostic about organizations and people until he saw them under fire; so he had formed no opinion on Whiplash, or even on Jed, though his youth and overabundance of nervous energy tended to grate.

Stoner noticed a small pile of rocks ahead, off on the right, seemingly haphazardly piled there.

"Security cam," he said.

"Yeah. They're all along the road," said Jed. "We're being watched via satellite too."

Stoner cracked the window slightly, listening to the rush of air passing over the car. The road changed abruptly, taking a sharp turn down into a suddenly exposed ravine. Barclay had to slow to barely ten miles an hour as he made his way through a series of switchbacks. Undoubtedly that was the idea, and Stoner noticed the random rock piles were now much closer together.

They must have remote weapons as well as sensors here, thought Stoner.

These guys knew what they were doing, at least in terms of guarding their perimeter. There'd be holes, though. There always were.

The dirt road at the base of the slope extended for roughly a quarter mile, then suddenly trailed off. Jed drove about two hundred yards further, then stopped the car. They looked to be in the middle of nowhere.

"Wrong turn?" asked Stoner.

"No. You wanted to do it the hard way. I told you, if we didn't go through Edwards—"

"Easier to keep it compartmented."

"If we don't go through Edwards or get a direct flight, this is the way we have to do it." Barclay hit his radio scan, pushing the FM frequency to exactly 100.00. All they could hear was static.

A small cloud of dust appeared directly ahead. The ground began to shake. As Stoner stared, the cloud separated into two Ospreys, roto-tipped aircraft capable of hovering like helicopters. These were unlike any Ospreys Stoner had ever seen, however; beneath their chins were swivel-mounted chain guns similar to those used in Apache gunships, and there were triple-rack missile launchers on their wings and the side of their fuselages.

Stoner started to unlock the door.

"Uh, no, not until they say it's okay." Jed reached across and grabbed him. "They'll blow us up if you get out."

Stoner let go of the door handle. One of the Ospreys whipped past, its big shadow covering the car. The other slowed to a hover about twenty yards away. The reflection of the sun made it hard to see, but from where Stoner was sitting there didn't seem to be a pilot.

"Blue Taurus, license plate X-ray Tetra Vector, exit your vehicle and stand by for identification," said a sharp, clear voice on the radio.

"That would be us," said Jed, unlocking the door. Stoner watched and then copied his actions, taking a few steps away and holding out his hands. He looked upward as the hovering Osprey moved forward slowly, its gun rotating. There was a camera pod behind the weapon.

The Osprey leapt upward. Stoner waited as the wash from the second aircraft pushed his pants and shirt to the side.

"Okay, let's go," said Jed, who was already trotting forward. The first Osprey landed about fifty yards ahead; the second, meanwhile, had plopped down behind them, depositing two fully armed Air Force special tactics team members to inspect and investigate the vehicle.

The door to the Osprey sprang open as Jed and Stoner approached. "Welcome, Mr. Barclay."

"Hey," said Jed.

"There's nobody flying this thing," said Stoner as he climbed inside.

"This is Dreamland," said Jed. "What did you expect?"

Prince Hotel, Las Vegas
1800

THE SILKINESS OF HIS WIFE'S BODY WORKED LIKE A drug, loosening knots Danny didn't know he had. He ran his hand slowly over her belly and breast, gently skimming along the surface. The tips of his fingers tingled, as if electricity were flowing from her. He pulled her hip toward him, rolling on top to make love again. His mouth dove into hers. Jemma's tongue slid along the bottom of his lip; something tight in his neck let loose and he fell inside her, his whole body plunging into a warm cave. He rolled through it, luxuriating in the liberating heat.

How long it lasted, Danny couldn't say. At some point, he felt as if he were floating at the top of an ocean; shortly afterwards, he washed up on a beach, still basking in the warmth of the summer sun.

"Good," said Jemma.

"Good," said Danny.

"We could do this more often."

"Exactly what I was thinking."

"Yes."

"Yes."

Jemma reached over to the floor, where they'd set the room service tray with its decanter of tea. Danny slid his arm under the pillow, wallowing in the decadence of the large bed. Living halfway across the country from his wife sucked—but it sure did make things sweeter when they saw each other.

"I talked to Jim Stephens the other day," said Jemma, slipping back in bed with her tea, an herbal blend that smelled like orange and cinnamon. Its perfume added to his intoxication.

"Uh-huh," said Danny, not really paying attention.

"There's a primary coming up this fall. A perfect shot. Happens to be the district where I'm staying—and it's an open seat."

"You should run," he said, starting to drift toward sleep.

"Not me," she said. "You."

"Me?"

"Yes, you." She took a sip of her tea. "You did talk to Jim Stephens, right? I know you did, because he told me he had an excellent conversation with you. And he's very, very high on you."

Stephens—election. Jemma's master plan to make him the next President of the United States.

"I can't run for office while I'm in the Air Force," said Danny, still drifting.

"Oh, Jimmy can fix that. Don't worry."

Danny reached his hand over to his wife's breast. His fingers slid gently across her nipple, brushing it erect.

"Changing the subject?" she asked.

"Fact-finding mission," he said.

"Oh? And what facts are you looking for?"

"Whether you're still horny or not."

"Again?" she said.

She reached over and put her tea on the side table. As she turned back, Danny's cell phone began to buzz.

Danny sighed, and immediately slid upright.

"Daniel."

"They wouldn't call unless it was important."

"Everything's important." She reached her hand down to stroke his leg.

"Mmmmph." Danny pulled the phone over from the stand on his side of the bed.

"Freah," he said after clicking the talk button.

"Captain, sorry to interrupt, but there's a Whiplash order," said Lieutenant McNally. "Colonel needs you ASAP."

"I'm on my way." Danny clicked the phone off and rolled out of bed.

"Oh, no," said Jemma.

"I'll call as soon as I can," said Danny, grabbing his pants.

"At least put underwear on," she called after him.

Danny, embarrassed—he had in fact forgotten—let go of his pants and dropped to the floor to retrieve his underwear.

"How do you manage without me?" said his wife, laughing and shaking her head.

Dreamland
2000

"THE POLITICAL SITUATION IN BOTH INDIA AND CHINA IS complicated, as you'd imagine," continued Jed Barclay.

"Just a summary, Jed," said Dog, trying to keep the NSC deputy on line. Barclay was a genius and a strong advocate for Whiplash and Dreamland, but his dissertations on international politics tended to sprawl.

"Yes, sir. Basically, the extremists in India are trying to improve their position in the upcoming elections. They calculate that China is a weak and easy mark due to the conflict with us and Taiwan—well, you're all familiar with the so-called Fatal Terrain event."

The dozen top officers gathered in the secure briefing room nodded. Though the details were still highly classified, most knew how Brad Elliott had chosen to give his life to help prevent an apocalyptic war—their interpretation, not the media's.

"Of course, the Islamic Alliance and the connection with China plays right into this, yada, yada, yada, because now hitting the Chinese is the same as hitting Muslims as far as most Hindus are concerned. Those who care anyway," continued Barclay. "And we've—uh, I better skip some of the political wrangling."

He glanced at Dog, who nodded.

"On the other side of the equation, the Chinese, domestically, need something to show they're in power, that they're not slipping. Because now, right, they look weak. As we saw with the incident in Tibet . . ."

"Which incident was that?" asked Rubeo.

From anyone else, it would have been an innocent question—in fact, Dog himself wasn't sure what Barclay was referring to, but Rubeo took a perverse pleasure in watching others squirm. An ever-so-subtle look of satisfaction flickered across the scientist's face as Jed stuttered, the train of his thoughts bunching and crashing down a siding he hadn't seen coming.

"Don't worry about Tibet, Pakistan, Taiwan, or any of that bullshit," said Stoner. It was the first time the CIA official had spoken since he arrived. "The action's out in the South China Sea. India and China are fighting a war out there, sinking each other's merchant ships. They've been rattling sabers and now they're using them. Everything else is just bullshit."

"Please," said Rubeo, in a way that implied many things other than courtesy or respect.

"I think we can get a full rundown on Tibet later, along with any other geopolitical matters anyone has an interest in," said Dog. "Let's move to our assignment."

Anyone else would have interpreted this as a mild reprimand. Rubeo, however, saw it somehow as a vindication, and slipped back into his seat with a barely concealed gloat. Before Jed could continue, the door alarm buzzed; the doors slid back and Danny Freah appeared.

"Sorry I'm late," said Freah.

"We're just getting to the good part, Danny," said Dog. "We're being asked to mount a surveillance mission in the South China Sea, observing a new weapon the Indians have."

"It's not limited just to that," said Jed. "Information on everything going on—that's what Whiplash covers."

"The new technology is a prime concern," said Stoner.

"Um, everything's of interest," said Jed. "The order covers the entire situation; the Chinese as well as the Indians. This is a twenty-four/seven operation, completely covert and not coordinated with Pacific Command or any other command."

"Why not?" asked Major Merce Alou, who had taken over command of the Megafortress development project when Major Cheshire left to head the operational wing.

"Security," said Stoner.

"Uh, well, uh, there are several concerns," said Jed. "We're absolutely not attempting to provoke anything, or increase tensions, which putting ships out there would do. Pacific Fleet's resources are already concentrated in the Indian Ocean and around Taiwan. The threat of an invasion remains viable."

"That's a bullshit estimate," said Stoner.

"I agree, but it's not my call," said Jed. "Also, the Director, um, the National Security Director, would prefer not tipping off the Indians that we know, uh, about Kali. Moving Naval assets would, at least arguably, tip them or the Russians off. Which would be the same thing."

"Kali?" asked Zen.

"It's halfway between a sub-launched Harpoon and a Tomahawk missile," said Stoner. "It's underwater-launched, like a torpedo. We think it can travel four or five miles underwater before it surfaces, which makes the launching sub that much harder to detect. It pops up, skims along the surface of the water, and hits its target. It seems to be able to correct toward its target close in; we believe it has an active radar phase, but we still need to gather data. That's your mission."

"At least for now," added Jed. "There's a debate—"

"Let's deal with what we're assigned to do, not maybes," Colonel Bastian said. Jed had told him earlier the NSC had debated asking Whiplash to protect all shipping in the area—a tall order, and one possibly beyond their abilities. NSC had held off doing so—largely, according to Jed, because doing so would have stepped on the Navy's toes.

"Piranha," said Rubeo. "It's the obvious choice."

"Not ready for a mission like this," said Dog.

"Piranha is what?" said Stoner.

"Underwater surveillance probe and weapon," Dog told him. "I don't think you need to know the details."

"We can clean up the computer issues in a few days," said Rubeo.

"The mission has to start right away," said Jed. "We were thinking Elint Megafortresses."

"I concur," said Dog. "Merce?"

"We'll use Raven and Quicksilver," said Alou, referring to the EB-52's optimized for electronic intelligence-gathering. "We deploy a mini-KH for optical surveillance at the same time."

"Negative on the tactical satellites," Dog told him. "We don't have any launch chassis."

"We do have satellite coverage of the area," said Jed. "It'll be available through the Dreamland network."

"If we're looking for really close views of something while it's traveling, we can take Flighthawks," said Zen. "Straightforward."

"What do we do if these weapons are used?" asked Alou.

"At the moment, just observe them," said Jed.

"Wait—they're firing at civilian targets or military targets?" asked Zen. "I think I missed something here."

"What difference does it make?" asked Stoner.

"It makes a shitload of difference," said Zen.

"There are military ships in the region that could be targets," said Jed. "Until now, all of the ships that have been sunk were civilian."

"Damn."

"The vessel sunk by the Kali was a merchant freighter owned by the Chinese government smuggling weapons to Islamic extremists," said Stoner. "The same ship delivered explosives used to blow up a government building in New

Delhi six months ago. Still worried about civilians?"

"Yeah, I am," said Zen.

"We'll need a force briefing before we deploy," Dog told Jed.

"Do we operate out of Guam?" asked Major Alou, referring to the air base on the island. "Anderson?"

"We'd prefer not to, due to the nature of the mission," said Jed. "We'd prefer a sanitized site not connected to USPACCOM or any present operation."

"Deniable," added Stoner.

"I've already checked into possible sites for a secure forward base," continued Jed. "We have a site in the Philippines away from, uh, away from the population centers and sea lanes. It's actually an old airstrip, pretty long. Just needs to be, um, tidied up a little. Remembering what you did in Turkey, I thought—"

"You want us to blow up another mountain?" Danny asked with a laugh.

"That won't be necessary this time."

"I want to drive one of the bulldozers," said Breanna.

Half of the room laughed.

The other half said, "Me too."

"I want to be in one of the Megafortresses," said Breanna as the laughter died.

"You have a heavy schedule with the UMB," Dog said, surprised that she had volunteered.

"There's only one flight test planned over the next seven or eight days," said Bree.

"This could easily last longer," said Jed. "I'd be thinking in, uh, the time frame of two or three months, at least until tensions die down."

"If that's the case, you really need me. You won't have enough trained Megafortress pilots unless you rotate in and out," said Breanna, looking at Alou.

"She's right, Colonel. We could work around her schedule. Actually, if this lasts any length of time, we'll have to work around a lot of schedules."

"All right. Map out plans for a deployment," said Dog. "I want planes over the area twenty-four hours from now, and I want them landing at that Philippines base when their shift is done."

III
Ghosts in the jungle

**Aboard Quicksilver, above the South China Sea
August 23, 1997, 1100 local (August 22, 1997, 2000
Dreamland)**

UNTIL YOU ACTUALLY DID IT, PATROLLING THE OCEAN
sounded like the sort of easygoing assignment a pilot and
crew could do with their eyes closed. Especially a crew
like the one aboard Quicksilver. Breanna Stockard had
flown the Megafortress platform for so long, the plane and
its complicated systems seemed to have grafted themselves onto her body, and vice versa. Chris Ferris, her
copilot, had been with the program nearly as long, and
had worked with Breanna through all of Whiplash's important deployments. The newcomer on the crew, Torbin
Dolk, had proved his worth in Iran, and even he seemed
tied into the crew's shared ESP. They took turns sleeping
on the long flight to South Asia, and while they couldn't
quite be called bright-eyed and bushy-tailed, they were
nonetheless ready when they finally began their surveillance track.

Thirty minutes later, they were bored stiff, butts dragging lower than the troughs in the waves. Even Breanna
had to fight to keep her attention focused on the mission
and the plane she was flying.

All of the Dreamland Megafortresses were hand-built from older B-52's. All had their own personalities as well as configurations, but they could be broken down into three main categories.

The general-purpose Megafortresses were essentially highly efficient bombers with the capability of acting as mother ships for up to four Flighthawks. Iowa was the leader of this class, intended to be configured for roles such as attack and long-range patrol.

The second category of Megafortress added a powerful onboard radar to the EB-52 skeleton, giving it nearly the ability of an advanced AWACS, but able to operate in an extremely hazardous environment. To accommodate the radar dome, these craft, around the forward wing area, had a prominent bulge. Though it was nowhere near as immense as the massive saucers that sat atop a standard E-3 Sentry, Galatica or "Gal" belonged to this category. Her powerful radar altered the flight characteristics of the aircraft as it revolved, necessitating changes in the control computer to compensate.

The third category of Megafortress added electronic interception and eavesdropping equipment, along with a suite of ECMs that could turn a Spark Vark green with envy. These planes included Raven and Quicksilver. Their automated telemetry gathering skills were on call here.

They would record all electronic transmissions from and to the Indian weapon, augmenting the data gathered by the EB-52's powerful radar suite and the visual data from the Flighthawks. They weren't just spy planes, however; armed with Tacit-Plus anti-radiation missiles, they could do the job of two or three different planes, protecting an attack package as effectively as a coordinated group of Wild Weasels, Spark Varks, and Compass Call aircraft.

There were other possibilities for the type. The Army was very interested in adapting the plane for the Joint Surveillance Target Attack Radar System or JSTARS role, another mission currently filled by aircraft of the 707 type.

JSTARS E-8As, which had made their debut during the Gulf War, used Army and Air Force technology to track ground warfare units and targets; they could do for ground-attack forces what AWACS did for fighters. In theory, a Megafortress could accomplish the same thing while getting even closer to the action and delivering weapons itself. In fact, a good portion of the JSTARS technology had originally come from the Air Force's Pave Mover and related programs, which were already incorporated in the development base of the "standard" EB-52.

Various other improvements for the Megafortress were in the works, including new engine configurations, but the program itself was now fairly "mature." With production models ready to go, it had a certain set character to it—and, of course, it already had its own project manager, Major Alou.

The B-5 Unmanned Bomber Platform was wide-open, a vast cloud of potential waiting to be shaped, like the Megafortress had been when Bree joined the program. It was also the sort of program a captain could ride to a colonelcy and beyond.

Was that important? Was that what she was worried about?

No way. She wanted to be promoted.

Even though it would strain her marriage.

Zen was due for promotion soon, and with his record no one was going to stand in his way. That would almost certainly mean going to Washington. He hadn't served in the Pentagon, and for someone like Zen the Pentagon was a necessary and expected ticket to be punched. He'd be there already if it hadn't been for his accident.

What did that have to do with anything? She'd be at Dreamland and he'd be in D.C., one way or the other.

Give up the B-5? Why? Because it wasn't a "real" plane?

Maybe she was worried about something else. Maybe there wasn't room to have a two-career family.

So she'd do what? Quit? Play Suzy Homemaker?

Bullshit. She was to Suzy Homemaker as Zen was to . . .

A Pentagon paper-pusher. He'd never last a week there, even in a wheelchair.

"Coming up to Cathay," said Chris Ferris. His voice had a cackle to it, accented by the interphone circuit shared throughout the airplane. He'd spent considerable time coming up with an elaborate list of code words for the various coordinates on their mission chart and, for some reason, thought they were amusing as hell. "Cathay" was the release area for the Flighthawks. "Byzantium" was the southernmost point of their patrol orbit; "Confucius" was the northern point.

It could have been worse. Bree had put her foot down on a list of kung-fu heroes.

"Ten minutes to launch area," she told Zen, who was below on the Flighthawk deck.

"Ready to begin fueling, Quicksilver," he told her.

"All right. Chris?"

"As Li Po would say, 'The sun rises with anticipation.' "

"Li Po would be a Chinese philosopher?" Bree asked innocently.

"My barber," he answered, guffawing.

ZEN WATCHED THE COUNTDOWN IMPATIENTLY, WAITING for the Megafortress to begin the alpha maneuver that would increase the separation forces and helped propel the Flighthawk off the wing of the big plane. The vortices thrown off by the Megafortress were a complicated series of mini-tornadoes, but the computer and untold practice sessions made the launch almost routine. As the Megafortress dipped and then lifted away, Zen dropped downward with the Flighthawk, hurtling toward the sparkling ocean; the plane's engine rippled with acceleration. He pulled back on the stick, rocketing ahead of the Megafortress. No amount of practice, no amount of routine,

could change the thrill he felt, the electricity that sparked
from his fingers and up through his skull as gravity grap-
pled for the plane, losing—temporarily at least—the age-
old battle of primitive forces.

And yet, he was sitting in an aircraft more than three,
now four miles away, flying level and true at 350 knots.

"Launch procedure on Hawk Two at your convenience,
Hawk Leader," said Bree.

"Ready when you are, Quicksilver."

They launched the second Flighthawk, then worked
into their search pattern, a 250-mile narrow oval or "race-
track" over the ocean. The earlier spin around the surveillance area had shown there were a half-dozen
merchant vessels in the sea lanes but no military vessels.
Likewise, the sky was clear.

"We have a PS-5 at seventy-five miles," said Chris,
reading off the coordinates for a Chinese patrol plane
coming south from the area above Vietnam. Known to the
West as the PS-5, the flying boat was designated a Harbin
"Shuishang Hongzhaji," or "marine bomber," SH-5 by the
Chinese; the SH-5 had limited antiship and antisubmarine
capabilities. With a boat-shaped hull and floats beyond the
turboprops at the ends of its wings, the PS-5 belonged to
an early generation of waterborne aircraft.

Anything but fast, the PS-5 was lumbering about three
thousand feet above the waves at 140 knots. Zen noted
the location, which was fed from Quicksilver's radar systems into C^3. The long-range sitrep map showed the patrol
aircraft as a red diamond in the left-hand corner of his
screen, moving at a thirty-degree angle to his course.

Just beyond it were two green circles, civilian ships on
the water, one a Japanese tanker, the other a Burmese
freighter, according to a registry check performed by
Lieutenant Freddy Collins. Collins handled the radio intercept gear, and had been tasked with keeping tabs on
ship traffic as well. The other specialist, Torbin Dolk, handled the radar intercepts and advanced ECMs, backing up
and feeding Chris Ferris, the copilot.

"Getting some hits just beyond our turnaround point," warned Torbin. "Radar just out of range."

"Unidentified ship at grid coordinate one-one-seven-point-three-two at two-zero-zero-one," said Collins. "Could be a warship."

"Roger that," said Zen. He pushed the Flighthawks further ahead of the Megafortress, running close to the edge of their control range at ten miles.

"Looks like a destroyer," said Collins.

"On its own?" asked Bree.

"There may be something beyond it but I can't pick it out."

"Definitely something out there—I have two Su-33's at two hundred thirteen nautical miles right on our nose," said Chris. "They don't see us—turning—looks like they're high cap for somebody."

"Have another destroyer—looks like we have a location on the entire Chinese Navy," said Collins.

"Radar contact is Slotback; we're out of range. Computer thinks Su-33's or Su-27Ks, same thing," said Torbin.

"That would fit with the *Shangi-Ti,* the Chinese pocket carrier," said Collins. "Should be right about the edge of their patrol area."

The Su-33—originally designated Su-27K by the Russians—was a Naval version of the potent Su-27. Most of its modifications were minor, helping adapt the fighter to carrier landings and midair refueling. It could be configured for either fighter or attack roles, and despite its alterations remained as maneuverable as any piloted aircraft in the U.S. inventory. The Chinese air-to-air missile systems were not particularly advanced, but nonetheless got the job done, and the 30mm cannons in their noses tossed serious hunks of metal in the air.

"Okay, that puts the carrier one hundred nautical miles beyond Confucius," said Chris Ferris, collating all the data.

"Typical CAP?"

"Usually two Sukhois in the air; they should have two others ready to launch. They have to go one at a time, so it takes them a bit to cycle up. Endurance is limited. We don't have a lot of data on what sort of refueling procedures they use. Carriers are brand-new."

"What do you say we change our patrol area to get a better look at them," said Bree. "Roll tape from four or five miles away. What do you think, Hawk Leader?"

"Hawk Leader copies," Zen told his wife. "I'll wave to them."

"Roger that."

Northern Philippines
1200

DANNY FREAH CURLED HIS FINGERS AROUND ONE OF the handholds at the side of the helicopter as it took a sharp turn to the left, riding the nap of the jungle valley toward their destination. It was his first ride in the Dreamland Quick Bird, a veritable sports car compared to the Pave Lows and the MV-22 Ospreys he was used to.

Starting with a McDonald-Douglas MD530N NOTAR (for no tail rotor) Little Bird, the engineers had made several modifications to the small scouts. The most noticeable was the reworking of the fuselage, trading its thin skin for faceted carbon-boron panels similar to the material used in the body armor Whiplash troopers dressed in. Even though comparatively light, the panels were too heavy to cover the entire aircraft. However, the protection offered by strategically placed panels meant the aircraft could take a direct hit from a ZSU-23 at a hundred feet without serious damage.

Uprated engines compensated for the weight penalty; the single Alison turboshaft that motivated a "normal" Little Bird was replaced with a pair of smaller but more powerful turbos based on an Italian design. The techies joked the motors had been taken from supercharged spaghetti makers; they were in fact intended for lightweight hydrofoils and had a tendency to overheat when pushed to the max. However, the little turbos delivered over seven hundred horsepower (actually, 713.2) apiece, compared to the 650 generated by a standard Alison, itself no slouch. The fuselage now had a triple wedge at the bottom, the blisters helping accommodate additional fuel as well as adding hard-points for Hellfire missiles and other munitions. A pair of 7.62mm chain-guns were embedded in the oversized landing skids, so that even when on a transport mission, as it was now, the aircraft was never unarmed.

It was impossible to effectively reduce the helicopter's radar signature; flying more than a few feet off the ground would make it visible to any powerful active radar. The NOTAR helped funnel its heat signature, however, making it difficult to detect with infrared gear. It was relatively quiet as well, and could cruise at just over 170 knots; its top speed was beyond 220, though no one was entirely sure, due to the performance limits placed on the engines until the overheating problems were solved.

The Quick Bird couldn't quite keep up with the Osprey, which cruised around four hundred knots, nor did it have the range of the Pave Low or even the ubiquitous Blackhawk, but the little scout was clearly an improvement over the AH-6 Special Forces-optimized Little Bird, and that was high praise indeed. Easily transportable by cargo plane, two had been packed inside "Quickmover," the MC-17 that brought Danny and his team to the Philippines. Without breaking a sweat, off-loading them at the Philippine Air Force base had taken the crew less than ten minutes.

Danny glanced at the paper map in his lap, trying to correlate it and the satellite snaps he had on his clipboard with what he was seeing out the bubble of the helo cockpit. The southeastern islands of the Philippines were pristine jewels of unfettered nature, wild amalgams of jungle, volcano, and desert island. The Quick Birds' destination sat on the side of one of these gems, now less than five minutes away. Somewhat overgrown, the base had served as first a Japanese, and then an Allied, airport during World War II. Afterwards, it had seen use as a reserve and emergency airstrip and then a remote training area. Its concrete ran nearly 2,500 yards, more than enough for the Megafortresses to land and take off—once the jungle was cleared away and steel mesh put down to even out the rough spots.

"There it is," said the helo pilot, pointing ahead. "We got that spot at the north end we'll try for, Cap," said the pilot.

"Good," said Danny. The satellite photo seemed to show about seventy-five yards of clear area at the northern end, but even without pulling up his binoculars, Danny could see there were thick vines covering a good portion of it.

"Couple of clear spots I think," added the pilot, dropping his airspeed to hover.

"Let's survey the area before we land," said Danny. "I know you don't have too much fuel, but I'd like to get a feel for the terrain first."

"Not a problem," said the pilot, radioing the second helo.

The airstrip edged out over the sea, paralleling a cliff that hung over a rock-strewn, sandy beach. The light-blue water revealed it was partly protected by coral reefs. Just to the south was a jutting stone, an oddly shaped piece of yellow rock that would provide a good point for one of their radar surveillance units. A road had once wound into the jungle near the southwestern end of the strip; from the air it seemed almost entirely overgrown.

Though it wasn't visible, a village lay about seven miles to the south, at the extreme tip of the island. According to their briefing papers, there were less than a hundred people there. The rest of the island was uninhabited.

"All right, let's get down and get to work," Danny told the pilot.

The Quick Birds managed to find a clear spot on the gray-brown concrete big enough to land nearly side by side. Gear off-loaded, the two choppers tipped forward and rose, leaving Danny and his six men alone with a collection of flamethrowers, buzz saws, and other jungle-removing gear.

"All right, we have forty-five minutes before the helos get back with the rest of our gear," Danny told his men. "Half hour after that, the mesh for the runway should start arriving. Powder and Bison, I want a landing area hacked out so the helos can get down without breaking our stuff. Nurse, you and Jonesy do a perimeter sweep south and west. Pretty Boy, Blow—you guys do the same north and east. No chances, okay? I'll set up the com gear."

Powder picked up one of the four flamethrowers they'd brought to burn off the undergrowth, and hoisted the pack onto his back.

"Hold off on that, Powder," Danny told him. "Don't go starting fires until we have firebreaks and everything else in place."

"Just making sure it works, Cap," said Powder, flicking the trigger. The device didn't light at first, and Danny half-worried that the sergeant would set himself on fire before he got it going. "Woo—what I'm talking about," said Powder as a long red flame jetted from the nozzle.

"Sometimes I swear to God I'm a goddamn kindergarten teacher," said Danny, shaking his head.

"Powder never made it to kindergarten, Captain," said Bison, taking out the chain saws. "Got left back in pre-school."

Powder put the flamethrower back down. He took one of the large chain saws Bison had laid out and fueled. "Wait till I get this little humdinger goin', Cap. Gonna call me Mr. Jungle."

"Mr. Jungle Rot, more like it," said Bison.

"Just get going," Danny told them. "I want enough space for the MH-17 to land before nightfall so we can get the trailer in."

The trailer was an RV adapted for use as Whiplash's mobile command post.

"This is what I'm talkin' about," said Powder, revving his saw.

Aboard Quicksilver, above the South China Sea
1230

ZEN COULD SEE THE TWO SUKHOIS ON HIS LONG-RANGE scan as he approached. They were flying a figure-eight pattern over the aircraft carrier task force, their patrol circle never more than twenty miles from the surface ships. Unlike an American battle group, there was no radar plane aloft, and the carrier would be vulnerable to an attack by any aircraft equipped with American Harpoon missiles or even Exocets, which, at least in theory, could strike from about twenty-five miles away. Of course, the Chinese were probably counting on the radars in the Su-33's to pick up approaching aircraft before they were in range to attack, a not unreasonable expectation—unless the aircraft attacking were American.

The Flighthawks were not equipped for surface attack, and the Megafortress was not carrying AGMs; nor were they authorized to attack the Chinese, or any ship for that matter. If they were, the Chinese would be out one pocket carrier. The stealthy Flighthawks began turning at five miles from the carrier, still undetected by any of the screening radars. Zen split the Flighthawks, riding Two ahead of Quicksilver and trailing with One, just in case the Sukhois finally got curious. But they didn't.

"Two helicopters operating with the carrier," reported Collins, who was analyzing some of the signal intelligence and magnified visual information they'd gathered.

"Probably looking for subs," said Ferris.

"Torbin, do you have a plane near eight-four-zero, mark, three-two? Over that atoll?" asked Ferris.

"Uh, something way down south there, beyond our range—probably just a bleep or an echo," said the radar-intercept specialist. Zen could hear him punching the keys at his station. "Nothing. I'll keep an eye on it."

"No ships there," said Collins.

"Probably just a weird flake out," said Ferris.

They continued south, tracking over the mostly empty ocean. Zen tried to stay sharp by having the Flighthawks change positions, but this was a long and boring patrol, especially after the long flight to get out here.

"Okay, we have two ships traveling together, cargo containers. Tanker beyond that," said Collins finally, feeding Zen the coordinates. He put Hawk Two in trail behind Quicksilver, then took One into a shallow dive toward the two freighters. Traveling roughly a mile apart, the ships were stacked with cargo containers, trailers that could be ferried by truck or train once ashore. The containers could carry just about anything, and it was impossible to tell from the air what they held.

Hawk One nosed through some thin clouds, continuing downward through three thousand feet. He could see an Australian flag flapping at the rear of the tanker about three fourths of a mile away. He slid his right wing up slightly, gliding over the starboard side of the vessel, the belly video cam freezing on the ship. Collins, meanwhile, checked all of the ships against their listings, keeping track of what was down there.

"Not a known bad guy in the bunch," he said.

"Lot of little boats ahead," said Zen, nudging back on the throttle so he was making just under three hundred knots. "Let's take a look."

The small boats were clustered around several atolls at the western side of their patrol run. Two or three were fishing boats, flat-bottomed boats similar to Chinese junks. The others looked like open whaleboats with large motors, odd vessels to be this far from land, Zen thought.

"Brief says there's pirates and smugglers all through there," said Collins. "Sometimes they off-load at sea."

Contraband cargo often found its way to any of the various shores via such boats; though the dangers were many, the rewards were high. Drugs, arms, and ammunition were perennial favorites, but the real moneymakers here were mundane items, like cigarettes, booze, and, of all things, women's tampons. There was also the occasional cargo of humans and, for the big operators, automobiles.

"I'll run over low and slow again," said Zen. "See if we see any weapons."

Most of the boats had two or three people in them; in a few cases they seemed to be tending nets. No weapons were visible.

The Chinese aircraft carrier had made good progress in the hour or so since they'd last seen him. Zen pushed the two Flighthawks into a one-mile separation, running seven miles in front of the EB-52 at 28,000 and 31,000 feet as they approached the group. The Sukhois were noodling along at about four hundred knots a good five thousand feet below the lowest U/MF.

"Turn at two miles," said Bree. "Let's get a full read on their radars, their electronics, everything."

"Still not tracking us," said Torbin.

The Su-33's passed over the carriers as Zen started to make his turn. All of a sudden they hit their afterburners.

"Got their attention," said Chris. "We're on their radar. Two bandits, bearing—"

"Yeah, I got 'em," said Zen, who simply held his flight pattern as the Megafortress continued in its southern bank. The Chinese fighters apparently didn't pick up the smaller planes with their passive gear or their eyeballs, because as they passed, Zen tucked down over their wings. Had he lit his cannons, the carrier would have had to scramble all available SAR assets posthaste.

The Sukhoi pilots jinked downward sharply, kicking out flares and tinsel, undoubtedly mistaking the small fighters for missiles.

"More aircraft coming off the carrier," warned Torbin.

"They think the Flighthawks are missiles," said Zen. "Better ID ourselves as three planes."

"Roger that, Hawk Leader," said Breanna. "Chris—"

Before the copilot could respond, the RWR lit up.

"We're spiked," said Chris.

"Break it," said Breanna coldly. "Evasive maneuvers. Tell them we're not hostile."

"Yup."

The plane shifted left and right as Zen brought the Flighthawks around. The Sukhois had fired their missiles, then broken off—good, safe tactics, and in any event, Zen wasn't in a position to pursue, since he had to stay close to the mother ship and wasn't authorized to fire anyway.

"Broke it. We're clean," reported Chris. "Second set of fighters."

"No radar missiles," reported Torbin. "At least not active."

"Tell 'em we're peaceful," said Bree.

"I am," said Chris. "They're not answering."

Zen felt the big plane jerk hard to the right. The forward viewscreen from Hawk Two showed the pair of radar missiles ducking downward, deeked by either ECMs or chaff, or both.

"Bandits Three and Four are coming at us," said Chris. "Twenty miles, accelerating. Looks like they want heater shots."

"I'll duck them off," said Zen, flicking his wrist as he jumped back into Hawk One. One of the Sukhois was closing on the rear of the Megafortress and climbing at the same time, pushing the Saturn AL-31FM turbofans to the redline. Zen had a good angle to cut him off; he flicked the nose of Hawk One downward, running a direct intercept on the Sukhoi's canopy. C^3 gasped—to the computer it looked as if the pilot was going to put the plane's left wing directly through the persipex. Once more, the relatively limited radar in the Chinese plane had trouble finding the slippery, Miata-sized interceptor until it was almost in its face; the pilot threw his plane over so sharply that the Sukhoi began to spin. Zen whipped past, then circled back. The other Sukhoi broke off. As Zen turned

Hawk One back toward the Megafortress, he expected to see the Su-33 recovering and climbing out at the left side of his screen, but it wasn't there. He selected the wider angle to find it spinning furiously toward the water.

"Bandit Three is in trouble," said Chris.

"He's going in," said Zen. "He's wet." He jumped into Two momentarily, making sure that none of the other Sukhois were close enough to threaten the Megafortress. Then he took over One from the computer, riding down toward the sea as the plane augured in.

"No chute," said Chris. "Shit. Shit."

The Sukhoi pilot's own stupidity had led to his apparent death. Still, Zen felt a hole opening in his stomach.

"Two more planes coming off the carrier," said Torbin.

"Chris, tell them we're not hostile," said Breanna.

"They're either deaf or refusing to respond," said Ferris.

"Did you try the preprogrammed Chinese message?" she asked.

"Yes, ma'am. SAM indications—they're trying to lock us," he added.

"Break them. I want to stay in this area and help them locate the pilots."

"Going to be rough, Quicksilver," said Zen, who saw on his screens the two fresh Sukhois were trying to get their radar missiles on the Megafortress as well.

"Roger that," replied Bree. "Keep broadcasting. Evasive maneuvers. Tinsel. ECMs. Keep the assholes off us, Torbin."

"Roger that," said Torbin.

Zen spun Hawk One back north, directly over the area where the Chinese interceptor had hit the water. There was no sign of the plane. The churning waves looked a bit darker than the surrounding ocean, though that might have been Zen's imagination.

"Homers in the air. Jamming—geez, they're persistent buggers," complained Torbin.

"AA-8 Aphids—way out of range," said Chris.

The Russian-made antiaircraft missiles were IR homers whose design dated back to the late 1960s and early 1970s. Designed for extremely close-range work, they were generally ineffective at anything over a mile. They were, however, highly maneuverable, and when one managed to stick on Hawk One's tail, Zen found he had to twist to less than fifty feet over the waves before the missile gave up on him. It skipped into the water like a rock flung by a schoolboy across a lake; the warhead separated and bounced several times before disappearing into a swell nearly a mile from the original point of impact.

By then, Zen had climbed back toward the spot where the Sukhoi had gone in. A thin ooze had appeared on the surface; the camera caught twists of metal, plastic, and fabric as he flashed by.

The poor son of a bitch.

The poor *stupid* son of a bitch.

"Gun battery on the lead destroyer is firing!" warned Collins, his voice cracking. "I don't know what the hell at; we're about five miles out of range."

The Chinese destroyer, a member of the Jianghu III class, began peppering the air with rounds from its 37mm antiair gun. Quickly, two other escorts joined in. Their shells arced far away from the American planes, undoubtedly more an expression of frustration than a serious attempt to shoot down anything. Either because of the gunfire, or perhaps because they were running low on fuel, the first two Sukhois headed back toward the carrier. The plane that lost its wingmate also circled back toward the surface ships.

The two freshly launched Sukhois pushed menacingly toward the rear of the Megafortress. Zen's long-range video scan showed the planes had launched with only thin heat-seekers on their wings.

"Stinger radar is tracking," said Chris. "They're just out of range."

"Still not responding?" Bree asked.

"Negative."

"Jeff, what do you think?"

"Sooner or later they're going to hit something," he told her. "But I think we can hold these two off, then hope they get a helo over the wreckage," he added. Zen had worked with Bree long enough to know he was just reinforcing her own thinking. "Then we resume our patrol."

"I concur. Collins—you getting all the transmissions?"

"Oh, yes, ma'am. They're going to love this back at the Puzzle Palace," he added, referring to the NSA's analysis section. Dreamland's mission orders included provisions for forwarding intercept data to the spy agency, which would use them to update estimates of the Chinese military and its hardware.

Hawk Two was flying two miles north of the orbiting Megafortress, sitting between Quicksilver and the two Chinese planes. Zen told the computer to keep Hawk One in an orbit over the wreckage bobbing to the surface, then jumped back into Hawk Two. He nudged back on his speed, tilting his wing slightly to let the bandit on the left catch up. The Chinese pilot pulled up cautiously—a hopeful sign, since he could have angled for a shot.

Zen tried broadcasting himself, "spinning" the radio so that it scanned through the frequencies the Chinese were known to use. When he got no response, he went onto the Guard band, the international distress frequency that, at least in theory, all aircraft monitored.

"Hawk Leader to Chinese Su-33. If you can hear me, please acknowledge in some form. I understand you may not speak English. One of your aircraft ditched and I have the location marked for you."

Nothing, not even a click on the mike. At the same time, the Chinese seemed to understand that the American planes were not being aggressive; the Sukhoi pilot made no move to close on the Megafortress, or the Flighthawk for that matter, which would have been vulnerable to a close-quarters gun attack.

For about a third of a second.

"I have the coordinates for your aircraft," Zen said. He

read out the exact longitude and latitude where the aircraft went in. "He went into a high-speed spin at low altitude and hit the water," said Zen.

"Liar! You shot him down."

The voice was sharp in Zen's ears. It had come from one of the Chinese pilots, but when Zen asked them to repeat as if he hadn't heard, there wasn't even static in response. He repeated the information from before, then began turning with Quicksilver, watching the Sukhois carefully.

Neither made a move. Quicksilver's sophisticated eavesdropping gear picked up transmissions between the planes and the carrier. The code was in the clear, making it relatively easy for Collins to process. Locked on the frequency, he fed the voice stream into the automated translator, which produced readable text that could be tagged, corrected, and augmented at his station. He then piped it on the fly to the copilot, who was also getting a feed of the radar data Torbin processed. It was almost like sitting in the enemy's control room.

"Pair of helos coming out from the ships," reported Chris. "One off the carrier, one I think from the cruiser. Uh, our library says these are Panthers, Aerospatiale AS 565's, performance similar to the Dauphin, Dolphin—looks like basically the same aircraft here. French. Vectoring for the coordinates of the crash. Sukhois are supposed to, uh, wait—no, excuse me, they're supposed to watch us, that's all. Not engage."

The Panthers were, in fact, Chinese versions of the sturdy French utility chopper. They rode slowly toward the wreckage, skimming around the area three times before settling into hovers above some of the flotsam. Two figures jumped from one of the aircraft, undoubtedly divers recovering some of the wreckage.

"I have a radar at two hundred miles south," reported Torbin. "Uh, belongs to a missile—SS-N-127 That's wrong, but it's definitely targeting."

"Give me a heading," said Breanna. "Hawk Leader—"

"I'm with you," said Zen, pulling Hawk Two around and tucking tight to the EB-52 as it began to accelerate south.

"Lost it," said Torbin.

"The container ships," reported Collins a few minutes later. "I have an SOS. Fire. People in the water. Doesn't look good."

Philippines Forward Operating Area
1350

A LIFETIME AGO, AMERICAN AIRCOBRA P-39s had flown off the hard-packed dirt beneath Danny's feet. An unusual design for an American aircraft, the original models were hopelessly outclassed and outnumbered by the Japanese Mitsubishi A6M Zero-Sen, otherwise known as the "Zero," one of the best early designs of the war. The Aircobra was nonetheless a decent performer and a tough aircraft. Those that had flown from this base had played an important role helping to mop up Japanese resistance and provide air cover over a wide swath of the nearby Pacific.

Other aircraft had used the base as well—P-38's, some P-40's, B-25's, B-26's, and on several occasions B-29's. But if the ghosts of old machines could be said to haunt a place, it was the spirit of the P-39 that remained: tough, somewhat misunderstood jungle fighters who spit 37mm bullets from their nose and drummed through the air with a guttural hum.

Danny Freah didn't believe in ghosts—and yet he sensed something watched him now as he trudged up the hillside. He slid his helmet visor down and clicked into IR scan. The computer's shape-recognition program flashed a bright blue pinhole in a brighter blue circle at the top right-hand corner, showing that it was operating, but aside from a few rodentlike creatures about fifty or sixty feet away, the jungle was empty. Danny held his new MP-5 in his right hand as he climbed up slowly, stepping gingerly. The wrap on his knees held them tight, their thick bands doing some of the muscles' and ligaments' work holding the two halves of his legs together. The injury didn't bother him as he sidestepped down the hill; in fact, he thought it was easier than working on the stair machine, which was part of his regular rehab assignment.

Jemma would be heading back home by now. He could see her jaw set, her slight nod to the man asking if he could take her bags at the hotel.

A flicker of blue print at the right side of his viewscreen sharply brought back his attention. A yellow shape materialized from the foggy green and black shadows.

"CAT" said the legend below the small shape at the base of the tree.

Danny switched from IR to magnified optical, popping the scene magnification to five times. The computer was close—the Philippines leopard cat was roughly the size of a house tabby, though it wasn't likely to run up to Danny and ask for a bowl of milk. It stared in his direction, peering curiously from between the rattan and tree trunks. It curled its lip, hissing, then darted away.

Something else moved, fifty yards farther down the slope. Danny flicked back to IR mode, scanning slowly. A figure floated across his screen, ghostlike.

It took a moment before he realized the figure was actually in the trees. The computer, meanwhile, realized the figure was human. It didn't note any weapons.

The ghost began moving downward. The program now had measurements to work with: just under five feet, one hundred pounds.

More a kid than a man, and unarmed, Danny thought. He watched as the Filipino began to move through the woods, pushing through the underbrush. He followed slowly, as quietly as he could. There weren't supposed to be people here.

Danny hunkered down as he came to a narrow stream. It coursed down a run of odd rocks; the far bank was exposed. He waited until the figure was no longer visible, then picked his way across and continued downward in the direction the figure had gone.

He debated whether to try talking to the Filipino or not. He'd memorized a few words on the way out; while it was likely the person would know English—a large number of Filipinos used it as their second or even first language—Danny reasoned that using the national language would at least show he was trying to be friendly. The words for good morning—*Magandang umaga po*—stuck in his head; he couldn't quite remember the combination for good afternoon, which was very similar—*Magandang hapon po* or something like that.

Hapon, like harpon, only without the R.

Magandang hapon po.

He could link to Dreamland Command and get a native speaker whispering in his ear if he had to. He'd take the first shot on his own, make the effort.

Danny pushed toward a thick clump of vegetation clustered around a row of gnarled tree trunks. He struggled through about ten or twelve feet of thick bamboo before he could see beyond. Finally, he saw a swamp and pond about twenty yards across, beyond the edge of the thickest brush. Two small patches of dull brown appeared about twenty-five yards to the left just above the shoreline, partly obscured by rocks or old tree trunks. High magnification showed they were sheets.

IR view picked up the embers of a fire beyond them. A cooking fire, probably; the vegetation was too thick to see clearly.

A whistle broke the silence. Danny looked toward the water as a duck darted downward, grabbed something from just the surface, and then flapped its wings in an arc away, the prize in its beak.

The person he'd been following was crouched at the edge of the water, thirty-five yards away.

Watching him? Or the whistling duck?

Danny thought of standing and waving. Before he could

decide, the figure turned and moved away, walking slowly, without alarm, past the sheets. There looked like there might be a hut there, but Danny couldn't get an angle to see.

He'd have to find out more about the camp. Maybe go in there, find out who these people were. At the moment, though, there were more important things to do—he could hear the distant thump of helicopters bringing in supplies.

Couple of people in the jungle weren't much of a threat, especially if they stayed where they were. He'd set up a sensor picket, keep tabs on the ridge and the valley until he decided what to do, or got some advice from the colonel. They might have to move these folks out.

They could use that stream for a sensor line. Put some video cams on the swamp and pond. There looked like only one way across the water and deep muck, off on the right, not counting the sharply rising slope to the left.

Danny began moving back up the hill, pausing every so often to make sure he wasn't being followed. It was presumptuous to think of moving the people who lived here. How the hell would he feel if someone snuck into his neighborhood, spoke a few words in halting English, claimed to be long-lost friends, then said, sorry, you gotta go? We have a top-secret airfield in your backyard and we can't have you tripping over it.

But that was the way it went sometimes.

Dreamland Command Center
August 22, 1997, 2321 local (August 23, 1997, 1421 Philippines)

AS COLONEL BASTIAN TOOK A FRESH GULP OF COFFEE, he told himself the scratch in his eyes was due to the ventilation system's lack of humidity. Under other circumstances, he'd have been snoring in bed. He'd put in a long day, and unlike the crews that had flown out to the Philippines, didn't have an opportunity to take a nap; he always felt he ought to be the one in the Command Center when the shit hit the fan—as it was now. He rubbed his eyes, then began pacing near the large screen at the front of the room.

The Chinese aircraft had gone down on its own, obviously because the idiot pilot decided to play cowboy with the Megafortress. The Chinese were out-of-their-minds furious about it; they'd already filed a protest note in Washington claiming it had been shot down. While the politicians postured, Dog considered the more important development: the sinking of the container ship. The attack seemed to have been the work of the weapon they were supposed to be gathering data on, the Kali missile, apparently launched at long range by a diesel-powered snorkler—*seemed* and *apparently* being the operative words, since Quicksilver had been too far away to gather meaningful data on the weapon or launch platform.

Had Breanna simply ignored the Chinese aircraft and continued on her patrol, that wouldn't have been the case.

Not that she necessarily should have. Still . . .

According to the analysts who had examined the data, the radar indications and probable warhead size showed interesting parallels to the Russian SS-N-12, a very large antiship missile known as "Sandbox." But the SS-N-12 was far too big to fit into a submarine or be launched from beneath the water.

Presumably anyway.

"Sir, stand by for communication from the White House Situation Room," said the lieutenant at the com console. "Mr. Barclay."

"Go," said Dog.

The lieutenant's fingers pounded on his keyboard. Jed Barclay's pimple-strewn face flashed onto the screen. He had deep black bags under both eyes; back East it was around three in the morning.

"Colonel, uh, Jed Barclay here."

"Go ahead, Jed."

"Pacific Fleet's making some noise. The boss man

wanted me to give you a heads-up. USCINCPACCOM's throwing a territory fit."

"Acknowledged," said Dog, who actually would have preferred to say something else.

"Whiplash order is being reviewed. They're going to look for an opinion from you," added Jed.

"Opinion on what?"

"Whether the Megafortresses can stop ships from being sunk."

"Okay, we'll start working on it." Colonel Bastian wasn't sure they could; they had no ASW weapons on the Megafortresses. Besides, protecting shipping was a Navy task, and if that became the primary mission, the Pacific Fleet would surely get the job. Their most likely role would be working with PACCOM as they had with CENTCOM in the Middle East, though the personalities here were considerably more prickly.

"I think the Navy may suggest escorts, flagships, like they did in 1987 with tankers in the Persian Gulf, the oil crisis," added Jed. "But most of the fleet is still up near Taiwan and Japan, uh, due to the situation on the mainland. The other major assets are near India and the Gulf— I guess you know that. So, uh, they're scrambling to figure out where to allocate what. I don't know how long it will be before there's a decision. Might be days or weeks."

"Okay," said Dog.

Barclay blinked.

"Maybe you ought to catch some Zs, Jed," said Dog. "Have you slept since you got back?"

"Thanks, Colonel." Barclay managed a weak smile. "You look a little tired yourself."

"A little."

"You have any more information about the Chinese plane?" asked Jed.

"No. I imagine the pilot didn't make it," said Dog. "Zen had a Flighthawk nearby and we don't have any video showing an ejection, let alone a chute."

"Yeah. Tough luck for him."

Dog nodded, though he felt more sympathetic. While the Chinese pilot wasn't exactly an ally, it seemed a waste that he had died. Dog hated the idea of any pilot dying in an accident, even if he'd caused it himself.

"Um, State may contact you," added Jed. "They're a little behind the curve on this, so they may need a full, uh, briefing. Director says do it, but you have to watch their clearance."

"What exactly does that mean?"

"Nothing on Kali," said Jed.

"Then what's the sense of briefing them?"

"Yeah. Not my call," said Jed, which Dog had learned was Jed's standard response when he agreed something didn't make sense, but his boss hadn't listened to the reasons. "I guess you have to do what you can do."

"All right, Jed. We should have the cargo planes on the Philippines tonight," added Dog.

"I'll keep you updated," said Jed.

"Thanks." Dog killed the connection himself with his remote control, then clicked onto the Quicksilver circuit to update them.

Aboard Quicksilver, over the South China Sea
August 23, 1997, 1430 local (August 22, 1997, 2330 Dreamland)

CARGO STRETCHED ACROSS THE WATER LIKE SO MANY icebergs. The fantail of the ship jutted upward from the water, its large screw looking like a bizarre metal daisy waiting to be plucked. Zen brought the Flighthawk down for a pass at two thousand feet, his airspeed bleeding back under two hundred knots. He could see bodies in the water; two or three appeared to be clinging to something, and there was a man on one of the floating cargo containers.

"I think we have survivors," he told Breanna. "I'm going to take another pass and try and get better video. You might want to radio any ships that are coming."

"We're in the process of making contact now," she told him. "We're going to pipe your feed up here."

"Hawk Leader," acknowledged Zen.

He checked Hawk Two, still in trail above and behind Quicksilver, then turned Hawk One around for another run. The feed off the robot plane was being pumped back to Dreamland, where it could be analyzed for potential survivors, as well as any hazardous cargo or weapons.

The merchant ship that had been sailing ahead of the container vessel when it was struck had made a large, cautious turn in the water and was approaching the debris field slowly. It hadn't yet lowered boats into the water. In answer to the SOS, another vessel, a tanker, was about ten miles away, coming north at fifteen knots. Several miles beyond the tanker, but making better time, was a cruise ship. Collins had ID'd the tanker and cruise ship already—the *Exxon Global* and the *Royal Scotsman*—and now Ferris clicked in to say they had acknowledged his message that there were survivors in the water. The closer merchant ship, meanwhile, did not answer on any of the frequencies the copilot tried, even as it continued at a snail's pace toward the bobbing containers.

"Hawk Leader—we're getting something twenty miles west of that tanker—odd reading on the water," said Ferris. "Could be our sub getting ready to surface. We want to change course to check it out."

"Yeah, go for it," said Zen, immediately turning toward the coordinates.

Hawk One cruised in range just in time to see a submarine rise gently above the waves, the black, elongated oval of its conning tower pushing aside the water. Zen slid around the sub at just over three thousand feet; Collins ID'd it as a Russian Kilo, a diesel-powered boat that according to his brief usually didn't operate this far south.

"This the bastard that sank the container ship?" questioned Zen.

"Not sure who it is," said Collins. "We don't have any

transmissions. I'm piping your feed to Dreamland, but they can't ID it either. Probably Chinese, not Indian."

"You think the Chinese sank the ship?"

"Stand by, Hawk Leader," said Collins, undoubtedly so he could talk to Dreamland people uninterrupted.

Zen took two passes low and slow, but failed to pick up any identifying marks. Like nearly all modern designs, the sub had no bow gun or surface weapons, besides its torpedoes and mines, and seemed to be taking no hostile action. It didn't use its radio either; the only emissions coming from it were from a relatively short-range surface search radar, which Torbin announced was a "Snoop Tray."

"Checking on his handiwork?" Zen asked.

"Can't tell for sure what he's doing," answered Torbin. "But I don't think these guys carry cruise missiles. Assuming he's Chinese."

"Thinking is, definitely Chinese," said Collins, coming back into the discussion. "Container ship almost certainly got nailed by a cruise missile, so odds are this guy's clean. Container ship was supposedly going to Pakistan, so the implication is that might have been a motive; that, or target practice."

Zen had dealt with the Chinese and their proxies before; he didn't trust them not to have sunk the ship.

"Ship captains are requesting instructions," said Ferris. "One of them got the sub on his radar; now they're all chattering about it."

"Tell them to proceed with the rescue," snapped Breanna. "Collins, if you can figure out what the hell radio frequency they're using, advise the submarine to help out or get lost!"

"We don't have a precoded message for that," said Collins. "Not in Chinese."

"Do it in English. Use every frequency you can think of—Russian and Indian as well as Chinese. Hell, try Dutch and French too."

"Yes, ma'am," said Collins.

"Sub's moving southward, changing course," said Zen. He brought Hawk One down to five hundred feet and rode the sub bow to stern. There were three or four men in the tower; no weapons visible. Hawk One was moving too fast to get a good look at uniforms, let alone faces, and the freeze-frame didn't make it any clearer. "Looks like they're headed toward the damaged ship. If they try to interfere with the rescue, I'm going to perforate their hull."

"It may come to that," said Bree. "Let's drop down a bit and make sure they know we're here."

"They'd be awful blind not to," said Zen. He did a quick check on Hawk Two; its systems were all in the green and the computer had it in Trail Two, one of the preset flight patterns programmed into the Flighthawk's onboard systems. To save communications bandwidth, a number of routine flight operations and patterns were carried aboard the robot, allowing it to perform basic functions without being told precisely what to do. In Trail Two, it homed in on the mother ship, staying precisely three miles off the V-shaped tail, varying its altitude and position as it flew, pretty much the way a "real" pilot would.

"Uh-oh. Got another sub surfacing," said Chris as the Megafortress spiraled down toward the ocean. "Five miles beyond the cruise ship."

"On it," said Zen, jumping into Hawk Two as the Megafortress changed course to get a look.

In the few minutes it took to get in range, the submarine was already fully surfaced. Its conning tower was longer than the first sub's, shaped like a rounded dagger with the knifepoint facing backward. Otherwise, the sub itself seemed to be roughly the same shape and size as the Kilo.

"Not in our library," said Chris. "We'll want to route video on this to Dreamland."

Zen had the Flighthawk down to two thousand feet. Tipping the wing gently, he cruised around the submarine, trying to go as slow and steady as possible. There were no markings on it, let alone a flag, but he felt sure this was what they'd been sent to find—the Indian hunter-killer that was blowing up Chinese ships.

"Zen, they think it's a modified Kilo," said Chris Ferris. "But the conning tower looks like an Akula, which is a nuke boat. They're real interested in this; it's off their maps."

Zen nudged lower for another pass. They'd just scored a major intelligence coup, but Zen wasn't particularly impressed.

"What's the Kilo doing?" Zen asked.

"Moving toward the wreckage," answered Ferris. "Still on the surface. Think they'll spit at each other?"

"I wouldn't mind that," said Zen. "As long as they don't interfere with the rescue."

"Collins, see if you can you hail them."

"Trying to communicate with them now," said Collins. "Nobody's acknowledging. Wait, here we go."

Collins switched off for a few moments, then came back on the interphone to explain he had spoken to the captain of the cruise ship, who said he would do nothing to endanger his passengers or crew. He'd asked if the Americans would guarantee their safety.

"Tell the captain we'll do what we can," Bree said.

"He doesn't seem to think that's good enough," he reported back. "He's holding off. I gotta think the others are going to do the same, Captain."

The sitrep showed Collins was correct: the surface vessels were no longer moving toward the debris field.

"We have a pair of Sukhois inbound," warned Chris. "Coming at us at zero-ten, one hundred miles away, about five hundred knots."

"Air-to-surface radars active," said Torbin. "Two more planes behind them."

"I confirm," said Chris.

"I can jam," said Torbin.

"Hold on till they're in firing range," said Breanna. "I'll

make the call then. In the meantime, let's see what Dreamland thinks."

"Gotcha, Cap."

Zen turned Hawk One back toward the floating debris field. As the sun slipped steadily downward, a storm front approached, and while this was a warm part of the ocean (near the surface, the water temperature was roughly thirty degrees Celsius or eighty-six degrees Fahrenheit), it would feel cold if you stayed in it long enough. No way the people clinging to the tops of the container ships and the debris in the water were going to make it through the night. They had to be rescued now.

"Orders remain to take no hostile action," Breanna reported.

"Okay, but how do we get these guys to close in and pick up the survivors?" said Zen.

"Working on it, Jeff," she told him.

"If we can get the subs to take their dispute outside, we can probably reassure the civilians," said Chris. "Maybe get them to move this catfight to the south."

"You want to try suggesting that to them?"

"I can give it a whack," said the copilot. About a minute later, he came back over the interphone to announce no one had answered his broadcasts.

"Well, let's show these jokers we're serious," said Bree. "Zen, I'm going to take it down low and buzz both of them, all right?"

"Hawk Leader."

"Chris, keep track of the Sukhois. Open bay doors."

"Open bay doors?"

"I want them to think we're prepared to fire. We're going to two thousand feet—no, one thousand. I want them to count the rivets."

"Yes, ma'am."

It was a serious calculated risk—at one thousand feet the Megafortress would be easy pickings for a shoulder-launched SAM. On the other hand, the move was sure to get their attention. Collins began broadcasting an all-channels message, telling the submarines to stand off while the surface ships made the rescue.

"How are those Sukhois?" asked Bree as she dipped her wings toward the waves.

"Five minutes to firing range," said Chris.

"Keep an eye on them," said Bree. "Hang with me, Flighthawks."

Zen rolled Hawk One just ahead of the big Megafortress as she pulled level. He tightened Hawk Two on Quicksilver's tail; if one of the subs did fire a heat-seeker, he hoped to be close enough to help suck it off.

The video on Hawk Two caught one of the crewmen aboard the first Kilo covering his head as Breanna came over. The others had thrown themselves to the deck. The second submarine had started to change course south when they reached it.

"Maybe they got the message," said Collins.

"They broadcasting?" Bree asked.

"Negative," said Collins.

"We have communication from a Navy plane," said Chris. "They're en route; about two hundred and twenty nautical miles to our south-southwest. Call name is Pegasus 202."

"Tell them to stand off until we see what the Sukhois are doing," said Bree.

As Zen edged back toward the debris field, he saw one of the freighters was once again moving toward the survivors. A small boat was being lowered from its side.

"Okay, this is shaping up," he told the others, passing along what he was seeing. Breanna began a wide, banking track to take the Megafortress back up to a more comfortable altitude.

"Hold on. Somebody's broadcasting to the civilian ships, in English," said Collins. "Telling them to stand off. They want them to move out of the area. It's the sub, that Kilo—definitely Chinese."

"Pipe it in," said Bree.

The accent made the words difficult to decipher

quickly, but it was clear the speaker did not want the civilians nearby. Breanna clicked her transmit button when he paused, identifying her plane, then asking the speaker to do the same. There was no answer at first, then the speaker repeated, more or less, what he had said before, adding that the Chinese Navy had the situation under control.

"Other sub is diving," said Chris.

"Those suckers are going to start shooting at each other," Torbin warned. "Sukhois are tracking."

"Collins, tell the civilian ships to move back," said Bree. "Torbin, see if you can jam those radars so they can't lock—"

"Missiles in the air! Sukhois are firing—AGMs—ship missiles, I mean. Shit!"

Dreamland Command
August 22, 1997, 2358 local (August 23, 1997, 1458 Philippines)

"PACCOM WANTS TO TALK, SIR," SAID THE LIEUTENANT just as Dog was going to take a quick break. "Admiral Allen."

"Don't they sleep out there?" asked the colonel, returning to his console.

"It's only about nine in Pearl."

"Rhetorical question," said Dog. "Let 'er rip."

The screen at the front of the room blinked white, then transformed into a high-resolution video feed showing a small office area filled with a half-dozen frowning Navy commanders. The script at the bottom of the screen identified the source as CinCPacSit, a top-level secure facility for Pacific Command. Admiral Allen, with his sleeves rolled up, stood in front of a large map table, his face as red as the flag used to provoke the proverbial bull.

"What the hell are you doing out there?" Allen demanded.

"Excuse me?" said Dog.

"Bullshit on that."

"With all due respect—"

"Stow it, Bastian. What is happening out there? Why are you picking a fight with the Chinese?"

"I'm not, sir."

"Are you trying to be the second coming of Brad Elliott?"

Colonel Bastian hadn't expected Admiral Allen to be happy about the incident, but he didn't anticipate the personal attack. Nor did he appreciate the comment about General Elliott. "Sir, I'm operating under strict orders," he told the screen, controlling his own rising anger.

"What yahoo gave the order to start a war with China?" demanded Allen. "I want an explanation, Bastian."

Allen made an obvious attempt to control his temper, his hands pulling down the sides of his shirt.

"As you can read on the Web net," Dog said, pausing between nearly every word, "two Sukhoi Su-33's took off from a Chinese carrier and approached our aircraft while on routine patrol. They seemed to think the U/MFs were missiles, they took evasive action, and one of the Chinese pilots put his plane into an unrecoverable spin. His loss was regrettable."

"I don't believe it happened that way," said Allen. "You're telling me the Chinese pilots are that bad?"

"I'm not critiquing the flying abilities of the Chinese, sir."

"Why wasn't I notified immediately?"

"By me?"

"Damn straight. You didn't even clear the mission with my people."

"It's not my role to inform you." Dog wasn't exactly sure what had happened—generally, the theater commander would be notified of an important operation by Washington, and the Navy certainly had had input prior to the Whiplash Order being issued. It was possible Allen had been bushwhacked by Washington—but it was also possible he was trying to exert control over Colonel Bastian and the operation.

Which wasn't going to fly.

"This isn't over, Colonel," said Allen. The feed died with a pop that sounded very much like an explosion.

"I wouldn't think we'd be that lucky," Dog told the blank screen.

Aboard Quicksilver, above the South China Sea 1500 local

BREANNA STEADIED THE PLANE AT NINE THOUSAND FEET as they sorted out the attack. The Chinese planes had launched eight missiles and then immediately begun to turn back north.

"I've got a lock on one Sukhoi," reported Chris. "We can shoot him down."

"Negative," said Breanna. "Let's focus on the missiles."

"Eight in the air, skimming down in a pattern similar to Exocets," he told her. One of the standard Megafortress simulation routines used the Scorpion AMRAAM-pluses to shoot down French-made Exocet antiship missiles. Though slightly outside of the Scorpion's design parameters, properly handled, the execution was not difficult.

Except they only had four Scorpions, and ordinarily would use two apiece on the targets to assure a hit.

"What's their target?" Breanna asked.

"I'd guess the sub," said Chris.

Torbin concurred. "There's no way they're going to come close to the sub, though," he added. "It's going to take them another four minutes to get into the area. If they're Exocets, or something like them, they'll run on inertia guidance, pop up, and then hit whatever they can in the area."

"They're moving at just over five hundred knots," said Chris. "We can get two."

"Let's target them singly," Breanna told him.

"Not a high-percentage shot."

"Target them," she told her copilot.

"Tracking. They're low."

"Bay."

"Bay open. We're locked."

"Go."

"Fire Fox One," he said, indicating that a radar missile was being launched. The Scorpions rolled off the launcher as soon as it rotated into position.

"ECMs," said Breanna after the last air-to-air missile had left.

"Working," said Torbin. "Not going to have much of an impact until they pop up and look for a target. May not work even then. I'm not sure what we're looking at."

"Do your best," said Breanna. "Chris, see if you can plot out a course to have us sweep in front of them and dish out Stinger air mines. Maybe we can put enough shrapnel in the air to knock them down."

"I was just playing with that. I think we can get a shot at two, but there are two on outside patterns sweeping around in an arc," he told her.

"Missiles are tentatively ID'd as VJ-2's, back-engineered Exocets," said Torbin. "But I don't know. They were launched from sixty miles, which ought to be beyond their range."

"Let's not get too hung up on their exact specifications," said Breanna. "Are they communicating with the Sukhois for guidance?"

"Negative," said Collins.

"Alert the civilians," she added. "Though I'm not sure what good that's going to do."

Chris hit a button that popped a flight path onto Bree's navigation screen. "Here's the course, Captain. Kind of a stutter step with a V in it. I don't know."

"Doable," said Breanna as the three-dimension overlay swirled around on the lower-right screen area. Her mind and body translated the sweeping arcs into a succession of forces; her muscles rehearsed the pulls.

"Two minutes to pop-up," said Torbin.

"Hawk Leader, this is Quicksilver," said Bree. She could feel her tongue and cheeks tightening, a clipped precision taking over her brain. "We're going to try and take out two of those remaining missiles. It doesn't look like we can reach numbers three and eight on that targeting screen Chris downloaded to you."

"They're mine," said Zen.

"Missile one is a home run!" interrupted Chris as their first AMRAAM hit its target.

"Thanks, Jeff," Bree told her husband. "Hang on. This is going to be a bit of a ride."

She took a breath, then put her hand on the throttle slide, goosing the engines as she tucked her wing, pirouetting the big plane in the sky. The massive Megafortress responded as nimbly as an F/A-18, turning with the grace of a veteran ballerina. Bree felt the impact all across her body, the cells in her speed suit inflating as they pulled over seven Gs.

She'd never feel that flying the B-5. She'd be sitting in a bunker at Dreamland, commanding the plane through a series of dedicated satellites. Gravity would be just another formula on the screen.

"Chinese sub is diving," said Collins.

"Smart man," said Torbin.

"Missile Two missed. Suck," said Ferris.

"All right. Full suite of ECMs," she told Torbin.

"We're singing every song we know, backwards and forwards," he answered, working his gear.

"Chris, give us chaff as we start the sweep. Anything we can do to confuse them."

"Okay. We can get that number-two missile in the sweep."

"Hang on."

The Megafortress's flight computer projected the intercept course on her HUD display as an orange dash along a crosshair at the center of the screen. Breanna moved her hand on the stick gently, holding the plane precisely onto the line. The approaching missiles were not yet visible to the naked eye, but the radar handed their positions to the computer, which obligingly painted them as red arrowheads on the screen. Truth be told, this was almost as fly-by-numbers as anything she did in the UMB. Breanna didn't have to be in the plane at all—and, in fact, didn't really have to do anything more than tell the computer to follow the dotted line.

She loved the pull of this plane around her, the feel and idea of it as it swayed in the air, the long, swept wings and their variable leading and trailing edges tilting Quicksilver at a thirty-degree angle as the chaff canisters popped out in the air, spreading a metallic curtain above the ocean. She loved the hard hit of gravity as she cranked the plane 180 degrees, holding her turn so tight the computer complained, dishing up a stall warning. She snickered—she knew this aircraft better than any computer program, and it was nowhere near its performance envelope and was miles away—miles—from stalling or even losing more momentum than she wanted.

"Thirty seconds to intercept!" said Chris, his voice rising like the high soprano of a boy in a children's choir, the excitement overwhelming him.

What computer could do that?

"Here come the zags," Bree told her crew. She slammed the plane hard south, dipping her wing momentarily and then gliding into a banking climb. The plane's tailbone jutted down, tracking the targets.

"Firing," said Chris.

Breanna held the plane against the staccato rumble, rising and sliding across the air, standing the massive, heavy plane up at nearly fifty degrees as the engines groaned, walking Quicksilver across the sky as if she were a dolphin skipping across the waves. Gravity and adrenaline punched against each other; the plane barely balancing the contrary forces.

Sex might be better than this, but some nights it could be damn close.

*   *   *

ZEN PUSHED THE FLIGHTHAWKS AWAY FROM THE MEgafortress. He had to turn the U/MFs, then trade altitude for acceleration as the missiles came on, as if they were pursuing fighters. The VJ-2's were flying low, relatively straight courses. Shooting down the small, fast-moving missiles was not an easy task; C^3's tactics section estimated the odds at under fifty percent apiece.

Forty-three and thirty-eight, to be exact.

The two missiles were separated so far apart that Zen had to stick one U/MF on each. He'd have to let the computer take one of them—thousands and thousands of hours of tests and experience showed it was nearly impossible to control both robots successfully in a high-speed furball.

Quicksilver's tracking gear guessed at the missiles' targets from their courses. The missile arcing in from the west was flying for the tanker; the other had the cruise ship in its sites.

No-brainer. Give the computer the one on the tanker. It had the easier shot besides.

"Computer, take Hawk Two. Complete intercept. Destroy target."

"Computer acknowledges."

Zen jumped into Hawk One as the plane whipped through a turn to get on the Chinese VJ-2's tail as it came on. There was so much electronic tinsel and ECM fuzz in the air, the computer warned the command signal had degraded; Zen pushed away the warning, pushed away everything but the streaking gray blur that whipped into the bottom corner of his viewscreen. He had his throttle slide at max, his stick pressed forward slightly, the Flighthawk at a shallow-angle dive over the rear of its target. His pipper glowed yellow, then pulsed, then went back to yellow. He pushed his nose down harder, trying to get his gun on the missile. The white blur of the cruise ship illuminated the other end of his screen, the ocean swirled into blue.

He had yellow. He had red. He pressed the trigger as the missile tucked hard right. Zen shoved his stick to follow, his tail flying up, the Flighthawk wallowing in the air.

A red triangle. Zen nailed down the trigger, pushing a stream of 20mm bullets into the rolling silver-gray blur sliding diagonally toward the right corner of his screen.

Firing 20mm bullets at an aircraft while flying between four and five hundred miles an hour is an iffy thing. The laws of motion get complicated; not only are you dealing with the momentum of both aircraft, but the actions of the bullets and gun greatly complicate the equation. A relatively small aircraft like the Flighthawk could be greatly affected by the spin and recoil action of the revolving Gat, even though these were reduced in the modified M61 it carried in its nose. The bullets, meanwhile, reacted in several dimensions at once, torn between their own momentum and that of the plane. With a target as relatively thick as the tail section of a Sukhoi fighter-bomber, the complicated physics made a direct hit hard enough; reduce the target size by a factor of thirty or so, and hitting the bull's-eye became exceedingly difficult.

None of which consoled Zen for missing.

Though the waves were now less than a thousand feet away, Zen hung on, still holding his nose down. The cruise ship grew rapidly into the size of a brick. He sprayed shells at the sea, and saw the swells grabbing them. At a hundred feet, Zen got a proximity warning, pulled up slightly, and kept firing. The splutter of bullets sailed all around the spinning gray cylinder. Suddenly, the stream connected. The missile shot into a somersault and then exploded. Zen yanked back on the stick, said, "Computer, take One," and jumped into the cockpit of Hawk Two.

The computer had already started to fire. Its target jerked left, then nosed up. Zen overrode the computer, pressing the trigger though his pipper was yellow. The ocean suddenly was all he could see—the missile was riding straight into the water.

He jerked upward, thinking the ship had been saved. But even as he did, he caught a large splotch of black in his face, and realized he was a lot closer than he'd thought to the tanker. Even before climbing back and spinning around to get a good view of the battle area, Zen realized the missile had survived just long enough to find its target, slamming into the side of the vessel at five hundred knots.

Philippines
1730

MARK STONER STEPPED OFF THE HELICOPTER SWIFTLY, ducking reflexively as the whirling rotors whipped grit against his face and clothes. He moved quickly toward the edge of the concrete, lugging his two Alice packs with him. The concrete ran surprisingly smooth, though there were a few spots where men were working on burning up roots and vines, and at the northern end a bulldozer and a buzz saw or two were hacking down a thick row of overhanging trees. Overall, the strip looked long, wide, and amazingly well-prepared.

The Whiplash people had established a sensor perimeter, using audio sensors, land radar, and optical and IR mini-cams tied by land lines to a sandbagged area about ten yards off the southern end of the airstrip. Stoner spotted it and began walking in that direction, ignoring the wind whipping from the wash of the Chinook that had deposited him on the island. Captain Danny Freah, the young Air Force officer who headed the deployment team, stood with his hands on his hips looking over the shoulder of a Whiplash trooper as they surveyed the array of video tubes.

Stoner recognized the captain's frown; he'd seen it on the face of every one of his superiors when he was in the Navy. Bastards must be issued it the day they graduate officer's school.

"Captain," said Stoner.

"Hey," responded Danny. "Be with you in a second." He leaned over his man and began tapping one of the two keyboards. About twice the size of a computer keyboard, it had two rows of oversized buttons at the top and several fat sections of others on either side of the QWERTY layout. There were tiny legends on several, but most merely had letters and numbers, like "A4" and "DD-2."

"Impressive," said Stoner when Danny straightened. "Shows you the whole perimeter?"

"Yeah," said Danny.

"What's that?" One of the video screens was focused on two pieces of cloth stretched in a clearing beyond a small pond.

"Looks like a little village," said Danny. "It's beyond the ridge, down the rift, maybe a mile, little less."

"I can get them moved," said Stoner. He reached into his pack for his satellite phone.

"That's not necessary. Not yet," said Danny.

"No, it is."

"My call here," said the captain.

"No, it's not."

Danny's eyes narrowed and his jaw set—another officer expression Stoner was very familiar with.

"With all due respect, Mr. Stoner, I'm responsible for security here. My call."

"This is my mission," said Stoner flatly. He pushed the cover of the phone up, and dialed his Agency liaison in Manila, the deputy station chief.

He'd hit the last digit when the captain's thick black hand folded around the phone.

"No," said Danny.

Stoner took a breath and straightened his body, fully relaxed except for his grip on the phone. If he jerked his knee up and pushed his left elbow, the Air Force officer would fall to the ground with a collapsed windpipe.

"Let me spell it out," said Danny, still holding the phone. "There are no more than a dozen people there. At the moment, they've made no move to come up over the ridge, and they have no way of communicating with the outside world. The other side of their camp is covered by another swamp. I have the only path out under video surveillance, and I have the beach opposite them under watch as well. If we move them, we'll make a lot of noise and potentially a lot of fuss. It's definitely an option, but I'd like to hold it off until necessary. I can take them prisoner in a half hour if need be. They're unarmed, and they're not getting away."

"You don't know what you're dealing with," said Stoner. He heard the words of his Zen master at the back of his head, telling him to breathe, telling him to maintain the center of the burning candle flame in his chest.

"Granted," said Freah. "But this is the best way to proceed if we're going to keep this base covert."

The captain was a young guy, with an impressive war record. He probably also thought he could deck Stoner if it came to that.

Stoner smiled.

"Captain, please let go of my phone," he said gently. "We'll do it your way—but let me just tell you something." He paused, waiting for the officer to let go of the phone. Released, he brought his arm down and bowed his head—then in a flash put his hand at Danny's neck, fingertips precisely on the two common carotid arteries. "Do not touch me again. Sometimes reflexes can be deadly."

He pulled his hand back quickly.

The Whiplash trooper who'd been watching the video cams was standing behind him, his MP-5 pointed at Stoner's head.

"Good point," said Danny—whose pistol was out and pointed at Stoner's stomach.

Aboard Quicksilver, over the South China Sea
1732

THE FLAMES LICKING UP FROM THE BLACKENED METAL were surprisingly small. The smoke, on the other hand, furled in all directions, a massive squat funnel that stretched all the way toward the debris field where the first ship had gone down. Zen took Hawk Two through the thick hedge of black, brown, and gray; not even the high-tech array of sensors on the Flighthawk could penetrate it.

"Can't quite get a visual," he told Breanna. "I think she's broken in two, but still attached, if you know what I mean. Like a twig that snapped but it has the top bark attached."

"Copy that," she replied. "Be advised they're repeating their SOS and saying they're abandoning ship."

"Hawk Leader." He banked as he cleared the heavy smog. A small portion of the rear of the tanker was visible below the smoke; he came back and crossed through the clear space, maybe eight or nine feet over the waves. A Zodiac-type rubber boat had been set into the water and was pulling away.

"I see the crew," said Zen. "What's up with that cruise ship?"

"They're still southeast," said Collins. "Moving at about four knots."

Zen pushed the Flighthawk skyward, toying with the idea of buzzing the liner. But that would serve no purpose; you really couldn't blame the captain for getting the hell out of there.

"Tell him there's a Zodiac with the crew of the tanker heading in his direction," Zen said.

"The captain says he'll stand by to pick up survivors, but they have to come to him," said Collins.

Zen brought Hawk Two back over the Zodiac. There were six or seven men in the boat.

Six or seven. How many manned a ship like that? Had to be more.

Damn. Damn.

"Hawk Leader, we're getting pretty far into our fuel reserves," said Breanna. "We're talking to Dreamland now—we can land at the Philippines."

"Hawk Leader."

"How's your fuel?" she asked.

"Yeah, I have to refuel," he said.

"We'll get into an orbit. We'll hold here until the last possible second," added Breanna.

"Yeah."

Zen pushed Hawk Two into a bank, sliding toward the Zodiac. Someone in the front of the small boat waved. He wagged his wings in recognition.

Poor SOB was probably cursing him out.

"Navy Orion is now zero-five away," said Chris. "I gave them the lowdown," he added. "They claim they can see the smoke from where they are."

"Yeah," was all Zen could say.

Dreamland Command
August 23, 1997, 0158 local (August 23, 1997, 1758 Philippines)

WHEN LIEUTENANT COLONEL BASTIAN PUT HIS HANDS to his neck and stretched them backward, his vertebrae cracked so loudly the lieutenant at the communications desk jerked his head around.

"Just a little stiff," said Dog. He glanced toward Major Lou "Gat" Ascenzio, who'd come in to spell him nearly an hour before. Gat—he'd earned his nickname as an A-10A "driver" in Iraq—was a recent arrival at Dreamland, assigned to head the tactical satellites and related projects. "I'm going to grab some Zs," Dog told him. "Anything comes up, beep me, all right?"

"Yes, sir. You ought to get some rest."

"Thank you, Major," snapped Dog—Gat's habit of restating the obvious annoyed the hell out of him. But as Ascenzio started to frown, he added, "It's all right, Gat. I know I'm tired. I'm sorry."

He took the elevator upstairs, then walked out to the Taj's lobby, where the security staff jumped to attention. One asked if he needed a driver; Dog declined.

"Walk'll do me good," he said.

The air had a dry, crisp quality, a sharpness that took away his fatigue. The stiffness that had twisted his upper body and legs evaporated before he'd gone more than a half mile.

His mind, however, remained in knots. Three men were missing from the tanker the Sukhois had hit; an untold number on the container ship had died, and the survivors still hadn't all been picked up. Then there was the Chinese Sukhoi pilot, apparently still lost at sea.

Arguably, Quicksilver had saved countless lives by shooting down the other antiship missiles. Somehow, that didn't assuage his conscience.

What if Allen was right? What if the plane incident started a war with China—a real war this time, the kind of war Brad Elliott had tried to prevent? The Chinese military was still potent; after all, that was undoubtedly their point now in the South China Sea.

What if they simply encouraged their Islamic allies in a campaign of terror? Six months, a year from now, something might happen in a quiet corner of the U.S. Would it be his fault?

They'd done everything they could to save lives, not take them. Yet the Chinese were unlikely to see it that way. Hell, not even Admiral Allen saw it that way, and he wasn't exactly China's best friend.

Dog turned down the access road toward his bungalow, a low-slung contemporary-style ranch that looked over a boneyard: hulks of old aircraft nestled in the starlight. Most were simply planes that had been parked here for storage and then forgotten. The inventory showed several B-29's and B-50's, as well as three C-47's (or DC-3's, as they were known in civilian guise). There were also the remains of Dreamland failures, aircraft tested here that didn't quite make the cut or no longer had much value. The shadows were a graphic reminder of the old Latin maxim, carpe diem; your time came and went very quickly.

Dog walked up the short crushed-stone path to his door, his shoes crunching stones that reportedly had been smuggled in a duffel bag by the past commander of Dreamland, General Brad Elliott. It was undoubtedly an apocryphal story, but Dog liked it; it added a touch of eccentricity to a commander well known for his efficiency and precision.

He hit his access code for the lock, then pushed in the door. Cool air hit him in a wave, refreshing him. As he turned and locked up, someone grabbed him from behind, wrapping his arms around his neck.

Her arms around his neck. He pulled his assailant to his chest.

"Hi," said Jennifer Gleason as they kissed. "About time."

"How long have you been waiting?"

"Hours," she said, and even though he knew it must be a lie, he apologized and kissed her again. He slipped his hands into the back of her jeans, beneath her ultrasensible cotton briefs, feeling the coolness of her skin. She folded into his body, sliding her own fingers to his buttons. Colonel Bastian moved his hands to her sides and lifted her shirt over her head; she writhed out of it like a snake shedding its skin. He undid her bra, her peach-sized breasts gently unfolding from the material. They kissed again, tongues meshing, lips warming each other, and still kissing they began walking toward the bedroom. They made love in a long moment that shattered the boundaries of time, then gave way to a warm bath of sleep.

Hours later, Colonel Bastian found himself walking down a long stairway, the entrance to a subway, maybe the Metro in Washington, D.C. The stairs were much longer than at any stop he'd ever been on. He knew he was dreaming, but felt fear.

He'd lost something and had to turn back. At first, he didn't know what it was. As he reached the second landing, he saw the luminescent white rectangle thrown on the concrete floor by a light panel below the banister rail.

He was looking for his daughter. It wasn't Breanna as

he knew her now—it was Breanna as a four-year-old. In real life, he'd rarely, if ever, been with her at this age. He'd been divorced right after she was born, and sent overseas besides; he didn't see much of her until she was twelve or thirteen, when he was back in California, and then D.C. In the dream, she had been with him when he started down the steps, and now he felt panic that she wasn't there.

He kept going up the steps, turning and twisting with each flight, expecting, hoping to find her. His knees and calf muscles started to hurt, the tendons pulling taut.

Why had he let go of her hand? How could he have come so far without her?

He told himself it was a dream, and yet that made the panic more real. He walked and he walked, the staircase unending.

Jeff Stockard joined him, not as a boy but as a man. In the dream, Jeff could walk, wasn't Bree's husband or even in the Air Force, but just a friend of his, a man trying to help. He asked where he'd last seen her, and assured Dog she'd be just up the next flight.

He pushed on, starting to run. "Where is she?" he said out loud.

Finally, he woke up. It took forever for his eyes to focus. When they did, he saw Jennifer had gone.

It wasn't a surprise really—she was a workaholic, used to keeping odd hours; he knew he'd probably find her over in one of the computer labs working on the latest project. In a way, her habit of sneaking out late at night was a blessing; it lessened the chances of others getting embarrassed if they happened to trip over her in the morning.

But he wished she were here now. He wished he could fold himself around her warmth, sink into her, fall back to sleep.

He pulled the covers over him for a moment, but when his mind drifted back to the dream, he pulled himself out of bed, got dressed, and headed back to Dreamland Command.

Philippines
August 23, 1997, 2008 local (August 23, 1997, 0508 Dreamland)

FROM THE OUTSIDE, THE WHIPLASH MOBILE COMMAND center looked like an RV trailer painted dark green, with twelve squat wheels and an array of satellite dishes and antennas. Inside, it looked like a cross between a power-plant control room and a frat-house living area. About two thirds of the interior was wide open, dominated by a pair of tables just big enough for a serious game of poker. They could be joined together and extended by panels that folded up and out from their sides. At the far end from the door was a counter with several video monitors; a large, flat television screen sat against the wall. The monitors were worked from a dedicated control station that looked like a slightly oversized personal computer desk; the gear tied into Dreamland Command via a dedicated secure satellite link.

On the other side of the partition was a bathroom, a storage area crammed with spare parts for the computers, a com section, and a tiny "suite" that was intended as a bedroom for the Whiplash commander. Since the trailer always had to be manned, Danny Freah had found it more expedient to sleep in a tent on their last deployment and intended to do so this time as well—assuming, that is, he ever went to bed. He'd been up since they landed.

Quicksilver's crew sat at the pushed-together tables, going over their patrol for Stoner—and just as importantly, themselves. Though exhausted, they'd described the encounters minutely, several times pausing to work out the exact details. Stoner listened impassively; his only comments were aimed at the Kali weapon. Unfortunately, the Megafortress had gathered relatively little data on the missile.

"So why are these guys shooting at each other?" Zen asked him finally.

"They don't like each other," said the spook blandly. "Advances their agenda."

"Yeah."

Stoner shrugged.

"All right, it's getting late," said Bree. "We can all use some sleep."

"I have to finish uploading the data," said Collins.

"Yeah, me too," said Torbin. "The radar hits we got on the way back kind of distracted me."

"Which hits were those?" Stoner asked.

"Couple of anomalies we read as we tracked back here. Looked like radars coming on real quick and then turning off, but they were real weak. Collins got some radio signals as well. We think they're spy stations."

Stoner stared over the map spread across the table.

"No ships out there?" he asked.

"Not that we saw," said Breanna. "You have a theory?"

"There could be spy posts on these atolls here." He pointed his finger at some brown dots on the map. "That might be one way the Indians or Chinese are keeping track of what's coming down the pipe. Or the Russians. Or us."

"Us?" asked Zen.

"You never know."

Danny looked over at the islands, which were part of the Spratly chain extending southward. The Spratly Islands—more like a vast series of atolls—were claimed by several different countries, including China, Vietnam, and the Philippines. For the most part uninhabitable mounds of rock, they were valuable because vast gas and petroleum deposits were supposedly located beneath them.

Not that most of the claimants needed such a good reason to disagree.

"We can dogleg off a mission and check it out," said Zen.

"What if it's defended?" asked Breanna.

"That's why we use a Flighthawk."

"We could get on those islands with the Osprey," said Danny. "Give them a real look. MV-22's due here in about an hour."

"Yeah," said Stoner. Danny thought it might be the first time he'd said anything nonbelligerent since he'd landed.

"I think we ought to recon it first," said Zen. "You guys got enough to do here. Besides, we don't even have a real location for you, do we, Torbin?"

The radar intercept expert looked like a blond bear, shrugging and shaking his head. "I can get it down to a few miles. We can pass it on to Major Alou, have them take a look if they get a chance."

"All right."

"Sooner's better than later," said Stoner.

The others looked at him. Danny saw Breanna rolling her eyes.

Good, he thought to himself. It's not just me. The spook is a jerk.

Aboard the trawler *Gui* in the South China Sea
August 24, 1997, 0823

CHEN LO FANN SAW THE TWO AIRCRAFT APPEAR OVER the water, his powerful binoculars straining to follow them as they rocketed upward from the carrier.

The limitations of the Russian-made planes had been clear before the accident with the Americans, but Beijing had reacted with shock and dismay, sending a long, rashly worded message filled with outrage.

To his credit, the admiral in charge of the task force had not tried to hide what had happened; he could easily have blamed the Americans for the accident or even claimed they had shot down his plane. Instead, the transmissions back and forth to the mainland made it clear that he was a man of integrity. While his actions could be questioned—he clearly should not have authorized his attack planes to fire at the Indian submarine from long distance—his honor could not.

Undoubtedly he would be rewarded for his honesty with disgrace.

Reinforcements were on the way.

Opportunity, Fann thought, yet the Americans had complicated the picture.

What if they prevented the inevitable confrontation? What if they forced the navies back?

Until the arrival of the Megafortresses, the American posture seemed clear. The Pacific fleet, concentrating on protecting vessels bound for Korea and Japan, was too far north to intervene in a clash, nor did its commanders seem of much mind to do so. Diplomatically, there was a lean toward India, and relations with Mainland China were as low as, if not lower than, at any time since Nixon's trip to Beijing a generation ago.

But the Megafortresses represented unwelcome change.

Chen had promised conflict. His position with the government rested entirely on that promise.

This was not a time for panic. Surely, fortune continued to smile. Within a day, if not hours, there would be two aircraft carriers sailing southward. The Indians must react to their presence.

Chen was sure the submarine would act tomorrow; he was staking his career on it. At that point, fortune would take over.

The Taoist master Lao Tzu said the river was king because it knew how to take the low path. The river did not shrink from its strength, but it bided its time.

The sea was merely the river at large.

The Megafortresses and their small escorts presented a difficult problem, but as Chen considered it, he realized they represented opportunity as well. Perhaps there was more potential than the mere conflict he had seen. Perhaps there was an opportunity others might only dream of.

Dreamland
August 23, 1723 local (August 24, 1997, 0823 Philippines)

JENNIFER GLEASON LEANED BACK FROM THE COM-
puter, rubbing her eyes.

"So?" asked Ray Rubeo, standing on the sides of his
shoes. "Work or not?"

"It'll work," Jennifer told him.

"Good, let's go tell your sweetheart. He's still up in his
office. I'll have Commander Delaford meet us there."

Jennifer felt her entire body flashing red.

"You know, Ray, you can be a real jackass," she said,
grabbing the Zip disk as it popped out from its drive.

"What?" asked Rubeo.

"We're not in junior high."

"Hmmmph," said her boss. He touched his small gold
earring nervously, but said nothing else as they walked to
the elevator. The computer labs were housed in the same
underground complex as the Megafortress project, a convenient arrangement when Jennifer's main responsibilities
were the computers governing flight operations for both
the Megafortresses and the U/MFs. Now, however, her
duties were much more diverse. She often found she had
to travel either to one of the other bunker areas or to Taj,
the main administrative building that also housed Dreamland Command and some of the labs dedicated to the
UMB. While she could have a car or an SUV, Jennifer
found it much more convenient to get around by bike. As
they walked down the ramp, she reached into her pocket
and took out two large rubber bands, which she used to
keep her pants legs from fouling the chain.

"You're not cycling, are you?" hissed Rubeo.

"Why not?"

"We'll take my car."

"No, I don't think so."

Rubeo said something under his breath.

"You shouldn't talk to yourself, Ray." Jennifer stopped
and rolled the bands over the legs of her jeans, refusing

to make eye contact. "It just reinforces the eccentric stereotype." She took out another band for her hair and tied it back, then picked up the bike and rode over to the Taj.

She parked her bike—there was no need to lock it at Dreamland—and went inside to the notoriously slow elevator as Rubeo appeared in the lobby doorway. Finished with its complicated security protocol, the elevator doors began to close. Under other circumstances, Jennifer would have pushed the hold button, and clearly Rubeo expected her to, walking toward her nonchalantly.

Too damn bad, she thought to herself, letting them slam closed as she looked right at him.

Chief Master Sergeant Terrence "Ax" Gibbs met her in the hallway outside Dog's office.

"Ma'am, pleasure to see you," said Ax. "Colonel's inside; I'm just on my way to get him a little coffee. You want a little something?"

"Not really."

He smiled. "A pineapple Danish maybe?"

"Well, you twisted my arm. Thanks, Chief."

"You know, you really should call me Ax," he said.

"I'll try to remember."

He smiled, bowed—actually, really, truly, bowed—then vanished through the door to the stairway.

Jennifer went into Colonel Bastian's outer office, a medium-sized bullpen dominated by Gibbs's desk. Sally, a staff sergeant who oversaw much of the paperwork in Ax's absence, greeted her and told Jennifer the colonel was inside on the phone.

"I have to wait for Dr. Rubeo and Commander Delaford anyway," said Jennifer. She sat down in one of the metal folding chairs lined up against the wall. The metal chairs had recently replaced a set of plush velour seats. Jennifer suspected that was Ax's doing, not Colonel Bastian's. The chief master sergeant had a simple but straightforward philosophy regarding visitors—discourage them as much as possible. Most of the scientists grumbled privately about the hard seats; the military people didn't seem to notice.

"So you beat me," said Rubeo, entering the office. He looked out of breath, as if he had taken the stairs, though that was unlikely. "Congratulations."

"I didn't know it was a race."

"The colonel is off the phone," said Sally.

"He expects us," said Rubeo. "Is Delaford in there?"

Before the sergeant could say anything, Rubeo pushed inside with a brisk but short knock. Jennifer followed a few paces behind; there was no reason to wait now.

"We're ready to deploy Piranha," said Rubeo before he even sat down. "The new E-PROMs will be done within the hour. All we have to do is select a recovery site for them to default to."

"Already?" said Colonel Bastian.

Rubeo touched his small gold earring. "Of course."

Anyone else saying that might have smiled. The scientist was dead serious and even a little dismissive.

Jennifer watched as a small smile curled at the corner of Colonel Bastian's mouth. She hated calling him Dog; Tecumseh was such a beautiful, different name, and it described him perfectly—tough and solid, protective, yet capable in a gentle way. It suggested thick muscles and, at the same time, nooks where you could let your fingers linger.

"Some of the Navy people are drawing up plans for a makeshift warhead," added Rubeo. "There are guidance issues, however."

"I doubt it'll be necessary."

"Gives them something to do," said Rubeo. "Otherwise, they tend to bother my people."

That wasn't true—the Navy people and the Dreamland scientists got along very well.

Ax opened the door, backing in with a tray of coffee and soda. Lieutenant Commander Delaford came in behind him, looking rumpled and tired. He'd left the computer lab about an hour before to take a nap.

"Don't you ever knock?" Rubeo asked Ax.

"Hey, Doc, got you some of that green tea you like. Got some coffee for our Navy friend. Needs it. Pepsi for you, ma'am. Diet, of course."

Ax winked as he gave her the soda and Danish. She noticed she was the only one with pastry.

"Thanks, Chief."

"Ax. Call me Ax. More papers for you, Colonel. When you get a breather." He disappeared through the door.

"I'm just telling the colonel we're ready to deploy," said Rubeo. The tea actually seemed to have an effect— he seemed almost human.

Almost.

"I'd like to make another recommendation," Rubeo told Colonel Bastian. "I want to add the UMB to the search matrix. It can survey the entire area and stay on station for nearly twenty-four hours. We could incorporate some of the testing schedule—"

"The B-5 has only had a dozen flights," said Dog. "No way."

"Colonel, the idea of Whiplash is to test new technology in real situations," said Rubeo.

Dog grimaced—his own words were being used against him.

"The UMB has a long way to go," said Dog. "There have been difficulties with the engines, as well as delays with the control surfaces."

"The hydrogen-fueled engine would not be necessary for this mission," said Rubeo. "Otherwise, Colonel—"

"And besides," said Colonel Bastian, "the UMB's pilot is in the Philippines." He glanced at Delaford, silently reminding him with a half-nod that he knew nothing about the UMB and had not heard any of this highly classified discussion. Delaford had been at Dreamland long enough to nod in reply.

"The UMB pilot is superfluous," said Rubeo. "Four different scientists, myself included, are trained to handle the plane. During simulations—"

"The simulations are not the real thing. We've got a lot of other things to worry about right now. Let's not get too complicated. End of discussion, Doc." He put his arms down on his desk and leaned forward. "Good work getting Piranha ready."

"Yes," said Rubeo.

"Thanks," said Jennifer. His glance•at her felt like a physical thing, a caress. "We got a few breaks."

"I want to deploy Iowa as soon as possible," said Dog, turning to Delaford. "We can use it to gather more data on the Indian submarine. We have a location from the last encounter."

"I'm with you, Colonel," said Delaford.

"Tonight if we can. I'll fly it myself."

"Ensign English and I will be ready," said Delaford.

"We'll want technical people as well." Colonel Bastian turned to Rubeo. "How many other command sets for the device?"

"We'll have the backup and one additional unit ready within twenty-four hours," said the scientist. "But they'll have to be installed in the Flighthawk bays. We can do two more planes. We'll need two full teams, though. I'd say about—"

"I'm in," interrupted Jennifer. "On the technical team, I want to go."

"It's not your project," said Rubeo.

"Baloney—I handled all the communications compressions, and the native intelligence sections on the probe. I just fixed the E-PROM for you. I should be there."

"I'd agree," said Delaford.

Rubeo rolled his eyes but gave up—on her, at least. "Colonel, if I may—your place really is at the Command Center. Captain Teijen can fly the aircraft."

"I think I'll make the call on personnel, Doctor, especially on military assignments. If you care to recommend more technical people, I'm all ears."

*   *   *

Dog listened as Delaford and Rubeo ran down the possibilities of technicians to handle the mechanical systems of the Piranha device. They were talking about twenty people, a small portion of the development team but far larger than a normal field deployment under Whiplash. It was one thing to send military people into a combat zone, and quite another to put scientists there. Nonetheless, if they were going to use Piranha, they had to support it adequately.

"All right," said Dog finally. "Pick the people you want. You and Ensign English will fly in Iowa. We'll go straight out and deploy the device, assuming we can get a reasonable fix on the sub's location."

"We'll be ready."

Dog rose, indicating the meeting was over. There were two lit buttons on the bank for encrypted calls, indicating calls on hold. As the others got up and filed out, he put his eyes down at his desk, pretending to study the papers there. He didn't want to be caught eyeing Jennifer, but it was difficult. Finally, he glanced up, and saw the slight sway of her hips through the doorway. It wasn't in any way provocative, it was just walking—but desire rushed into his veins nonetheless. He sat back down in his seat, took a sip of his coffee, then punched one of the buttons on hold without waiting for Ax to tell him who it was.

"Bastian."

"Um, Colonel, good," said Jed Barclay. "Sir, uh, standby for the President of the, um, United States."

Dog sat upright in his seat.

"Colonel, how the hell are you?" said President Kevin Martindale breezily. The President had taken a liking to Colonel Bastian early in his administration, and his tone always implied that they were friends.

"Sir, very well."

"Good. Now I've had the full briefings, and even young Jed here has filled me in, but I'd like to hear from you— the Chinese plane. What happened?" asked the President.

Dog explained carefully and as fully as he could, then

segued from that into a description of the ensuing engagement between the Sukhois and the Indian sub, which had resulted in the sinking of the oil tanker and the probable loss of three men.

"Thank you, Dog." The President's voice remained friendly; they could been discussing a hunting trip where they'd come up empty.

"Sir, we do have plans in place now to track the Indian submarine," Dog added.

"Well, you carry on, Colonel," said the President. "I'm afraid I have some pressing matters."

"Yes, sir, thank you, sir," said Dog reflexively. It was doubtful that the President heard his last few words; the line had snapped dead before he finished.

His intercom buzzed. Dog picked it up and barked at Ax. "Why the hell didn't you tell me that was the President on hold?"

"Didn't know it was the President," said Ax. "It was Mr. Barclay, as far as I knew. And he wasn't on hold more than ten seconds. Line two is Admiral Allen. He's spitting bullets."

"Why?"

"Born that way."

"Listen, Ax, I'm going to be deploying to the Philippines—"

"Camp Paradise, huh? Pack a bathing suit, and a raincoat—there's monsoons this time of year."

"Thanks. Make sure everything's in order. Is Major Ascenzio still in the secure center?"

"Far as I know, Colonel. How long will you be gone?"

"A few days."

"Just wanted to know how many signatures I'll need to forge."

"Very funny, Ax."

Dog punched the phone button and got a tired-sounding lieutenant on Admiral Allen's staff.

"The admiral wants to speak to you, sir," said the Lieutenant.

"That's why I'm here," said Dog.

"Tecumseh, what the hell is going on?" said Allen, coming on the line a few seconds later.

"Not exactly sure what we're talking about, Admiral."

"I hear from my sources you're looking for authority to fire at Chinese vessels."

"Not at all, Admiral."

"Don't give me that crap. What are you trying to do, Colonel? Start World War III?"

"Admiral—I don't know where that rumor came from," said Dog. "I haven't asked for authority to do anything."

"What happened with the tanker?" asked Allen.

"The Chinese aircraft were firing at an Indian submarine," Dog told him.

"Which conveniently disappeared."

"We have tape of the incident," said Dog. He wondered if Allen was being sabotaged by enemies over at the Pentagon—or if *he* was the target. "The details should have reached you by now."

"They haven't. I want to see it."

"I'm sure if you called over to the NSC—"

"Don't give me that bullshit," said Allen.

"Admiral, my hands are tied."

"From now on, you check with my people before running any more missions."

"I can't do that, Admiral," said Dog. "And I won't."

The line went dead.

Philippines
August 25, 1997, 0600 local

FROM THE WAY HE LOOKED AT HIM, ZEN COULD TELL Stoner was wondering how he managed to get from his wheelchair to inside the airplane, and how he maneuvered once there. It was the sort of question everyone had, though almost no one asked.

There were a lot of things no one asked. At first, this was fine with Zen—he couldn't stand bullshit sympathy, which was always in the air whenever an AB—an able-bodied person—asked about his useless legs. Gradually, however, people's avoidance of the topic began to annoy him, as if by not saying anything they were pretending he didn't exist. Now his attitude was complicated. Sometimes he thought it was funny, sometimes he thought it was insulting, sometimes he thought it was ridiculous, sometimes he thought it was almost endearing. Watching how a person handled the awkwardness could tell you a lot about them, if you cared.

In Stoner's case, he didn't. He didn't like the CIA agent, probably because he'd copped an attitude toward Danny. He was one of those "been-there, done-that" types who spread a know-it-all air everywhere he went. Stoner had suggested he come along to get a firsthand look at things; Major Alou and Bree had thought it a good idea.

"We go up the ramp, Stoner," Zen told him, pushing his wheelchair toward the ladder that led down from the crew area of the Megafortress. When Zen reached the stairway he swung around quickly, backing into the attachment device the Dreamland engineers had added to all of the Flighthawk-equipped EB-52's. The Zen Clamp, as they called it, hooked his chair into an elevator they'd rigged to work off electricity or stored compressed air, so no matter what was going on with the plane he had a way in or out. Two small metal panels folded down from the sides of the ladder; Zen backed onto them and then pulled thick U-bolts across the fronts of his rear wheels.

"Gimp going up," said Zen, hitting the switch. He had to push back in the seat to keep his balance and avoid scraping his head; there wasn't a particularly huge amount of clearance and, once moving, the elevator didn't stop.

His greatest fear was falling out onto the runway. While it might be more embarrassing than painful, it was one bit of ignominy he preferred to avoid.

At the top, he backed onto the Flighthawk deck. He'd put on his speed-suit already, but Stoner would have to take one of the spares they kept during Whiplash deployments. He unlatched the wardrobe locker at the back of the compartment—an EB-52 special feature—then wheeled back as Stoner came up.

"You have to put on a suit," he told the CIA officer. "We pull serious Gs. Helmet too. I'll show you how to hook into the gear when you sit down."

Stoner selected the suit closest to his six-foot frame, pulling it over his borrowed jumpsuit. Zen stopped him when it was done, inspecting to make sure it was rigged right. It was, and he knew it was since he'd watched him suit up, but something about the spook's presumption ticked him off.

"Life-support guy will be here by tomorrow," said Zen, clearing Stoner to pass. "He'll measure you up for a suit if you're going to be flying with us."

"This is fine."

"Your seat's on the left. Don't touch anything." Zen watched Stoner slip into the straight-backed ejection seat and begin to snap up. Ordinarily, he sat first—it was easier to maneuver into his seat if he could lean all the way over into the other station, but he could do it just as well with someone sitting there.

"Incoming," he said, backing his wheelchair against his own seat. He set the wheel brake on the left side, then pushed his weight forward, beginning the pirouette into his seat. The techies had tried several modifications, including an experiment with a sliding track that let the ejection seat turn. They'd also played with a wheel-in arrangement that allowed Zen to use a special wheelchair during the mission, but they couldn't make it ejectable.

Of course, he wouldn't stand much chance going out. Unless, ironically enough, it was over water, where he could use his upper body to swim—something he did a lot of during rehab.

He swung into place, curling his chest across and landing slightly off-kilter, but it was close enough. He wedged himself into place and pulled on his straps, then turned to

Stoner, who'd already worked out the oxygen and com hook-ins on his own.

"All right," Zen told him over the interphone. "Preflight's going to take a while. You're just a spectator."

"Yes," said the CIA officer.

"You see how to adjust your headphones?"

"Got it."

"You can check the oxygen hookup by—"

"Yes, I know."

Been-there-done-that. Right.

Zen punched up C^3 and went to work.

UPSTAIRS ON THE FLIGHT DECK, BREANNA finished going through the main preflight checklist, then stretched her neck back and turned to Chris, who was doing another double check of the mission course they'd programmed earlier.

"So?" she asked.

"Ready to rock, Boss. You think we ought to give these atolls names?"

"Numbers are fine."

"I'm thinking rock songs with a common theme. Say all Rolling Stones songs. Get it?"

"No," she said.

"First up, 'Angie.' A, Angie. Get it?"

"Chris, maybe we should do the preflight again."

"Your call. Next rock would be 'I Wanna Hold Your Hand.'"

"That's a Beatles song."

"You are into this, huh?"

"How's the weather?"

"Still sucks," said Chris. "At least it's not raining here."

As he said that, lightning flashed in the distance.

"Somebody heard me," said Chris.

"That or they're reacting to your song titles."

"Hey, I could do puns. *Do not ask for whom the a-toll*

tolls. John Donne," he added, giving the name of the poet for the butchered line of verse.

They came off the runway swift and smooth, the big plane's wings catching a ride on the stiff breeze blowing the storm front in. Breanna felt the wheels push up, the engines rumbling easily as they headed over the storm front. They got clear of the clouds and turbulent air, rising swiftly and then tracking toward the atoll.

"Angie in fifteen," said Chris as they hit their way-marker.

"Quicksilver, this is Hawk Leader. Ready to fuel and prepare for launch," said Zen.

"Copy that," she said. "How's our passenger?"

"Breathing."

Zen's voice told her Stoner had rubbed him the wrong way. The feeling seemed to be unanimous among the Whiplash people who'd dealt with him. Breanna was trying to withhold judgment. So far the only trait she'd formed an opinion on was his eyes—they were nice.

"Begin fuel sequence on Flighthawks," she said. "Prepare for launch."

THE GEAR BLEW STONER AWAY. THE VIDEO BEING FED from the robot plane onto the large tube in front of him looked remarkably clear and focused, even though the aircraft feeding it was moving at nearly five hundred knots.

Barclay had been right; the Dreamland people did know what they were doing. Touchy bastards, full of themselves, but at least they were competent. He could live with that.

Zen had said the large display was infinitely configurable, but it wasn't clear exactly what that meant. Though it was intended as a second Flighthawk station, its flight-control section had been locked out, and there was no joystick or any switch gear to control the robot. He had figured out how to stop, slow, and replay the main video feed on a second, dedicated screen on his left. A slider and a small panel very similar to standard VCR controls worked the tube; he could also select a bird's-eye or sitrep view and a map overlay. Undoubtedly the damn thing made coffee too, if you hit the right combination of switches.

An atoll began to grow in the left-hand corner of the main screen. Stoner heard the pilot grunting and groaning as he flew. He ducked his body with the aircraft, as if he were in the cockpit, not sitting here miles away.

Stoner wanted to ask him about his nickname, Zen. Practitioners of the way were rare in the military, and it was possible, maybe even likely, it was just a nickname. It seemed an improbable one, unless it had come before the pilot had lost the use of his legs. Jed Barclay was his cousin, but hadn't said very much about Zen on the way out.

"Slowing for our run," reported Zen. "No radar spotted, nothing active."

"I have nothing," said Torbin, whose gear scanned for radar emissions.

"Negative as well," said Collins, who was essentially an eavesdropper on radio transmissions.

"Rain's moving in pretty fast," added the copilot. "Wet down there, Zen."

"I brought my umbrella."

The storm front a few miles to the north covered the rest of the atolls with heavy rain and fog. Even their high-tech gear would have trouble seeing through it.

"Looks like a lean-to on that northern end," said Zen. "Stoner?"

He turned to the smaller screen, rewinding and then magnifying. Three trees had been laid across a large rock near the water.

"Might shelter a canoe, swimming gear," Stoner told him. He worked the slider, getting a wide-angle view. "Don't see anything else."

"Stand by for a second run-through."

"Hawk Leader, we have an unidentified flight one

hundred-twenty miles southwest of our target atoll, very low to the water," said Ferris. "Course unclear at the moment. Not getting an identifier."

"Hawk Leader."

"Hold that—positive ID. U.S. Navy flight. An F/A-18," said the copilot, who had used special gear designed to "tickle" an unknown plane and find out if it was friend or foe.

"Hawk Leader. We're done on Angie. What's next— Bella?"

"That would be Atoll Two," snapped the pilot. "Jeff, I'm going to take it up another five thousand feet over this storm. It's pretty fierce."

"Hawk Leader."

Stoner pushed his head toward the main video screen as the robot surveyed the next collection of rocks and coral. He felt the big plane tilt backward, the acceleration pushing him against the seat. If Zen felt it, he gave no indication as the Flighthawk looped twice around the atoll, its cameras covering every inch of ground.

"Nothing," said Zen finally.

"I concur," said Stoner.

"On to the next stop," said Ferris, the copilot. "Should I tell our guests what they'll win if the prize is behind door number-three?"

"Go for it," said the pilot.

"A goat."

"No sex jokes, please."

Her voice was so serious it took Stoner a second to realize Captain Breanna Stockard was joking. She was gorgeous, cool, and obviously well-trained. Stoner had never liked the idea of women in the military, and as a SEAL had never actually had to deal with any, but Breanna Stockard might make him rethink his attitude.

Too bad she was married.

The third target was much larger than the others, more an island than an atoll. It had a U-shaped lagoon and what seemed to be skid marks from a boat on the beach. There was a tarp covering something about twenty yards from the water, half-hidden by the trees.

"No radar operating," said Torbin.

"That tarp is big enough for one," said Zen.

"Yeah, interesting," said Stoner. "Can you get a close-up?"

"Copy that," said Zen.

A severe wind whipped the trees. Zen's grunts and groans increased. Stoner guessed it was hard to hold the small plane on course at low speed, but the video remained steady and in focus. They couldn't find anything besides the tarp.

The nearby fourth target proved to be a pile of coral perhaps ten by fifteen meters. There was nothing on the jagged surface.

By the time they reached the fifth atoll, rain had begun to fall. The computer compensated, but the view on the large screen was still grainy. Oddly, the smaller screen seemed easier to read. Stoner watched the Flighthawk come over the island at just under 180 knots and two thousand feet.

"There's a buoy in the water, a line up the beach," said Zen.

Stoner put his face practically on the screen and still couldn't see it.

"Here," said Zen. He did something with his controls and muttered something to the computer that Stoner didn't quite catch; the large screen flashed with a close-up of a small round circle in the water, boxed in by hash marks drawn by the computer.

"Could be part of a long-wave device," Stoner told him.

"Panel—there's a radar set. Look at it. Yeah, small. Infrared."

The screen blurred.

"Too much rain," said Zen. "Torbin, you have anything?"

"Negative. No transmissions of any type."

"Same here," said Collins.

They took two more runs over the island, switching back and forth between optical, infrared, and synthetic radar scans. None of them produced a very clear picture as the storm began to kick up fiercely, but there was definitely some sort of installation here.

"Maybe a long-wave com setup," suggested Stoner. "Surface radar, sends information out to ships."

"That a radio mast in the tree?" asked Zen.

Stoner had trouble seeing the tree, let alone the antenna. "Don't know," he said finally.

"Who's it working for?"

"Good question. I'd guess the Chinese. Have to see the equipment, though. Could be the Indians. Early warning, something comes south. Radar might scan a hundred miles, give or take. Like to look at it up close, on foot."

"Yeah," said Zen.

Zen took Hawk One up off the deck, rising through the clouds to get out of the storm. Even with the computer's help, it was a bitch flying low and slow in the shifting air currents, their violent downdrafts and rain pounding on his head.

There were two more atolls nearby, both now covered by heavy fog, clouds, and rain. He took a breath, checked his gear—instruments were all in the green, everything running at spec—then plunged back downward. He ran over both a little faster and higher than he wanted, but saw nothing.

"We still have some time," Bree told him as he came off his last pass. "We can check out those islands to the east as we head for the patrol area. Beyond that, though, we'll have to call it a day."

"Hawk Leader." Zen punched his mission map into the lower left-hand screen, got himself oriented, then checked his fuel panel. It'd be tight, but he could wait to refuel after the flyovers, then launch Hawk Two. He touched base with Ferris to make sure that would be okay, and got an update on some ships they'd seen. Most were civilians, sailing well clear of yesterday's trouble spot.

"Two Indian destroyers off to the southwest, in the thick of the storm," the copilot added over the interphone. "If they stay on their present course, they'll reach the patrol area about five hours from now, maybe a little sooner. Depends on the weather, though. They may not get anywhere."

"Maybe they're heading for that atoll we saw with the radar," suggested Stoner.

Zen grunted. He resented someone else cutting into his conversation. He avoided the temptation to cut him off the circuit, which he could do with the Flighthawk control board.

"More likely they're scouting for the carrier group to the south," injected Ferris. "About a day's sail behind, according to the intel brief."

"I wouldn't rule anything out."

Zen took Hawk One back toward the ocean, riding down through the angry carpet of whirling wind and water toward the target, a doublet of coral and rock. The thick drops of precipitation rendered the IR gear useless, and the optic feed was nearly as bad. The synthesized radar did the best, but the Flighthawk's speed made it nearly impossible to get any details out of the view. The computer assured him there were no "correlations to man-made objects" on the first group of rocks. Approaching the second, he saw a shadow that might be a small boat, or perhaps a large log, or even a series of rocks. He came in higher than he wanted, catching an odd wave of wind. Two more flyovers into the teeth of the storm failed to reveal anything else.

"I think it was rocks," said Stoner.

"We'll analyze it later," Zen told him.

"Hawk Leader, we're starting to get close to pumpkin time," Breanna told him.

"Roger that. I need to refuel," said Zen, pointing his nose upward.

**Aboard the submarine *Shiva,* in the South China Sea
0852**

"UP SCOPE."

Admiral Ari Balin waited as *Shiva*'s periscope rose. His
arms were at his chest, his eyes already starting to narrow.
He placed his fingers deliberately on the handles as the
scope stopped climbing, then began his scan with delib-
erate, easy motions.

The gods were beneficent; they had lost the noisy Chinese submarine, and were now in the middle of a storm
that would further confuse anyone trying to track them. It
was the perfect preparation for the next phase of their
mission, a sign that theirs was indeed the proper path.

Satisfied there were no other ships nearby, Admiral
Balin stepped back. Captain Varja, the submarine's commander, took his turn at the periscope. Where Balin was
slow and graceful, the younger man was sharp and quick;
it was a good match.

They had done well so far. The weapon had worked
perfectly, and the information that had come to them provided two perfect hits. The real test, however, lay ahead.

"Clear," said Varja, turning away from the scope.

"You may surface," Balin told him. He felt almost fa-
therly as the diesel-powered submarine responded to the
crew's well-practiced routine; they began to glide toward
the surface.

As built, the Russian Kilo class of submarines pos-
sessed an austere efficiency. Their full complement was
no more than sixty men; they could manage twenty-four
knots submerged and dive to 650 meters. While their re-
liance on diesel and battery power had drawbacks, they
could be made exceedingly quiet and could operate for
considerable periods of time before needing to surface.

Shiva—named after the Hindu god of destruction—had
been improved from the base model in several respects.
Her battery array was probably the most significant; they

nearly doubled her speed or submerged range, depending on how they were used. The passive sonar in her nose and the other sensors in the improved tower were surely important, with almost half again as effective a detection range as those the Russian supplied—and the Chinese copied. For Balin, the advanced automation and controls the Indian shipyard had added were most important; they allowed him to operate with half the standard crew size.

They too were the fruits of Hindu labor and inspiration, true testaments to the ability of his people and their future.

"We are on the surface, Admiral," reported Captain Varja.

"Very good."

Balin's bones complained slightly as he climbed the ladder to the conning tower, and his cheeks immediately felt the cold, wet wind. He struggled to the side, fumbling for his glasses.

As he looked out over the ocean, he felt warm again; peaceful. Dull and gray, stretching forever, the universe lay before his eyes, waiting for him to make the future coalesce.

The Chinese aircraft carrier should now be less than one hundred miles away.

He put the glasses down, reminding himself to guard against overconfidence. His role was to fulfill destiny, not to seek glory.

"We will stay on the surface at present course for forty-five minutes," the admiral told the captain. "The batteries will be back at eighty percent by then."

"I would prefer one hundred percent," said Varja.

"Yes," he answered mildly before going to the hatchway and returning below.

**Aboard Iowa, approaching the Philippines
August 25, 1997, 0852 local**

DOG RAN THROUGH THE INDICATORS WITH HIS COPILOT, Captain Tommy Rosen, making sure the plane was in good shape as they headed onto their last leg of the flight. In truth, the meticulous review of the different instrument readings wasn't necessary—the computer would automatically advise the pilots of any problem, and a quick glance at the special graphic displays showed green across the board, demonstrating everything was fine, but the routine itself had value. Checking and rechecking the dials— or in this case, digital readouts—focused the crew's attention. It was a ritual practiced by pilots since shortly after the Wrights had pointed their Flyer into the wind at Kitty Hawk; it had saved many a man and woman's life, quite a number without their even realizing it.

Checks complete, Dog spoke to each crew member in turn, making sure they were okay. Again, the ritual itself was important; its meaning was far deeper than the exchange of a few words. It was ceremony, a kind of communion, strengthening the link that would be critical in a difficult mission or emergency situation.

All his career, Dog had been a fast-plane jock, piloting mostly single-seat interceptors. You were never truly alone, of course; you had a wingman, other members of your flight and mission package, gobs of support personnel both in the air and on the ground. There was, however, more of a feeling of being on your own; certainly you were more independent than in a big aircraft like the Megafortress. Flying the EB-52 was an entirely different thing. As pilot, you were responsible for an entire crew. Your family, in a way; they were always in the back of your mind.

"All right folks. We're about twenty minutes out. After we land and have the plane checked, I'd like to try and get back up in the air as quickly as we can. I know we've all taken naps, and we're going to pretend we're refreshed, but—seriously, now—if anyone feels tired, talk to me when we're down. I know how hard it is to adjust."

He didn't expect anyone to admit they were beat, but still, he had to offer them the possibility. Most of the target area was covered by a slow-moving storm that made it difficult to patrol, and would certainly hinder the launch of the Piranha device. Being ready to go might be academic.

The portion of the panel at the left side of the dash that Dog had designated for the com link flashed gray and the words "DREAMLAND COMMAND LINK PENDING" appeared at the bottom. Dog authorized the link, and Major "Gat" Ascenzio's face beamed into the LCDs.

"Quicksilver thinks it has a location on the Indian submarine," said Gat. "On the surface, about seventy miles from the Chinese carrier. They're having a difficult time with the weather; hard to get a definitive read."

"Can you patch us together?" Dog asked.

"That's what I was thinking," said Gat. He turned away from the screen and the image popped gray. An instant later, the space was filled by a slightly scratched flight helmet.

"Hey, Daddy."

"Captain Stockard, good morning. We understand you have a possible location on the submarine."

"That's affirmative. A long-distance contact. The Flighthawks haven't seen anything and our radar looks clean, though the storm's pretty fierce. We'll transfer the data. Be advised the Chinese have aircraft aloft north of the target area."

"Copy."

"They haven't challenged us. We've been giving them a wide berth; they're doing the same."

"Good."

Dog waited while Rosen and Delaford worked on the details from the uploaded information. "We're about two hundred and thirty miles away, as the Megafortress flies," said the copilot finally. "Half hour we're there. If we push up the power we could get in range to launch Piranha in twenty minutes; maybe even a little quicker. Assuming they moved at top speed after submerging, we still have about a thirty-mile radius, and we can cheat north toward the Chinese, where they'd likely be going."

"Give me the course."

"On your screen," said the copilot, feeding it in.

"Quicksilver, be advised we are heading for that position. You should continue your patrol," he added.

"Quicksilver," acknowledged Bree.

"Thanks."

"Any time, Dad."

"She says that just to bust my chops," Dog told Rosen as they brought the big plane onto the new course.

"Oh, I think she likes you," said the copilot.

As Dog and Rosen brought the plane onto the new course, Delaford and Ensign English fired up the Piranha gear. The prelaunch procedure took precisely twenty-eight minutes; Dog adjusted his power to fit Delaford's timetable, figuring they could conserve a little fuel since there was no reason to arrive at the target area before then.

"We have a good plan laid out," Delaford said. "The question is how long we can stay on station when we find it."

"We're working on a tanker," Dog told him. "If we work in shifts once we make contact, we ought to get about twelve hours in before having to just shut it down."

"We can go as long as you want," promised Delaford. "We can put the probe into automatic, go home, then come back. Then we fish for it with the buoys."

"Okay."

"In the meantime, the MC-17 comes in with the new gear for the other planes. We hand off to them."

"You don't think the MC-17 can get there in twelve hours?" said Dog.

"It may, but then who handles the operation?"

"I thought you said the Flighthawk pilots can do it."

"Well, Captain Fentress has already," said Delaford. "But I'd still like to go over it with him."

"I'm sure Curly can pick it up," Dog said, referring to the UM/F pilot's nickname. "As for Zen, he's a quick learner."

"Not a problem," said Delaford. "Just wanted you to know we're ready for anything."

"Good," the colonel told him.

Rosen gave him a radar update. They did not have a read on the sub, but the Chinese had two aircraft above its carrier, now just over a hundred miles away.

"I doubt they're seeing us through the storm," added the copilot.

"They'll pick up our radar eventually," said Dog.

"I hope so. I've been working on my Chinese."

"No kung-fu jokes, okay?"

"Colonel. I'm serious."

"We can launch any time," said Delaford, finally finished with his checks.

"We're about sixty seconds from the initial point on your target sweep," Dog told him. "Where do you think he is?"

"Depends on what his mission is. If it were just spying on the Chinese, I'd guess he'd sneak in close enough to see the escorts, but I'm not sure."

"Is he in range for Kali?"

"If it were a Tomahawk, yes. If it were a Harpoon, no. If it's something in between, who knows? But that's why we're here."

Dog listened as Delaford continued to theorize about what might be going on. He guessed the attacks on the merchants were tests of the missile system—the ships could have been reliably and easily sunk by torpedoes. If that were the case, they were probably dry runs for a much more important attack—which meant the proximity to the aircraft carrier was significant.

"On the other hand, he could have shot his wad, reported back, then been given new instructions to shadow the carrier if it came south," added Delaford. "Hard to say. We have no data."

"Data's why we're here," said Dog, double-checking their position on the search grid.

"I think we may have finally caught the Sukhois' attention," said Rosen. "Looks like they're changing course."

"Will they be close enough to see us launch?"

"If they flood the gates," said the copilot. "On afterburner, sure."

Before Dog could decide on a strategy to keep the Chinese from seeing them launch the probe, another communication flashed on the board from Dreamland Command.

"Authorized," said Dog. Major Ascenzio's face came on the screen, his lips pursed in a tight frown.

"Got a communication for you, Colonel," said the major. "You're not going to like it."

Dog didn't even have to guess. "Okay. Clear it in."

Jed Barclay's face appeared. He was in the White House situation room.

"Colonel, Whiplash is being chopped to Central Pacific Command. Um, directly, sir. You're going to have to work under Admiral Allen."

"You're kidding me."

"Um, your, um, projects remain code-word-classified."

"How exactly is that going to work, Jed?" Dog said.

"Yeah, I know. It sucks. But Secretary Chastain is on the warpath and Admiral Allen—you don't even want to hear about it." The young man shrugged. Arthur Chastain was the Defense Secretary. "Um, the um, admiral wants to talk to you. I have the connection."

"Yeah, go ahead," said Dog.

To his credit, Allen wasn't grinning when his face flashed on the screen.

"Colonel, I'm going to place you under Admiral Woods' tactical command," said Allen, dispensing with any preliminaries. "I'm aware of your mission, though frankly I'm still hazy on some of the details. Or so it would seem. Including the reason that you are personally in the air right now."

"Just taking my turn in the rotation," said Dog, as levelly as he could manage.

"Admiral Woods will contact you shortly," said Allen. "Until that point, you are to do nothing. Nothing. Return to base immediately."

The screen blanked.

"Colonel?" asked Rosen.

"We're being chopped to the Central Pacific. Admiral Woods is going to be our boss."

"That wouldn't happen to be the admiral whose fanny you spanked during the exercises a while back, would it?" asked Rosen. "Man, the gods must be crazy."

"They're just having a little laugh at our expense," Dog told him. "Tell Quicksilver to return to base. Commander Delaford, everyone, we're on hold," he added to the crew. "Looks like our assignment's being changed. We're being chopped to Pacific Command."

"Those Sukhois are headed our way," said Rosen.

"Details to follow," said Dog, turning the plane south. He told Rosen to try contacting the Chinese interceptors with a benign message.

"Not responding."

"Spin it through the channels," said Dog. "You know the drill."

Rosen had the radio broadcast a preprogrammed message in English and Chinese saying they were on a routine observation mission and would take no aggressive action. As they waited for a response, the Dreamland channel popped up again. Once more, Gat's tight grimace greeted Dog.

"We have a communication from the fleet. We're not able to guarantee it's encrypted at this time," said Ascenzio from Dreamland Command.

"They know that?"

"If the Navy speaks English," said Gat. "I'm not totally convinced."

Despite everything, Dog laughed. The transmission came voice-only.

"I want you on the ground ASAP," said a gravelly voice that could only belong to Woods.

"Admiral, I'm advised your transmission is in the clear."

"I'm aware of that," said Woods. Though he didn't actually use any four-letter words, they were somehow implicit in his reply. "Stand down, Bastian," added the admiral.

Under other circumstances, Dog would have written the remark off. Aware the Chinese might be listening in, he felt it important to state his position clearly.

"I'm on a routine observation mission, and have taken no aggressive action and contemplate taking none at this time," he said. "We have no hostile intent. Dreamland EB-52 *Iowa*, setting course for FOA as ordered," said Dog. He snapped the com link closed. "What are the Chinese fighters doing?" he asked Rosen.

"Still coming."

"All right."

"Their radars are cooking. They're trying lock on us."

"Hold off on the ECMs unless they launch," said Dog.

"You want the Scorpions to target?"

"Not necessary."

"Awful close, sir."

"They're just trying to scare the shit out of us," Dog explained. "They've heard our transmissions, and know we won't attack. So now they're going to be brave."

"Couple of AMRAAMs up their butt will take care of that."

"My thoughts exactly. But that's not what we're going to do."

Sure enough, the Sukhois charged in. Locking their radars on the Megafortress was definitely a hostile act. Dog would have been within his rights to shoot the bastards down, but he trusted his read of the situation, and felt vindicated when they turned off their radars.

He wasn't surprised when they popped back on a few moments later, this time in gun mode.

"Man, what a bunch of hot dogs," said Rosen. The radar on the Chinese planes derived from Russian gear and had been so thoroughly compromised Rosen could use it to find out what the enemy pilot had for lunch. "The lead plane is about ten seconds from Stinger range," he added. "I could make him nervous."

"That would just give him a reason to fire," said Dog. "Then we'd have to shoot him down. Make the Navy boys more pissed off than they already are."

"Geez—gun radar's off," said Rosen. "Now what?"

"Now he's going to see how close he can get, and take a picture," predicted Dog. He held the EB-52 steady as the Sukhoi came in off their left wing. Sure enough, the hot-dog Chinese pilot produced a small camera, waved, and began clicking away. His wingman, meanwhile, was trailing at a more respectful distance.

It took Dog every ounce of his self-control not to flick the stick.

"Bastard's giving us the finger," said Rosen.

"Probably means hello in Chinese."

Rosen laughed. Dog laughed too. As they did, the Sukhoi started to slow, losing altitude.

"Tell him not to slide too close," said Dog. "Tell him if he goes underneath, the vortices will beat the hell out of him."

Rosen immediately began to broadcast, but it was too late. The Chinese plane ducked below Iowa—then disappeared.

"Idiot," said Rosen, studying his radar screen. "Uh, he's still in one piece, though. Looks like he's recovering west. Yeah, he's climbing."

The Chinese wingman then broadcast—in English—supposedly telling the carrier they had been fired on.

"Not true, not true," said Rosen over the frequency. "He was hotdogging."

"Stay calm," said Dog.

"Radar—we're spiked. We're spiked."

"All right," said Dog. "ECMS. Break it. Nothing else."

Dog could tell Rosen wanted to argue—the Chinese

planes were not only targeting them with missiles, but had lied about being fired on. Rosen clearly expected to see a missile coming up the chute any second.

But Dog didn't.

"Uh, they're heading back," said Rosen. "Lost the radars."

"Used to play these games all the time with the Russians," Dog explained to his copilot. "First one to hit a weapon or fuzz the air lost."

"We lost?"

"Depends on your perspective. I don't know if you were keeping track, but they went so deep in their fuel reserves they may have to glide back to their carrier."

Philippines
0930

DANNY FREAH STOOD OVER BISON'S SHOULDER, watching the video screen as the small figure made his way up the hill.

"What do you think, Cap?"

"Gonna have to do something," said Freah.

"Want me and Nurse to go down and clip 'em?" said Powder, standing nearby.

"Tell you what, you and Nurse come with me. Bison, alert the troops; feed the video into my helmet. And be careful this isn't diversion."

"Gotcha, Cap."

"We'll have to use the radio frequency in this jungle."

"Good thing you got the old bag to put it in," said Bison.

"Annie is not an old bag," snapped Danny. Though she seemed to totter as she walked, the white-haired grandmother had saved their necks more than once or twice.

"I meant it in a nice way," said Bison. "Really. Seriously."

"Fuck with her and I'll break your skull," said Powder.

"Hell, she'll break my skull," said Bison. "I like her, really."

Danny grabbed his smart helmet and gun. "All right, listen up," he told Nurse and Powder, who were checking their weapons. "This is a capture-and-release program. No firing unless I say."

Nurse nodded; Powder gave a thumbs-up.

"Button up," Danny said.

"Ah, they're not even armed," said Powder, pointing back toward the monitor.

"Button up anyway. I don't want any accidents."

Danny made his way to the trail on the east side of the base. Before starting into the jungle, he clicked the back of his smart helmet, selecting a preset that created a small window in the lower-left portion of his viewscreen. The window opened with the feed from the security station.

The Filipino was still making his way up the slope slowly, obviously afraid of being seen.

"How we doing, Bison?" Danny asked.

"What you see is what we got."

"All right. If he reaches the line before we do, drop back to Cam Three up the hill."

Danny paused, waiting for his men to catch up. He cycled through the presets for a 3-D map of the area that acted as a sitrep with the other team members' locators notched in, then set it to toggle back and forth. While the visor and the portable computer controlling it were capable of more complicated displays—he could overlay the map and video, for example—there was a limited number of presets. He'd have to pull out the palm-sized controller from inside his vest to do anything complicated. From experience, he'd learned this was the quickest and easiest way to set things up.

"All right, let's hold the noise down below the level of a herd of elephants," said Danny, pushing down. "I got point. Powder, you're tail gunner."

"Man, that's Nurse's job," said Powder. "He's always sniffin' behinds."

"Zip it." Danny eased his way off the trail near one of their hidden cameras, crouching as he worked across a slick rock, then down a rather steep slope. He felt himself losing his balance and pushed backward, landing on his rump. To him, it sounded like an earthquake, but the figure in the surveillance cam, still more than a hundred yards away, didn't react. The thin, short figure continued picking his way across a shallow ravine, heading in the general direction of the base. The Filipino's face was hunched down and in shadow; it was impossible to say whether he was a man or boy, let alone decipher what he might be up to. Danny shifted his weight, but before he could get back on his feet, he began to slide in the mud. He slid all the way to the stream, now a fair-sized torrent because of the rain.

"Mud," he explained to his men. He moved north with the stream, watching the GPS readings until he was almost directly north of the Filipino. The stream was no more than three feet wide here; he reared back and jumped, landing with a heavy plop on the muddy bank.

"Nurse, I want you to cross where you are," said Danny, clicking up the sitrep. "Powder, I want you to stay on the other side, in case our subject slips past us. He'll have to slow down for the stream."

"You guys get all the fun," said Powder.

"Tell me when you're across, Nurse."

Danny pushed down through the clumps of trees, about fifty feet from Camera Three; the subject was just now coming up to the camera that had first caught him, Camera Twelve, meaning he was about seventy yards ahead, just to the right of Danny.

"How we looking, Bison?"

"Just the one native, coming at you," said Bison. "Jones'll back you up."

"Get a good look at him?"

"Negative. Don't see a rifle, though."

"Hang tight up there."

"Colonel Bastian's inbound," added Bison. "CT's say he's, like, ten minutes away."

"Thanks."

"Captain, I see a good little spot with a bunch of trees we can use as an ambush," said Nurse. "Ten yards due south of you. If you want to wait for him to make his way up."

"Yeah, that'll work," said Danny. The Filipino was moving a little faster now; he passed Camera Twelve and headed toward Three. After they got in the tree line, though, their subject stopped.

"Hears the plane," said Nurse.

The A/C-130 thundered in behind the ridge.

Danny crouched, waiting to see what their subject would do.

If he turned around and started back, should he grab him?

Surely they'd have heard the planes earlier.

Have to take him in, no matter what. These people were getting curious, and had to be dealt with.

"Moving. He's going to come up through the bushes there," said Nurse.

"All right, here's the plan." Danny whispered; their target was now about twenty yards away. "I'll duck back around, then come up behind him. You come down when I flush him. We'll get him between us. Fire only if he produces a weapon."

"What if he runs?"

"You don't think we can catch him?"

The sergeant, being a sergeant, didn't answer.

"Knee's all healed, Nurse," said Danny, moving out.

He was nearly abreast of the figure and barely eight yards away when the Filipino suddenly stood straight up.

Shit, thought Danny. In the next second, he plunged down the slope. He took no more than a step before the Filipino began running as well.

"He's running," managed Danny, lungs already ready to burst. He slipped as he ran, but held on to his balance, crashing through bushes. The Filipino, unencumbered by body armor, smart helmet, and gun, started to pull away.

Nurse suddenly appeared to Danny's left, flashing down the hill. He got to within two feet when the Filipino threw on the brakes. Nurse lost his balance and flew forward, his arms catching part of a shirt but failing to hold on.

It was just enough of a delay to let Danny catch up. He leapt forward and pulled the native down by his legs, clamping his hand on his chest.

Her chest. It was a young woman.

Danny rose, throwing back his helmet's shield so he could get a good look at her.

She started to squirm. Danny wrapped his hand firmly around her shirt. She pulled away, ducking around to get out of his grasp.

Nurse jumped up. Before Dog could do anything else, he smashed the woman's skull with the butt-end of his MP-5. She crumpled to the ground.

"Shit," said Danny. "You didn't have to do that."

Nurse pointed down at the prone body; there was a pistol in her hand.

"Maybe you did," was all Danny could think to say.

IV
Chopped

DOG AND HIS COPILOT KEPT IOWA IN THE HOLDING PAT-
tern over the island, orbiting as a pair of C-130's low on
fuel made their way onto the runway. It had been roughly
an hour since the change in orders, but already Admiral
Woods was making his mark on the base, flying in Seabees and Marines to improve it so the base could also be
used for patrols. An Orion and its support team had already arrived; another was due soon. Cubi Field, the former Naval Air Station at Subic Bay, was much larger and
would have offered considerably better facilities and potential, but the political ramifications of a large U.S. force
reappearing during election season made the Dreamland
base the place to be. Dog couldn't help but think another
factor was involved: Putting Navy people on the ground
next to Whiplash was another way Woods could keep
Whiplash under his thumb.

He seemed to want to do so personally—Dog noticed
a C-12 VIP transport in the parking area as they took a
turn waiting to be cued in to land.

"Admiral wants to see you in his headquarters ASAP,"
shouted a combat-dressed Marine as Dog came down

Iowa's ladder a short time later. The Marine added the word "Sir" and snapped to attention, saluting and manipulating his M-16 so quickly it seemed a stage prop.

"Yeah, thanks," said Bastian, tossing back a salute.

"Sir, I have a vehicle."

"Thank you, son. I'll get there on my own."

"Sir?"

Dog ignored the Marine, scanning the area for Danny Freah or one of his people.

"Uh, sir, my orders—"

Dog turned toward the Marine, intending to tell him what he could do with his orders, but the pained expression on the young man's face somehow pushed away his annoyance. "Tag along," said Dog, quite possibly speaking as mildly as he'd ever spoken to someone in uniform. "We'll get there. It'll be all right, son."

The Marine's expression didn't change, but he was smart enough to follow without further comment as Dog strode up the long, dirt access road that paralleled the runway. A Herc transport hunkered in as he walked, its broad shoulders delivering more supplies for the Seabees swarming over the base. Two crews with surveying equipment were setting up near the aircraft parking area; another was already working on the far end of the runway. Large metal poles, the skeleton framework for a building or hangar, were being off-loaded from one of the C-130's that had just landed. By the end of next week, the Navy would have a base here twice the size of Norfolk.

Sergeant Jack Floyd, otherwise known as "Pretty Boy," guarded the entrance to the mobile Dreamland command unit. He snapped to attention as the colonel approached, then cast a rather jaundiced look at the trailing Marine. Pretty Boy had his carbon-boron vest on; his helmet hung off a loop at the side like a nail gun off a carpenter's tool belt.

"Hey, Sergeant," said Dog. "Where's Captain Freah?"

"He and the guys snagged a local in the woods, Colonel," said Pretty Boy. "Looked like she was spying on us.

They're bringing her up to the med tent. Liu says she's got a concussion or something. Went for the stretcher, whole nine yards."

"Okay," said Dog, starting toward the small flight of stairs to the trailer.

"Uh, sir," said Floyd. "Something you oughta know, uh, the admiral—"

"About time you got here, Bastian," said Admiral Woods, opening the door to the trailer.

The Marine jumped to attention so quickly Dog thought he heard the air snap. Pretty Boy scowled deeply, his back to the admiral.

"Hello, Admiral," said Dog. "Good day to you too."

Woods said nothing, disappearing inside. Dreamland's ultra-top-secret facility was now crowded with Navy people. The lone member of the Whiplash team inside was Sergeant Geraldo Hernandez, who sat at the com panel toward the back.

"Out," demanded Dog. "Everyone the hell out of here."

"Belay that!" said Woods.

"Belay bullshit," said Dog. "This is a code-word-classified installation. *Everyone the hell out.*"

"Belay that!"

Woods, his hands balled into fists that perched on his hips, stood in front of Dog, his face the color of a ripe strawberry. Dog's was undoubtedly the same shade. It was only with the greatest effort he kept himself from physically pushing the Navy people out the door.

"Admiral, let's be clear about this," he said. "The gear in this trailer, let alone the network it connects to and the information it accesses, are covered by six different code-word clearances, none of which I guarantee you or your men have," said Dog. "You're not even cleared to know the existence of the damn classification."

"And let *me* be clear about this," said Woods. "You work for me."

"The chain of command is going to make little difference in Leavenworth," said Dog.

Dog wasn't particularly tall; fighter pilots rarely were. Woods was only an inch or two taller than Dog, though his frame held at least thirty more pounds. The two men glared at each other, their eyes only a few millimeters apart.

"Colonel, uh, I have a link pending here from NSC. Need your voice confirmation," said Hernandez. Among other things, the Whiplash team member had helped make a daylight rescue under fire during the Gulf War, but his voice now had a worried tremble to it.

Dog managed to unball his hands.

"I have to get that," he told Woods. "The computer won't let the communication proceed with anyone else in view, even if I wear headphones."

"Understood," said Woods.

The two men held each other's glare for a few seconds more. Then simultaneously, Dog turned toward the com area, and Woods nodded to his men. They filed out quietly, undoubtedly glad to escape without having been scorched. Hernandez looked at Dog, silently asking if he should go too. Dog decided it might be an appropriate diplomatic gesture and nodded.

Woods stood quietly by the table, out of line-of-sight of the com screen. Dog, meanwhile, picked up a headset and spoke his name into the microphone. Jed Barclay's face snapped into view.

"Hi, Colonel."

"Jed. What's up?"

"Wanted to brief you on the situation with China and India. Um, and um, to uh, well, the way you got the news, I would've preferred to give you a better heads-up."

"Understood," Dog told him. "You're just the messenger."

"Yes, sir."

"It's all right, Jed. I'm a big boy," said Dog. When he'd first met Barclay, he hadn't thought much of the NSC aide; he was a pimple-faced kid who stuttered when he spoke. Hell, he was still a pimple-faced kid who stuttered when he spoke. He was also a computer whiz, quite possibly as adept at the science as Jennifer Gleason, though his interests were more in international politics than hand-constructed integrated circuits. Barclay combined the technical knowledge with a surprisingly deft feel for foreign relations, and could analyze the international implications of anything from ATM machines to U/MFs. What he did for Dreamland and Whiplash—basically acting as a liaison for the NSC director and the President—involved perhaps one one-hundredth of his skills.

"Well, okay," said Jed. He began running down the situation between China and India, starting with the present force structure.

Dog stopped him.

"I have Admiral Woods here," he said. "Maybe he ought to listen in."

"Okay. Sure. Good idea," said Jed. While he authorized the feed from his end, Dog took off his headset and called Woods over.

The admiral too had calmed somewhat. He came over without saying anything, frowned, then looked at what was now a blank screen.

"You'll have to give your name and rank to the computer," Dog told him. "Just do it once, and do it in as natural a voice as you can. If the voice pattern is not already in the system, you'll be asked for a retina scan and a fingerprint. You put your hand there."

Dog pointed toward a small glass panel at the side of the auxiliary keyboard to the com set. Woods nodded.

"Authorize additional com link," began Dog, starting off the procedure. He nodded at Woods, who spoke so slowly the computer asked him to repeat in a natural voice.

Dog suppressed a grin as Woods repeated his name, this time somewhat sternly. When he finished, the admiral started to laugh.

"Jesus," said Woods. "It's come to this."

"Please maintain level composure," snapped the computer.

"What the hell does that mean?"

"It needs to look at your eyes. Poor choice of words," said Dog.

Woods began to laugh. "What does it know? It's a computer."

Dog started to laugh too, though not quite for the same reason. The words had been chosen by Ray Rubeo, who was twice as arbitrary as any computer in existence.

Jed Barclay's face came back on the screen.

"So here's the thing," said Barclay, launching back into the point he'd been making earlier. "The Indians use new technology, the Chinese feel they have to retaliate. Up the ante. They're in big trouble domestically, and if they can't go to war against us, they figure they have to find somebody they can push around. It's one thing to get outgunned by us, and quite another for the Indians to do it. They have a second carrier en route; we suspect two more subs—nukes this time."

"Two? The Xias?" asked the admiral, referring to the most advanced submarine the Chinese were known to have.

"Actually, Admiral, we think they're Trafalgar clones. We're still trying to develop information on them. That's uh, what we want from Whiplash. I mean, from the Dreamland contingent."

"Where would the Chinese have gotten British attack submarines?" asked Woods.

"Well, these aren't Trafalgars per se," said Jed. "Though we think they do have the pump-jet propulsion system. We're pretty sure about that. The question is whether they're some kind of Chinese take on the Akula or a totally different design. We're really interested in the diving capability and we don't have a sound signature, for obvious reasons."

"You guys are losing me," said Dog. "Give me a little background, okay?"

Woods explained the Akula was a very good Russian nuclear attack boat, capable of high speeds and deep depths. The British submarines were also among the best all-around attack subs in the world, though the Trafalgar class represented a slightly different philosophy, one that emphasized silence over sheer performance. Its pump-jet propulsion system was notably quieter than a traditional propeller-driven boat. With their hulls covered in a special rubber material and a range of other improvements, the submarines were about as quiet as anything in the ocean, including diesels using batteries.

"They can dive to about the same depth as the Akula," said Woods, "though the Brits tend to be more conservative than the Russians. Pick your poison really—they're both excellent subs. If the Chinese have anything similar to either, they're pretty potent weapons."

He turned back to the screen. "But nowhere in any briefing that I've seen has anyone said the Chinese have such advanced submarines. We haven't seen them at sea, certainly. They had plans to purchase two Akulas from the Ruskies, supposedly, but that hadn't gone through. This is out of left field."

"Which is my point," said Jed. "The two boats left Behai eighteen hours ago. We have a good read on their initial direction, but beyond that we're empty."

"Behai? On the Gulf of Tonkin? There's no facility there."

"Yes, Admiral, exactly. The thinking is a shallow-water facility in some sheds about fifty yards from the waterline. They're doing a history run on satellite photos. It's at least technically feasible. Otherwise the subs just appeared from nowhere. Pacific Fleet has the northern coastline bottled up," Jed added. "So we don't think they could have snuck down past."

Woods furled his brow.

"What's more important," Dog asked. "Kali or the subs?"

"The six-million-dollar question," said Jed. "NSC is split. CIA wants both."

"That's not very helpful, Jed," said Dog.

"Tactical situation to dictate," said Jed. "Uh, the exact assignment would be Admiral Allen's call. He's already been informed."

"Okay," said Dog.

"That's all I have," said Jed.

"Thanks." Dog cut the connection by pushing a button on the console. "My plan was to use Piranha to track the Indian sub," Colonel Bastian told the admiral. "We can do the same for the Chinese. We have two units available; they can operate for roughly eighteen hours. We're bringing in additional control units so we can run the Megafortresses in shifts gathering the data. We hope to have other probes out here shortly."

"Right now, our orders are to keep the sea lanes open. That's our top priority," said Woods. "But I would say the more information about the Chinese submarines the better. From what Barclay just said, they'd probably be hunting for the Indian sub anyway. We might be able to catch them all together."

"Okay."

"Akulas can be a true pain in the ass," said the admiral, speaking as if from personal experience. He took a step away, thinking. "Can the Megafortresses look for the submarines while keeping tabs on surface shipping? Send back data, I mean."

"You mean tell you what ships are down there while we're running Piranha? That's easy."

"That's what we'll do. My carrier group will soon be close enough to handle the surface patrol. We'll move in ASW units to help you."

"Okay," said Dog.

"I'll talk to Admiral Allen right away. I know you're one of the Jedi, Bastian," he added. "I'll try not to hold it against you."

"I'm not really involved in Beltway politics," said Dog.

Though the exact usage varied, "Jedi" was a term often applied to a group of military officers and others connected with defense issues who advocated different approaches to traditional forces and thinking. It was generally used in a disparaging way.

"You think the Navy's obsolete," said Woods.

"Not at all."

"I've read the report that led to Whiplash," said Woods. "Asymmetric technology edge," he added. The phrase, which had been one of the section subheads, had become a buzz phrase in the administration—unfortunately, without the context that followed the headline.

"The report clearly noted that conventional forces still have a primary role," said Dog. "The idea is to develop next-generation weapons and get them into use as soon as possible. Piranha's a good example."

"I know you don't like me," said Woods. "I'm not asking you to. I understand you have a lot of experience. Good experience; and success. Candidly, Colonel— you're a very capable officer with an enviable track record. But you work for me now."

"Yes, sir," said Dog.

"Map out a plan to look for the subs. If we find one, Indian or Chinese, we'll stick with it. The others are bound to show up eventually," said Woods. With that, he turned and walked quickly out of the trailer.

THE GIRL'S BREATHING AND HEART RATE WERE NORMAL, and though unconscious, she didn't seem to have been severely injured. They brought her to a small tent at the far end of the base, letting her rest on the air-cushion stretcher that carried her. Liu and the others had turned from warriors to mother hens, watching for signs of her revival.

Bison had told Danny about the change in their orders, but the captain hadn't had time to think about the implications until he reached the medical tent. There were

Navy people all over the place, off-loading equipment from transports, revving up bulldozers, and staking out building sites.

Ordinarily, Danny Freah didn't put too much stock in interservice rivalry. In the modern military, the Joint Service Command structure meant that Air Force people and Army people and Navy people often mixed in together. Danny had worked with Marines several times since coming to Dreamland; before that, he had drawn assignments with several Army Special Forces teams, including one from Delta.

However, besides heading the Whiplash ground team, he was responsible for Dreamland security, and this many people running around presented a serious problem, no matter what uniform they wore. Even the observation post and its displays were classified. While allowances had to be made for "live" operations, he had to make sure everyone up and down the command chain understood there were fences.

"Okay, Sergeant," he told Liu. "Keep me posted on the girl while I sort the security stuff out."

"Gotcha, Cap."

Danny's ear bud vibrated with a page.

"Colonel's looking for you," said Bison. "He's headed your way."

"Good. What's our status with the Megafortresses?"

"Our guys'll watch 'em after they come in," said Bison. "Marines know they're out of bounds. Colonel Bastian kicked the admiral's staff out of the trailer."

"What staff?" said Danny. "What the hell were they doing in the trailer?"

"Uh, Captain, did you want Pretty Boy to shoot them?"

"Damn straight," said Danny, who wasn't kidding. "Shit. Why the hell didn't you tell me, Bison?"

"I told you the admiral was going there."

"Just the admiral, you said."

"I'm sorry, sir. I thought you meant the whole staff could wait there."

"Bison. Shit."

Danny's anger was temporarily diverted by a moan from the stretcher.

"Girl's waking up," said Liu.

"I'll get back to you," Danny told his sergeant.

The Filipino jerked upright on the cot, disoriented and angry. Liu put his hand on her shoulder. She pushed forward, and his grip tightened just enough to stop her from moving any further. The anger on her face changed to fear, then something like curiosity, then back to anger.

"Are you okay?" Danny asked her.

She frowned. Her reaction convinced Danny she spoke English, like most, though not all, of her countrymen.

"You're okay," he said. "Does your head hurt? You may have a concussion."

"Captain Freah?"

Danny turned toward the door of the tent. A Marine captain and two of his men had come in.

"I'm Freah."

"Name's Peterson. Justin Peterson." He held out his hand, which Danny shook professionally. "Prisoner?"

"Not exactly," said Danny. He gestured toward the door and they went out to talk. The wind was whipping up with a fresh storm; Danny could taste moisture on his lips and his breaths were heavy with the approaching rain.

"I'm in charge of securing the base area," said Peterson. "I understand you guys have some high-tech gizmos set up."

"The sensors themselves aren't that high-tech," said Danny. "Cameras, some IR gear. But what we have controlling them—that's classified."

"Oh?" Peterson's tone was somewhere between a challenge and genuine puzzlement.

"Yeah, I know. It's a pain in the ass, but I'd like to get some compartmentalization," said Danny. "I'm thinking my guys work the gear. We feed the information to your guys. I don't know what personnel you'll have."

"A company. We can get what we need, though."

"Company's fine. I'll go over the perimeter with you, and you can decide how you want to handle it. We had a similar arrangement with some guys from the 24th MEU (SOC)," added Danny, pronouncing the words as if they were "Mew-sock." "Seemed to work out. We can get you some of our como gear, but not the helmets we use."

Danny smiled. "You'd never give 'em back," he added.

"Okay. I heard a little about you," said Peterson.

"Me or my unit?"

"Both. You sure you're not Marines under those black vests?"

Danny knew he was being buttered up—but still, Peterson seemed all right. They'd get along okay.

"So what's with your prisoner?" asked the Marine.

"Native we found approaching our perimeter," said Danny. "She's not really a prisoner. Technically."

"Don't think she's a guerrilla?"

"No," said Danny quickly. He'd decided he was holding on to her himself until he had things figured out. Giving details of what had happened—such as the fact that she had a gun—would jeopardize that.

He wasn't just going out on the limb personally here, but potentially endangering the entire mission. Yet he knew that wasn't the case. She hadn't been trying to attack them; she was just protecting herself, as he would have done.

Danny was sure he was right. He just needed some time to talk to her, to prove it. Until then, they'd keep an eye on the village. They could take it out quickly enough.

"How can you be sure she's not a guerilla?" said Peterson.

Danny shrugged. "There's a tiny little village on the other side of that hilltop there, down the slope, across a swamp."

"Going to have to evac it, no?"

"Well, I didn't want to," said Danny. "Kinda sucks telling people they have to leave their homes."

Peterson took off his soft campaign cap, scratching his

head. For a Marine, he had relatively long hair—it might measure a full inch. Most of it stood straight up, as if at attention.

"We gotta do what we gotta do," said Peterson finally.

"Yeah. I know. At the moment, I want to make sure she's okay, then find out what she's up to, move off of that."

"Who we talking about?" said Colonel Bastian.

"Colonel."

Peterson saluted sharply. Danny introduced him, then told him about the girl—still leaving out the detail about the gun. "She can't stay here," said Dog. "What has she seen?"

"She just came to. She hasn't gone out of the tent," said Danny. "I want to see what she was up to."

"Captain, excuse me a second," Colonel Bastian said to Peterson.

"Yeah, I have some things to check out," said the Marine. "Captain Freah, if I could meet you at the Whiplash observation post in an hour maybe? If you can get the radios for us, I'd appreciate it."

"That'd be good."

"There more to this than you're saying?" Colonel Bastian asked after the Marine and his two men left.

"How so, sir?"

"You sound a little protective."

"No, sir."

"Why was she unconscious?"

"We had to knock her out to take her into custody," said Danny.

"You weren't thinking of setting her free, were you?"

"Absolutely not," said Danny truthfully. "I'm honestly not sure what to do with her, though. I mean, frankly— she hasn't done anything except cross an invisible line we set up in the jungle. I'm not sure what I can do. And the local government—from what I've heard, it's best not to get them involved."

Colonel Bastian had a way of pushing up his cheeks

and squinting when he heard something he found difficult to believe. Danny saw that look now.

If this had been Dreamland, Danny would have had the girl in a hood before being transported to the medical area. While she was isolated there, her prints would have been checked against innumerable databases. She'd be in Dreamland-issued clothing. She'd be guarded by two tiers of guards. He'd have a list of legal charges—civilian as well as military—pending against her. All might ultimately be dropped, but they'd be signed and sealed, ready to be used if necessary.

This wasn't Dreamland. Still, he was definitely being lax, at least by his standards.

He felt—what? Sorry for her?

She would have killed him, though.

"All right, Captain. For now, keep her isolated. We're going to have to consult with Admiral Woods on what to do with her," said Bastian. "But under no circumstances is she going anywhere without my specific approval."

"Of course, sir."

"Even if Woods tells you something else."

"Yes, sir."

Dog frowned. The steady hum of a Megafortress grew in the distance. "We've been chopped to PACCOM, but we're supposed to maintain strategic security," added the colonel. "I'm not exactly sure how we're supposed to accomplish that. Especially given that Admiral Woods is a class-one—"

The roar of a Megafortress landing on the nearby runway drowned out the end of Dog's sentence, but it wasn't particularly difficult to fill in the blank.

Philippines
1200

BREE ABSENTMINDEDLY RAN HER HAND ALONG THE back of her husband's wheelchair, listening as the Navy intelligence officer continued his briefing about the layout of Chinese and Indian forces in the area. Her father stood next to him, arms tightly folded and eyes fixed in a glare. He'd already snapped twice at errors the man had made when talking about the Megafortresses' capabilities. He appeared fully capable of strangling him if he misspoke again; his glare looked more potent than the Razor anti-aircraft laser.

Breanna hadn't seen him so belligerent since his first few weeks at Dreamland. He didn't like Woods, that much was clear—he frowned every time the admiral started to speak. Breanna had heard about the admiral's antics during the Piranha test, and so she understood there'd be some competitive animosity, but this seemed to go beyond that. Woods, though a bit gruff and obviously used to having his way, seemed competent and intelligent, traits her father normally held in high regard.

There were two battle groups in the South China Sea; the Chinese were at the north, the Indians at the south. Numerically, the Chinese held a serious advantage. They now had two small aircraft carriers with supporting destroyers and a cruiser. The Chinese carriers were a little less than seven hundred feet long and drew about twenty thousand tons fully loaded; by contrast the U.S.'s *Lincoln* measured over a thousand feet and displaced more than a hundred thousand tons. Size-wise, they were more equivalent to American assault carriers like the *Wasp* than what the U.S. considered front-line aircraft carriers. They were, nonetheless, potent, able to project serious airpower and the centerpiece of a major task force.

The Indians currently had eight destroyers and two guided-missile cruisers heading toward the Chinese fleet. About a day behind them was an ancient aircraft carrier named *Vikrant*, originally named *Hercules* when built by the British in 1946. The Indians had bought it soon afterward, operating her for nearly forty years before taking her into dock for repair and refurbishment. Another round of repairs and renovations had just been completed, adding a British-style ski jump to her flight deck, among other things. Also tiny by American standards, she was a bit bigger than the Chinese carriers but probably roughly their equivalent.

Her aircraft complement was unknown, but certainly included first-generation Harrier jump jets. There were also reliable reports that a version of the MiG-29K had been adapted by the Russians specifically for the Indian aircraft carrier. The MiG had lost a fly-off to the sea version of the Su-27/Su-33 as the preferred multirole fighter for the stillborn Russian carrier navy, but many analysts felt the smaller MiG-29K would have been a far better choice; its only shortcoming—albeit a serious one—was its more limited endurance.

"We haven't seen those planes yet," said the intelligence officer, tapping on the map spread out on the table. "One theory is they're being kept belowdecks to escape satellite surveillance. If so, there wouldn't be more than six. I have to admit, our intelligence on the *Vikrant* isn't good. The Indians brought the ship into dry dock last year and claimed it was beyond repair. We know a lot more about a sister ship, or close to a sister ship, called the *Viraat*. It has eighteen Harriers and some Russian ASW helicopters. It's back here, near India. We don't expect it to be a player at this time."

"What about the submarines we're supposed to find?" asked Zen.

"Ah yes, the subs." He pulled an overlay out from under the map. It was a large, clear transparency with yellow and red circles. "The two new Chinese attack subs were spotted around here," he said, pointing to an area of the Chinese coast just to the right of Vietnam, "eighteen hours ago. You'll appreciate that I can't discuss the specific intelligence methods used to find them," he added.

It was a snotty allusion to Dreamland's security protocols, and drew a snort from nearly everyone in the room. The Fleet hadn't found the subs at all—they'd been spotted by satellite, and all the details were readily available to the Dreamland team.

The intelligence officer continued, comparing the submarines to high-tech British attack boats powered by an ultraquiet propulsion system. Roughly as silent as the Indian ship on battery power, Piranha would have to stay closer than twenty miles to track them. The Indian submarine was bound to be easier to find initially, since it had to eventually come up for air and recharging.

"Your job is to find all the submarines and keep tabs on them," said Woods. "You'll work with our standard ASW patrols. We have two submarines en route, as well as several surface ships that can be tasked to shadow the submarines once they're located. Those assets are all some distance away, however."

"Iowa, with Commander Delaford and Ensign English, will take the first shift," said Colonel Bastian. "Because the launch and initial tracking are most critical. We'll hand off to Quicksilver and Zen, then Raven."

Major Alou and his crew were currently out on patrol, keeping tabs on the Chinese and Indian fleets.

"Assuming the new control set is in and you're comfortable," added the colonel, looking at Zen.

"I'll be comfortable," said Zen, who had been grousing about the Piranha controls ever since he'd heard he was going to have to "pilot" one. Delaford had brought along a sim program, which Zen had already begun working with. Typically, he'd nailed the high-proficiency score on his first try. "What about the Flighthawks?"

"From what Rubeo told me, we have to leave them on the ground," said Dog. "It won't be that big a deal. We'll just have to forgo close-in CAP and configure the missions accordingly. We figured we could place double-launchers on the wing hard-points for Scorpion AMRAAM-pluses, since the bay will be loaded with buoys. That's four missiles, and we should be able to get some long-range escort, or at least standby escort, from the Fleet."

Woods nodded. One of the Navy officers took over, running down some details about flight operations. A squadron of F/A-18's was en route from Hawaii and would be available for whatever contingency arose. He also briefly ran down some of the differences in Navy rescue procedures; downed Naval aviators used different "spins" for contacting rescue units. Though the difference was subtle, it could be vital in an emergency; coming up on a radio at five minutes after the hour when people were listening for you at ten might mean the difference between life and death.

"Gentlemen," said Woods, bringing the briefing to a close, "now that we understand each other. Let's get moving."

Gentlemen? Bree felt her face turning red. The admiral was looking straight at her.

Gentlemen, huh? We'll see about that.

"There's another matter I'd like to address," said Stoner. The CIA officer had sat quietly in the corner of the room, saying nothing and seemingly overlooked.

"There are some spy sites, or possible spy sites, on the atolls along the western end of the patrol area. At least one has radar. Captain Freah suggested they be investigated and I concur."

Woods frowned at Stoner.

"I suggest we use the Birds and the Osprey," added Danny. "We think there's probably a whole string of them, but looking at one would tell us a lot about the others."

"What sites? Who are they working for?" asked Woods.

"We're not sure," said Stoner. "My guess is they're with the Chinese, but that's why we'd like to go in. Major Stockard and the Quicksilver crew have data on them."

They discussed the sites briefly. Woods seemed to actively dislike Stoner, and pointed out twice this was not a CIA operation. Stoner didn't respond to the provocations.

His sunburned face had a harsh ruggedness that was attractive, Bree thought, even when he frowned. And those eyes—gray-blue. Pretty.

In the end, Woods agreed investigating the sites would be useful—but at the moment they weren't authorized to strike forces on either side of the conflict.

"Draw up a plan for my review," he said. "Gentlemen, good-bye."

"DRAFTED INTO THE FUCKING NAVY," SAID ZEN, ROLLING toward the tent that had been designated as their temporary quarters. "I'm a fucking sailor."

"At least he got your sex right," said Breanna, walking alongside his wheelchair.

"Navy bullshit," grumbled Zen, pushing inside.

"How's the tooth?"

"Still there." Zen pushed his tongue back toward the filling.

"So he must've done a good job, huh?"

"Why?"

"It's not bothering you. So going to the dentist isn't a bad thing."

"Yes, Captain. Right again."

She ran her hands from the back of his neck across his face, her thick, strong fingers lingering on his cheeks. Zen felt reluctant to let the bad mood drop, but her touch softened the muscles in his face. She moved closer and pushed her body against him, leaning her breast into the side of his face.

"Maybe having nothing to do for a few hours isn't so bad," she said.

"Ya think?" said Zen. He pulled her downward for a kiss. Except for the tooth, it was perfect; a long, slow melt into the softness she kept behind the bomber-pilot face.

"Mmmmm," she said.

"Mmmmm," he repeated, his fingers sliding to the top of her flight suit. They had just started south when there was a scream outside.

Zen jerked back and grabbed the wheels of his chair;

Breanna rushed ahead of him, running to the medical tent ten yards away. Two Whiplash team members, fully armed, came on a dead run, one dropping to his knee just outside the tent and talking into his microphone. Danny Freah barked something and the door to the big tent flew open. Freah, Sergeant Liu, and a Navy corpsman pushed out dragging a small Filipino. It was the woman they'd captured below, her shirt hanging half off.

"She grabbed a scissors," said Liu. "She tried to stab the captain."

"Guerrilla," said Stoner, appearing behind Zen.

"Maybe she just doesn't like the idea of being man-handled," said Breanna. The young woman had collapsed to the ground. Bree went to her and kneeled down.

"Careful, Captain," said Danny.

"Were there all men in there?" asked Bree.

"I don't think that was the problem," said Liu. "We took a gun from her earlier."

Breanna squatted in front of the Filipino. "Are you okay?"

The young woman didn't answer.

"Restraints," said Danny. Liu nodded and went back inside the tent.

"CPP," said a Marine officer who'd joined the semicircle. "Commie."

"No. She's a Muslim," said Stoner. "Ask her."

"What difference does that make?" said the Marine.

Stoner said nothing, but came over and lowered himself into a squat next to Breanna. Danny, standing behind the Filipino and still holding her shirt, stooped slightly. A light drizzle had started to fall; the rain was warm, like the sprinkle from a shower.

"What are you doing on this island?" asked Stoner. "You don't come from here."

The young woman spit at him, but the spook didn't react.

"We're not your friends, but we're not interested in hurting you either," he said. "Tell us why you're here.

Otherwise we'll turn you over to the Army."

She said nothing. They stared at each other a few seconds more; then Stoner rose.

"She's a guerrilla," said Captain Peterson. "You'll have to give her over to Western Command, the Filipino Army. Her people were probably planning a raid."

"She's not CPP, and she wasn't planning a raid," said Stoner.

"Who the fuck are you?" Peterson said.

Stoner gave the Marine a half smile but didn't answer his question. He turned to Zen instead—he was the ranking officer, but even so, Zen thought it odd—and told him, "The people in that settlement are probably all related; came here from one of the other islands. Luzon or someplace. They'll have a horror story." Stoner then turned abruptly and walked away.

"Whether she's a Commie or not," said Peterson, "you're going to have to turn her over to her government."

"She's my prisoner," said Danny. "I'm not sure what I'm going to do with her yet."

Peterson took a long breath obviously designed to underline what he was going to say next. "Captain, you have to follow proper procedures. And if there's a village that's threatening our post, then—"

"We'll survey the village to see if it's a threat," said Danny. "In the meantime, this woman may have to stand charges."

"For grabbing some scissors?" said Bree.

Danny glared at her.

"I want to talk to Colonel Bastian," said Danny. He turned to Liu. "Put her in the tent. Keep her hands cuffed. Behind her."

STONER WALKED ALONG THE PERIMETER OF THE AIR-strip, letting the light rain soak his face and clothes. He knew he wanted it to purge his anger. He also knew it wouldn't work, not completely.

Desire was the cause of all suffering. He stared into the droplets of rain, gazing out at the ocean. The furling waves had no desire; they were just drops of water pushed by physics.

Like him.

Not like him. He hated Woods—he hated all of the Navy people. And the Marines. Especially the Marines.

Irrationally, ridiculously. He had been a SEAL, and yet he hated the Navy. His assignments with the Company made use of his Navy expertise. Yet he hated the Navy. With no reason, beyond a hundred thousand insults and injuries, all to his ego, all meaningless in the great flow of life.

He would never be a true Buddhist, since he could not denounce his ego. Maybe he didn't want to be a true Buddhist—which, ironically, would make him closer to being one. The koan of it was a beautiful, humorous circle.

Stoner held his fingers together, his arms down at his sides, absorbing the rain. He actually liked Freah for not wanting to turn the idiot girl over to the Filipino Army. He liked all the Dreamland people—Zen Stockard especially. The major had just sat there, listening, not forming a judgment. The guy knew shit every second he was awake, but he didn't bitch about it.

And his wife, his beautiful wife . . .

Stoner let the idea float out toward the water. Desire was the cause of all suffering, the Buddha taught, and this was still the most difficult lesson to reconcile.

DANNY KNEW FROM BISON HE WOULDN'T FIND COLONEL Bastian in the trailer, but he went there first anyway. Then he walked very deliberately—to the tent that had been designated as Colonel Bastian's quarters. He knew he wouldn't find the colonel there either. So by the time he went to look for him where he had known all along he would be—Iowa, getting ready to takeoff—it was too late. The Megafortress's four engines rumbled and flared as Danny watched from twenty or thirty yards away; slowly being towed toward the runway, preparing to take off.

"Hey, Cap," said Powder as Danny watched the Megafortress put her nose into the wind. "Getting wet, huh?"

"Yeah," said Danny. If he wanted, he could use his smart helmet to talk to the colonel right now, ask him what to do. But he didn't.

"So what's with the girl?" asked Powder. "Tried to shoot your head off?"

"Something like that."

"Like that girl in Bosnia, huh?"

"Yeah," said Danny, who hadn't even thought about that incident.

Oh, he realized.

Oh!

"Spooky replay, huh?"

Danny put his hand over his eyes, shielding them from the rain. Powder had been with him in Bosnia.

"You know, I hadn't even thought about it," he told the sergeant. "I didn't even remember that."

"Shit."

"Yeah." Danny laughed.

"Really, Cap? You blocked the whole sucker out?"

More or less. It had probably poked at him when he realized the person he'd grabbed was a woman, but he hadn't really remembered, or thought about it, maybe because he was too focused on doing his job. Or maybe the memory was just too much.

The other woman was a Muslim too.

"Shit," said Danny.

"Captain?"

"Let's go get some coffee," he told Powder. "Assuming these Navy guys know how to make it."

HE'D BEEN IN ITALY AS PART OF A SPECIAL TACTICS Squadron, and through a series of related and unrelated

developments, wound up being assigned with two of his
men to accompany a UN negotiating team. The UN people were to meet with government officials at a police
station in an obscure hillside town. The day before Danny,
Powder, and another STS sergeant named Dave Chafetz
went into the town with two plainclothes Yugoslavian policemen to familiarize themselves with the area. The policemen were scared shitless about something, even
though they were in ostensibly friendly territory.

Scouting the ingress and egress routes went quickly.
The police station was located near the town's biggest
intersection, which, despite the Yugs' assurances, was
highly problematic. Danny and his team members took
mental notes of several evacuation points, including the
police station roof. They planned to have a pair of Black-
hawks and some scout helicopters no more than two
minutes away, and a ground unit with armored vehicles
within striking distance. With Danny taking pains not to
tip off his assessments to his Yugoslav escorts, it took
about four hours to scout the whole place. Danny's efforts
were more professional than practical; it wouldn't take a
genius to know roughly where an emergency rendezvous
or pickup would be planned.

The policemen kept asking nervously if he'd seen
enough, hinting almost to the point of insistence that it
was time for them to return to their UN base. Finally,
Powder suggested they look at the building next to the
police station; it was a grocery-type store, though from
the window and door facing the street, the shelves looked
pretty bare.

The policemen argued it was time to leave. Danny exchanged glances with his two men, then told the Yugs
they were going in.

"Fine," said one of the policemen. "We'll wait out
here."

More than likely, they were just being paranoid, but
you could never tell. The building had to be inspected,
and it had to be inspected now.

Danny and his men were dressed in fatigues with armored vests, but weren't carrying rifles. They could and would call on air support if things got crazy, but he knew doing so would greatly complicate things, probably cancel the meeting tomorrow, and set the process back considerably.

He left his Beretta in its holster, trying to play it as innocently as possible. The door squeaked on its jamb as he pushed inside, and a bell at the corner of the frame rang, but there was no one in sight. He walked in, boots creaking against the old floorboards—there was a basement; they'd have to investigate.

Danny had memorized a set of cumbersome phrases in Serbo-Croatian, meant more to show he was friendly than to really communicate. He rehearsed one—*"Vrlo mi je drago što vas vidim,"* or roughly, "pleased to meet you"— as he walked toward a glass display counter about three quarters of the way back in the room. The display was empty, as were the shelves nearby. The place had a slightly sweet smell to it, the sort of scent that might come from cooking cabbage. The faint odor mixed with something more like dirt or mud.

Something moved on his right. He spun, his hand down near his belt and gun.

A figure came from behind a tattered curtain, a thin shadow. He thought it was a boy at first, then realized it was a girl, a young woman really. Maybe five-one, barely ninety pounds. Her hair was very short, unusual for the area.

"Vrlo mi," he started, faltering almost immediately with the pronunciation. He had memorized a phrase for "are you the owner?"—*"da li ste sopstvenik?"* which was intended to apply to the taxi drivers. He tried to remember it, but before he could, the girl held her hands in front of her, then backed away.

"I'm not going to hurt you," he said, putting up his own hand.

The girl stopped. The store was unlit, making it difficult

to see her face well, but Danny thought she had understood what he said.

"We're just Americans. Yanks," he told her. "United States. U.S. We were just, uh, looking around. Do you have anything to sell?"

It was lame, but it was all he could think of. Powder, who was a few feet behind him, said they were looking for coffee.

"Powder," said Danny. "This isn't a deli."

"Hey, Cap, you never know. I could go for a good hit of joe right now."

"We just want to look around," Danny told the girl. "Okay?"

She stared at him, and then nodded, or seemed to nod.

"You stay with her, Powder, while I check out the stairs."

"You sure, Cap?"

"I'm sure."

The urge to take out his gun was overwhelming, but Danny managed to resist, determined to show the young woman he meant no harm. He walked toward an open staircase at the side of the room. A candle and matches were on a small ledge at the base of the steps; he lit them, then, calling ahead, went upstairs. In the glow of the candle, Danny saw the floor of a large room was covered with bird shit; he looked up and saw little remained of the roof. Still, he walked far enough inside to make sure no one was hiding in the shadows, then returned to where Powder was monitoring the young woman.

"Basement next, Powder."

"Yes, Cap."

In the basement, Danny found a mattress and some bedclothes about four feet from the bottom step. There was nothing else; no furnace, no washing machine, not even a store of food—just the stone and dirt walls of the foundation.

Danny relaxed a bit as he walked back up the stairs. Idiot policemen were probably just anxious to go home—

or more likely, complete whatever black-market transaction was waiting for them near the checkpoint. Smuggling was a common sideline for the authorities here.

Once back on the main floor, Danny started toward the door, then remembered he hadn't looked beyond the torn curtain the girl had emerged from.

As he turned and took a few steps toward the concealed area, Powder said something, then shouted. Totally by instinct, Danny ducked as the woman charged past his sergeant. He reached out and grabbed her leg, sending her tumbling against the shelves. A small revolver fell from her hand.

"Shit," said Powder.

Now standing, Danny clamped his foot on the woman's arm. The two Yugoslavian policemen charged inside, raking the ceiling with submachine guns. After shouts from the Americans finally managed to calm them, one of the policemen grabbed the woman and hauled her out. Danny—pistol now out—pulled back the curtain.

A boy, three or four years old, sat on the floor in the middle of a small, squalid kitchen, his thumb in his mouth.

By the time Danny got outside, the young woman was gone, and several policemen had poured out of the station next door. As Danny tried to sort out the situation, one of the policemen said the woman was a known Muslim. Danny tried to find out what would happen to her, but was ignored. Finally, he and his men had no option but to leave. The meeting between the UN and government officials was never held.

Powder had grabbed the pistol and found three bullets loaded, but the firing pin was broken and it probably couldn't have fired.

Months later, Danny saw a Reuters news story about bodies being unearthed in a field near the same village. There was a murky photo of a recently opened ditch. In the corner of the photo were the bodies of a young woman and a small boy, both nude.

Was it the woman and her son? The photo was too poor for him to tell. They could have been anyone in that war, any of a thousand victims, mother and child, sister and brother, innocents slain because of religion, or revenge, or just for the hell of it. It was the reason the U.S. got involved in the first place; to stop shit like that from happening, but reasons, and intentions, and the future didn't make much difference to the people in that ditch.

Aboard Iowa, over the South China Sea
1600

AS SHE POKED INTO A SOLID WALL OF RAIN JUST OVER the ocean, Dog slid Iowa back down through the clouds, holding her steady through a series of buffeting winds. Piranha was ready to dance, but they couldn't find her a partner; the Navy ASW planes with their sonar buoys had been delayed. Delaford said the Indian sub captain might try to take advantage of the weather to snorkel and recharge batteries. So, with nothing else to do, they were trying to find him on the surface. The laborious process of running tracks over the empty water hadn't yielded any results, however, and Colonel Bastian was starting to feel tired.

"I felt that yawn over here, Colonel," said the copilot. "I thought we were heading into a hurricane."

"Very funny, Rosen. Just keep tabs on those Sukhois."

"Aye, aye, Cap'n."

"We're not in the Navy yet," Dog told him.

"No, but we're low enough to be a ship," said the copilot. It was only a slight exaggeration—they were at a thousand feet, using every sensor they had, including their eyes.

"Shark Ears," the Navy Orion with the sonar buoys, checked in. They were still a good forty minutes away.

"Maybe we should set up a refuel," suggested Rosen. "Extend our patrol and come back and work with them for a while, assuming they don't totally scrub because of the weather. It's pretty rough down there, and it's going to get worse."

"Good idea," said Dog.

The tanker was flying a track well to the northeast. With the help of Iowa's sophisticated flight computer system, Rosen quickly plotted a course to rendezvous about thirty minutes away. Eager to get away from the water and the severe weather below, Dog leaned back on the stick and the airplane bolted upright. The air was fairly clear away from the leading edge of the storm, their view unimpeded.

"We may have a contact on the surface," said Rosen. "Ten miles, two degrees east of our nose, just about in our face."

Dog immediately began to level off and nudge toward the contact. Delaford, monitoring the feeds on his equipment downstairs, couldn't find anything. Dog swung Iowa around, holding the Megafortress on her wing, and cruised over the coordinates at about a thousand feet.

"If there was something there, it's gone now," said Delaford finally. "I don't think we should launch Piranha until we have something more definite."

"I concur," said Rosen.

"All right. Let's give Shark Ears this point as a reference," said Dog. "In the meantime, let's go tank."

As they started to climb once again, the two Chinese fighters flying over the nearest aircraft carriers changed their course.

"Looks like we've finally aroused some curiosity," said Rosen. "Their new course will put them in visual range in eight minutes."

There was no pressing need to refuel, so Dog decided not to lead the fighters out to the tanker. He told Rosen to cancel the rendezvous for now, and resumed what was essentially a holding pattern just over the worst of the storm. Big fists of gray clouds ran northwest by southeast for as long as the eye could see; a light haze sat to the northeast of the front, a dark blanket to the southwest where the storm was coming from.

The Chinese planes weren't moving particularly fast, an indication they weren't intending hostile action, though there were no guarantees. Rosen tried hailing them at twenty miles, but to no one's surprise, the Chinese pilots did not respond. A second two-ship of Sukhois was also heading out, a few minutes behind the first. Their carriers were just a little ahead of the storm, and it occurred to Dog the Sukhois wouldn't be able to spend all that much time with them if they didn't want to land in the teeth of the heavy weather.

The enhanced optical feed from the Megafortress's chin camera caught the lead Sukhoi at ten miles. The computer ID'd the missiles under its wings as R-73s, known to NATO as Archers. They were heat-seekers with excellent off-boresight capability, at least, in theory, better than all but the latest-model Sidewinders at sniffing out heat sources. They could be launched from any angle, including head-on.

Which was pretty much where they were now.

"Six miles and closing," said Rosen. "Man, it pees me off they won't answer our hails. I've been practicing my Chinese and everything."

"Just keep tracking," Dog told him.

The two lead Chinese fighters broke to Iowa's right about a mile ahead of them, turning in a wide circle. Not coincidentally, the move put them in an excellent position to close and then fire their heat-seekers, though they made no obvious move to do so.

"Computer thinks the second group of Sukhois is packing Exocets," said Rosen, referring to the second flight of Sukhois. "Optical IDs are not perfect."

"Could be they're hoping we have a line on the Indian sub," said Dog. He kept Iowa steady as the second group of planes abruptly tipped their wings and shot downward toward the water. The nearest civilian ship was about two miles behind them; the Chinese fighters showed no interest in the tanker.

"What do we do if they sink him?" Rosen asked.

"I guess we take notes," said Dog. "Delaford, how good are Exocets against submarines?"

"I'd say next to useless, unless something keeps the sub on the surface for an extended period. You saw what happened the other day," said the Navy commander. "The helicopters are what they'd really want out here, but we're too far from the carrier group for them to operate comfortably. It's just not in their normal doctrine."

"Then why did they blow it the other day?" Dog asked.

"Well, they probably had the planes in the air, just like now, and decided to take their best shot. My guess now is they were planning to land soon anyway, they saw us dip down like we found something, so they decided to come out and see what's up. We're close to a hundred miles from the carrier, which is beyond the range of conventional submarine torpedoes. So, this far from the carrier, a submarine ordinarily wouldn't be a threat, unless it was one of ours or maybe a Russian. See, that's why Kali is so significant; it changes the equation for them."

"Hey, I have a question," said Rosen. "Why didn't the Chinese submarine take out the Indian sub the other day?"

"Assuming it didn't," said Delaford, "since we don't really know what happened under the water, my bet is that it was returning from the Indian Ocean and had fired all of its torpedoes earlier. Three ships sank out there last week."

"So why didn't the Indian sub fire at the Chinese?" asked Dog.

"Again, we're assuming they didn't," said Delaford. "We don't know what happened under the water later. But given that, my guess is the sub wasn't a big enough target. They'd want the carrier. Or their orders didn't call for firing on a combat vessel unless they were specifically attacked. They hadn't fired on one."

"Still haven't," said Dog.

"Right."

"Our Orion ASW plane is twenty minutes away," said Rosen. "Tomcats are reporting they have the Sukhois on their scopes at long range."

"Quite a party," said Delaford.

"Lay it out for them," Dog said. Before Rosen finished, however, the Sukhois had changed course to return to their carrier.

Iowa directed the Navy sub hunter to the spot where they'd had the tentative contact. Twenty minutes later, Shark Ears reported a contact.

There was only one problem—it was a Russian sub.

"They know this guy," Delaford reported. "It's a Victor III. May just be keeping tabs on things, or not."

"Nothing else?" Dog asked.

"Nothing yet."

Aboard *Shiva* in the South China Sea
1630

KALI WAS THE GODDESS OF DESTRUCTION, SHIVA'S wife, the embodiment of the idea that true life begins only with death.

It was an apt name for a weapon, and a perfect name for the missiles in *Shiva*'s forward tubes.

Admiral Balin looked again at the chart where their position had been plotted. Balin studied the map carefully; his target should lay just within the range of his weapons, though he still needed fresh coordinates to fire.

The *Vikrant* and her escorts would be twenty-four hours away. It was time.

Varja remained with the radio man, translating the coordinates received by the ELF. ELF—extremely-low-frequency—transmissions were, by technical necessity, brief, but this one did not need to contain much information—simply a set of coordinates and a time. With those few numbers, the device could be launched. Once fired, the weapon was on its own, relying first on its stored data to take it to the target area, then using its low-probability-of-intercept radar to take it the rest of the way. As their earlier tests had shown, as long as the target ship was within five miles when the radar activated, it would be hit.

"Precisely as the earlier coordinates predicted," said Varja finally. "It is a good day, Admiral."

Balin watched the crewman mark the map, then nodded.

"Launch in three minutes," said Captain Varja, passing the word to the weapons controllers and the men in the torpedo room.

Aboard Iowa
1645

"SHARK EARS REPORTING POSSIBLE CONTACT," SAID Rosen.

He gave Dog a set of coordinates almost due north, taking them roughly parallel to the Chinese carrier task force about forty miles away. An Australian container ship was plying the seas about ten miles ahead of them, going roughly in the direction of the carriers, though undoubtedly it would steer well clear as it approached.

As Iowa changed direction and waited for an update, another set of Sukhois came over to check them out. Unlike the earlier pilots, these jocks were cowboys, clicking on their gun radars at long range. The Tomcats riding shotgun for the Navy patrol plane further south didn't particularly appreciate the gesture, though they maintained good discipline, staying in their escort pattern. They could afford to, knowing they could splash the Su-33's in maybe ten seconds flat if that was what they decided to do; the Chinese planes were well within reach of their long-legged Phoenix missiles.

"Contact—I have—a launch—two launches," said Rosen suddenly. "Shit—tracking—we have a cruise missile—

two cruise missiles, breaking the surface. Fifty miles, bearing on nine-zero, exactly nine-zero."

There was no time to consider whether the missiles were aimed at the Chinese carrier or the Australian ships; both were in range.

"Target Scorpions," said Dog.

"Need you to cut, uh, need you at two-seventy," said Rosen, giving Dog the turn they needed to launch their missiles. "Tracking One. Tracking Two. Okay, okay. No locks. Come on, baby."

Dog pushed his stick to the left, riding the big plane hard. He nosed the plane down at the same time his hand reached for the throttle bar, picking up speed for the launch. The AMRAAM-pluses sat in their launchers near the wingtips, their brains seething for the targeting data.

"Okay—locked on Two!" said Rosen.

"Fire."

"Launching. Launching. Two missiles away. Good read. Still looking for One. Still looking—can you cut twenty north—north, I need you north."

Dog pushed the jet hard, following his copilot's directions. Rosen gave another correction—they were almost out of time, the missile hunkering low against the waves, accelerating. Dog slid the stick back, his body practically jumping in the ejection seat to slap the Megafortress onto the proper bearing.

"Locked on One! Locked!"

"Fire," said Dog softly.

The first Scorpion came off the wing with a thud so loud, Dog first thought there had been a malfunction, but it burst ahead a second later when the main rocket ignited, its nose rising briefly before settling down.

The Sukhois had rolled downward and were now five miles behind the Megafortress, closing fast.

The RWR blared.

"Flares," Dog told Rosen calmly. "Hang on everyone."

He threw the big plane onto its wing as the Chinese interceptors launched a volley of missiles. After seeing the Megafortress launch, they had incorrectly concluded it had fired on their ship.

"Two more Sukhois," said Rosen as Dog whipped them into a seven-G turn. "Bearrrrrring—"

Gravity slurred Rosen's words as Dog whipped the plane back and then pushed the wing down, not merely changing direction, but dropping altitude dramatically. The Megafortress temporarily became more brick than aircraft, whipping toward the waves just barely under control. The two Russian-made heat-seekers sailed well over them; by the time they realized they'd missed their target and lit their proximity fuses, Dog had already wrestled Iowa level in the opposite direction. He was nose-on to one of the Sukhois and had he harbored any hostile intent—or a cannon in his nose—he could have waxed the Chinese pilot in a heartbeat. Instead, he merely pushed the throttle glide for more giddyap. The Sukhoi shot below as Dog pushed upward toward a stray bank of clouds, looking for temporary respite.

He hadn't quite reached cover when the RWR announced there were radar missiles in the air. Rosen cranked the ECMs. They fired off chaff, and once more began jucking and jiving in the sky. The easily confused radar missiles sailed away harmlessly.

"Two is cooked! Splash cruise missile two," said Rosen, somehow managing to keep track of his missile shots despite working the countermeasures.

"Where are the Sukhois?" asked Dog.

"Two are heading back to the carrier. Ditto the one that just launched the homers," said Rosen, meaning the radar missiles. "Tomcats are sixty seconds away."

Dog hit the radio. "Dreamland Iowa to Tomcat Top Flight—do not take hostile action. Stand off."

"Missile three is terminal—missed, shit," said Rosen.

Dog ran out of clouds and tucked toward the ocean, his altitude dropping through five thousand feet. A geyser shot up in the distance.

"Four is-is," stuttered Rosen, eyes fixed on his targeting

radar screen. "Four—yes! Grand slam! Grand slam! Got both those suckers!"

"Relax, Captain." Dog swung his eyes around his instruments, getting his bearings quickly. The sitrep map showed the Tomcats now within twenty-five miles. There were two Sukhois directly over the Chinese carrier *Shangi-Ti*. A flight of four, undoubtedly from the *T'ien* to the north, was coming down with afterburners lit.

"They're looking for us," said Rosen.

"ECMs."

"I'm singing every tune I can think of," said Rosen. The computer was jamming the Sukhois' "Slotback" Phazotron N001 Zhuck radars, making it impossible for them to lock on the Megafortress, or anything else nearby, including the much more obvious Orion to the south.

As Dog banked, he turned his head toward the side windscreen, looking at the sea where the missiles had originated. "Tell our Chinese friends we just saved their butts."

"Yes, sir."

"Delaford, you have a line on the Indian submarine?"

"Not a specific location, but they're definitely in range for Piranha. We'll have tons of data on Kali now," he added. "Very interesting."

"No response from the Chinese," said Rosen. "Helos launching—looks like one of the destroyers changing course."

"I don't see much sense launching Piranha now," Dog told Delaford. "The Chinese will be throwing depth charges left and right."

"By the time they get near the sub, it'll be long gone," said Delaford. "But I concur, Colonel. At this point I'd suggest we stand off and watch."

Dog gave the lead Tomcat pilot a quick brief after being asked for a rundown.

"I'd prefer we didn't have to shoot them down," he added.

The Navy pilot didn't respond.

"You got that, Commander?" Dog added.

"Lightning Flight acknowledges transmission," said the pilot. "With due respect, Colonel, it's my call."

"Listen, Captain, at this point, we do not need to escalate. Hold your fire unless the Chinese get aggressive."

"Just because you have a fancy ol' plane, doesn't mean you're king of the hill," said the Tomcat jock.

"Set the ECMs to break their missiles if they fire," Dog told Rosen over the interphone.

"The Chinese?"

"The Tomcats."

"Yes, sir. Four helos now, coming out from the task force. Hold on here. Got some transmissions." Rosen listened a moment more, then laughed. "The Chinese are demanding we tell them where the Indian sub is."

"Tell 'em damned if we know. Just like that."

"Just like that?"

"Verbatim." Dog switched his radio to the shared frequency again, this time talking to the Orion pilot. They decided to hold off dropping more buoys—no sense helping the Chinese any more than they already had.

In the background, Dog heard a transmission from one of the Tomcat pilots to another group of Navy fighters coming from the south: "Watch out for the cranky AF transport driver."

Dog didn't mind being called cranky. The slur on the Megafortress was hard to take, though.

"They're damn lucky we're out of Scorpions," said Rosen, who'd flipped into the circuit just in time to hear the crack. "Show 'em cranky."

Dog looked to the west at the slowly approaching storm. All things considered, it was probably better they hadn't launched Piranha; tracking it through the storm would have been difficult.

"Can you get me a weather update?" he asked the co-pilot.

"Worse and worser," replied Rosen before proceeding

to retrieve the more official version—which used a few more words to say the same thing.

"Plot a course back for the Philippines," Dog told him. "We'll let the Navy guys take it from here."

"Sure you don't want to shoot down one of the Tomcats before we go?" joked Rosen.

"Very tempting, Captain," said Dog, starting to track south.

Aboard the trawler *Gui* in the South China Sea
1715

IT HAPPENED CHEN LO FANN WAS STARING AT A MAP showing the respective positions of the Chinese and Indian fleets when the message came that Americans had shot down the Indian missiles before they could strike the carrier. He read the note calmly, then nodded to dismiss the messenger. He resisted the impulse to go to the radios; there would be no further details, or at least none of any import. Instead, he locked the door to his cabin, then sat cross-legged on the deck in front of the large map.

It was undoubtedly the first time he had sat on the floor of a cabin since he was young man, and probably the first time he had done so when not playing dice. He could feel the ship here, and through it, the sea, the endless energy of the complicated sea.

Perhaps the information was incorrect or incomplete. He needed more. The Dragon ship was still too far off; he had to rely on his network.

He stared at his map, eyes blurring. The coldness of the ocean seemed to come up through the deck, though he was a good distance from the water.

While his men gathered their information, he could only wait.

V
Death in the family

WHEN JENNIFER GLEASON FINALLY MANAGED TO UN-
fold herself from the jump seat on the C-17's flight deck,
her legs felt as if they had been stapled together. Her
stomach and throat had changed places, and even her eyes
were giving her trouble. Jennifer was a veteran flier, had
been in the Megafortress during combat, and survived a
disabling laser hit, but this was by far the worst flight she
had ever endured.

It wasn't just the uncomfortable fold-down seat or the
turbulent air. She'd spent the entire flight worried about
Colonel Bastian; a vague uneasiness, indefinable. It was
new to her; she'd never really had anyone to worry about
before, not like this. None of her other boyfriends—the
term seemed ridiculous applied to Tecumseh, who was
anything but a boy—had aroused such emotions. Until
Tecumseh—she hated calling him Dog—Jennifer had
been organized and specific about her thoughts and emotions. Now her head fluttered back and forth, and her body
hurt like hell.

Outside, the rain had just stopped; the wet leaves glis-
tened in the morning light. The base had been taken over

by the Navy—there were several large patrol aircraft parked in front of two Megafortresses, along with a pair of F/A-18's and a blue Navy helicopter. Three or four bulldozers were revving nearby, assisting a construction crew to erect a hangar area.

Colonel Bastian was waiting for Jennifer at the Whiplash command post. So was most of the Dreamland contingent, and a few Navy officers besides, so she had to confine her greeting to a very proper "Sir."

"Jennifer, we've been waiting for you," said the colonel. "Or rather, your equipment."

She snickered at the unintended double entendre, but it went right by Dog and the others. He introduced two Navy officers as liaisons with the fleet, informing Jennifer they had clearances for Piranha.

"If you can give us a quick timetable," he added in his deep voice. She had trouble turning her mind back to the project, and the reason she'd come.

"It's straightforward. First up, we get the control gear into the planes. By tomorrow night we should have two new probes. Beyond that, there are some tests and fixes I'd like to try. Oh, and I have a fix, no, not a fix, just a tweak, on the wake detectors—I'll put that in first. Shouldn't take too long; it's a software thing."

"So how sensitive is the passive sonar?" asked one of the Navy people.

"Good enough to follow submarines of the Trafalgar type at twenty miles. I have the diffusion rates, all the technical data here."

The officer had obviously asked the question to see how much she knew, and Jennifer, not so subtly, called his bluff, reaching into her knapsack for her laptop.

"We've had a few problems with amplitude when the temperature shifts quickly, such as when you go into a different thermal layer. We think it's hardware, though I've tried two different versions of the chip circuitry and had the same results, so I'm not sure. Here—maybe you have some ideas. Look at the sines, that's where it's obvious."

She started to unfold the laptop. The intel officer had turned purple. Delaford rescued him.

"I think for now we better just stay focused on equipping the other planes," he said.

Jennifer gave the other man an overly fake smile and packed the laptop away.

"How long to install?" Zen asked.

"Three hours per plane," she told him. She took a long strand of hair and began twisting it, thinking. "We're going to route the com units through the Flighthawk backup gear and use the panels for the display. We didn't have time to actually test it, but I think it'll work."

DOG WANTED TO GRAB HER, JUST JUMP HER RIGHT there—it was as blatant as that; raw, an overwhelming animal urge. His eyes bored into the side of her head; she hadn't looked at him after coming in, probably because she felt the same way.

"All right. We need a fresh weather report. Storm should almost be out of the tracking area, which will make our job easier, at least until the next one comes through. They were talking about a twenty-four-to-forty-eight-hour window, which means one full rotation. Then, the probe goes home." Dog resisted the urge to pace—there simply wasn't room in the small trailer. "Our Navy friends have worked on some ideas about where some of targets may be located. We're going to work with a group of P-3's flying at very long range on the west side of the Chinese battle group, from here over to the Vietnamese coast."

Dog's hand slid across a massive area of ocean as dismissively as if it were a small parking lot.

"If we find something or get a good hint, we launch. Quicksilver is up next. They replace us on station in six hours. Raven comes on six hours later. If there's no launch, Quicksilver still helps the Navy with patrols, but we'll take the next shift. By sometime tomorrow, or maybe the next day, *Kitty Hawk* should be in the patrol area and that will change things. I'm not sure exactly what the admiral has in mind at that point."

Dog's lineup would mean at least twelve-hour shifts for the crews, with three or four hours prep, six hours on patrol, two or three hours to get back and debrief. No one complained—which didn't surprise Dog in the least.

He glanced over at Jennifer. She was looking at him, squinting ever so slightly.

Of course she was looking at him. Everyone was.

Dog forced himself to nod, shifted his gaze to Fentress, and nodded again. When he turned toward Breanna, he saw she was frowning.

"Captain?" he asked her in surprise.

"Nothing."

"Captain Williams will give us the latest on the Chinese and Indian forces," Dog said, turning to the Navy officer. Williams had come from the G-2 section of Admiral Allen's staff to facilitate intelligence sharing.

"The storm slowed down the progress of the task forces." He pulled out a small manila folder and handed some papers around. Dog glanced down at his and saw it was actually a cartoon rendering of the situation—on one side of the South China Sea was Donald Duck, on the other Mickey Mouse, both posturing on top of aircraft carriers.

"You draw this yourself?" said Zen, an obvious snicker in his voice.

"Just keeping things in perspective," said Williams. He dished out another version—this one a detailed sketch based on the latest reports. "Probable area of the Indian submarine is that crosshatch just to the east-southeast of the lead Chinese carrier, which is where they launched from. They haven't found it yet, at least as far as we know. Good submarine captain—and I think we have to assume this fellow's at the top of the heap—would use this storm to skitter around, get a new location. The Chinese don't have an all-weather ASW capability, not from the surface anyway. Their submarines may be a different story, but as you can see from the diagram, they're still at best a day away from joining the aircraft carriers. Even then, frankly, their probability of intercepting the Indian boat is not going to break double digits."

The Indian aircraft carrier had managed to link up with the cruisers and destroyers. If everyone steamed toward each other at flank speed, they could be firing at each other within twenty-four hours.

"More likely, they'll just shadowbox," said Williams. "Plenty of opportunity for you to get information about the submarines. Yesterday's show of force by Iowa seems to have dampened some of the war fever; the diplomacy's at high pitch." Hoping to fire a diplomatic flare of his own toward the Dreamland contingent, Captain Williams added, "By the way, that's a good name for a Megafortress. Her Navy namesake would be proud."

THE SAILOR HANDLING THE CHOW LINE IN THE MESS tent saw Danny Freah approach. "More eggs, Captain? Be your third helping."

"Problem with that?" said Danny lightly.

"No, sir," said the Navy seaman, lifting the metal cover on the serving tray. "No, sir. Good to see someone with a healthy appetite."

"It's good cooking, sailor," said Danny, though truth was the eggs were rubbery at best. Most likely they were powdered or flash-frozen or whatever the hell they did to eggs these days. Still, he took another full helping, then went back to his table.

He was putting off talking to Colonel Bastian. He'd already put it off since last night, when he could have caught the colonel before he turned in. This morning he could have grabbed him before his briefing session. Danny could have—*should have*—interrupted him.

Powder was right about the girl. That was no reason,

none at all, not to do his job. She wasn't the same woman, and he wasn't in the same situation.

But she didn't present a threat, nor did her village. He knew that in his bones.

They couldn't keep her in the med tent; he had to deal with her before Peterson went over his head, which he might already have done.

Or Stoner. The spook thought he was God, just about. Spy with attitude. He would get involved soon too.

Danny was trained to be cautious, to think about what he was doing before he acted. He was also trained to act, not to sit on something for a day—days, really, if you argued he should have moved the village right away.

He sure as hell wasn't trained—wasn't *paid*—to get caught up in emotions and buried memories. Maybe Jemma was right; maybe it was time for him to quit.

And do what? Run for office? What good would he do?

Right wrongs, like Jem always said.

That was what he was doing now.

"Hey, Cap, you probably want to get over to the med tent," said Bison, leaning down next to him. "Stoner's hassling the prisoner."

"Shit," muttered Danny, getting up quickly.

He found Stoner sitting across from the woman in a chair. She was talking in English, her face red. Danny started to say something to the CIA officer, but Stoner stopped him by putting up his hand.

"They burned the houses first," continued the woman. "The houses were huts, not even as sturdy as this. Two people we have never seen again. These are the people you call saviors."

"I didn't call them saviors," said Stoner. His voice was flat, as unemotional as a surgeon asking for a fresh scalpel.

"We want only to live in peace. Is that too much to ask?"

"You're not in a good place," said Danny, taking another step toward her. Her cheekbones were puffed out and her hair brushed straight back; her anger made her seem more like a woman.

"Where would you have us live?" she demanded.

"I don't know."

"If you turn us over to the government, they will massacre us." She looked at Danny defiantly for a moment, then turned back to Stoner and began to cry.

"Mr. Stoner, a word," said Danny. He turned and went out of the tent. When the CIA officer appeared, he walked a few feet away.

"She telling the truth?" Danny asked him.

"I told you there'd be a sob story."

"Sob story—two people being killed is hardly a sob story."

"What would you call it?" Stoner asked.

"A fucking massacre—an atrocity."

Stoner shrugged.

"We're not turning her over to the government, or the army," said Danny.

Stoner said nothing.

"We're not," said Danny. "We'll move them ourselves. Fuck those bastards—we'll move them ourselves. Well? Say something."

"What do you want me to say?"

"Say you agree."

Stoner shrugged.

Danny felt his anger rising so high he almost couldn't control it. "What the fuck, man? What the hell—aren't you human?"

"We can move them. But sooner or later, the Army will find them again. We won't have control over what happens then."

"You know—"

Danny clamped his hand into a fist, stifling his anger. Would it do any good to tell Stoner what had happened in Bosnia? Probably not.

It didn't matter. He'd move them himself.

"You going against me on this?" Danny asked.

Stoner shrugged. "I'm not for or against it. It's not really my business. There's a communications network. I have NSA intercepts that are reporting on ship activity and transmitting."

"From here?"

"They haven't been able to pin down the location, which is pretty interesting, I guess. There are two kinds of transmission—radio, and something that goes underwater. Not all of it's decoded."

"And she's involved in that?"

"I doubt it, but we won't know till we look in her village."

Danny frowned, as if Stoner were saying he should have done this before.

Which, in a way, he was.

"The gear's pretty sophisticated," said the CIA officer. "They wouldn't be able to hide it."

"Those atolls," said Danny. "If there's some sort of network, they'd have to be involved."

"Probably."

"All right." Danny nodded. "We'll go to her village ASAP. But here's the deal—if what she's saying checks out, we move her ourselves."

Stoner shrugged. Danny took that to mean it was okay with him.

DOG FIGURED HE COULD SNEAK FIFTEEN MINUTES AWAY with Jennifer while the rest of Iowa's crew got the plane ready. He shouldn't, of course—but rank had its privileges. Besides, Rosen and the others were fully capable of handling things on their own.

Now, if he were really taking advantage of the situation, he would ask someone else to fill in for him as pilot, which he wasn't.

"Miss Gleason, if I could have a word," he said as the others began filing out of the trailer.

"*Miss* Gleason?" she said, her face red.

"Um, Ms. Sorry."

"*Miss* Gleason?"

"Uh-oh, Colonel, you stepped in it," said Zen.

"Hmmmph," said Breanna.

"I had an idea about adding something to the com section of the computer," said Dog. "A language translator. As part of the regular communications area. We had—"

"Which communications area?" she snapped. "In the flight-control computer, or the master unit? Tactical or the mission-spec areas?"

She wasn't angry with him, he told himself, she was just busting his chops.

She was, wasn't she?

"Well here's the situation," the colonel told her, starting to explain how they had tried to talk to the Chinese yesterday.

"Important officers in the Chinese military all speak English," she insisted, absentmindedly taking a stray strand of hair and pulling it over her ear.

"They may speak it, but in the heat of battle, they don't understand it too well."

"You can have language experts on call at Dreamland."

Damn, she was being difficult. "In the heat of the moment, it would be easier if you could press a button and what you said was translated and broadcast," said Dog. "It would prevent misunderstandings, and there'd be no time delay."

"Mmmm," she said.

"Can you insert some sort of translator into the communications sections?"

"I'd have to think about it."

Busting his chops, definitely. He could see the start of a grin on her face, a slight hint.

Man, he just wanted to jump in bed with her.

"We should be ready to preflight in ten minutes," said Rosen from near the doorway.

"I may be delayed," the colonel said. "I have to check back with Dream Command."

"You can do that from the flight deck, Daddy," said Breanna. "Sorry. Didn't mean to say 'Daddy,' Colonel," she added in a tone of voice that left no doubt that she'd done it on purpose.

"Colonel Bastian, I need a word," said Danny Freah, squeezing inside. "Has to be private, sir."

"Well, I was just leaving," said Jennifer.

Dog managed to sit down in the chair without stopping her.

"Have a good sleep?" asked Danny.

"Yes, Captain, I did," said Colonel Bastian. "Go ahead."

"The girl we picked up, from the village."

"We still have her?"

Dog listened as Danny explained in detail what had happened, what the girl had told Stoner, and what Stoner's team had discovered on the atoll stations.

"I should have told you she tried to shoot me," said Danny when was he done. "I'm sorry, sir."

"Why didn't you?"

"I—it's a little hard to explain."

"You better try, Captain."

"Yes, sir. This isn't an excuse." Danny's body seemed to deflate. "In Bosnia, there was an incident, an innocent woman trying to protect a kid."

As Dog listened, he noticed Danny kept shifting his hands awkwardly. He'd never seen the captain so ill at ease.

Dog rubbed his forehead, unsure exactly what to say, much less to do. Conceivably, his captain could be charged with dereliction of duty for not taking the situation seriously.

On the other hand, if this woman was just a housewife in the village—hell.

"Search the village," Dog told Freah. "Secure it."

"What about the atoll? I'd like to check it out ASAP."

"All right. I'll talk to Woods. If you're looking for force backup—"

"I have what I need," said Danny. "We'll use the Marines here."

"Not without Woods' okay."

"They're authorized to secure the island."

"Not the atoll."

"Right," said Danny. "One other thing. I want us to move the people in that village when we're done. If we just turn them over to the Filipinos, they'll be slaughtered."

"I doubt that's true. I . . ."

"We can move them ourselves. I'll scout a new spot for them on the south part of the island. We can have them there tonight," Danny said firmly.

"Let's find out what's in the village," said Dog. "Inspect it, then contact me."

"Can we move them? I have to know what I'm going to do with them."

"It's not my decision," Dog said. "It's up to Admiral Woods, and probably Admiral Allen. They'll deal with it."

"But they'll take your advice."

"They may, they may not," said Dog. "More likely the latter."

"YOU DON'T LIKE HER AT ALL, DO YOU," SAID ZEN, ROLLing alongside Breanna as she walked to the Navy's mess tent.

"Please, Jeff, we've been over this a million times," she said. "Let's talk about something else, okay?"

"Green-eyed jealousy. Hell hath no fury like a jealous lady."

"At least you know your clichés." Breanna swung through the door without holding it for him. A fresh batch of pancakes was just being put out; she loaded a double-high stack on her plate.

"Packing it in, huh?" said Zen when she returned to the table. He was sipping a cup of black coffee.

"On a diet?" she asked, taking a bite of her pancakes.

"Trying to get back my girlish figure."

"These are good," she said. She tried changing the subject. "How's FDR?"

"We're fighting the Depression," said Zen. "You know what's amazing?"

"The fact that you're actually reading?"

"I read all the time before I met you," said Zen.

"*Sports Illustrated* and *Penthouse* don't count."

"*Penthouse* Letters," he told her. "Big difference."

"I was wondering where you picked up your technique."

"Roosevelt never really gave up trying to walk, not until he was in the White House," said Zen, suddenly serious. "I think he really thought he would walk again. He kept telling people, next year. Next year. You know the thing he did with his legs, leaning on people? I bet he really thought that was walking. I bet he did.

"Geez, Bree, you got to chew those things."

She stopped mid-bite—half a pancake slipped from her mouth.

Zen laughed and took a sip of coffee.

"Me, I'm a realist. I know I'm not going to walk again."

"Except when you were in ANTARES."

"Yeah. Well, the drugs did that," he said. He looked into his coffee cup, then put it down and picked up a spoon, fishing out a fly. It was a minute or so before he began speaking again. "I understand what Frank was thinking."

"Frank?"

"Hey, all that reading gets me an' old Franklin on a first-name basis," said Zen. "Except only his enemies called him Frank. I think." Another bug dive-bombed into his coffee. "These flies must love this coffee."

Jeff held it out, laughed—then tapped the spoon at her, as if tossing the bug.

"Hey!"

He'd actually slipped the bug off the spoon, which he delighted in pointing out.

"You shoulda seen your face."

"Ho, ho," said Bree.

"Finish eating and let's go recreate. I have to practice the Piranha controls in an hour."

"Oh, you're suave," she said.

"Comes from reading *Penthouse* Letters."

Philippines
1103

THEY RAN IT AS A CLASSIC ENCIRCLEMENT, USING FOUR squads of Marines as well as Danny's people. Two groups were dropped east of the village, each led by one of Danny's Whiplash troopers, while two other groups came down from the ridge. Using so many people decreased the likelihood they would achieve surprise, but Danny reasoned the available resources made it the way to go. It was a conservative choice, one that couldn't be faulted. As he boarded the Quick Bird helo to supervise the mission from the air, he realized he'd probably chosen to do things this way to compensate for screwing up earlier.

Not screwing up. Just not acting aggressively.

Danny had his helmet plugged into the helicopter's com circuit, which allowed him to talk on the radio channels and the interphone. He wasn't just observing—both Quick Birds were packing rockets and chain-guns. A Megafortress and a pair of Flighthawks piloted by Captain Fentress were also supporting the mission. The two teams coming in from the coast were aboard Marine Super Stallions, helicopters the size of Pave Lows, but with an additional engine.

Stoner sat in the back of the helo. He had suggested bringing the girl with them, but Danny wasn't convinced she'd be much of a guide. Besides, she'd inadvertently see a lot of their technology.

Another conservative choice. Late.

"Squad One is down," said Powder, who had the northeastern approach.

"Two is down," said Liu, heading the southeastern team. As always, the Marine helos had made their deliveries precisely on time.

As the remaining teams reached the stream, Danny checked in. Fentress's bird's-eye view of the area showed the swamp and the area surrounding the village looked quiet. The village itself was almost completely hidden; Fentress would have to get much lower and use the IR sensors to give them a meaningful view.

"No boats," said Stoner as they circled off the coast of the island.

"Yeah," said Danny. He switched the feeds on his helmet visor back and forth in quick succession, checking for any sign of movement. A small zigzag of smoke made its way up from the trees, most likely a cooking fire. Danny would have his men check the ashes, make sure the locals weren't burning documents.

"We're ready," said Powder, a good ten minutes ahead of schedule.

"Hold your position," Danny told him.

"Got it, Cap."

Danny clicked into the feed from Powder's helmet. He could see two thatched roofs to the left of the team's position. Something moved on the right—a kid maybe, or an animal. The range-finder said Powder's squad was seventy-two yards away. Trees and low brush blocked the approach, but a clear path down to the ocean was just to the team's left. Two Marines would grab anything that used the path as an escape route.

"Squad Two ready," said Liu.

Danny ordered the two squads that had come from the ridge to move across the stream toward the swamp. Five minutes later, they were in position at the south edge of the wetlands.

"Hawk Leader, we're ready for your run."

"Copy that." Fentress sounded a lot like Zen over the radio, though the two men could not have been more different. Fentress was rail-thin, and looked like he'd fall over in a breeze. Zen looked like a running back, and except for his legs, might be in as good shape. Personality-wise, Fentress bordered on flighty, though while flying the UM/Fs, he made an effort to project a calm, almost cold, demeanor.

"Feeding you video," said Fentress.

The island came into sharp focus as the Flighthawk approached. The optical feed was at maximum magnification, making objects ten times larger than in real life. The U/MF was at five thousand feet for its first run, still relatively high.

Nothing from the village—no small-arms fire, no shoulder-launched SAMs. Good.

"Teams, move forward," said Danny as the plane came in. "Confirm when you reach Alpha Point."

He told the helo pilot to move forward also. A slight twinge of adrenaline hit his stomach; he leaned against his restraints as the chopper pushed toward its own Alpha Point near the coastline.

The IR feed on the Flighthawk's next run painted the village as a green sepia Currier & Ives scene, assuming Currier & Ives did the Philippines. Three huts, another structure that might not have sides, a fenced area, probably for animals. He saw something that looked like a goat, but no people yet.

No people? Shit.

"Ready," reported Liu.

"You guys are cheatin'," said Powder. "They must've gotten a head start."

"Powder," said Danny.

"We're ready," said the sergeant. So were the other teams.

"Hawk Leader, I need that low-and-slow run, give me your best shot," said Danny. "Three and Four, move in, I'll locate the natives for you in a second."

"Machine gun," said Bison.

"Everybody hold. Hold!"

Danny keyed the feed from Bison's helmet to his, but he couldn't make out what Bison had spotted.

"You sure, Bison?"

"I got something moving, Cap," said Powder.

"What's going on?" said Stoner.

Danny held up his hand, needing him to be quiet. He was in automatic mode now, punching buttons. The scram of things had a swirling logic of their own, and you wanted to keep yourself on the edge, away from the whirlpool.

"Everyone hold on," Danny told his people. "Hawk Leader, we're ready for you now, Captain."

"Hawk leader," acknowledged Fentress.

The Flighthawk dropped to a hundred feet over the island, literally at treetop level. Though it was moving slow for an aircraft—just under 150 knots—the feed nonetheless blew by in a blur. Danny calmly hit the freeze frame as the first building came in view.

Three figures in one hut, one figure in another. Four, maybe five in the pen.

Three more up near Squad Four.

"Floyd, you have three natives on your right, above that ridge there. Everybody else is in the hut, or the pen—those are animals in the pen. I don't have Squads One and Two in view. Hang tight."

Danny clicked forward on the feed, still didn't have them. He could wait for another run or just go.

Waiting was conservative, but it meant giving the people in the village more time to man weapons, plan a defense.

"Three and Four move in," Danny said, finding another solution. "One and Two hold."

"Aw, shit," said Powder.

"Hawk Leader, another run, further east," Danny said.

"Copy that," said Fentress.

The Flighthawk came over again—two people were

walking south toward Liu's team. Danny fed the details to Liu, then ordered One and Two to move in.

"Take us there," Danny told the helo pilot, who gunned the engine on the small helicopter. The scout rocketed forward so fast Danny flew back in the seat.

"Go, go, go!" Bison was yelling. Danny clicked in the Flighthawk feed, saw an explosion on the west side of the camp. Going at the machine gun, the team used flash-bangs and smoke grenades. Voices shouted in his ears. He struggled to stay above it all—outside the scram.

"Quick Birds, hold your fire," said Danny. "That smoke is from our grenades."

He clicked into the feed from Bison—the trees moved swiftly, then he saw ground, smoke—an old tree trunk in front of his team member.

The machine gun.

"Shit fuck," said Bison.

"All right, everyone relax now, relax," said Danny.

"Got two guys here," said Powder. "Older than the hills."

"Powder, watch it—natives coming at you," said Liu.

"We're on it."

Danny pushed up the helmet screen, looking through the windscreen of the Quick Bird as the pilot pointed to the ground. Stoner leaned over, trying to make out what was happening.

"Can you get us down?" Danny asked the pilot.

"I can hover over that roof there," he replied. "You'll have to go down the rope."

"Yeah, do it," said Stoner.

"Do it," said Danny.

There was gunfire to the right of the helicopter. The pilot hesitated, then pitched his nose toward it, steadying into a firing position.

"Hold off," said Danny, touching the man's arm. "Powder, what the fuck?"

"Wild stinking dogs," said the sergeant. "Mean motherfuckers."

"What about the people?"

"They're all right," he said. "We're okay. We have two, three natives secured. No resistance, Cap. 'Cept for the barking dogs. Man, they bug the shit out of me."

Danny let go of the pilot's arm. "We'll use the rope," he said.

BY THE TIME STONER GOT TO THE GROUND, THE VILlage was secure and the huts had already been searched. The unrehearsed, ad hoc operation had gone remarkably well, so well, in fact, Stoner thought the Whiplash people might actually give his old SEAL team a run for the money.

A run, nothing more.

Even the Marines had done well. The only casualties were six dogs, probably kept by the villagers for food.

The locals were sitting grim-faced in a small circle in front of one of the huts. They were all old, easily in their fifties if not well beyond. The place was what the girl had told him it was—a refugee village started by people who had fled from another island.

Captain Freah was consulting with his people, dividing the surrounding area into quadrants for a detailed search. To Stoner, it seemed a waste of time, though he wouldn't bother pointing it out.

"Looks pretty clean," said Danny.

"We have to hit the atolls," said Stoner. "Sooner rather than later."

"Yeah," said Danny, his voice still flat. While the captain turned and went back over to his men, Stoner looked at the huts. They couldn't have been here for more than a few months.

"We'll go out through the beach," said Danny when he came back. "It's quicker. Marine helo will shoot us to the base. I have to leave one of my guys here to supervise, and one at the security post. That'll give us a total of six people, including yourself."

"We can use the Marines," said Stoner.

"I have an okay for an armed recon already," said Danny. "If we add Marines, that has to be cleared. They'll probably want to fly in more forces, set up a whole operation. It'll be thorough, but it'll be overkill—and it won't happen till tomorrow night. You told me you wanted to go sooner rather than later."

"I do."

"Then let's do it."

Aboard Iowa
1409

THEY GAVE THE CHINESE CARRIERS A WIDE BERTH, working their way close to the Vietnamese coastline before heading back west. It occurred to Dog this very same B-52 frame might have pulled many missions here decades ago, dropping its sticks on North Vietnamese targets, maybe even mining Haiphong Harbor. Dog had an unobstructed view of the coastline from roughly 25,000 feet; it seemed like a faceted jewel, a piece of intricately cut jade. He'd missed Vietnam, and wasn't the nostalgic type besides, but even to Dog, it looked like the last place on earth a war would break out.

Then again, so did the empty ocean in front of him.

"Two minutes to our search area," reported Rosen.

"Delaford, how's it looking down there?" Dog asked him.

"We're ready when you are, Colonel."

"We're talking to your friends in the Orions. They haven't found anything for us yet."

"Tell 'em to listen harder," said Delaford.

"I'd give 'em new hearing aids if I thought it would help." Dog did an instrument check, then turned his gaze back to the side window, looking down at the now-peaceful sea. His quarry was somewhere below, but where?

Armed with the satellite information as well as intercepts from SOUS and another hydrophone net, the Fleet intelligence officers had analyzed the probable course of the Chinese submarines. They had decided, given the mission, the subs would work as direct a course to the carrier group as possible, and probably get regular updates as they closed. This scenario presented several opportunities for finding the subs; not only would their route be somewhat predictable, but the subs would probably poke their masts above the surface from time to time. The intel officers looked for specific choke points—in this case, places where it would be easy to find the subs as they passed—and concentrated their resources there. It sounded good, but so far, it wasn't working. There was so much sea to cover, and without support vessels and submarines to assist, the Orions had a relatively limited view.

Dog wondered about the possibilities of extending Piranha's range—not by the factor of two, which Delaford had said was doable, but by ten or even a hundred. It would be much more effective to launch it now and let it go find its target on its own.

Actually, they could, theoretically, do that. Just launch and search. Set a course southwest, toward the Chinese carriers; they'd find the subs sooner or later.

"Tommy, what do you think of launching Piranha blind and letting it look for the subs on its own?" Dog asked Delaford over the interphone.

"You mean completely without a contact?" asked Delaford. "The problem is, Colonel, it's such a wide area to cover. Considering Piranha can only stay in the water for eighteen hours—well, twenty or twenty-one . . ."

"It'll stay longer than that," said Dog.

"Right. I mean, it can only pursue at speed for that long, then runs down."

"But if we figure, say, an eighteen-hour patrol, so the last six hours or so it's near the carriers—I don't know, can you plot something like that out? How close would we have to be?"

"Let me talk to English."

"Orions are clean," reported Rosen. "You know what we need? Hot dogs."

"Oh, that'd be great on a long mission," said Dog sarcastically.

"Break up the monotony."

"Colonel, we think we have a good drop," said Delaford, coming back on the line. He laid out a plan to launch Piranha at 260 nautical miles from the carrier task force and run it on an intercept. When it reached a point twenty miles from the carriers, it would then sweep ahead in an arcing search pattern.

"The only problem is what we do if, after we launch, the Orions find the Chinese subs and they're really far away."

"How far?" asked Dog.

"Well, anything over fifty miles and not heading in our direction is going to be problematic," said Delaford.

"But we'll know where they're headed."

"Only if our guess that they're after the Indian sub is right."

"I say we go for it," said Dog.

"I agree."

Woods and Allen might not, but Dog couldn't see the use of flying around all day and not launching. They had to take a shot sooner or later.

"Give us that launch point again," Colonel Bastian told Delaford.

Twenty minutes later, Dog and his copilot took Iowa down to five hundred feet, surveying the ocean and preparing to launch a buoy and the device. After a last check with the Orions to make sure they hadn't found anything, Dog dipped the plane's nose. Piranha splashed into the water like an anxious dolphin, freed from her pen.

"Contact with Piranha," said Delaford, reporting a link with the robot. "We're running diagnostics now. Looking good, Colonel."

They ran the Megafortress in a slow, steady oval at

approximately five thousand feet above the waves. As they completed their second pass, Rosen got contacts on the radar—a pair of Shenyang F-8's were heading south from China.

"I have them at one hundred twenty-five miles," said Rosen. "They're between eighteen and twenty angels, descending."

"They see us?" said Dog.

"Not clear at this time," said Rosen.

"Check and record our position," said Dog, who wanted the record clear in case of attack. They were, irrefutably, in international air space.

"Absolutemento."

"Which means?"

"You got it, Colonel."

"Still bored? I thought the launch would perk you up."

"Just call me Mr. Perky, sir." Rosen worked in silence for a few minutes, still tracking the pair of interceptors as they headed south, not quite on an intercept vector. It was possible a land-based radar had picked them up as they opened their bay to complete the Piranha launch. On the other hand, it was also possible the planes were merely on a routine mission. The F-8IIMs looked like supersized MiG-21's, though their mission was considerably different. Intended as high-altitude, high-speed interceptors, they were not quite as competent as the more maneuverable Sukhois that had recently tangled with Iowa. Nonetheless, they were capable aircraft, and their Russian Phazotron Zhuk-8 multimode radars would be painting the Megafortress relatively soon.

"We have a surface ship, thirty miles west, thirteen degrees from our present heading," said Rosen. "Unidentified type—trawler-size."

"Yes, we have it on the passive sonar," said Delaford. "We're looking at our library now. Probably a spy ship."

"Not in the library," said Ensign English after comparing the acoustical signal picked up by Piranha with a library of known warships.

"We can swing over and take a look," said Dog.

"Good idea, Colonel," said Delaford. "We'll keep the probe on its present course."

"Keep an eye on our F-8's," Dog told Rosen as he nudged the stick to get closer to the ship.

"They're turning it up a notch—on an intercept now at forty miles."

"Surface ship tracking us for them?"

"No indication of that," said Rosen.

By the time the ship appeared in the distance, the F-8's were roughly ten miles out. The two planes had cut their afterburners and were now descending in an arc that would take them about a half mile off Iowa's nose, if everyone stayed on their present course. The fact they were heading in that direction, rather than trying to take a position on Iowa's rear, seemed a significant tactical shift to Dog. Maybe shooting down the cruise missiles yesterday had won some friends.

Not that they necessarily wanted them.

The ship in the distance looked like an old trawler. Ensign English, working off the video feed piped down by the copilot, identified it as a Republic of China or Taiwan ship, one of a class of spy vessels the Taiwanese used to keep tabs on their mainland brothers.

"He may be looking for the subs," said Delaford. "He's got active sonar."

"Can they find us?" asked Dog.

"I don't believe so."

"F-8 pilots are challenging us," said Rosen. "In pretty good English too."

Dog turned his attention to the Chinese fighters, giving them the standard line about being in international airspace and having no "hostile intent."

The Chinese replied that the Yankees were overrated and would have no chance in the World Series this year.

"Couple of comedians," said Rosen.

In the exchange that followed, Rosen proved to be a ridiculously committed LA Dodger fan, predicting the

Dodgers would "whup" whomever the American league managed to put up. The Chinese pilot—he was apparently the wingman in the two-plane flight—knew more than enough baseball to scoff at Rosen's predictions. The man inexplicably favored the Cleveland Indians, and in fact, seemed to know the entire lineup.

As the two pilots traded sports barbs, the F-8's took a pass and then came back to work themselves roughly parallel to the Megafortress's cockpit. This was undoubtedly their first look at an EB-52, and the pilot complimented Rosen on his "choice of conveyance."

"Quite a vocabulary," said Dog.

"Claims he went to Stanford."

After the tension of the past few days, the encounter seemed almost refreshing.

Excitedly, Delaford brought the laughs to an end.

"We have a contact. Definite contact," he said. "Shit, yeah!"

The GPS readings showed the submarine exactly thirteen miles to the south by southeast.

"They've made good time submerged," Delaford answered. "These are them—Trafalgar signature. Wow! Colonel, this is pay dirt. Pay dirt. These submarines don't exist—this is a serious coup."

"Relax, Commander. There'll be plenty of time to pick up the Navy Cross at the end of the mission," said Dog. Not that he didn't share at least some of Delaford's excitement—especially since it meant his decision to launch without a sighting from the Orions had been vindicated. One less thing for Allen to look down his nose about. "Make sure we're recording."

"Oh, yeah. Big-time."

"Thirty-five knots, submerged," said Ensign English.

"Is that fast?" asked Dog.

"It's good. It's very good," said Delaford. "And they may not even be trying. We're twenty miles behind, at forty-two knots, our max. I'm going to settle in at sixteen miles behind them. If they're like our guys, they'll accelerate a bit, then stop. Jesus, I wonder if they consider this slow."

"F-8's holding their position," said Rosen.

"I'd like to shoot south and drop a buoy ahead of the subs," Delaford added.

"We'll wait until the F-8's go home," Dog told him. "They ought to be leaving pretty soon; their fuel should be just about out."

"Copy that," said Delaford. "This is great, Colonel. This is really great."

Aboard *Shiva* in the South China Sea
1530

THE DISTANCE FROM THEIR TARGET, THEIR NEED TO avoid the escort ships, and the storm all greatly complicated matters. When they were finally able to analyze all of the data, Admiral Balin was faced with the inescapable, if unpalatable, conclusion that their vaunted weapons had somehow missed. To add further insult to this grave disgrace, one of the Chinese escort ships somehow managed to get close enough to him as he doubled back to reconnoiter; two of its Russian-made ASW rockets had exploded close enough to do some damage to *Shiva*. One, but apparently only one, ballast tank vent was stuck in a closed position, a circulating pump in the environmental system had broken, and it seemed likely there had been damage to the radar mast. The ELF gear was apparently no longer functioning, as they had missed a scheduled transmission. Casualties were negligible; one man had suffered a broken arm.

Any competent Navy would have sunk them.

He was now out of Kali missiles, but had six torpedoes, one for each forward tube. In the chaos and the storm, he had lost contact with the Chinese fleet, but would find it again soon enough.

The torpedoes on board were primitive Russian twenty-one-inch unguided fish, which required him to get considerably closer than the Kalis. To guarantee a strike, he intended to close to within three thousand yards, if not closer.

Getting that close to a warship involved many dangers, but these were not to be thought of now. Soon, if not already, his own fleet would be pressing home the attack; no matter the odds, Balin owed it to them to press home his mission.

To be truthful, part of him was glad. From he moment he had launched the last missile, an inexplicable sadness had come over him. He had fulfilled his greatest ambitions; there was nothing else left to achieve. Even if he had been given a hero's welcome, or promoted to command the entire Navy, he would, in effect, be retired. He had fought all these years to remain at sea—to remain alive. Retiring, even as a hero, seemed something akin to a slow and meek death.

Retirement was no longer a possibility. That notion somehow felt supremely comforting as he plotted a course to intercept the enemy.

Airborne, northwest of the Philippines
1623

THEY RIGGED THE MV-22 WITH BUDDY TANKS ON THE lower fuselage, allowing the Osprey to refuel the Quick Birds en route to the atoll. It was a great plan in theory, one that worked perfectly in any number of computer simulations. In the real world, however, it was trickier than hell.

The small helos struggled to stay connected to the drogues fluttering behind the Osprey. The gyrating wash of the two massive propellers tossed the small bodies up, down, and sideways. The pilots compared the energy needed just to work the stick to a ten-mile kayak race; their arms were burning even before the fuel started to flow. Watching the sweat pour off his pilot, Danny wondered what he'd do if the man collapsed in midair. When the Quick Bird was finally topped off, it lurched so violently to the right, Danny thought they'd been clipped by something.

"We're five minutes out," said the pilot, no sign of stress in his voice.

"All right, listen up," Danny said over the Dreamland frequency. "Flighthawks give us real time ninety seconds ahead of the assault, so we see what's there when we go in. Boom-boom-boom, just like we drew it up."

He'd drawn it up simple: one helicopter from the south, one from the east. The one from the south overflew the small dock and landed on the beach area. The other went directly to the building seventy yards from the water. The helos would suppress any defenses—the Flighthawk snaps Zen had taken showed there were no gun emplacements or heavy weapons, so resistance should amount to no more than hand-carried light machine guns. With the defenses neutralized, the two teams would rapid-rappel to the ground.

Stoner had concluded there should be no more than six people on the island, given the small size of the building and the lack of cover elsewhere. Danny concurred. The takedown should go quickly.

In case it didn't, the Osprey would circle in from the north, prepared to use the chain-gun in its chin if things got tough. Fentress and the Flighthawks, with their 20mm weapons loaded for bear, would be available for fire support as well.

The island was shaped like an upside-down L, with the observation post near the tip of the leg. The head of the letter had a rocky beach that could serve as a set-down point for the helos and Osprey once the atoll was secure.

"Hawk Leader to Whiplash One," said Fentress over the common frequency. "Captain Freah, I'm ready when you are."

"Roger that," said Danny. He glanced at his watch, then back at the sitrep map in his smart helmet, which showed they were about twelve miles from the atoll. Fentress would start his pass when they hit five miles. "We're just over three minutes from Alpha. We'll keep you posted."

"Hawk Leader."

Fentress wasn't Jeff Stockard and would never be, but he was definitely capable; Danny had no doubt he'd do this job well.

So if Danny left, would somebody else walk right in and pick up the slack?

Yeah.

"Team Two checking in," said Powder, in charge of the second squad. "Hey, Cap, can we go for a swim when this is over?"

"Only if there's a school of sharks nearby," said Liu.

"That's what I'm talkin' 'bout," said Powder.

"Hey, Cap, you ever have grilled shark?" asked Bison. "Serious food. You get a little lemon, maybe some herbs. Very nice."

"I thought you only ate burgers and pizza," said Danny.

"Burgers, pizza, and shark."

They were eight miles from the atoll.

"All right. Sixty seconds, Hawk Leader," said Danny.

"Copy that."

Danny turned to look at his pilot, an Army officer who'd come over to Dreamland specifically for the Quick Bird program. Before that he'd flown with the special operations aviation group that worked with Special Forces, 160th Special Operations Aviation Regiment (SOAR). The captains gave each other a thumbs-up; Danny sat back, clicked his viewer into the Flighthawk feed, and curled his thumbs around his restraints.

"Alpha," he told Fentress.

"Alpha acknowledged," said the Flighthawk pilot. And the show began. "Welcome, my friends, to the show that never ends. . . ."

All Danny saw at first was a blur of blue and white whipping across the screen. The blur settled into a hatched pattern of waves as the Flighthawk leveled off, then slowed. A brown bar appeared in the distance, growing into a cat stretched across a purple rug, morphing into the side of a mountain at the top of a black-blue desert. Light glinted like crystal arrows from the blue background. Then, the image seemed to snap, and now everything was in perfect focus. A small dock sat before him, a rubber speedboat tethered to one end; above it sat a green-yellow cottage, a shack really, made of palms—no, panels designed to look like palms in the distance. Fishing poles, oddly oversized, sat in the water near the dock. There was a rock at the water's edge.

No, not a rock. A housing for a radar.

"Infrared feed," Danny told Fentress. The pilot must have anticipated him, for as the words left his mouth, the image flashed into a gray greenness, a murky monotone as if the robot aircraft feeding it had dipped into the bottom of an algae-choked pond. It took nearly three seconds for the computer to artificially adjust its sensitivity, forming the blurs into an image. It froze frame, backed out twice—all obviously at Fentress's command—then analyzed the picture, supplying white triangles that showed a total of five people on the island: two near the docks, one in the hut, and two about twenty yards further north, possibly observing the water.

"We're dancing," said Danny. He fed the analyzed picture to the rest of his team, briefly summarizing the situation. The Osprey was tasked with neutralizing any resistance from the two men on the northern side of the atoll.

"Everyone hold your fire unless we're fired on," he reminded them. "You know the drill. Two—if they move toward the boat, sink it."

"Aw, Cap," said Powder. "Can't we take it out for a spin first?"

"Hawk Leader to Whiplash One. You need another run?"

"Negative, Hawk Leader. Hold your orbit as planned. We're going in."

"Godspeed."

The Quick Bird pilot threw everything he had into the helo's turbine engines, flooding the gates with the remains of a thousand long-gone dinosaurs. The tail whipped around and the helicopter tilted hard, pulling two or three Gs as it swooped into an arc. Once pointed at his target, the pilot began to back off the throttle, and somehow managed to come at the island like a ballerina sliding across the stage.

The effect on his passengers, however, was more like what might be felt in the cab of a locomotive throwing on the brakes and reversing steam at a hundred miles an hour. Danny felt his boron vest pushing hard against his collarbone as the restraints took hold.

It felt damn good.

"We're hot!" said the pilot as something red erupted on the left side of the island.

"Missiles in the air!" said Danny. He could see small pops of red near the dock. "Guns—fuckers! Let 'em have it!"

The mini-gun at the side of the Quick Bird's cabin spit bullets toward the cottage. A burst from the ground, and the helo pirouetted to the side, flares popping as it whipped into a quick series of zigs and zags to avoid a shoulder-launched SAM. The missile sniffed one of the flares and shot through it, igniting above and behind the helicopter. The small scout shot downward in a rush; Danny threw his arm out in front of him as they hurtled toward the cottage area. The pilot slid the aircraft twenty feet from the ground, hurtling almost sideways over the rooftop. As they passed the cottages, Bison, sitting behind Danny, pointed his MP-5 out the open doorway and burned a magazine at one of the men on the ground. Flames burst from the cottage. Danny caught a glimpse of the man dropping his rifle and falling backward as the chopper spun away.

"Let's go, let's go," screamed Danny, undoing his restraint to go down the rope.

*   *   *

STONER GRABBED THE ROPE AFTER SERGEANT LIU DIS-
appeared. Even though he wore thick gloves, the friction
burned his hands. He had taken the team's smart helmet
and carbon-boron vest, but because the Whiplash issue
seemed a bit bulky, had opted to use his own gloves.
Obviously, a mistake, but it was too late to bitch about it
now. He felt the dock under his boots and let go, collapsing into a well-balanced crouch.

Ten times hotter than he'd imagined, everything was
exploding. In the back of his mind, he heard his boss's
boss, the Director of Operations himself, bawling him out
for going ahead with only six guys in broad daylight.

Yet the atoll's defenders throwing up all this lead and
blowing up so much equipment—for surely that was what
they were doing—argued that hitting them as soon as they
could had been the right thing to do.

Should have hit it last night then.

Liu was at the head of the dock, onshore already. The
boat was on Stoner's right. He pulled his knife and went
to it, slashed the two lines, then kicked it away. Something pushed him down onto the bobbing boards—it was
the helicopter rocking back after firing a salvo of rockets.
Thick cordite and smoke, and something like diesel fuel,
choked his nose. A fireball erupted; the water churned
with a stream of steady explosions. Now all he smelled
was burning metal.

These bastards had SAMs and all sorts of weapons.

"Hey, forward, damn it!" yelled someone.

It was Powder, waving through the smoke on the beach.
Stoner pushed himself to his knees, stumbling toward the
land.

BY THE TIME DANNY MADE IT TO THE GROUND, THE GUN-
fire had already stopped. The defenders' stores of ammunition and weapons continued to explode, and the

cottage burned bright orange, flames towering well overhead.

They'd rigged it. Bird One tried smothering the fire by
flying over it, but this only made the flames shoot out to
the side and was dangerous as hell. Finally, Danny told
them to back off. The inferno continued, doubling its
height in triumph and sending a burst of flames exploding
above.

"Team One, move back," he told Bison and Pretty Boy.
"Get back to that fence of vegetation. Powder, what's
your situation?"

"Two dead gomers. Can't see what else is going on
with all this smoke. We're on the beach near the dock."

"You got a way out of there?"

"Same way we came."

"How's Stoner?"

"Got a smile on his face," said Powder. "I think we
oughta draft him, Captain."

Danny doubted the CIA officer was doing anything but
frowning. The truth was, the operation was a fiasco. The
only saving grace was that none of theirs were injured—a
minor miracle, given all the lead and explosives in the air.

What listening post was worth this?

"We'll wait for the fire to go down; then we'll inspect
the building," Danny said. "Everybody just relax. Powder,
those bodies near you got IDs?"

"Negative. Look Chinese, but no dog tags or anything.
No names."

There was one more burst of fire from the walls of the
hut, followed by an explosion that seemed to shake the
island up and down an inch. Danny half-expected a volcano to open up in front of him.

Then everything was quiet. In less than two minutes,
the flames had consumed themselves. Danny pushed the
visor back on his helmet, and unbuttoned two buttons on
his vest. He walked toward the ruins of the cottage, now
a thick line of black and gray soot in the sand. The air
was still hot, as if he was walking into a sauna.

"Looks like they had an underwater long-wave-communication system," said Stoner from down on the beach. "Most of it's in pieces, but if that's what it is, they're very sophisticated."

"You figure that's what they were protecting?" Danny asked.

"I don't know," said Stoner. "Sure blew everything up in a hurry."

"They must have realized we were coming when the Flighthawk came in," said Danny. "Or they picked up the helos with their radars."

Powder and Liu had moved up from the beach toward the cottage, and were now poking at the dust of its remains.

Powder scooped up something in his hand and started toward Danny.

"Hey, Captain, look at this. . . ."

Danny raised his head just in time to see a mine explode beneath his sergeant's foot, blowing him in half.

Aboard Iowa, over the South China Sea
1800

ONCE THE CHINESE PLANES TURNED BACK, DOG pushed the Megafortress south, tracking ahead of the submarines to a point about seventy-five miles away from the carrier's air screen. Dog began running a figure-eight at two thousand feet, then ducked lower to drop the transponder buoy. It settled under the waves and began transmitting perfectly from its wire net. Delaford made sure he had the probe on the new channel, then sank the first buoy.

"We're looking good," said Delaford as Iowa climbed back up through five thousand feet. "Buoy is gone. We have our two contacts now at fifteen miles, still moving at thirty-one knots now. Interestingly, the two subs are sticking pretty close together," he added.

"Why is that interesting?" said Rosen, listening in. Delaford gave a short lecture in submarine tactics. It began fairly basically—splitting up made it more difficult for the two submarines to be followed—and progressed into a dissection of the wolf packs used by the Germans during World War II. Delaford had a theory the two subs might be talking to each other somehow, though there was no indication of that from Piranha. He had interesting ideas on short-range acoustical and light-wave systems that sounded more like science fiction than doable technology, even to Dog. His chatter, though, helped relieve some of the boredom of the routine; Dog's job now consisted primarily of flying the same figure-eight pattern again, and again, and again, holding a steady course while Piranha did its thing.

Meanwhile, the submarines continued on a beeline for the position of the Chinese carriers. The Iowa began plotting the next buoy drop, deciding how close they would get to the Chinese task force.

As Dog found the coordinates for the next launch, a communication came in from PacCom, restricted for Dog.

"What the hell is going on up there?" said Admiral Woods, flashing onto the small video screen in front of the pilot's console. The computer automatically restricted the communications to his headset.

"We've deployed Piranha and are tracking two Chinese submarines. I'm told they're making good time—thirty-two knots."

"The MiGs."

"The F-8's? They played cowboy and Indian for a while, then went home. We reported that."

"Your orders were to steer clear of all Chinese aircraft."

"Admiral, I think you're being a little picky," said Dog. "The fighters came out and met us. We took no action against them. What would you have me do?"

"I would have you follow orders."

"With all due respect, sir," said Dog, who felt anything but respect was due, "I think you're just looking for things to criticize. I can't seem to tie my shoes without you objecting."

"My people don't talk that way to me, Colonel."

"Maybe they should."

"You want to go toe-to-toe with me, fine."

"Admiral, really. What's the problem here?"

"You're used to running the show, Tecumseh. I understand, but you're under my command now."

Dog stared at the screen. Woods stared back.

"Well?" said the admiral finally.

"I was following my orders as best as I knew how. That's all I can say."

"I'm sending a patrol plane to help track those submarines," answered Woods.

"I don't see that as necessary, Admiral. We're tracking sufficiently."

The line snapped clear before Dog could finish.

An atoll in the South China Sea
1800

DANNY'S BRAIN SPLIT IN HALF, ONE PLAYING AN ENDLESS track of sorrow, the other stepping back calmly, decisively, peering at the scene from above. The second half realized—belatedly—the area near the cottage had been thickly laid with mines and booby traps.

"Stay where you are. Everybody!" the calm half yelled. "Stay!" He pointed at Stoner, who'd impulsively taken a step toward Powder. Liu, who'd been about ten or twelve feet away when Powder got hit, lay slumped over on the ground, moaning.

Get Liu out, then decide what to do.

Danny flipped the shield on his helmet back down. Any metal in the area ought to be a little warmer than the rest of ground, and metal might translate into mines or trip wires—he pushed the IR sensor, went to maximum sensitivity, and began scanning slowly.

Nothing.

God damn, screamed the other half of his brain. *God, God damn*.

Try again, said the other half. He readjusted the setting, took a long breath, then moved his helmet slowly.

He could see rocks, or something like rocks. Flipping back and forth from IR to optical, he realized there were some rocks that had a triangular shape at the bottom. These were mines, or attached to mines.

Liu, twenty yards away, curled between two of them. Danny continued to scan. There were two other mines behind where Powder had been blown up.

There were more mines over to his left. And a row of mines directly in front of him; another step and he would have blown himself up.

Powder had saved him.

He had a pretty straight path to Liu on his right, assuming he wasn't missing any of the mines.

Danny lowered himself to his knees, then pulled his knife out of its scabbard. He began crawl-walking slowly, examining the area in front of him as carefully as he could. It couldn't have taken him more than two minutes to reach the sergeant, but they stretched out forever. Liu turned toward him as he came forward.

"Don't move," Danny told him. He pointed near Liu's head. "There's a mine right there."

"Helicopter," said Liu, suggesting he be pulled out from above.

"Yeah, but I'm afraid of the rotor wash and we don't know if there are any timers," Danny explained. "We can do this. Just relax."

"I got nicked in the arm and in the leg," said Liu. "I think I'm okay."

"Just hang there a minute," Danny said. He bent over the first mine, sliding around it. Until he started to move sideways, his balance had been perfect, but now he started to lose it; he tottered forward toward the trigger of the explosive. With a quick jerk, he changed his momentum. His leg slipped and he fell backward.

He'd missed the mine by a good measure, but still he expected an explosion. When it didn't come, he started to laugh uncontrollably. The spasms shook his body, emptying it not only of tension but of doubt. Sure of himself now, Danny got back up and made his way to Liu, scooping him into his arms.

"Powder?" asked the sergeant.

"No," said Danny. He'd left a good trail and it was easy to take Liu back. He paused and got his bearings before moving, made sure the area to the south was clear. Once he started, he moved quickly.

"You okay, Captain?" said Bison when he reached him. The trooper had inflated a stretcher.

"Get him out," Danny said. "Get the mine detector on the Osprey down here too."

"Inbound," said Bison. The MV-22 was just approaching the dogleg part of the atoll.

"All right. Get him back ASAP. Just go," Danny said.

"I'm okay," Liu protested.

"Go." Danny returned to the spot where he'd retrieved Liu, then began moving down toward Stoner.

"You got a mine detector in that helmet?" Stoner asked.

"I got infrared."

"That works?"

"Seems to," said Danny.

"This ain't worth getting blown up."

"Now you fuckin' tell me that," said Danny. "There's a wire over there. I can't tell what it's attached to."

"You see it?"

"Not well," Danny admitted. "Temperature in metal's a little different than the sand. I got it on maximum. Problem is, there's rocks on top of some of these mines, or they're set up the same. Pretty clever. I'm doing okay so far."

"Yeah," said Stoner.

"Yeah." Danny was now ten yards from the CIA officer. Part of Powder's leg lay directly to his right. "How the hell did they work around these mines?"

"Maybe they weren't armed. Get attacked, they hit the radio and turn it on," suggested Stoner.

"Yeah," said Danny, working closer. Even though the way looked clear, his paranoia felt overwhelming.

"Protecting something."

"I think that was a long-wave-communications device out by the shore they blew up," said Stoner. "Looked like big fishing poles? Use it to communicate with submarines."

"So this was an Indian post?"

"Guys looked Chinese to me."

The Osprey, already loaded with Liu, buzzed low over the water and headed out, its large rotors whipping it toward its top speed of 425 knots, twice as fast as any helicopter in the world.

"He gonna be okay?" Stoner asked.

"He said he would. He's just about a doctor, so he's probably right," said Danny as he reached Stoner. "Now we go back the way we came," he told him. "Easy."

"Yeah."

"My footsteps."

"I'm right behind you."

Bison had started toward them with his gear, moving very slowly and marking the mines with reed-thin flags. It was as if he were laying out an odd golf course.

"They must've had some pretty high-tech stuff here," said Stoner as they walked. "They sure as shit fought to protect it."

"Yeah, they did."

"That hump down by the water didn't blow completely. Was probably a radar."

"Yeah," said Danny.

"Look at it once the mines are clear."

"After we secure my sergeant's body, yes."

Aboard Quicksilver, over the South China Sea
2002

"WE'RE READY," SAID JENNIFER. "WE SHOULD HAVE IT."

Zen stared at the screen. "Nothing. Didn't work, Jen."

"All right, hold on."

Zen pushed back in the seat. The sim program included a short-handoff module, but it wasn't much of a workout—on the program, the screen appeared and you went.

No screen, no go.

"All right, let's try again," said Jennifer.

Zen's main screen turned green. White axis lines dissected it into four quadrants. Two white blobs sat in the upper quarter, percolating like tiny Alka-Selzer tablets.

"Hey, got the radar feed," said Zen.

"Sonar!" corrected Jennifer.

"Yeah, sorry. Got it. Okay, this is the synthetic thermal feed?"

"Right."

"Looks like I'm flying in soup. Except for the grid, there's no reference."

"You're swimming, not flying."

"Whatever. Running diagnostic set. You out there, Delaford?"

"I'm watching everything you do," said the Navy commander from Iowa, which was orbiting the ocean a short distance away.

Zen's Flighthawk controls had been replaced by two oversized keyboards and a control stick larger, but considerably less flexible, than the Flighthawks'. While Piranha's full range of commands could be entered through the keyboards, Zen's interest—and training—was confined to a very small subset, which could be handled by preset buttons carefully marked with tape. He could flip between a view synthesized from either passive sonar or temperature-deviant sensors. The computer automatically processed the contact data, displaying a small amount of its information in captions beneath each of the white synthesized images on his main screen; more information on each could be called up on the auxiliary screen. His speed controls were also worked by dedicated keys on the left board.

"How you looking over there, Quicksilver?" asked Delaford.

"Uh, well, the sea is kind of a brownish green," said Zen.

Delaford laughed. "I can tell you how to change the colors if you want."

"I'm just fine," Zen told him.

"All right. Those two white blobs are our submarines. We're twelve miles behind the closest one. This is as close as we want to get. They're oblivious to us. All their attention is ahead. Pretty soon they'll be turning around," added Delaford. "They'll pull a quick spin in the water to make sure there's no one behind them."

"What do I do then?"

"Just stop. Their active sonar can't see us beyond roughly five miles, if that. Truth is, we could probably get right on their hulls and they'd never know we were there."

"Okay."

"Temperature sensors are not nearly as sensitive. Here, look at the screen."

Delaford fed in the display. It took Zen a second to realize the orange funnels in the milky greenish-brown field were the target subs.

"Very obvious what sensor you're looking at," noted Delaford.

"Clever."

Delaford ran through some of the routine, then repeated things Zen had already heard from one of the Navy briefers as well as Jennifer. Zen felt a little like a high school backup quarterback being crammed with information on the sideline after the star went down. Best thing to do, he thought, was just get into the game and work it out on his own.

"Okay, so eventually these guys split up. It's not going to matter who you go with, but once you do, you have to stay with him. Just make sure the other sub doesn't come back around and try and sniff you out," said Delaford.

"I thought they couldn't see me."

"Hear you. Probably, they won't."

"Probably?"

"If we could sneak past an American destroyer, I wouldn't worry about a Chinese sub," said Delaford. "On the other hand, that's kind of why we're here, to figure out what they can do."

"All right, I'm ready."

"I would go with the sub that heads west," said Delaford. "That's the one that will be likely to be closest to the Indian ships, so if they're going to do anything fancy, that's the one that'll do it. We want to see if they lay mines, fire torpedoes, that sort of thing. Be an intelligence bonanza, as long as you don't get in the way."

"Okay. I'm ready."

"When they surface, just hang back. They come up every so often to use their radio. You know the auto-destruct sequence, right?"

"Yes, we do," shot in Jennifer.

"Our preference is to pick up the probe when we're done. You can hit the home sequence. You remember?"

"Yeah," said Zen. "You know, I'm really ready to go. Let's just do it."

"All right, do a ten-degree dive for a hundred meters, then return to three hundred meters depth," said Delaford.

Zen pushed the joystick forward, remembering he needed to move very slowly. A bright red number appeared on the grid line as soon as he pushed on the stick. To its right, what looked like a compass with an artificial horizon appeared, showing the attitude of Piranha's nose. The depth climbed—or rather, dropped—through 310 quickly, but the attitude of the probe barely budged. It was like flying in thick honey. Or swimming in thick honey—Zen had trouble conceptualizing what he was doing.

"Good enough," said Delaford as he hit the mark, then brought the probe back. "Every movement is very gentle. Very Zen-like, Zen."

"Ha-ha," said Zen.

"So when do I get to fly the Flighthawks?"

They ran through a few more maneuvers and the detection modes. Delaford then transferred complete control and watched over Zen's shoulder for a while.

"We've got great data so far," the Navy commander told them. "What we get from here out is just icing on the cake. Anything you find out—how deep they go, weapons—it's all icing on the cake."

"Chocolate or vanilla?" asked Jennifer.

Delaford laughed, then signed off.

DOG'S BRIEF TO BREANNA WAS SIMPLE AND QUICK, FILLing her in on the positions of the Chinese, where they'd dropped Piranha's com buoys, and their encounter with the fighters. There were some civilian commercial vessels at the far eastern end of the patrol sector, heading south but obviously trying to avoid the Chinese fleet. They also counted three Taiwanese spy ships in the search range. Breanna already had the tanker tracks and contact info, and there asn't much to say about the weather forecast, which was still predicting clear skies for thirty-six hours or so.

He told Breanna that at least one SSN had been detailed south to try to intercept and trail the Chinese subs; Delaford thought Woods would end the Piranha mission once he was sure the attack sub was on the trail. In the meantime, other ASW assets were moving in on the eastern side of the Chinese fleet. It was possible they too would make contact, at which point their job would, likewise, be ended. The idea was to switch to the least sensitive method of data-gathering as soon as possible.

That, and to make sure Dreamland couldn't grab all the credit.

"One thing you want to watch for, Captain," he added when he had exhausted his official brief, "is Admiral Woods. He seems to have a stick up his ass. He takes it out and beats me with it at every opportunity. He blamed us for the contact with the Chinese interceptors."

"Well, you shouldn't have buzzed Beijing," said Breanna.

"Stay clear of the carrier air screen if at all possible," Dog told her, not particularly appreciating the joke.

"That's kind of up to them, isn't it? If the subs keep going the way they're going, it'll only take another two hours or so before we're in their patrol area," said Bree. "Sooner or later they're going to see us."

"Understood," said Dog.

"Anything else, Daddy?"

"Captain, I'd appreciate it—"

"Bag the Daddy stuff. Yes, sir. Sorry, sir."

He longed to ask to speak to Jennifer—she was on board Quicksilver, helping Zen—but it was too much of an indulgence.

"All right, Quicksilver. See you later."

"Roger that."

Dog broke the Megafortress out of her figure-eight track and found his bearings for the Philippine base. They were just climbing through twenty-five thousand feet when the computer buzzed with an interruption on the Whiplash command link. The words INCOMING TRANSMISSION. PRIORITY: DOG EARS appeared on the HUD screen.

Danny Freah's voice, but no image, came through after Dog authorized the feed.

"Colonel Bastian?"

"Daniel. How we doing?"

"Not good, sir. We've lost one of our men. Sergeant Talcom. Powder."

Dog listened as Captain Freah described the operation in cold, sober tones.

"I understand," he said when the captain was finished. "I'll notify Admiral Woods. Where are you now?"

"We're still at the site, waiting for the Osprey to return from transporting Sergeant Liu."

Dog listened as Danny told him what they'd found— not much actually. They still had the mission tapes to analyze. The dead enemy soldiers who hadn't been charred beyond recognition seemed to be Chinese; they figured the atoll had been a spy site.

"We think there's a whole chain of them, running north," said Danny. "Stoner thinks that, but they're not using known Chinese codes; or Indian codes for that matter. CIA's pretty interested."

"I'm assuming you don't require any assistance," said Dog.

"Affirmative. We're ready to bug out."

"I'll see you back at the FOA."

"Yes, sir."

"Hang in there, Danny." The words were trite, way too automatic—he had to say something but couldn't come up with anything profound. "Iowa out."

He killed the connection, then went through the plane's status with Rosen. He checked on the other members of the crew, talked to Delaford about the way Zen had handled Piranha, asked Ensign English what it was like a hundred meters below the ocean during a storm—all delaying actions before telling the rest of the Dreamland team their friend was dead.

He punched through the circuit that connected back to Dreamland, bringing the command center on-line in what amounted to a conference call with the other Megafortresses and the mobile base back at the Philippines.

"I have some very sad news. Today, Technical Sergeant Perse 'Powder' Talcom lost his life to an enemy mine in a reconnaissance mission in the South China Sea. Powder was an exceptional man, an important member of the Whiplash action team, a cutup at times, and a ferocious fighter."

Dog stopped abruptly. He couldn't sum up a man in a sentence, and there was no need to. The people listening knew him pretty well, most of them probably better than Dog did.

"Colonel Bastian out."

Aboard Quicksilver 2012

"GOD, SERGEANT POWDER," SAID JENNIFER. TEARS started to slip from her eyes. "He was so sweet—he was one of the people who helped deliver that baby in Turkey. God."

She started sobbing, then brought her hand up to clear her eyes so she could see the display. The communication algorithms didn't require any tweaking—the Piranha system as a whole was probably the least bug-ridden project she'd ever worked on—but she ran a test on the signal strength anyway.

"You okay, Jen?" asked Zen. He was sitting a short distance away on the Flighthawk control deck.

"Oh, yeah, I'm all right."

"It sucks. Powder."

"Yeah."

The sobs bubbled up again. She pushed her teeth together, trying to force them away. She barely knew the sergeant, barely knew most of the enlisted men in Whiplash and at Dreamland.

What if Colonel Bastian were killed? What if his plane went down? It was not impossible—the EB-52's weren't invincible. A mechanical problem, a screwup in the computer system that helped run the plane. . . .

She'd worked on that system. Maybe she hadn't tested it properly, maybe there was something she'd messed up. God, she'd worked so hard she must have forgotten a million things, screwed up in a million ways.

"Jen?"

"I'm okay," she said. She reached to push her hair back, forgetting she was wearing a helmet. "I'm all right," she insisted again.

"It'll help a little if you focus on the mission," said Zen.

"Since when did you become a fucking shrink?"

The remark was wildly inappropriate, but Zen didn't say anything, and she couldn't find a way to take it back.

BREE SETTLED ONTO THE FIGURE-EIGHT PATTERN above the Piranha buoy. The sea was almost glasslike, and though it was getting dark, the sky was so clear, if you squinted just right you could see clear to Australia, or at least think you could.

Thoughts of Sergeant Powder's family crowded into her head as she went through some routine instrument checks with her copilot. She didn't know Powder very well—he was a bit crude, a class clown, not the kind of man she liked—but he was a member of the team, of their family.

She could imagine his mother getting the news.

The nights by Zen's bedside came back to her.

"Engines so in the green I think they're sprouting buds," said Chris, subtly hinting that she'd started to daydream.

"Roger that."

He read the fuel states—having tanked before coming on station, they had more than ten hours of flying time. Breanna glanced at the long-range radar, which showed the Sukhois patrolling over the Chinese carriers one hundred miles away. It was unlikely they didn't know the Megafortress was there, or why.

Powder's poor mother would never know what happened. They wouldn't be allowed to tell her much.

"Captain, we're intercepting broadcasts from that Taiwanese spy ship," said Freddy Collins, handling the Elint board. "Should I roll tape?"

"Go for it," said Breanna. The transmissions were actually recorded on computer disk, but there was no ring to "imprint electrons."

"Whole lot of talking going on," added Collins. "But they're using a very sophisticated code."

"Can't break it?"

"As a matter of fact, no, not with our equipment," said Collins. "The computer claims it's using some sort of bizarre fractal code on top of a 128k-byte thing—and they're skipping frequencies on some sort of ultrarandom basis besides. The boys at the NSA are going to want to see this."

"Probably talking about us," said Chris.

"Torbin, what kind of radar is that Taiwanese vessel using?" she asked.

"Negative on that. Don't have any transmissions. Sukhois have standard Slot Back radar. They're not close to picking us up. You want data on the carrier and the escorts?"

"They tracking us?"

"Negative. I'd compare the carrier's radar capabilities to the AN/SPG-60 the Navy uses. Not particularly a problem for us; they can't see their own planes beyond fifty miles. No airborne radar capacity."

"You sound a little disappointed."

"You always like to go against the best."

"Don't get too cocky."

"Yes, ma'am; thank you, ma'am."

Torbin was a big blond Norseman, a rogue throwback to the days of the Vikings they'd shanghaied from a terminal Wild Weasel posting in Turkey. He fit right into the Dreamland crew.

All they'd give the poor woman was a folded flag and some well-meaning salutes.

* * *

ZEN NUDGED THE JOYSTICK EVER SO SLIGHTLY TO THE right, trying to keep the closest white blur in the center of his screen. Like the Flighthawks, Piranha had a set of preprogrammed routines, one of which allowed it to simply trail its designated target. Still, he preferred to manually steer the probe—otherwise, he really had no function.

They were about twenty miles from the end of their effective communication range; they'd have to drop another buoy soon.

The submarines were changing course, making a slight arc that took them due east. They were well behind the carrier group—Zen started to slow, remembering Delaford's warning they would probably spin around to look for him, but they didn't. They had their throttles open, plunging ahead at thirty-eight knots. Much faster and he'd have trouble keeping up.

Zen hit the toggle, changing the synthesized view from sonar to temp. The nearest submarine looked like an orange funnel in a greenish-brown mist; the other was such a faint blur, he wasn't sure he would have seen it without the computer legend. The computer used all of its sensors to keep track of the targets, and could synthesize a plot from any angle. Jeff briefly toggled into front and top views. It was important—but difficult—to remember the views were based only on sensor information; he wasn't looking at reality, but a very simplified slice of it. Anything outside of the sensor's sensitivity was missing from the scene. That meant, for instance, when he looked at the thermal image, anything precisely the temperature of the water wouldn't show up.

He went back to the passive sonar feed, the easiest to use when controlling the probe. The lower portion of the screen looked foamy and white, a by-product of the sound reflections the device picked up. As Jennifer had explained, it was a kind of refracted energy, similar to glare bouncing off sand. The computer could only filter so much of it out, but a good operator could compensate for the blind spot by changing the position of the nose every so often. In effect, pushing the spotlight into the darkness. Zen nudged the nose down slightly, peering into the basement, then tucked back to keep his targets in sight.

They were turning again, this time south. Zen made another course correction, then studied his sitrep map on the far-right screen. He guessed the subs were making an end run around the back of the carrier task force.

Zen glanced over at Jennifer. She seemed more herself, her nose almost touching one of the computer screens. The only signs she was still upset were that she wasn't talking to herself or sipping her diet soda.

"Hey, Jen, we're going to have to drop a buoy soon," he said.

"Yeah," she said. "I just want to make sure they're going to hold roughly to this course. I'll work it out with Captain Stockard."

"You have to watch the carriers."

"I know."

"I know you know."

"There's a comeback for that, but I don't remember what it is."

Zen turned his attention back to the screen. He realized he'd slipped a bit off-line, and started to correct a little too quickly. The probe went too far right, then wallowed a bit as he overcorrected. He backed off, easing his grip.

A warning tone buzzed in his ear. He started to frown, thinking the computer was scolding him, then realized it was showing a new contact.

"Jennifer—I have a new contact. No range markings," he said. He flipped back into the thermal mode—there were only two funnels. He went back—the third shadow was off to the left; it didn't seem to be moving.

Jennifer punched buttons at her station. "Roughly thirty-eight miles away, but the probe isn't sure. Very quiet, angled away—could be a submarine using only its battery. I'm guessing it's the Indian sub."

"Not one of ours?"

"Hang on."

He could hear her pounding her keys.

"Doesn't appear to match. We can check with PacCom, though, see if the position would match. I think it's the Indian. It's got to be. Can you hold your position while I talk to the Piranha people and see if I can get more data?"

"The Chinese subs are trucking," he told her.

"Well, hang back a little while I get Commander Delaford. They're not using active sonar?"

"They haven't since we came on."

The probe's nose began to oscillate; he'd moved it too fast. Zen gently applied pressure to get it into a wide circle, where it stabilized.

"The Indian sub is supposed to be further south and to the east," said Jennifer. "Commander Delaford says it's possible it is one of the American attack subs at a good distance, beyond what the probe is reading. He can go through the data later. Stay with the Chinese. We're going to check in with PacCom."

"We're going to need that buoy soon," Zen said, pushing up his speed.

Aboard the trawler *Gui* in the South China Sea 2100

IT WOULD NOT BE AN EXAGGERATION TO SAY THINGS had gone in completely the opposite direction from what Chen Lo Fann had intended. Now that he had all of the data and weighed all of the evidence—the attack on his post, the interception of the missiles, the communications showing the American and Chinese pilots joked freely—it was clear a secret agreement had been reached between the two countries. They somehow saw India as a common enemy, and if they joined together against India so quickly after the animosity of a few months past—what would that mean for his Free China?

Annihilation, surely.

The course must be reversed. To do this, however, he

would have to go well beyond his mandate. He would have to violate his orders. In a way that was most unambiguous.

There was no choice, though. He would use the robot planes; not to spy, but to provoke the Communists. They would think they were American U/MFs; they would attack in turn. The Americans would have to retaliate. It would be a replay of the events a few months before, but this time the Americans would have no reason to stop. This time, they would annihilate the Communists. China would once more be unified under a free government.

His own government would be displeased with his methods. Despite the outcome, he would be punished. But Chen had no choice. Disaster loomed, and he could not count on fortune reversing herself without his own action.

As he went to board the helicopter that would take him to the dragon ship, Fann told himself that this was the way it must be.

Aboard Quicksilver
2100

"REDTAIL ONE TO QUICKSILVER. YOU READING US there, Air Force?"

Breanna clicked the talk button. "We have you, Redtail," she said, acknowledging the communications from the S-3B, an ASW aircraft launched from the USS *Independence*. The two-engined Lockheed Viking was an incredibly versatile craft developed primarily for antisubmarine warfare. Packed with electronic equipment, it could launch and monitor up to sixty sonar buoys; it was also equipped with an inverse-synthetic-aperture radar for finding surfaced submarines at long range. When feeling aggressive, the S-3s could pack everything from antisub torpedoes to Harpoons and even Rockeye cluster bombs. They could also carry nuclear depth charges, though as a general rule these were not deployed.

Like all Vikings in the Navy, this one was scheduled

to lose its ASW role in the next few months. In fact, if it hadn't been for the conflict with China, it probably already would have changed roles. Orions and helicopters were set to take on the task, though as this plane's presence showed, neither aircraft could quite completely take the versatile little Lockheed's place.

This particular S-3B happened to be a member of a storied squadron, the oldest dedicated carrier ASW group in operation, the Fighting Redtails. While their planes and detection gear had changed dramatically since the squadron was first organized in 1945 (it didn't gain its nickname until 1950), the pilots and crew members still showed the determination born in a period of worldwide strife.

They also liked to rag on the Air Force whenever possible.

"What the hell you doing out over water, Air Force?" mocked the Redtail pilot. His plane was roughly fifty miles to the southeast, approaching at about 320 knots. "You lost?"

"We hear you Navy boys needed your hands held," replied Breanna.

"Hey, Air Force, either you're a woman or real popular with the choir."

"Want to hear me sing?"

"Only if it's 'Anchors Away.' "

"Sorry, my plane is programmed to self-destruct if I sing that. You want a fix on our contacts or what?"

"Roger that, good-lookin'."

"My, what a charmer," Bree said to Chris. "Give the joker what he's looking for."

"A punch in the mouth."

"Just the coordinates for now," she said. "You can protect my honor later."

As Chris filled Redtail in on the submarine contacts, Torbin told Breanna the Chinese were scrambling a pair of fighters after the S-3.

"Redtail, be advised you have some tagalongs," Bree told the Navy flight.

"We always dig a little faster and a little harder when people are watching," answered the pilot.

"Come again?"

"Line from 'Mike Mulligan,' " explained the Navy aviator. "You know, Maryanne and the Steam Shovel. Kids book."

"You got me."

"You don't have kids?"

"Negative."

"I'll give you one of mine."

Two Sukhois from one of the Chinese carriers rode out to shake hands with the S-3. Chris tracked them for the Viking, then helped Breanna get ready for the buoy drop, now less than five minutes away. After they opened the bay doors and started to nose downward, the radar picked up a new flight taking off from the *T'ien,* the Chinese carrier that had recently entered the arena.

"Sikorsky SH-3," said Chris, his voice jumping an octave. "Wow. Where'd that come from?"

"Range?"

"One hundred miles. That's a Sikorsky. The Chinese don't have it," added Chris. The venerable SH-3 had served with many countries, but wasn't listed in the inventory of Chinese aircraft. "Those are ours."

"Want me to tell them to give it back?"

"Captain, I have an active search radar off a Sea King AEW Mark 2 British helicopter," reported Torbin. "Hey, this is pretty interesting stuff—the Chinese have a Sea King bag on that Sikorsky. Searchwater. Getting parameters."

Torbin was using the slang term for the special airborne early warning system installed in Royal Navy Sea Kings. The British had pioneered the use of AEW systems on helicopters, installing what they called Searchwater radar with a data link to their Harrier aircraft. Mounted in what looked like a large spaghetti pot off the starboard side of the aircraft, the radar gave roughly a hundred-mile coverage when the helicopter reached ten thousand feet.

"Chinese don't have this sucker," added Torbin.

"Yeah, so you think the Queen defected?" asked Breanna.

"More like someone from Spain. They use this configuration. Wait, though. You know, it's not exactly a Searchwater."

"Does he have us?"

"Uh, negative on that. Our profile's too small for him."

"Okay, everybody take a breath," said Breanna. "Let's drop the buoy, then recheck your gear and make sure our IDs are right. Major Stockard, Ms. Gleason, we're about thirty seconds away from the drop."

**Philippines
2120**

DANNY FREAH'S LEGS WOBBLED AS HE STEPPED OUT of the Quick Bird; he had to grab on to Stoner to keep his balance. The rest of the team was waiting near the edge of the runway. For some reason, he had expected Powder's remains to be waiting there as well, though, as protocol demanded, the dead man had already been removed to a proper area to await disposition.

"Colonel's inbound," reported Bison. His eyes looked red, but his face was set in its usual frown.

"Okay."

"Marines found a place for the villagers," added the Whiplash trooper.

"The Marines?"

"Peterson worked it out with some Navy people. The word came down. No government, just do it. They're about to take off now."

"Where?"

Bison thumbed toward a "Frog"—a general-purpose transport helo that looked like a Chinook shrunk to half size. "Blow's with 'em," said Bison, referring to Sergeant Geraldo Hernandez. "They thought you might like to go, so they waited a little. Been two or three minutes."

"Yeah, maybe I will. All right. Stoner?"

"I gotta make a report."

"How's Liu?" Danny asked Bison.

"Claim's he'd rather fix himself than let a corpsman near him."

"Good," said Danny. "I'll be back."

He began trotting toward the waiting Navy helicopter. The crewman at the door waved and helped him in; a moment later the helicopter lifted off.

THE VILLAGERS DIDN'T HAVE MUCH, BUT THE REAR OF the chopper wasn't all that big, and in order to fit, Danny had to stand next to the door. The Filipino girl he'd captured stood against the opposite wall, staring at him. Danny tried smiling at her, but she didn't respond.

The spot they'd found for the village was on another island about fifteen minutes to the south. Blow, squeezing over to Freah, told him some Navy Seabees were at the new village site already; they'd cleared it with a dozer, erected some temporary canvas tents, and were digging so they could pour foundations—three small prefab housing units had been located by the ever-resourceful engineers and were en route.

"Build a skyscraper if you let 'em," said the sergeant. "Peterson really kicked some butt. Gotta give it to the Marines. Except that they're Marines, they'd be okay."

"Yeah," said Danny. "Locals give you any trouble?"

"Not really. Just the silent treatment. I'm sorry about Powder," added Blow. "That sucks horseshit."

"Yeah."

"You see it happen, Cap?"

Was he asking because he was accusing him of screwing up?

Danny looked down at Hernandez, who was six or seven inches shorter than him. There wasn't any anger in his face, just confusion, a little sorrow.

"Yeah. He was a few yards away," Danny told his

team's pointman gently. "If Powder didn't get it, I would have. Sucks."

"Yeah. They sure as shit fired up the place. Crazy fucks."

"Dedicated," said Danny.

"Crazy fucks."

"Yeah."

The helo settled down. Unlike the last village, this one had a good view of the shoreline, which lay a quarter mile below the settlement area. Danny guessed the Filipinos might not appreciate that. They wanted a place where they could hide, and the clear view worked both ways, but it was too late to worry about it. He jumped out as the helo touched down, then helped the Navy people unpack the villagers' gear.

"Got a Lieutenant Simmons wants to see you," said one of the sailors on the ground. "He's a liaison guy. He helped set this up. Some paperwork, and I think he needs some advice on classification or some such thing."

"Yeah, okay. I gotta get back, though," said Danny. He put down the box of cooking gear he'd taken from the helicopter. As he rose, the girl he'd taken prisoner passed in front of him.

It was as if he wasn't there, just another ghost in the jungle. Danny felt anger well up—he'd busted his ass for these people, for her, and they just went on like he wasn't there.

"Hey," said Danny. He grabbed her arm. She jerked it back. "You gonna thank me?" he said.

She reared back her head. If it hadn't been for the wind from the blades of the helo, her spittle probably would have struck him in the face.

Aboard Quicksilver, over the South China Sea
2140

THE CONSENSUS WAS CLEAR—DEFINITELY A SIKORSKY, definitely something very similar to Searchwater, though not quite an exact match. It looked like it might be a bit harder to jam, according to Torbin, who immediately volunteered to try.

"Let 'em be," said Breanna. "Chris, get on the line to Dreamland Command and tell them about this. They're going to be very interested."

The helicopter climbed into an orbit over the aircraft carrier. As interesting as it was, the Sukhois that had charged after the Viking were a higher priority; and so Breanna sidled in their direction, making sure to stay within range of the Piranha communications buoy. As they got within ten miles of the Viking, the Sukhois started to sandwich the Navy plane in a high-low hello-there routine; one Chinese pilot came in over the S-3 while the other came in below. Even at five hundred knots, it was doubtful the separation between the three planes added up to ten feet.

"They're crazy," said Chris. "They'll hit 'em for sure. They can't fly that well in the damn daylight, let alone in the dark."

The radar showed the Chinese fighters merging with the Viking and, looking at the display, it seemed as if they had crashed. Instead, they had simultaneously sandwiched the S-3 swooping across in opposite directions. It would have been an impressive move at an air show.

"All right, let's see if we can get their attention so our Navy friend can drop his buoys," Bree said, reaching for the throttle bar. The engine control on the Megafortress was fully electronic, and unlike the old lollipop-like sticks in the original B-52, consisted of a master glide bar that could be separated into four smaller segments. Unless the individual controls were activated, the flight computer assumed that it had discretion to fine-tune any discrepancies in the engine performance to maintain uniform acceleration.

Not that any aircraft maintained by a member of a ground crew under the direct supervision of Chief Master

Sergeant "Greasy Hands" Parsons would dare show any discrepancies.

Breanna couldn't get close to the Chinese without getting close to the S-3 as well. Even so, she got close enough to send a serious vortex of air currents across their wings.

Not that it had any effect.

"They're really a pain in the ass, ain't they?" said the pilot in Redtail One. "They're not going to keep me from doing my job," he added.

Possibly hearing the comment, the Sukhoi below the S-3 accelerated and popped up in front of the Viking's nose. Redtail One fluttered; as the plane started to bank the Chinese planes seemed to swarm tighter. Two Sukhois flying over the *Shangi-Ti* changed course and headed in the S-3's direction.

Jennifer Gleason, meanwhile, had filled the S-3 pilot in on the submarines they were tracking and their present course. As the pilot tacked toward it, the other fighters arrived. Though he chopped his speed, he couldn't shake the weaving Sukhois.

ZEN, EAVESDROPPING ON THE RADIO COMMUNICATIONS, had an almost overwhelming urge to hit the gas and chase off the Chinese planes, and had to keep reminding himself he was controlling a robot probe under the water. Maybe because of the distraction, it took him a few extra seconds to realize the two subs he was following were splitting up.

"Bree—our targets are splitting. I'm with the one heading west. We're going to need another buoy soon."

"Roger that, Hawk Leader. Ms. Gleason, give all the data to our Navy friends."

"Already have, Captain."

*   *   *

"CAN WE HELP YOU SOMEHOW?" BREE ASKED THE RED-
tail pilot as the Sukhois swarmed around the Viking.

"Short of firing at them? Negative."

"Don't tempt me," Breanna told him.

"Yeah, my orders suck too," said the Navy pilot, referring to his rules of engagement, which, because of the
complicated political situation, strictly forbade him from
doing anything but running away. "Current ROEs are
bullshit on top of bullshit."

"I didn't know you had antiair weapons," said Breanna.

"At this range, I could hit them with my Beretta," said
the pilot.

One of the Chinese Sukhois nearly clipped the S-3's
wing as he rose up suddenly. The Redtail pilot cursed over
the radio and banked hard, just barely missing another of
the fighters. Undaunted, the two other Chinese planes
stayed right on this tail. As the S-3 leveled off, one
slipped beneath him.

"What do you think they'll do if we activate our gun
radar?" Bree asked Chris.

"Activate theirs."

As Bree considered it, one of the Chinese planes came
at the S-3 head-on.

"Man, they're out of their minds," said Chris.

Breanna checked her position, then switched back into
the radio circuit. "We're going to have to cut out of this
dance in a few minutes," she told Redtail One, starting
another pass in an attempt to pull the Sukhois away.

"Acknowledged," said the pilot tersely.

The interceptors took no notice of the bigger plane,
ducking and weaving with the S-3.

"We're going to have to leave you, Navy," said
Breanna.

"Been fun, Air Force."

Breanna tucked her wing and pushed the Megafortress
west toward the coordinates Jennifer Gleason had plotted
for the next buoy drop. She was just about to give the

order to open the bomb bay doors when Torbin's deep voice rattled in her headset.

"Sukhois have activated gun radars!" he barked.

"ECMs," said Bree. It was undoubtedly another ratchet in their harassment campaign, but she wasn't going to just stand there. "Hawk Leader, I mean Piranha, we're going to have put that buoy drop off for a second."

"Copy that," said Zen.

Bree pitched the Megafortress around, taking nearly eight Gs to get back on an intercept. "Chris—tell Redtail we're coming back. Then target these motherfuckers. Excuse my French."

The copilot's answer was garbled by the force of gravity as the big plane's momentum shifted. The Megafortress's electronic countermeasures filled the air with a thick radio fog, but at close range from behind the plane the Sukhoi pilots could have used straws and spitballs and still brought the Viking down. That didn't seem to be their intent—at least not yet. The lead Sukhoi accelerated on a diagonal, crossing so close over the S-3 they seemed to collide.

"Shit," said Redtail One over the radio. The plane tucked toward the waves, but then righted itself.

"Scorpions," Bree told Chris.

"Our orders—"

"Fuck our orders."

"Yes, ma'am." Another copilot might have pointed out the captain was about to set herself up for a court-martial—and was taking him along, but Chris had flown with Bree forever and helped her ignore any number of orders. "Let me offer a suggestion—we're close enough for the Stinger air mines."

"Stinger then. Good idea."

Chris brought the tail gun on line as Bree began banking.

"Redtail One, I'm going to come right over you and nail those mothers," she told the pilot. "Just hold your course."

"Negative, Air Force. Negative. Shit."

"Redtail?"

"I'm ordered to return to my carrier. Repeat, I just got the order to break off. I have to scrub."

"Scrub? You're kidding," blurted Chris.

The Navy pilot didn't respond, but his actions showed he was dead serious—he began a slow bank to the east. The Sukhois continued to dog him, not yet realizing they'd won.

"Quicksilver, what's going on up there?" asked Zen.

"Just the normal command bullshit," said Breanna. She scanned her instruments, trying to control her anger.

"We need to drop the buoy, Bree," Zen reminded her.

"On it," she said, pulling the big plane back toward the drop point.

Philippines
2300

IT WAS A LONG GREEN BAG, A SIMPLE THING, THE KIND of wrapping that emphasized the one enduring truth of man's existence.

"Shoulder, arms!"

Like everything Whiplash did, the service was a bit ad hoc—and utterly suited to the task at hand. All Dreamland personnel available gathered near the edge of the runway, standing between the long dark bag and the gray C-130 waiting to take it home. The powerful lights of the Seabee work crews turned the night a silvery yellow as four members of the action team, four of Powder's closest friends in the universe, walked to the edge of the cliff overlooking the sea. Each man shouldered a different weapon—an M-16, an MP-5, a Beretta pistol, and a Squad Automatic Weapon. One by one, they pointed their guns skyward and fired off a burst in his memory. Each weapon had been Sergeant Talcom's.

Danny Freah held the pistol. A sensation came over him as he pulled the trigger. He wanted to fling the gun in, throw it into the water, one last offering to the universe. But he was an officer, and he was a man of discipline and self-control, so he simply turned and led the others back. As the chaplain thumbed through his Bible, he couldn't help thinking this might very well be the first time Powder had ever sat through a reading from the Scriptures.

"I say unto you which hear," began the reverend, "love your enemies, do good to them which hate you. Bless them that curse you, and pray for them which despitefully use you. And unto him that smitheth thee on the one cheek offer also the other. . . ."

The words, from Luke 6, struck Danny off balance. Why was this idiot talking of mercy when his man was dead?

Turn the other cheek? Bullshit!

A new urge came over him. Danny wanted to grab the minister, throttle him, make him say something more appropriate, more comforting.

But Danny Freah was a man of discipline and self-control; he did nothing.

"Love ye your enemies, and do good, and lend, hoping for nothing again; and your reward shall be great, and ye shall be the children of the Highest: for he is kind unto the unthankful and to the evil."

The words drifted away. The chaplain stepped back. On a tape player found by one of the Marines, a recorded bugle began its lonesome wail. Powder's best friends in the universe each went to the corners of his remains, then gently placed him on board for the journey home.

VI
The verdict of fortune

South of Taiwan, aboard the command ship *Blue Ridge*
August 27, 1997, 1023 local

"WHAT YOU AND YOUR PEOPLE DON'T SEEM TO APPRE-
ciate here, Colonel, is that we're supposed to be the peace-
makers. Are you seriously interested in starting World
War Three?"

Woods's face puffed out with anger. The admiral
turned sideways for a moment, staring at the wall as if he
could see something through the ship's steel.

"I authorize you to conduct a simple reconnaissance
mission and you obliterate an atoll," continued Woods
finally. "Tell me—is your base located over radioactive
material? Do X-rays fry your brains?"

"Admiral." Dog stopped himself. There was no point
in trying to explain the mission again. Not only had he
told Woods everything, but the admiral had the tapes of
the incident and Danny Freah's report sitting on his desk.

"Well?" said Woods.

"Nothing," said Dog.

The admiral turned back to the wall. Maybe he really
could see through it—maybe he could see far beyond it
to the forces gathering on either side of the American task
force. "In two hours, the Indian and Chinese fleets will

be able to bomb the hell out of each other. The President has sent the Secretary of State—the fucking Secretary of State—to New Delhi to negotiate a cease-fire. You know what my orders are, Tecumseh?"

"No, sir," said Dog. It was the first time Woods had used his given name.

"If it were up to me, if it were truly up to me, I'd let them fight it out. Hell, I think it's in our best interests. I don't have to tell you about the Chinese. The Indians are trouble as well. As long as the extremists are in control, the Indians are trouble as well. But if I had to choose, at this point, I'd side with the Indians. Hell, I'm tempted to help them even now. My orders, though—and unlike you, I actually believe in following orders—are to keep the two sides apart, and to do nothing to increase hostilities. Nothing! Now how the hell am I supposed to do that? Put myself directly between them?"

"I'm not sure, sir."

"Twenty-four hours from now, that's where I'll be. *Kitty Hawk* and her escorts will be positioned to blow both of their fleets out of the water. Hell, I could do it now. If I got the order."

"Yes, sir."

"But blowing them up wouldn't bring peace, would it?"

"No, sir," said Dog.

"Which is my mission, whether I like it or not. Now how can I fulfill that mission with a bunch of cowboys running around shooting things up? Very good cowboys," added Woods before Dog could object. "Excellent cowboys. But your job was reconnaissance—spying. Not fighting."

Woods emphasized the words the way one might talk to a five-year-old. Colonel Bastian had pretty much reached the end of his patience.

"I thought the SEALs were bad," added the admiral. "You guys make them look like kids on their way to First Holy Communion."

"I don't know that that's accurate, sir," said Dog. "On

that atoll, my people were fired on; they responded. At sea, we shot down two missiles. Missiles that surely would have sunk the Chinese carrier; which ought to count for something."

The admiral frowned; Dog couldn't help but wonder if he would have preferred the carrier went down.

"In the air, every incident with the Chinese was initiated by the Chinese," said Colonel Bastian in a level voice. "You have the tapes and the data from every flight. We're not the cowboys, sir. We're just doing our job, as ordered."

"I'm not unreasonable, Tecumseh. Truly, I'm not. I had the Filipinos moved at your request."

"I didn't say you were unreasonable, Admiral."

"But?"

"You do seem to go out of your way to make me your whipping boy."

"That's because I don't like you," said Woods.

The two men stared at each other. Dog waited for Woods to soften what he'd just said, take it back by adding, "that's what you think, isn't it?" But he didn't.

"You're in over your head on this operation," the admiral said finally. "Don't get me wrong. You're competent, capable, even a hotshot. But Dreamland and Whiplash—you need perspective. You'll understand what I'm saying in five or six years."

"I understand now."

"The surveillance mission with Piranha will continue," said Woods. "That's a direct order from the President I can't and won't ignore, but the mission will be carried out under my personal direction. You're no longer in the loop, Colonel. You have a lot of work to do at Dreamland."

"What?"

"It's not necessary to embarrass you in front of your people. But I will. Go home."

Dog had to physically bite his lip to keep himself from saying or doing anything else. It was only after he boarded

his transport helicopter topside that he realized blood had
dribbled down his chin.

Aboard *Shiva* in the South China Sea
August 27, 1997, 1326

THEY CAME TO PERISCOPE DEPTH CAUTIOUSLY, AWARE
the sonar contact was a Chinese destroyer. Admiral Balin
confirmed the crew's prediction quickly; they were almost
perpendicular, and close enough for Balin to see the two
large guns at either end. The ship was surely a Jianghu
frigate.

Captain Varja gave the order to change their course.
They came around quickly and began closing on the Chinese vessel.

The Kali weapons and their assorted equipment had
robbed Balin of precious space, leaving him room for only
six torpedoes. He would fire two at the destroyer, holding
the others for whatever targets he would find later.

"Sir," said Captain Varja. "We have additional contacts.
A carrier."

"A carrier?"

"Making good speed," added the captain. "Other vessels as well. Beyond the destroyer."

Balin put his eyes back to the periscope viewer. There
was only gray beyond the destroyer.

They were using only their passive sonar. To use the
active array would surely alert the Chinese to their presence—but would also provide a good deal more information.

He wanted it too badly; he must be cautious.

Balin stepped away from the periscope. His eyes met
Varja's. The captain surely had the same thoughts.

"We must find it," said Balin softly.

"Agreed."

Varja gave the orders to use the sonar.

One carrier, less than three miles away. It was the
Shangi-Ti; the sound signature left no doubt.

There was another—another very large contact in the distance, more than likely a vessel of the same size as *Shangi-Ti*.

A second carrier!

Again the gods had been beneficent, guiding them here so they could strike both.

The sonar room gave a fresh warning—the frigate was turning in their direction.

"Return to passive sensors. Take us to a safer depth," he said, his voice a bare whisper.

Swiftly, the crew moved to obey.

Philippines
1326

THE WATER LAPPED AT DANNY FREAH'S WAIST CLEAR and warm; if it weren't for the roar of the approaching F/A-18's, he could have believed he was wading out from an exclusive private beach.

It wasn't exactly private, but thanks to a contingent of Marine guards and Dreamland security protecting the island and this cove below the airstrip, it was very exclusive.

Danny slid onto his side and began swimming parallel to the shore. When he'd gone about twenty yards, he turned back. He used large boulders on the hillside as markers, treading back and forth as if working out, though he didn't keep track of his many laps. He swam a backstroke to the south, the sidestroke or breaststroke to the north. He was not a big swimmer, and his muscles soon began to tire with the unfamiliar exertion. He kept on paddling, the burn creeping down from his shoulders to his arms, out from his hips to his thighs, and then all the way to his calf muscles. He swam until the tingling sensation weighed him down. Finally, he stopped abruptly, putting his feet down to stand on the coral and rock-strewn ocean floor, but his path had taken him into deeper water. He floundered for a second, water lapping over his face. He pushed up with his arms, and in a burst of energy began swimming and laughing at the same time. How ignoble would that be, he wondered to himself, to die recreating in a combat zone?

He didn't stand until the water was less than waist-deep. When he reached his blanket on the shore, he saw Bison heading down the rock-strewn path from the air-strip.

"Hey, Cap—Colonel Bastian looking to talk to you up at the command post," said the sergeant.

"Thanks," said Danny, toweling off. Bison stood a short distance away, staring at the water. Danny suddenly felt modest and, though no one was looking at him, pulled his shorts off below his towel and then pulled his uniform pants up, forgoing underwear.

"Water warm?" asked Bison.

"Yeah," said Danny, pulling on a T-shirt.

"Say Captain, mind if I ask you something?"

"What's that?"

"How come Powder chose that reading?"

"Sorry?" said Danny, thinking he'd misunderstood.

"Powder—Liu told me to make sure the chaplain got the verse right. That's what he wanted read? Turn the other cheek and all that shit? I don't get it."

Danny pulled on his shirt. "I don't know," he said. He hadn't realized Powder himself had chosen the reading.

"It's supposed to be a message to us, sure, all right, I can understand that," said Bison. "But from Powder? Man, he liked to shoot things up. Now he's telling us to turn the other cheek? Shit. Powder?"

Bison—who'd never gotten along particularly well with Powder while he was alive—looked a little as if he was going to cry.

"To be honest, I don't get it either," said Danny. "I miss him, though. Already."

"Yeah, weird. Powder. Fuck. It sucks, Captain."

"It does suck, Bison. Big-time."

"He told us about you in Sarajevo, how you saved his life that time."

"It wasn't Sarajevo," said Danny. He ran his pinkie around the corner of his ear, clearing out the water. Bison was waiting for the full story, but Danny didn't feel like telling it. He gave the short version. "We were in a town about twenty miles south of there. Guy came around the corner. I popped him. That was it, basically."

"I'm glad you did."

Danny laughed as he pulled on his shirt. "Yeah, me too. Because the son of a bitch would've popped me next. Had a stinking Uzi—where the hell do you think he got an Uzi, huh? Those things are supposed to be damn expensive."

By the time the captain reached the trailer, Dog was already giving the pilots the lowdown. Even before he heard the words, Danny knew from the colonel's face a heap of bullshit had gone down. Colonel Bastian always wore "the Pentagon stare" when he had to dish out a line he didn't agree with. Today it was mixed with something else Danny saw even less often, genuine anger, though Bastian wasn't venting.

"Bottom line, we continue monitoring the Chinese sub until further notice. Bree, your plane's out in three hours, relieving Major Alou. My replacement will take Iowa six hours after that. We'll keep turning it around until we're ordered to go home."

Zen raised his hand to interrupt. "Colonel, Jen and I have been doing a little thinking. With a little work, we may be able to squeeze the gear tightly enough and route things so Raven and Quicksilver can fly one of the Flighthawks and handle Piranha at the same time."

"Well, that's not really necessary," said Bastian.

"It would keep the Chinese off us," said Zen. "The way things are going, it makes sense for a Flighthawk to be along."

"Our orders are not to engage the enemy." Colonel Bastian's eyes were almost glassy—obviously that was the heart of the trouble.

"Flighthawks can help hold them off," said Zen. "Bree wouldn't have had to get that close to the Viking. Besides, if the sub surfaces, the Flighthawk can get up close and personal."

The colonel turned to Jennifer Gleason. "Is it doable?" he asked.

One thing Danny had to give Dog—there was no visible sign that he was sleeping with her; his voice was as gruff with her as it was with anyone.

Another thing he had to give Bastian—the ol' dog sure could pick 'em.

"We can do it, but only with Iowa because of the second control bay. I just don't have the space to get the computer into Quicksilver and Raven. I mean, if we had more time—"

Dog held up his hand. "How long?"

"Six or seven hours. Tommy Jacobs is coming in on the next flight with the pilot, and he's bringing a full—"

"Okay," said Dog.

"I'll take Zen's place on Quicksilver," said Fentress.

Bastian's Pentagon stare dissolved into a faint smile. He folded his arms in front of his chest. "So what else have you decided in my absence?"

"We didn't decide," said Bree innocently.

"We might have discussed it a little," said Fentress.

Colonel Bastian shook his head and turned to Danny. "Captain Freah, you missed a little at the top there. I have business at Dreamland. The mission continues; reconnaissance only. You will continue to provide security for the Megafortresses. I realize it's superfluous," he added. "I trust the Marines, but I want at least a token presence. Work out what equipment and personnel we need to keep here."

"Yes, sir," said Danny.

"All right, well, let's get cranking then. I have to pack. Commander Stein will be in charge of operations as of ten seconds ago." Dog glanced at his watch, then back at them. "I expect everyone to follow orders to the best of their ability. And in some cases, beyond."

ZEN LET HIS WHEELCHAIR SLIDE DOWN THE RAMP, RUSH-ing so close to Breanna he nearly spun her around.

"Hey, hot rod," she said, grabbing hold of the side. "Watch where you're going."

"Gimps have the right of way," said Zen.

"I thought you weren't going to say that anymore," Bree told him. "I hate that word."

"I calls 'em like I sees 'em," he told her.

"You like to piss me off, don't you?"

"Favorite thing in the world, next to kissing you," he said truthfully. "So you ready for the mission?"

"I can handle it."

"No shooting down Chinese planes."

"I will if I have to," she said.

Zen laughed, but he believed her. "You going to be okay without me riding shotgun for you?" he said as they continued toward the planes.

"I don't need you to watch my back," she said.

"Hey." Zen grabbed at her hand, but missed. "You mad?"

"No."

"Bree? I was just kidding about the gimp thing."

"I'm fine," she said, still walking.

"Hey, what are you mad at?"

She turned toward the mess tent.

Zen began to follow. Ordinarily, his teasing didn't have this kind of effect. Ordinarily, she simply teased back. But this wasn't teasing.

"Hey," he said, rolling to the door.

"Just feeding my face before the flight," she said, let-ting the screen door on the tent slam closed behind her.

*   *   *

STONER LET HIS BREATH FLOW FROM HIS CHEST softly, each cell in his lungs reluctantly surrendering its molecule of oxygen. A yellow light filled the center of his head. His body melted. Stoner's consciousness became a long note vibrating in the empty tent. He slipped into a deep, meditative trance.

It was then he realized what had happened.

Deliberately, he unfolded his legs, then rose. He stooped down for a sip of water from the bottle near his bed mat and roll—he didn't use a cot—then went to find Colonel Bastian.

"The lookout post belonged to the Taiwanese," Stoner told the colonel when he found him. "All of them. The Chinese don't need them. They must be helping the Indians."

Bastian nodded. "Have you spoken to Langley?"

"Not yet. But it makes sense. I'll talk to Jed Barclay too."

"Why would they fire on us?" asked Bastian.

Us, not *you.* Stoner liked that. He knew Bastian had, without complaint, taken the hit for what went down on the island. Protecting his people, even though they could have plausibly been blamed for messing up. He had grown to admire Bastian; he was a man he could work with.

"Because they fear discovery. Possibly they expected the Chinese, but more likely they knew it would be us. Taiwan can't appear to be taking sides or provoking a confrontation. They want to hurt Mainland China, but if they do something that looks to us like it's belligerent, like it's against our interests, we might crush them. Simply moving our fleet away would hurt them."

Bastian nodded.

"I'd like to join the next patrol flight," added Stoner. "The Taiwanese spy ships that have been tracking the submarine, I want to find out about them. I think there's some other operation under way."

"They're not part of our mission."

"Their goal isn't peace, or coexistence with the Mainland. They want the same thing the Communists want—one China. They just want it on their terms."

"That may be," said the colonel. "But at the moment, that's not our concern."

"I won't be just a passenger. There's no one here who knows more about Chinese and Indian capabilities than I do. I'm the one who found Kali. I'd be very useful tracking the Chinese submarines."

"Okay," said Bastian finally. "Work it out with Captain Stockard. Stoner—" Bastian pointed a finger at him. "This operation ultimately answers to Admiral Woods, not me."

"Took him longer to kick you out than I expected," said the CIA officer. "He must like you."

Aboard the Dragon Ship in the South China Sea
1326

CHEN LO FANN WALKED THE DECK OF THE FORMER tanker, his mind heavy with thought. Professor Ai Hira Bai. the scientist who led the team that developed the Dragons, percolated next to him, bouncing with every step. The launch procedure was not particularly difficult. The small robot was lowered from the side of the ship onto the surface of the water, where it rested on a pair of skis. A solid-propellant rocket propelled it into the sky; once it was safely above the spray, its jet engine was activated. The plane looked somewhat like a miniaturized Su-33UB, except its engine inlets were placed atop the wings and it had four angled fins—two on top, two on the bottom—rather than the more traditional double tailplane of the experimental Sukhoi.

And, of course, there was no place for a pilot.

Chen turned and looked at the horizon while Professor Ai conferred with some of his technicians. The water had a dark green tint to it today; he felt a fresh storm approaching.

In a hundred years, no one would remember the

weather or the color of the sea. They would think only of the destruction wrought as the two Navies met.

A storm indeed.

One of the men assigned to relay messages approached as Chen stared out at the water.

"Yes?" he asked without turning.

The man held out a slip of paper. Chen let his eyes linger, then turned and took the message.

The captain of one of his trawlers had seen the American Megafortresses drop an unknown type of buoy into the water. Photos of the buoy did not match any of the ASW types the Americans typically used. Interestingly, the trawler—equipped with an array of high-tech snooping gear that worked both under and above the water— had been unable to pick up any transmissions to or from that buoy, or a second one dropped sometime later, at least not at the distance he had been ordered to stay from any American asset. The captain wanted permission to investigate, and perhaps retrieve one of the buoys if the opportunity presented itself.

Chen weighed the matter. Despite being allies, the Americans were hardly forthcoming when it came to sharing new technology. The appearance of the EB-52's— which had not been used in marine patrol or ASW roles before—surely meant they were using some new device. Whatever it was—a passive sonar system perhaps?— would be of great value in dealing with the Communists.

He would not, and could not, provoke an incident with the Americans. But surely this was worth studying. What if he snatched the device, then claimed to have thought it was a Mainland weapon?

In the confusion of battle, such an explanation would be accepted, if only reluctantly. In such a case, the asset would be returned—after it was examined, of course.

Chen took a pen and wrote his orders to the captain, telling him to proceed. He handed the message back to the courier, who immediately retreated for the radio room.

"Ready, Commander," said Professor Ai, who'd been waiting.

"Then begin."

Fann turned toward the crane as the tarp was taken off the small aircraft. The large hook, very old and heavy, swung freely above, making him slightly apprehensive; its weight could easily damage the robot. The crew was well trained and practiced, however. Two men grabbed the hook as it came toward them, then fit it into the harness. One of them climbed up above the Dragon and onto the chain. It must seem like the greatest job in the world, riding on the hoist as it swung out, waiting as the four men in the water carefully undid the sling, then riding back to the deck.

For Chen, the elation would come later, much later—he hoped to see one of the carriers in flames before the end of the day.

Professor Ai looked at him, and Fann realized the scientist was waiting for his order to begin. Fann nodded. The scientist smiled broadly, then turned and waved to the crane operator, who stood a short distance away with a wired remote. The man pushed one of the levers and the motor on the crane whirled.

There was a loud grinding noise. Someone shouted. Smoke appeared from the crane house. Professor Ai leaped toward the robot, cursing.

Fann stood impassively, watching.

Who was riding the donkey now? Which way did Fortune blow?

"It's a problem with the crane," said the scientist a few minutes later.

"Yes."

"We have to use the backup."

"Do so."

"It will take time."

"Do it as quickly as you can," said Chen. He turned and went back to his cabin.

Philippines
1346

DOG TOOK A LAST CHECK OF THE SITUATION AT THE
Whiplash trailer, touching base with Dreamland Command before leaving. Major Alou and Raven were on station, Alou being extra careful to stay outside the patrol area the Chinese fighters had established. Piranha sat about ten miles away from the Chinese submarine. The sub had taken up an almost stationary position to the southwest of the carrier task force. A U.S. sub had already found the other Chinese submarine on the eastern side of the Chinese fleet. Within the next twelve hours, a second SSN should be on Piranha's target as well. Whiplash could close up shop.

The fate of the Indian sub remained a mystery. Though the profile wasn't a good match, the contact Piranha had seen was discounted as the American SSN, which had indeed been in the vicinity. Intercepts of Chinese Mainland transmissions by the NSA showed the Chinese believed the submarine had been sunk, but the analysts weren't completely sure. There was no hard evidence it had gone down, and it clearly had the capability to stay submerged for several days. It could still be shadowing the Chinese fleet, or it could have set sail south to return to India.

Whiplash had accomplished its mission. The data they had gathered would provide a hundred analysts useful employment for the next year or more. Just as importantly, they demonstrated the value of Piranha and its technology.

Yet Colonel Bastian felt as if he'd failed. Because he'd lost a man? Or because he'd had his tail whacked by Woods?

Definitely the tail-whacking. He'd lost men before—good men, friends. It was the cost of freedom, as corny and trite as that sounded. The sorrow of their deaths was as much a part of his job as the speed-suit he donned to

fly. But getting treated like—like what, exactly? A lieutenant colonel?

He missed General Magnus now. The three-star general
would have insulated him from this BS. He had in Turkey,
when Central Command tried to get its fingers in.

Problem was, at the time he'd thought Magnus was a
bit of pain as well. So the real problem was his ego.

"Something up, Colonel?" asked Jack "Pretty Boy"
Floyd, who was at the communications desk.

"Just getting ready to hit the road, Sergeant," he told
him.

"Yes, sir. Coffee's better over at the Navy tent," he
added. "Liu's the only one on the team who can make a
decent pot."

"Better pray he gets out of the hospital soon then, huh?"
said Dog.

"Yes, sir," said Floyd, who didn't quite take it as lightly
as it was intended.

"He'll be okay, Sergeant," Dog added. "You hang in
there."

"Yes, sir. Thank you."

Outside, the air was heavy with humidity; another
storm was approaching. Sweat began to leak from his
pores as he headed toward the Navy C-9B waiting to take
him to Manila, where he'd hop a civilian flight to L.A.

The schedule was tight. Unlike the Navy plane, the civilian 747 wasn't going to wait, but midway to his plane
Dog took a detour, deciding he really had to say good-
bye to one more member of his command.

Jennifer Gleason stood on the hard-packed dirt near
Iowa, hands on hips. Several access panels directly behind
the crew area of the plane were open; a portable platform
was set up below the EB-52's belly. Three or four techies
hunched over equipment on a nearby pallet, flashing
screwdrivers; a sailor carried a disk array the size of a
pizza box up the plane's access ramp. Gleason was shaking her head in obvious disgust.

"Hey, Gleason, what's up?" said Dog.

"These guys handle the computers like they're crystal," she complained. "They're designed to take over twelve Gs for cryin' out loud. We won't be ready for hours."

"You look pretty when you're fretting." Dog allowed himself a light touch on her shoulder. "You don't want them to throw the gear up there, do you?"

"Be faster."

God, she was beautiful.

"I have to go home," he said.

"Uh-huh." She flicked her hair back behind her ear. "I'm okay here."

"I know that," said Dog.

Something near the plane caught her eye and she turned back. "Excuse me, Colonel." She started to trot toward the plane. "Hey! Hey!"

Dog watched the sway of her hips in the fatigue pants, then abruptly started for the Navy plane. If he didn't get aboard now . . .

Aboard Quicksilver, above the South China Sea
1636

GUIDING THE PIRANHA PROBE WAS CONSIDERABLY EAS-ier than flying the Flighthawks. Fentress ran through some simple maneuvers and flipped back and forth between the views as Delaford watched from aboard the other Mega-fortress. They had made a few adjustments in the simulated 3-D screen since he had sat in on the development sessions, but it wasn't difficult at all to get comfortable. He even remembered, without prompting, how to split the screen so he could see a forward and a sitrep view at the same time.

The probe was within thirteen miles of the Chinese sub-marine, which was moving at three knots south. Another fifteen miles away was the lead Chinese aircraft carrier. The Piranha communications buoy had been dropped thirty-five miles further west, allowing the EB-52 to stay outside of carrier CAP.

Delaford had launched this probe a few hours before to replace the first, whose fuel had lasted slightly longer than they'd originally calculated. It was now moving southwest in low-power mode, and would be picked up by the Dreamland Osprey in a few hours, if the weather held. A new storm system was approaching rather quickly.

"You look like you're on top of it," said Delaford. "See you down the line."

"I'll be here." The line snapped clear; he was on his own.

UPSTAIRS ON THE FLIGHT DECK, BREANNA REVIEWED her fuel situation and went through a quick instrument check. With everything in the green, she turned the plane over to Chris and eased out of the driver's seat, intending to take a short break. Among Quicksilver's custom touches was a small refrigerator located at the back end of the flight deck. Breanna had often joked that, with missions sometimes stretching over twelve hours, a full galley ought to be provided, and one of the engineers had suggested adding a microwave.

She'd have a full galley when she flew the UMB. Even better, a full bathroom.

Hell, one of the geeks said she could fly it from her bedroom via laptop—now wouldn't that be a trip?

Breanna checked on Freddy and Torbin, both hard at work parsing their data from the Chinese and Indian forces. Freddy fed most of his communications intercepts directly back to Dreamland, where a team of language experts were monitoring the transmissions. Given that both sides realized they were being listened to, there was a surprising amount of traffic.

Breanna squatted in front of the refrigerator and took out a diet cola. She opened it and took a sip, then leaned against the bulkhead and looked at her crew.

Did she want to leave this behind?

Maybe. This was fairly routine. Almost boring.

Not that the business the other day had been.

It made sense from a career angle, certainly. It'd be easier on her back, which was crinked from the cot she'd slept on last night. She'd see Zen more. Not that she didn't see him all the time now.

The thought came to her in a sarcastic tone, almost as if someone else had said it. She was mad at her husband, though she wasn't exactly sure why.

Because he was working with Jenn-i-fer?

Whom she hated. But Zen was always working with Jenn-i-fer; it wasn't that big a deal.

Was it?

"Hey," said a voice behind her. It startled her so badly she nearly lost her balance.

Stoner, the CIA officer aboard to act as general intelligence consultant and Fentress's gofer.

"Mr. Stoner. We would prefer it if you kept your seat," she told him.

"You're up."

"What can I do for you?" she said frostily.

"I was wondering if I could listen in on some of the com intercepts from the trawler, if they're in the clear."

"You speak Chinese?"

"A bit."

"I doubt they're in the clear," she told him. "But we may be able to pipe them through. Go back to your station and I'll see."

"Can I view them?"

Civilians just didn't get it sometimes.

"We're too far from the actual position of the ships on the surface to see them. We have radar indications, that's all."

"If you get close to them, I'd like to take a look. I might be able to tell what kind of equipment they have. I'd be very interested."

He had a handsome face, deep blue eyes that seemed out of place with his dark hair.

"We'll try. Use the interphone from now on," she told him. "Downstairs."

He stared at her a while longer, then nodded.

"Kind of a jerk," she said as she sat back in her seat.

"Who?" said Chris.

"Stoner."

"Yeah? Seemed okay to me. First CIA guy I ever met."

"Give him a sitrep screen, all right? Show him where everything is."

Breanna checked with Collins about the intercepts. They'd only isolated one or two from the spy ships, and they were all heavily encoded. "Give Mr. Stoner a low-down, would you?"

"Not a problem."

Restraints snugged, Breanna checked their position as well as that of the other players. The Chinese and Indian fleets were moving slowly toward each other. Two Sukhois had begun shadowing the Megafortress in a long oval track three miles to the east. Same old, same old.

"Trawler's heading off south," Chris pointed out, referring to the Taiwanese spy ship. "Wimping out?"

"Just getting out of the way for the showdown" said Breanna.

STONER FOLDED HIS ARMS IN FRONT OF HIS CHEST, staring at the video screen. Both the Chinese and the Indians had their chessmen in place; they could start duking it out in an hour.

So what were the Taiwanese up to anyway? Egging the Indians on? Usually, they took a more laid-back approach, but they had spy ships all over the place, including one so close it was going to catch shrapnel when the fighting started.

Stoner stared at the fifteen-inch display screen where the sitrep view was displayed. It was a simple thing, a plot of positions against longitude and latitude, yet cobbling it together was not exactly child's play. To get all these different inputs, process them, put them on the screen so that even an untrained operator like himself could see what was going on—Dreamland indeed.

"Say, uh, Captain Ferris. Chris. This is Stoner. What's the green triangle on my screen?"

"On the sitrep? That's the marker for the Piranha buoy. It's tied into the tactical system so it comes on the display. Sorry if it's confusing."

"That Taiwanese trawler is going to run right over our buoy if they stay on that course. Is he tracking it?"

"No way," said Ferris.

"Well, he's going to run over it anyway."

BREANNA PUSHED THE PLANE DOWN THROUGH THE leading edge of the fast-moving cloud front, trying to get low enough for a visual on the players—and the trawler that was on a collision course for their buoy. "Stoner's right—they're aimed almost perfectly for it," said Chris as they broke through the clouds into the gray stillness above the water. The spy ship looked like a child's boat in a bathtub. "Should I try hailing them?"

"What are you going to tell them?" asked Bree. "That they're about to run over a top-secret communications system for a high-tech weapon?"

"I probably wouldn't want to say that," said Chris contritely.

If the trawler hit the buoy, they would most likely lose their connection—and Piranha. It occurred to Breanna the ocean was awful big and the buoy awfully small—and yet the ship was uncannily on course for the device.

"Could they track the transmissions, you think?"

"Well, the Navy couldn't," said Chris. "But in theory, it's possible. That ship has been around—they might have seen the buoy launched."

*   *   *

"FENTRESS—HOW'S YOUR CONNECTION WITH PIranha?" Bree asked.

"As far as I can tell, Captain, they're not interfering."

"Going through two thousand feet to nineteen hundred, eighteen hundred," said the copilot, belatedly calling out their altitude. "We're getting low."

"Is there enough time to auto-sink this buoy and launch another?" Bree asked Chris and Fentress as she leveled off.

"Sinking procedure takes a hundred and eighty seconds," said Fentress. "I have the screen up."

"We have to get the new one in the water first," said Chris.

"Pick a spot about five miles away. Make it ten."

"Hang on." He worked on his screens, plotting a course. "Five minutes total. If they're watching and they're interested, there's no guarantee they won't see us, Bree. They'll know what we're doing and get at least a rough idea of where we launch. The Chinese may too."

"I don't know that we have any other choice. Give me the course. Kevin, be ready with the self-destruct."

"I can't get that panel once we're trying to connect," he told her. "What I mean is, it'll take a few more seconds."

"They're just about alongside," said Chris.

If Zen were here, she'd have him send the Flighthawks to buzz the spy ship.

So where the hell was he when she needed him?

"Think they'll back off if we buzz them?" she asked Chris.

"Don't know," said the copilot. "Sure get them talking about us, though."

Breanna slid the Megafortress onto her left wing, pirouetting back toward the trawler and kicking up her speed.

"They may be armed," said Stoner over the interphone.

"Don't be so optimistic," said Breanna. She pushed the EB-52 to just three hundred feet over the white-capped waves, the plane a black finger wagging at the trawler not to be naughty. They could see the people on the deck duck as they roared over.

"One more time," she said, picking up the plane's nose and then pedaling into a tight bank. "And this time, we're going to one hundred feet."

"We can snap their aerial if you want," offered Chris.

"Don't tempt me."

"Two hundred fifty feet," said the copilot. As he continued to read the descending numbers, a bit of a tremble entered his voice. They cleared the upper mast by maybe ten feet.

"They stop?" Breanna asked.

"Not sure. They're on the deck."

"One more pass. Prepare to deploy buoy," said Breanna.

This time they cleared the mast by inches rather than feet, but the trawler had continued moving and was now practically alongside the buoy. Two or three crew members were leaning over the rail there.

"Getting static here," said Fentress as they cleared the shop.

"Activate the targeting radar for the air mines," said Breanna.

"Captain?" said Ferris.

"We'll get their attention, launch another probe while we're firing, sink the first, launch a third further away, then sink the second," said Breanna. "Calculate it so we come close, but don't hit them with the shrapnel."

"I'm not sure I can do that. I don't even know if I can get the gun on them."

"You can do anything, Chris." She swung the Megafortress through another turn so she could get her tail aimed at the spy ship.

"All right. We cross over the trawler, bank, take our shot, then launch."

"You disappoint me," she told him, hitting the throttle for more speed.

"How's that?"

"All that potential and no sexual innuendo?"

"Yeah, well, you should hear what I'm thinking."

Aboard *Shiva* in the South China Sea
1830

IT WASN'T UNTIL HE WAS FOUR MILES FROM THE AIR-craft carrier that the Chinese destroyer picked up Balin's submarine. Even then, the destroyer wasn't quite sure what it had found, or where its quarry was—the ship began tracking north, probably after one of the other subs Balin's men had detected in the vicinity. And so he managed to get nearly two miles closer before Captain Varja passed the word that the enemy escort was now bearing down on them.

"Prepare torpedoes," said Balin calmly.

"Torpedoes ready," said Varja.

"Range to target?"

"Three thousand, five hundred meters," reported the captain.

The others in the control room were trying to strangle their excitement; the few words they exchanged as they prepared to fire were high-pitched and anxious. Varja, though, was calm. Balin appreciated that; he felt he had taught the young man something worthwhile.

"We will fire at three thousand meters," Balin said.

A moment later, a depth charge exploded somewhere behind them. The boat shook off the shudder and the helmsman managed to stay on course, but Balin realized this had only been the opening blow.

"Launch torpodoes," said the admiral. "Sink them."

Aboard Quicksilver
1835

IN ORDER TO GET THE AIR MINES WHERE CHRIS WANTED them, Breanna had to practically stand the Megafortress on its tail, fighting all of Newton's laws—not to mention those of common sense. Breanna barely managed to control the big plane, sliding sideways across the waves at a mere thousand feet. She finally had to let her left wing sail downward; the front windscreen filled with blue before she could recover.

"Got a couple of shots on their bow," said Chris. His helmet was touching the display where the Stinger target box was displayed. "I don't think we hurt anybody. They all ran aft. Ship's dead in the water, eight, ten feet from the buoy."

"Get ready to launch," said Bree calmly.

"Okay, right."

"Fentress?" she asked.

"Not as much static. Geez, those bullets make a hell of a racket hitting the water. You should see them on the display screen—look like volcanoes erupting on top of you, then there's this wild crisscross pattern in different shades of red and blue. Very 1960s. I had to hit the manual filter and—"

Fentress stopped abruptly.

"We're at launch point," said Chris.

"Wait," she told him. "Fentress? Kevin? You okay down there?"

"Torpedoes in the water."

"What?"

"Back by the carrier," said Fentress. "Have two, three warning blocks."

"Launch the buoy," she told Chris. "Kevin, we're launching. You sure about the torpedoes?"

"Yes ma'am. Have another sub."

"Give the coordinates to Chris as soon as you can. Buoys first."

Aboard the Dragon Ship in the South China Sea
1838

REALIZING HIS PRESENCE MADE THE MEN NERVOUS, Chen Lo Fann had refrained from coming into the operator's suite until the robot planes were approaching the fleet. Now, his place was in this room.

They rose as one as he entered, bowing stiffly. After he returned their salute, they went back to what they were doing.

The long LCD screen at the center of the room was gray. He stared at it, wondering why he had not been told of the malfunction, before realizing he was seeing clouds.

"We will descend from the clouds in thirty seconds," said Professor Ai. Overcoming the mishap with the crane seemed somehow to have calmed him, or at least drained some of his energy. He spoke slowly now, more himself. "The carriers will be in the far corner to your left. There is one Sukhoi approaching, but its radar has not detected us."

"At what point will it do so?" asked Chen.

"We are not sure. We will be ready in any event."

"Yes," said Chen.

One of the radio operators at the far corner of the room held up his hand. "There is a report the Megafortress is firing on our ship near its probe," said the man.

Chen considered this. "Have them back away. Tell them to leave the area."

The robot supplying the video finally broke through the cloud bank. The operator adjusted the picture, compensating for the fading light. The Chinese aircraft carrier sat like a large, gray cow at the top of the screen.

His robot was equipped with two small missiles, adapted from antitank weapons. They would do almost no damage on a target so vast. The thought occurred to him that he could crash his plane into the carrier; it would not sink, but the fire would kill many men.

Relatives of his perhaps; much of his family had not escaped the Communists, and he knew that a few were now in their Navy. Fortune's irony.

"The Indian planes?" he asked Professor Ai.

"They are still in their patrol pattern to the south."

"Look!" said one of the men at the console. He jumped to his feet and pointed at the LCD screen.

Something blossomed beyond the Chinese aircraft carrier, the dull bud of an early spring flower.

There were two other wakes approaching it.

Torpedoes. Either they had come from the Indian submarine that had failed earlier, or from an American.

It must have been an American. For surely, the Indian was gone by now.

"Halt the attack," said Chen Lo Fann, his satisfaction so deep that he could not possibly hide it. "Stay only close enough to observe the destruction, but remain undetected if possible."

Aboard Quicksilver
1838

"CAN WE STOP THE TORPEDOES?" BREE ASKED.

"No way," said Chris.

"They see them," said Collins. "They're trying to get out of the way. Too late."

There was an explosion in the water, a geyser back near the carrier force. But Breanna was too busy to watch it.

"Long-range radar I can't ID," said Torbin.

"Indians?"

"Wrong direction," said the radar intercept officer. "I-band, okay. Woah, woah. APG-73—no way!"

"Torbin, what the hell are you talking about?"

"The radar—the computer is IDing the source as an F/A-18 unit. No way."

"One of those torpedoes hit the carrier, maybe two," said Chris.

"I have telemetry out near your contact," Collins told Torbin.

"I don't know what the hell kind of radar this is," said Torbin. "Shit. I mean, it could be an F/A-18. Chris?"

"No American flights within a hundred miles. I have nothing on radar. You sure about this?"

"Sure as shit."

"All right, everybody take a breath," Breanna said in her calmest command voice. "Fentress, did we sink that buoy?"

"Still trying to get the connection to the first one."

"Tell me when we're on."

"Explosion!" said Chris. "Carrier's hit."

"I need you to stay close to the buoy," said Fentress.

"Sukhois are trying to lock on us—we're spiked!" said Torbin. The RWR screen flashed with a warning as well, showing the bearing of the radar looking for them.

"Full ECMS," said Breanna. "Hang on, everyone."

Breanna threw the Megafortress into as sharp a turn as she could manage, dipping the wing and sliding in the direction of the buoy. Fentress, Collins, and Torbin all tried to speak at the same time; the computer gave her a warning that she was approaching maximum Gs. Breanna filtered everything out but the plane, trying to beam the Doppler-pulse radar that had locked on them. There was a missile warning—one of the Sukhois had launched.

"Chris, when you have a chance, broadcast the we're-the-white-hats message in every language you can think of," she said calmly.

"I am." His voice was three octaves higher than normal, which itself wasn't exactly a bass.

A silver needle shot across Quicksilver's bow, no more than fifty yards away. It was the missile.

"Optically aimed flak from that destroyer," said the co-pilot. "Way out of range."

"I see it," said Bree.

"Sukhois coming down through ten thousand feet. We're jamming. They're going to line up for an IR shot."

"Get the Stinger ready."

"On it."

"SAM radar active. I'm jamming," said Torbin.

"Fentress, we have to get moving here, friend," said Bree.

"I'm still having trouble with the link," he said. "We're

too high. I need you as close as you can get. The jinking's not helping."

"Getting shot down won't help either." She regretted snapping back like that, but there was no time to apologize—one of the ships launched antiaircraft missiles.

"SA-N-4, basically an SA-8 tweaked for shipboard use," reported Torbin. "We're at the far end of their envelope. Jamming."

"Chaff, flares, kitchen sink," she said.

Breanna began a turn, then realized she was moving toward the Sukhois. She pulled back on the stick abruptly, then twisted her left wing downward. The big jet did a half-gainer toward the waves, gravity and momentum pulling at its wings so badly, one of the sensors in the wing-root assembly freaked out. The alert board lit with possible structural damage and the computer squawked at her for exceeding the design limits of the plane—not an easy feat.

Breanna's body was pounded by the rush of Gs; she felt as if her head had been pounded by an anvil. A gray fuzz pushed in from her temples and something cold and prickly filled her lungs; she started to cough, but something scraped deep down in her throat. There were all sorts of warning lights now, but she rode the wild maneuver steady, forcing the plane through an invert as the Sukhoi she had spotted earlier fired its missiles from almost head-on. Fortunately, they were both heat-seekers, and despite their advertised all-aspect ability, were easily shunted by the flares Chris had managed to dish out into the air.

As the gray veil pulled back, Breanna saw a much darker one reaching up from the sea to smack her. Her maneuvers had taken her back toward the Chinese fleet. She was now dead-on for the flak; there was nothing to do but ride it out, struggling to keep the Megafortress level as they passed through the percolating air.

"Damage to our right wing," reported Chris. He was breathing hard. "Lost the Sukhoi at least."

"All right," said Bree, suddenly conscious of her own breathing. "Kevin, we need that connection, and we need it now."

"You have to get closer."

"They're launching more planes," reported Collins.

"Indians too. This is total war," said Chris. He was gasping for breath, hyperventilating.

"Dreamland Command to Quicksilver." Major Lou "Gat" Ascenzio's voice sounded a little tinny on her circuit; Breanna glanced at her com screen and saw that the message wasn't coded.

"Quicksilver."

"Get out of there."

"We're trying," she said. Then, remembering the line was in the clear—and hopefully being intercepted by the Chinese—she added, "We've taken no hostile act. We believe an Indian submarine fired torpedoes at a Chinese aircraft carrier."

"We confirm one hit and one near miss," said Gat. "Serious damage. Fires. Get out of there."

"Quicksilver," she said.

"I got it!" said Fentress.

"Sink the first buoy."

"I need you to get lower. Get over it."

"Bree," said Chris. He didn't have to say anything else; his meaning was clear—we have to leave *now*.

"I'm trying, Kevin," she told Fentress.

"Missiles in the air!" said Torbin.

Philippines
1840

"FUCK!"

Once again the video feed in his Flighthawk control helmet dissolved into a test screen. Zen slammed his fist on the console and leaned back, cursing.

"I know, I know," said Jennifer over the interphone.

She was in the bomb bay, helping one of the technicians adjust the link server. "We'll get it."

"Yeah," he said. He slid the headset back off his head, letting it fall around his neck. He was restless, frustrated.

It was more than the difficulties getting the Flighthawk linked back into the circuit—he could feel his heart pounding.

He thought of Bree.

He was pissed at her for acting like a jerk before.

That wasn't it.

She had been a jerk, but he wasn't pissed at her, not exactly.

He was worried about her.

He picked up the headset, put it back on. His heart pounded so badly, he could feel the phones reverberating against his ears.

"Hey, Jen, I'm going to take a break," he said.

"Okay."

"Yeah. I'm going to go get something to eat. Ring-Dings or something."

"Ring-Dings? I thought you couldn't stand Ring-Dings."

He couldn't—they were Bree's favorite pig-out food.

"I'm going to swing by the trailer and see what's up on the way," he told her.

"We'll have it ready by the time you get back."

Aboard Quicksilver
1840

A GIANT SNAKE WRAPPED ITSELF AROUND STONER'S body and squeezed, pushing his blood toward his mouth. He felt the warm liquid on his tongue, knowing he was forcing himself to breathe the long, quiet breath of purity. The universe collapsed on top of him, but Stoner sat as still as a pillar, remembering the advice of the bent old man who had taught him: you are the light of the candle, the flame that cannot be extinguished.

But no religion or philosophy, Eastern or Western, could overcome the simple, overwhelming urge of gravity. The plane jerked back and forth, trying desperately to avoid being hit while Fentress worked to sink both Piranha com buoys. He'd already managed to put the probe on the automated escape route—or at least that was how Stoner interpreted the groans and grunts he'd heard among the cacophony of voices in his earphones.

The sitrep was still on his screen. One of the carriers had been hit badly, though at least two planes had managed to get off in the chaos. Planes were swarming off the other. An Indian flight was coming north to meet them. There were missiles in the air, and flak all over the place. The destroyers on the eastern flank were attacking the submarine that had launched the torpedoes.

The lights in the cabin flashed off and on; there was a warning buzzer, another flash. The snake curled tighter.

Stoner pushed his hand to his face mask, making sure his oxygen was working. Two or three voices shouted at him from far away, urging him into the darkness. He forced his lungs to empty their oxygen slowly into the red flame of the candle in the center of his body.

Aboard *Shiva* in the South China Sea 1843

A FRESH ROUND OF DEPTH CHARGES EXPLODED OVER the conning tower; the submarine bobbed downward as if her namesake had smashed his powerful leg against its bow. Admiral Balin fell forward against the map table, then slid to the floor.

One of the electrical circuits had blown. It was impossible at the moment to assess the damage, but he would welcome death now. At least one of the torpedoes had exploded directly beneath the aircraft carrier; the damage would be overwhelming. The failure of the Kali weapons had been requited.

Calmly, Balin rose. Accepting fate did not mean wishing for death—he turned his attention to his escape.

Someone screamed nearby, seized by panic.

"There will be none of that," he said in a loud, calm tone before making his way toward the helmsman. "We will carry on as we were born to do. We will survive this."

Aboard the Dragon Ship in the South China Sea 1845

CHEN DID NOT WANT TO LOSE HIS DRAGON, BUT NOT even Lao Tze could have resisted watching the Chinese fleet reel under the attack. To see the glorious flames licking the side of the Communists' ship—how beautiful!

There was great danger in this vanity, however. The Chinese were launching missiles and firing guns in every direction, and even the American Megafortress was vulnerable. The Indians seemed to be en route as well.

The western horizon was covered with the dark clouds of an approaching rainstorm. Lightning flashed in the distance. Appropriate, thought Chen Lo Fann. Even the gods wanted to participate.

"We believe the American plane is tracking us," said Professor Ai.

"Return quickly," said Chen. "Issue the order to all of our forces. We have seen enough. We now wait the verdict of fortune."

Aboard Quicksilver 1845

"WE LOST ENGINE THREE," CHRIS TOLD HER.

Breanna didn't acknowledge. The Indian MiGs had sent a volley of missiles at long range at the Sukhois; there was so much metal in the sky now, it was impossible to avoid getting hit.

"It's sunk, it's sunk," said Fentress. "Both buoys are down!"

"Fighter on our tail," said Chris. "Out of air mines."

She could feel the bullets slicing into her, ripping across her neck. Breanna pushed the stick and stomped the pedals, trying to flip the big jet away from the fighter. But the Sukhoi was more maneuverable than the Megafortress, and the Chinese pilot was smart enough not to get too close or overreact. He wasn't that good a shot—maybe one out of four of his slugs found its target, a half dozen at a time—but he was content with that.

"Four's gone," said Chris.

"Restart."

"Trying."

Her warning panel was a solid bank of red. Part of the rear stabilizer had been shot away; they were leaking fuel from one of the main tanks. The leading-edge flap on the left wing wouldn't extend properly, complicating her attempts to compensate for the dead engines.

They were going in.

Breanna fought off the flicker of despair. She pushed herself toward the windscreen, as if she might somehow add her weight to the plane's forward momentum. The Sukhoi that had been dogging them passed off to the right; he'd undoubtedly run out of bullets, or fuel, or both.

About time they got a break.

Ahead, a jagged bolt of lightning flashed down from the clouds. It seemed to splatter into a million pieces as it hit the ocean, its electricity running off in every direction.

Zen, why aren't you here with me? I need you.

Jeffrey!

The altimeter ladder began to move—somehow the big Megafortress was managing to climb.

"Come on, baby," she told it. "Hang with me."

"I can't get four," said Chris, who'd been trying to restart the engine. "Fuel's bad. Fire in the bay. Fire—"

"Auto extinguish."

"I've tried twice," he said.

"Dump the AMRAAMS," she told him.

"No targets?"

"Let's not take sides at this point. Kevin—put Piranha in auto-return and sink the probe we just launched."

"Yes, ma'am."

As Chris fired one of the missiles, there was a slight shudder in the rear.

"Fire won't go out," the copilot told her. "I think the extinguisher system has been compromised."

"Okay," she said.

They absolutely had to go out, and they had to go out now.

"Dreamland Command, this is Quicksilver. Gat, you hear me?" she said over the Dreamland line.

There was no answer. It was possible the fire had already damaged the radio or antennas, but she tried again, then broadcast their position and that they were ditching.

"Bree, we're running out of fuel," said Chris. "And the temp is climbing. The fumes will explode."

"Prepare to eject," she told him. "Crew—prepare to eject."

The leading edge of the storm front punched at the persiplex glass in front of her. Windswept hail whipped in her face.

"I don't know if we're going to make it," said Chris.

The panic hit her then, panic and fear and adrenaline. Someone grabbed hold of her hair and pulled her up from her seat, dangling her in midair, twirling her around.

Jeff, honey, where the hell are you when I need you?

"Crew, listen to me," Breanna said calmly. "We're all going out together. Cinch your restraints. Put your legs and arms inside your body. Check in, everybody— Chris?"

"Ferris."

"Dolk."

"Collins."

"Fentress."

There was no answer from Stoner.

"Stoner?" she said.

Nothing.

"Stoner?"

"Engine two—" Chris started to tell her the engine had just died, but it was unnecessary—the thump jerked her so hard she nearly let go of the stick.

"Manage our fuel," she told him. "Fentress—where's Stoner?"

"He's here, he's here—his radio's out. He's ready."

"Crew, we're going out on three. I have the master eject, authorization Breanna Rap Bastian Stockard One One Rap One," she told the computer in her level voice.

The computer didn't answer, as if it were hesitating, as if it didn't want to lose its crew. Then it came back and repeated the authorization. All the seats would now be ejected when she pulled her handle; the Dreamland system would greatly increase the probability they could find each other after the chutes deployed.

"The weather's hell out there," she told her men. "Let the chutes deploy automatically. Just enjoy the ride."

Given the intensity of the storm they were flying into, it was probably suicidal to go out now. She reached for the throttle slide, pushing for more speed, hoping to maybe get beyond the storm, or at least through the worst of it.

"Fire in the Gat compartment," said Chris. "We're going to blow."

Breanna heard a rumble and then a pop from the rear of the plane. She reached down to the yellow handle at the side of her seat.

"Three-two-one," she said quickly, and the universe turned into a tornado.

VII
In the hands of the gods

Philippines
August 28, 1997, 1847

THE SCREEN BLANKED.

"Get them back," Zen told Bison.

"I'm not sure what's going on," said the sergeant sitting at the com panel.

Zen pushed his chair back and then forward at an angle, as if realigning himself would make the picture from Quicksilver reappear.

"Get them back," he said again, this time his voice softer.

"They're off-line," said Bison. "They were hit—they may be down."

Zen pushed backward and wheeled to the door. One of the two Navy people in the trailer said something, but Zen didn't hear the words and wasn't about to stop to ask him to repeat them. He had to reach awkwardly to open the door, pushing with his other hand on the wheel; he nearly fell out of his chair and down the ramp as he burst outside, downward momentum the only thing keeping him in the seat. He mastered it, got his balance, and continued to the oversized tent where Major Alou and the rest of the flight crew were just starting to brief for their mission. The fabric sides were rolled up.

"Merce—Quicksilver is down," said Zen. "We need Iowa now."

Without waiting for Major Alou to acknowledge, he wheeled back onto the path and headed for the aircraft.

It took nearly twenty minutes for the crew to get the Megafortress airborne. It was actually good time—the plane hadn't been refueled, and the work on meshing the Piranha and Flighthawk systems was far from complete. Every second stretched to torturous infinity.

In the air, the buffeting pressure of the fresh storm system held them back. Zen launched the Flighthawk and pushed ahead, scanning through the thick rain even though they were still a hundred miles from the coordinates of Quicksilver's last voice transmission. Other resources were being scrambled from the fleet, but at the moment they were the only ones on the scene, and certainly Bree's best chance.

The storm was so severe, both the Chinese and Indians had landed all of their planes. The thick cloud cover made it impossible for satellites to scan the ocean, and at points Zen had a difficult time seperating the waves from the muck he was flying through. Ten miles from the gray splatch of sky where Quicksilver had been lost, he felt his arms and shoulders sag. Zen leaned his head forward. The fatigue nearly crushed him, pounding his temples. He saw Bree on their wedding day, the blue and pink flowered dress tight against her hips in the small chapel. Her mouth trembled ever so slightly, and when the minister had her repeat the words of the vows, she hesitated over "richer or poorer."

Did not, she said that night, cuddled against his arms.

Did too, he told her.

Didn't, she said a thousand times later.

Too, he replied.

But there'd been no hesitation on sickness. Ever.

"Commencing visual search." Zen tightened his grip on

the U/MF's controls and pushed the plane through a reef of wind and rain. Clouds came at him in a tumble of fists; the small plane knifed back and forth as it fell toward the dark ocean. Finally, he broke through the worst of it, though this was only a matter of degree; at three thousand feet he found a solid sheet of rain. Leveling off, Zen gingerly nudged off his power. Not exactly optimized for slow flight in the best weather, the U/MF had trouble staying stable under two hundred knots in the shifting winds. Zen had his hands and head full, constantly adjusting to stay on the flight path. But he needed to go as slow as possible, since it increased the video's resolution and, more importantly, the computer's ability to scan the fleeting images for signs of the survivors.

At least concentrating on flying meant he couldn't think about anything else.

"Coming to the end of our search track," said the copilot above.

"Roger that. Turning," said Zen.

Zen selected IR view. The rain was too thick for it to fight through, and finally he decided to flip back to the optical view. Two long circuits took them slightly to the north. Iowa's look-down radar fought through the storm to scan the roiling waves, but the conditions were severe. Zen punched over the waves at just under a thousand feet, convinced the U/MF's video cams—and *his* eyes—were the best tools they had, at least for now.

A distress call came over the UHF circuit as one of the Sukhois ran out of fuel before he could complete a landing on his storm-shrouded carrier.

"Poor shit," said somebody over the interphone circuit without thinking.

Yeah, thought Zen to himself. *Poor shit.* Then he pushed the Flighthawk lower to the ocean.

Los Angeles International Airport
August 27, 1997, 0600 local (August 28, 2100 Philippines)

FLYING AS A PASSENGER ON A CIVILIAN AIRLINER WAS
bad enough, but Colonel Bastian had the bad luck to draw
an overly talkative seventy-year-old as a seatmate. The
woman spent roughly an hour detailing the cruise she had
just been on; when that topic was exhausted, she moved
on to the wallpaper she was putting in her bathroom, and
finally the oranges she had ordered for her daughter's upcoming birthday. Dog was too polite to tell her to shut
up. By the time he got off the plane, his ear had a permanent buzz; he knew if he checked in a mirror it would
be red.

He hadn't decided how to get over to Edwards; thinking
he might rent a car and drive, he headed in the direction
of the Hertz booth. On the way, his eye caught the fleeting
text on a TV screen set to deliver headline news.

"Fighting breaks out between China and India," said
the words.

Dog stopped so abruptly, a short man walking behind
him bumped into him with his suitcase. Instead of accepting the man's apology, he asked where the phones
were.

"Major Ascenzio has a jet en route," said Ax when Dog
dialed into Dreamland. "I'll transfer you down to him for
the details."

"Thanks, Ax."

"Colonel, one thing—Breanna was aboard the plane."

"What plane?" Dog asked.

For the first time since he'd known him, Chief Master
Sergeant Terrence "Ax" Gibbs was lost for words.

"What plane?" Dog demanded when he didn't answer.

"Quicksilver is down, sir."

Aboard Iowa, over the South China Sea
2308

TWICE ZEN THOUGHT HE FOUND SOMETHING, BUT THE brief flickers from the computer proved to be anomalies. Jennifer Gleason worked the freeze-frames back and forth silently, sometimes calling up the radar and IR scans on her own. But none of the sensors picked up anything substantial in the swirling torrent.

They refueled the small plane three times. Knocking off the refueling probe and diving through the thick storm, Zen felt as if he had plunged back into the underworld, battling the winds of hell. He funneled his eyes into the viewscreen, scanning with the computer, looking, looking, looking. The copilot kept track of the search tracks; his announcements of the approaching turns marked the time like a grandfather clock clanging on the quarter hour.

Zen saw nothing. The radar found nothing. Still he flew, back and forth across the angry ocean, repeating the tracks.

In sickness and in health, she'd said. And she'd meant it.

"Jeff, we're about three ounces from bingo." Major Alou's voice sounded as if he were speaking from the other end of a wide pipe.

"Where's our tanker?"

"There are no tankers," said Alou. "The storm's too much and we're too far. There's no choice—we have to get down. I've already stretched it out."

Zen didn't answer.

"There's a Navy P-3 out of Japan due in twenty minutes," he told him. "They're going to continue the search. As soon as the carrier can launch more planes, they'll have another search package out. The F-14's will stay over the area in the meantime. They'll hear a transmission."

Who the hell would manage to use a radio in this?

"Jeff, we'll find her. They will, or we will. But we have

to go. We'll be out of the storm at least, so we can refuel and take off right away. It may be far east. Okay?"

"Yeah, Roger that."

**Dreamland
0936 local**

THE FLIGHT FROM LAX TO DREAMLAND WAS QUICK—Ax had sent an F-15E, and the pilot, Major Mack Smith, had probably broken the speed barrier twenty feet off the tarmac. Ax met Dog in a Jimmy SUV as the airplane taxied toward the hangar; the truck whipped over to Taj so fast Dog never got his seat belt buckled. Even the notoriously slow elevator seemed to understand this was a real emergency; it started downward three seconds after Dog touched the button for the subbasement level where the command center was located.

Major Ascenzio, Ray Rubeo, and about a half-dozen mission specialists were waiting for him.

Rubeo stepped up and started to talk, telling the colonel they shared his concern for his daughter and the rest of the crew. The scientist was not only sincere, but actually seemed on the brink of becoming emotional—a development so out of character Dog felt worse than before.

"Thanks, Doc. Thanks, everybody. Let's get to work. Who's searching, what have we heard?"

"Iowa's just knocking off for fuel," said Gat. Major Ascenzio reached down to his desk and hit a key; a diagram of the search area appeared on the main screen at the front of the room. They had used data from Quicksilver's transmissions to plot its probable flight path after it was hit. Because of the clouds and Quicksilver's altitude and position, there was no usable information from the Crystal asset—a KH-12 satellite—covering the area, but there was some possibility a satellite used to monitor missile launches might have picked up explosions aboard the plane; they had a query in to the National Reconaissance Office to see. That information might help them tweak their search area, though Gat felt they had a decent handle on it.

One thing the major didn't mention: Like much of the rest of the Air Force, Dreamland's standard survival equipment included the PRC-90 survival radio. While the radio was a time-tested veteran, it had a limited range and was hardly state-of-the-art equipment. Newer versions utilizing satellite communications were hard to come by—a ridiculous budget constraint that might have proved fatal for Captain Scott O'Grady in Bosnia two years before. O'Grady's heroism and resourcefulness notwithstanding, a more powerful radio with a locator would have shortened his ordeal considerably.

"We'll find them," said Gat. "A P-3 from the Pacific Fleet is en route."

"That's it?" said Dog.

"The weather is fierce," said Gat. "Hurricane winds, hail, the works. Half the Pacific is covered by it. The carriers can't launch aircraft."

Dog folded his arms. The storm had even more serious implications for the people who had parachuted—if they parachuted—from the plane. Even if they somehow got into the water without injury, climbing into a life raft in mountainous seas could be an almost impossible task. And once you were in it—hell, you might just as well go over Niagara Falls in a barrel.

"PacCom has lost at least one plane as well," said Gat. "The storm is that bad. They feel they'll be in a better position by tomorrow afternoon."

"Tomorrow afternoon? Fuck that. Fuck that!"

The words flew from his mouth like meteors, spitting down on everyone in the room.

"We need to organize the search," said Dog, not apologizing. "We have three planes—two planes." He caught himself. His breath was racing but he couldn't corral it. "We'll run eight-hour missions out of the Philippines."

"Raven's not ours," Gat said. "And besides, the storm there is incredible. *Kitty Hawk* had to curtail operations,

I had Major Alou divert all the way over to Japan."

"Why didn't he just refuel in the air and continue the search?"

"We didn't have a tanker available."

"Punch me through to Woods."

"Yes, sir." Gat grimaced. "It'll be voice-only."

"Yeah, okay." Dog wasn't mad at Gat—he wasn't even mad at Woods, but he nonetheless barked at the Navy lieutenant who came on the line.

"Where's our search team?"

"Excuse me, sir, this is Lieutenant Santiago. The admiral is tied up."

"I understand that," said Dog. He pushed his arms tighter to his chest, as if by holding himself he could calm down. "I need help searching for my people."

"We have a plane en route. I'm in charge of—"

"Get Admiral Woods for me," said Dog.

"Uh—"

"Just do it."

The line went dead for a moment.

The others in the room were trying to be discreet, but he knew they were watching him. He had to fight for his people—even if it wasn't his daughter who'd gone down, he had to do everything he could to get them back.

"We have our hands full here, Colonel," said Woods, his voice snapping through the speakers. "I understand the difficult position you're in, but I've lost another plane as well, and one of our destroyers was fired on inadvertently—at least we think inadvertently—by the Indians. One of our submarines has missed two scheduled transmissions, and at least one helicopter is an hour overdue. In the meantime, the Chinese ships up near Taiwan are in a frenzy. We are looking for your people, Tecumseh. They're one of our priorities, just not the only one. The storm is complicating everything."

"My plane on the Philippines can get around the storm," said Dog.

"Those are my planes," said Woods. "Now I'm not going to press the point, but Major Alou and his crew took off without orders and without authorization. Granted, it was an emergency, and I certainly would have approved— but that will not happen again. Those are my assets. I need to be able to control what's going on, and that requires—"

Dog cut the connection. It was either that or punch something.

Rubeo broke the silence. "I have a suggestion," said the scientist.

"And?"

"The UMB is due for a flight in six hours. We can use it to conduct the search. The mini-KH photo package is already scheduled for telemetry tests—completely unnecessary, I might add, given that we've already proven it works without flaw."

"It won't see through the storm," said Dog.

"The imaging radar will. By coincidence, it happens to have been loaded into the plane just prior to your arrival. Merely to see if the double load would fit. The aircraft has to go up anyway. We are merely speaking here of an inconsequential change in the flight plan."

Dog considered the situation. The mini-KH gear not only could identify an object .3 meters in size—roughly a foot—but placed in the B-5, it could train its sensors wherever they wanted, without having to worry about the complications of earth orbit and maneuvering in space. Launching the plane and flying it over the Pacific was completely within his purview as Dreamland commander. There was only one problem—the UMB's pilot went down in Quicksilver.

"The computer can fly it," said Rubeo, anticipating Dog's objection.

"We need a pilot," said Dog. "Maybe Mack Smith—"

"Piffle." Rubeo's face contorted. "Smith would have it rolling into the ocean within minutes. Colonel, the computer can fly it. That's what it's designed to do."

"I want someone at the controls."

"Naturally. I'll be at the controls, with Fichera as backup," said Rubeo. "Along with the rest of the team. Precisely as designed. This is what the system was created for."

"Where's Zen?"

"Why Zen?"

"He's flown the B-5."

"He merely guided the computer by voice. As far as that goes, he's no more competent than I. Frankly, Colonel, I not only have considerably more experience flying the aircraft, but—"

"No offense, Doc, but I want a combat pilot at the controls." Dog turned to the lieutenant handling the communications panel. "Get Major Stockard."

"Colonel—"

"We've been over this, Ray. I appreciate your getting it ready—that was damn sharp of you. But I want an experienced pilot making the call when the shit hits the fan. The scramjets—they're still a problem?"

"They function within parameters."

"Plan the flight without using them."

"That's overly cautious," said Rubeo. "The problem was in sensors. They're due to be tested on the flight."

"Then set it up so that they're used on the back end of the flight—on the return to Dreamland."

"There's no reason not to use them in-flight," insisted Rubeo.

"If they fail we'll have to return home."

Rubeo's face paled ever so slightly. "As you wish," he said.

"Major Stockard is on the line, sir. They're just landing on Okinawa," said the lieutenant.

"It'll take ten or twelve hours to get here," said Rubeo.

"Eight," said Gat.

Ascenzio's voice surprised Dog—he'd actually forgotten the others were in the room.

"Hardly," hissed Rubeo. "But even if it were only eight, you want to lose all that time? We can have the UMB off the main runway in four hours, perhaps even less."

"Zen doesn't have to be here, does he?" asked Dog. "If he's guiding by voice. You just have to work out a connection, right?"

"It's not that simple." Rubeo frowned, then put his finger on his small gold earring. "I'd have to talk to Dr. Gleason. Maybe," he added, as if reluctant to concede his assistant would have the final say. "The communication protocols—if we use the channels reserved for the extra Flighthawks, and reprogram them into the network. Maybe. Yes."

"Put Major Stockard on the screen."

His son-in-law's helmeted face came on the screen. Zen was still piloting a Flighthawk and had his visor down; he looked a bit like a race car driver in his crash cage, head bobbing left and right before he spoke. "Stockard."

"Jeff, I want to talk with you, Major Alou, and Jennifer Gleason," said Dog. "Dr. Rubeo has an idea—"

"This is not exactly my idea," said Rubeo.

"*I* have an idea," said Dog. The others plugged into the line and he laid it out.

"I think we can do it," said Jennifer. "We may even be able to use the Flighthawk controls for limited maneuverability."

"Don't get fancy," said Dog. "There's no time."

"It's not fancy—we built the control section from the same module; it's meant to be portable."

"That storm's pretty fierce," said Zen.

"The KH Storm and Eyes modules are to be tested," said Rubeo, using the nicknames for the sensor arrays. "We'll see anything we want to see."

"Can I see them on my screens?" asked Zen.

"That part's easy," said Jennifer.

"Voice commands can be issued by myself—or even you, Colonel," said Rubeo. "There's no need to create a camel here—with all due respect to Major Stockard, I'd imagine he's tired."

"I'm fine."

"I want a combat pilot at the controls," insisted Dog. "Major Alou, Admiral Woods may call you to assist other missions. Could you accomplish them while you're handling this?"

"I don't know that we can be in two places at one time," said Major Alou.

"You won't have to be," said Jennifer. "It'll be just like a regular mission with Flighthawks—except you won't have to stay close to the UMB. We can do it, Tecumseh."

Her use of his name paralyzed him; he felt a strange mix of love and fear.

"Ray," she continued, "on the Piranha translation module, the 128 processor—"

"Yes. The assembler will—"

"But we won't need the weapons section."

"That's where we're routing the KH radar unit."

"I can do it, I can do it. We can use the channels reserved for the helmets. I can do it!"

"Don't play the schoolgirl."

"All right, listen," said Dog. "Major Alou—you land your plane, gas up, take off ASAP. Dr. Gleason and Doc—" He pointed at Rubeo. "See what you can work out. I want a go, no-go recommendation in two hours. Less if possible."

"It's go," said Zen.

"I appreciate the sentiment," said Dog.

"What do I do if I'm given a mission before then?" asked Major Alou.

"Take it," said Zen.

"We need to be on the ground for at least two hours," said Jennifer. "Maybe a little more."

"It'll take a while to refuel," said Alou. "And the weather may delay us too."

"Two hours, go or no-go," said Dog. "Let's get to work."

Aboard Iowa
August 29, 1997, 0207 local (August 28, 1997, 1107
Dreamland)

ZEN CHECKED THE INSTRUMENTS ON FLIGHTHAWK ONE, preparing to land on Okinawa. Jennifer was bouncing up and down next to him, already working out the problems on one of her laptop computers. He could feel her adrenaline rush, the excitement that came with facing the impossible, the sureness it could be overcome.

He'd heard it in their voices back at Dreamland too. They all had it. Even Rubeo, despite grousing that the computers would do a better job than Zen could.

The one thing they hadn't talked about was that Bree and the others were very likely dead already, blown to bits in the plane.

Which was why they didn't talk about it.

Somewhere in the South China Sea
Time and date unknown

SHE WAS THE RAIN, SOAKING THEM. SHE WAS THE WIND sheering through their skulls. She was the tumult of the ocean, heaving her chest to plunge them into the black, salty hell, then lifting them up into the pure gray clouds. Again and again she twirled them back and forth, lashing them in every direction until she became them all, and they became her.

When Breanna Stockard pulled the handle on the ejection seat, time and space had merged. She now occupied all possible times and all possible places—the moment of the ejection seat exploding beneath her, the storm reaching down to take her from the plane, the universe roaring at her pointlessness.

She could see the canopy of the parachute. She could see the ocean collapsing around her. She could feel her helmet slamming against the slipstream; she could smell the rose water of a long-ago bath.

Somehow, the raft had inflated.

Stoner had saved her with his strong arms, pulling against the chute that wouldn't release, but that finally, under his tugging, did release. Breanna had pulled at Ferris, who bobbed helmetless before her, but it had been Stoner who grabbed her. It was Stoner who disappeared.

She was the roll of the ocean and the explosion that sent them from the airplane. She was the storm soaking them all.

STONER FELT HIS FINGERS SLIPPING AGAIN. THEY wouldn't close. The best he could manage was to punch his hands on the raft, shifting his weight slightly as the wave swelled up. It threw him sideways and, whether because of good luck, or God, or just coincidence, the momentum of the raft and the swell threw him back into the small float, on top of the two pilots. Water surged up his nostrils; he shook his head violently, but the salt burned into his chest and lungs. Fortunately, he didn't have anything left to puke.

The sea pushed him sideways and his body slipped downward. An arm grabbed his just as he went into the water. In the tumult, it wasn't clear whether he pulled his rescuer into the sea or whether he'd been hooked and saved; lightning flashed and he realized he was on his back, lying across the other two, the man and the woman.

"Lash ourselves together," he told them, the rain exploding into his face. "Keep ourselves together until the storm ends."

The others moved, but not in reaction to what he said. They were gripping on to the boat, holding again as the waves pitched them upward.

"We can make it," he said. "We'll lash ourselves together."

He reached for his knife at his leg, thinking he would use it to cut his pants leg into a rope. As he did, he touched bare skin on his leg.

They'd already tied themselves together. Somehow, in the nightmare, he'd forgotten.

Aboard the Dragon Ship in the South China Sea
August 29, 1997, 0800

THE MESSAGE WAS NOT ENTIRELY UNEXPECTED, BUT IT nonetheless pained Chen Lo Fann greatly. In language bereft of polite formulas and its usual ambiguity, the government demanded an explanation for the activities of the past few days that "led to this dangerous instability."

Dangerous instability. An interesting phrase.

Obviously, the Americans were making their presence felt. Peace was in the American interest, not theirs; true Chinese prayed for the day of return, the reinstatement of the proper government throughout all of the provinces of China. Inevitably, this war would lead to the destruction of the Communists.

The angry gods of the sea had thrown a typhoon against the two fleets, halting their battle after a few opening salvos. In the interim, the Americans, the British, and the UN had all stepped up their efforts to negotiate peace.

Surely that would fail. The Communists had lost an aircraft carrier and countless men. The storm would multiply the damage done to their ships. They would want revenge.

The Indians too would fight. They understood this battle was about their survival. If the Chinese and their Islamic allies were not stopped, the Hindus would be crushed.

Chen Lo Fann stood on the bridge as the storm lashed against the glass and rocked the long boat mercilessly. He had always understood that, as necessary as they were, the Americans were not, at heart, their brothers. When their interests did not coincide, they would betray his country—as Nixon had shown a generation earlier, bringing the criminals into the UN.

Lao Tze had spoken of this:

The gods of heaven and earth show no pity. Straw dogs are forever trampled.

Now, his government was making him the straw dog. He needed leverage.

The American Megafortress had been shot down; undoubtedly its crew was dead. Americans were charmingly emotional about remains; a body or two, handled with the proper military honors, would go a long way toward insuring his position. Even an arm or leg. Such could be found and prepared if the authentic article were not available.

Two of his ships were in the area. As soon as the storm abated, they would begin the search. After a short interval, they would find what they were looking for, one way or another.

Meanwhile, he would sail for Taiwan, as ordered.

Or perhaps not.

Aboard Iowa
August 29, 1997, 1036 local (August 28, 1997, 1936 Dreamland)

"Not there, Jen," Zen told her.

"I'm working on it."

Jennifer jammed the function keys on her IBM laptop, trying to get the requested program data to reload. Zen tapped anxiously on the small ledge below his flight controls. He was usually very good at corralling his frustration—to survive as a test pilot you had to be—but today he was starting to fray.

Of course he was. If it was Tecumseh instead of Breanna down there, she'd be twenty times worse.

This ought to work—the program simply needed to know what frequency to try, that was *all* it needed, and she had it right on the screen.

It had accepted the array—she knew it had because when she looked at her dump of the variables, they were all filled.

So what the hell was the screwup?

Shit damn fuck and shit again.

"Dreamland Command—hey, Ray," she said, banging her mike button on. "What the hell could be locking me out?"

"The list is exhaustive," replied the scientist.

"Yeah, but what the hell could be locking me out?"

"You're not being locked out," he said. "The connection gets made. The handoff just isn't completed."

She picked up one of the two small laptops from the floor of the plane, sitting it over the big IBMer in her lap. It was wired into the circuit and set to show the results of the coding inquiries. Data was definitely flowing back and forth; something was keeping it from feeding into the Flighthawk control system.

The security protocols of C^3 maybe? The system had a whole series of protocols and traps to keep out intruders. Even though the UMB plug-ins were being recognized as "native," it was possible that, somewhere along the way, they weren't kicking over the right flag.

She'd put them in after C^3 was up. Maybe if she started from scratch.

Right?

Maybe.

But, God, that would take forever.

Kill the Flighthawk. They wouldn't use it anyway, right?

That would save shitloads of time.

"Jeff, I'm going to try something, but to do it, I have to knock the Flighthawk off-line. You won't be able to launch."

"Do it."

"I guess I should check with Major Alou in case, you know, it interferes with her mission."

"Just do it."

She guessed he'd be angry, but she went ahead and talked to Alou anyway.

"We won't need the Flighthawk," Alou told her. "Go ahead."

"We're doing an adequate job from here," said Rubeo when she told him what she had in mind. "We're already over the Pacific."

"I think this might work."

"You still have to take the computer off-line, enter new code, then reboot it. Twenty minutes from now, you'll still be in diagnostic mode."

"I'll skip the tests."

"How will you know you load right?"

"It'll work or it won't. If it doesn't, what have I lost?"

She found an error in one of the vector lines before taking the system down. She fixed it, then began the lengthy-procedure.

"Want a soda?" Zen asked, pulling off his helmet.

"Love one, but—"

"I got it," he said. He undid his restraints, pulled over his wheelchair—it was custom-strapped nearby—and then maneuvered himself into it. She'd seen him do this before, but never in the air. He looked awkward, vulnerable.

Would she have the guts to do that if she'd been paralyzed?

"We got Pepsi, Pepsi, and more Pepsi. All diet. Which do you want?" asked Zen.

"Pepsi."

"Good choice."

TEN MINUTES LATER, C^3 gave her a series of beeps— at one point she'd wanted to program in "Yankee Doodle" as the "I'm up" signal, but Rubeo had insisted—and then filled the screens with its wake-up test pattern.

Two minutes later, Zen shouted so loud she didn't need the interphone.

"I'm in. I'm there. I have a view." He worked the keyboard in front of the joysticks. "Wow. All right. This is going to work. I can select the still camera, and I have a synthesized radar. At least that's what it says."

She glanced over and saw his hand working the joystick. "Woo—this is good."

"Magnification on mini-KH Eye?" asked Jennifer. She couldn't dupe the optical feed on her screen yet—she had to get the feedback through Dreamland's circuit—but she did have a control window with the raw numbers showing whether it was focused.

Rubeo was cursing over the Dreamland circuit, using words she'd never heard from his mouth before.

"Ray?"

"I've lost the visual feeds, the synthetic radar, everything. Damn it, we're blind here."

"I can see," said Zen.

"Well, we can't," insisted Rubeo. "Jennifer, kill the program now."

"Hold on," said Colonel Bastian over the circuit. "Major Stockard, do you have control of the aircraft?"

"Yes, sir."

"I can override it here," said Rubeo.

"Jeff, we'll back you up, but you're the one I want on the line."

"Colonel, I don't believe that's necessary," said Rubeo.

"I want a pilot in the plane," said Colonel Bastian. Jennifer recognized the words—they were the colonel's mantra in his debates with Rubeo over the future of air warfare.

"He's not *in* the plane," said Rubeo.

"Close enough," said Dog.

Somewhere in the South China Sea
Time and date unknown

THE BLUR COALESCED INTO LUMPS OF REALITY, LIKE THE precipitate in a test-tube solution. The lumps had shiny edges, crystalline pieces—her head pounding in her helmet, a body pulling off the side of the raft, the waves turning from black to an opaque green.

Breanna's flight suit felt both sodden and stiff. She pushed her hands down, felt the ocean giving way beneath her—she was on a raft, a survival raft.

They were in the ocean. The storm was passing beyond them.

Were they alive?

Slowly, she reached to take off her helmet. Her fingers groped for several seconds before she realized she'd pulled it off earlier.

Breanna managed to sit up. The air felt like salt in her lungs, but she breathed deeply anyway.

Chris Ferris lay curled against the side of the raft. She leaned toward him, felt something heavy fall against her back—Stoner was sprawled against her, legs trailing into the water.

She pulled at Stoner's thighs, trying to haul them up over the side. She got one, but not the other, finally decided that would have to do.

A PRC-90 emergency radio lay beneath Stoner's calf. As Breanna reached for it, she felt something spring in her back, a muscle tearing. Pain shot from her spine to her fingers, but she managed to pick up the radio. She stared at it, her eyes barely focusing. It took a moment to remember how to use voice—even though it was only a matter of turning a small, well-marked switch—then held it to her head.

"Captain Breanna Stockard of Dreamland Quicksilver looking for any aircraft," she said. "Looking for any aircraft—any ship. We're on the ocean."

She let go of the talk button, listening for an answer. There wasn't even static.

The earphone?

Long gone. Was there even one?

A Walkman she'd had as a child.

Breanna held the PRC-90 down in her hand, staring at the controls, trying to make the radio into a familiar thing.

On the right side there was a small dial switch, with the settings marked by a very obvious white arrow. There were only four settings; the top, a voice channel, was clearly selected. The volume slider, at the opposite side of the face, was at the top.

Madonna was singing. She was twelve.

Snoop Doggy Dog. Her very first boyfriend liked that.

Breanna broadcast again. Nothing.

Switching to the bottom voice channel, she tried again. This time too she heard nothing.

Shouldn't she hear static at least?

The spins—they'd listen for her at a specific time.

The hour on the hour or five past or ten past or twelve and a half past?

She couldn't remember when she was supposed to broadcast. She couldn't think. The salt had gotten into her brain and screwed it up.

Just use the damn thing.

Breanna pushed the dial to beacon mode, then propped the radio against Stoner so that the antenna was pointing nearly straight up.

Was the radio dead? She shook it, still not completely comprehending. She picked it back up, flipped to talk mode, transmitted, listened.

Nothing.

"Chris, Chris," she said, turning back to her copilot. "Hey—you all right?"

"Mama," he said.

She laughed. Her ribs hurt and her eyes stung and all the muscles in her back went spastic, but she laughed.

"Mama," he repeated.

"I don't think so," Bree told him softly. She patted him gently. Chris moaned in reply.

"Sleep," she said. "There's no school today."

**Aboard *Shiva* in the South China Sea
1102 local**

THE STORM AND HIS ENEMY'S INEPTNESS, AS MUCH AS his skill and the crew's dedication, had saved them. Sitting below the cold layer of water just below test depth, waiting forever, listening to the enemy vessels pass—Admiral Balin had known they would survive. They sat there silently, pacing their breaths, so quiet the sea gods themselves would surely think they had disappeared. The admiral waited until the very last moment to surface, remaining in the deep until the batteries were almost completely gone. In the foul air he had begun to hallucinate, hearing voices; if they had not been congratulating him for his glory, he might have thought they were real.

A light rain fell; they were on the back end of the enormous storm. The waves pushed the low-sitting submarine violently, but the weather that hid them was welcome.

"Every man, a turn topside," he told Captain Varja.

Varja nodded solemnly.

The crew needed to thoroughly inspect the vessel, but to Admiral Balin's mind, no matter what they found, the damage was minor. At worst, a few more vents on the tanks were out of order; he still had his engines, propeller, and diving planes.

And he still had two torpedoes.

There was another carrier, and at least one large ship, a cruiser, several escorts. He would pursue his enemies until all his weapons and energy were gone, even if it meant death. For what was death but a promise of another rebirth? The next life would strive even higher after this glorious triumph of the soul.

"We will continue east, with our best speed," he told the captain.

Varja hesitated.

"Do you disagree the enemy lies there?" asked Balin mildly.

The question seemed to take the captain by surprise. He considered it for a second, then shook his head. Within moments, the submarine began to come about.

Aboard Iowa over the South China Sea
1102

SHE WAS THERE, SOMEWHERE THERE. ZEN ROLLED HIS head around his neck, trying to loosen his muscles. Flying the UMB was easier than flying the Flighthawk. In truth, he wasn't actually flying the aircraft. He was more like an overseer, making sure the computer did what it was programmed to do.

And it always did, precisely to the letter.

The computer had a detailed and rather complicated three-dimensional flight plan worked out for the search pattern. Starting at a peak of 180,000 feet—roughly thirty-four miles high—the UMB spiraled downward across the search grid to precisely sixty thousand feet above sea level. At that point, it ignited the rocket motor and began to climb again, once more spiraling upward. Zen's primary concern was monitoring the speed, since as the UMB dropped it began to lose some of its stability; it was hampered by its inability to use the scramjets to maintain airspeed through the "low" supersonic flight regimes.

He was the only one with real-time direct access to the plane's native sensors; Jennifer had spent the hours since their takeoff trying to work out the problems in the link, but still didn't have a solution. Rubeo had to content himself with the slightly delayed KH feeds; he wasn't particularly happy and shared his displeasure freely.

They had pinned down the point where the Megafortress went into the ocean, about 150 miles west of the Chinese task force. A close examination of the debris on the water, while confirming it was Quicksilver, failed to turn up any survivors.

Or bodies.

If they'd gone out somewhere before the plane hit the water—and as far as Zen was concerned, that was the only possibility—they should be somewhere between the impact point and their last transmission location. They had now carefully mapped the entire area, and even accounted for the effects of the wind and stormy sea, but there was nothing there.

According to the computer, there was enough fuel to continue the search for another six hours. As far as Zen was concerned, he could sit here for a week.

But what was the sense of going over and over the same territory? Obviously, they were looking in the wrong place, but Zen wasn't sure where the right place was.

Iowa, meanwhile, rode a surveillance track to the east of the battered Chinese fleet. The damaged carrier had sunk sometime during the night at the height of the storm; two of the destroyers were tied up together, apparently to help repair damage on one of the vessels. The Chinese were not in a good mood. Twice their aircraft had warned off Alou in rather abrupt English, though she had come no closer than thirty miles from the escort screen. In accordance with her orders, she moved off as directed. Iowa's position did not affect Zen or the UMB.

"How are we doing?" Alou asked as Iowa reached the southernmost point of her patrol area.

"We're just about done," Zen told him.

"Nothing, huh?"

"I think the problem is we're assuming they were flying a more or less straight line."

Alou didn't answer. Zen wasn't sure what he expected him to say, but the silence angered him.

He switched abruptly into the Dreamland channel, where scientist Greg Meades had taken over com duties for the UMB team.

"We have to shift the search area," Zen told him.

"We've re-created the route they were flying," said the scientist. "Based on our data."

"Then the re-creation is wrong. If she was ducking back

and forth, trying to avoid getting shot down, her path could be very different than what we computed."

"Could be," said Meade, though it was obvious he wasn't convinced.

"Let's try farther to the southwest. The plane could have swung back fifty miles, a hundred before they punched out."

"Yes, sir."

"You don't have to humor me," said Zen. He snapped the talk button off, then pushed it again. "I'm sorry. Set up a new search area, assuming they would have tried to go south as soon as they were hit."

Philippines
1130

DANNY FREAH CLEARED HIS THROAT. "ALL RIGHT, LIS-ten up," he told the eight men standing in front of the Dreamland MV-22. "We're backup to the main team. Routine SAR mission. Latest intel is this—beacon believed from the Seahawk lost in the storm was heard, and we have a location that's roughly a hundred miles from here. Other assets are already en route. Our speed's going to get us there quick, though, so we may get into the mix, especially if they run into trouble. There's a small island in the area, and it's possible—small possibility—there may be other people there. If that happens, we're definitely in the mix. Otherwise, what we're doing primarily is using our eyes. Okay? Not a big deal. Just backups." Danny paused. "You Marines who haven't come with us before—welcome aboard."

Danny smiled at the five Marine privates who had been detailed to fill out his squad. The oldest looked like he'd be eligible to shave in a year or so.

"A little word of advice," Danny continued, "because I'm not really going to get a chance to give a pep talk if things get hot. I know how much everybody here, my guys especially, like pep talks."

Bison and Pretty Boy were both grinning. Good to see them smiling after losing Powder.

"Your adrenaline's going to pump like crazy, your heart's gonna thump, you're going to want to get right in the mix," Danny said, addressing the young Marines. "I want you to stay within yourself, do your job. Listen to the sergeants. I don't want any heroes—I want men who follow orders. Basically, I want *Marines*. Got it?"

The kids nodded.

Did he want heroes? Of course he did. He wanted Powder. And Liu out of the hospital.

Turn the other cheek? Bullshit on that.

So what the hell had Powder done that for? Had that passage read at his funeral?

"All right," said Danny. "Let's kick ass. Blow, load 'em up."

"All aboard," said Sergeant "Blow" Hernandez, using an exaggerated train conductor's voice.

The Osprey pilot started the aircraft down the runway about a half-second after the hatch snapped shut. Danny cinched his seat restraints, then methodically took stock of his equipment. He'd done so on the ground—twice. Ordinarily, he didn't worry himself into a mission, but today the review was soothing. He checked his pistols, first his service Beretta, then his personal Sig. He inventoried his grenades, checked his watch and the backup battery for his smart helmet. He ran his fingers over the smooth surface of the outer shell of the helmet. He retied his boots, pulling hard on the laces.

"Two minutes, Captain," said the Osprey crew chief, relaying the message from the pilots.

"All right boys, we're just about on station," Danny said. He took the aircraft headphones, got up, and braced himself so he could see out the side windows. The sea was now so calm it looked as if it had been rolled out flat by a steam roller.

In the distance, he could see a dark blue Navy helicopter, part of the SAR team.

His own people had gone down somewhere about an hour north. But the odds were overwhelming they were dead; they'd gone down in the teeth of the storm.

Were the odds any worse than for the Seahawk?

"Navy's coming up blank," the Osprey pilot said. "We're going to start crisscrossing northwest of the area where they think the signal came from."

"Sounds good," Danny told him. He told his guys what was happening, got them up looking out the windows.

"Tradition has it," Danny told them, "that a downed pilot owes every member of the rescue team a case of beer. I'll double that for the man who spots them first."

"Kick ass, Captain," said Powder.

Danny turned in shock toward the back of the Osprey. He'd heard Powder's voice—absolutely heard Powder's voice.

"Who said that?"

No one spoke.

"I'm sorry," said Danny. "Was there a question?"

They were looking at him as if he'd seen—or heard—a ghost.

"All right then, let's put our eyes to good use," he said, struggling to raise his voice over the hum of the engines.

The South China Sea
Date and time unknown

THEY HAD TWO BOTTLES OF WATER BETWEEN THE three of them, four "nutrition" bars, a working flare gun, and a radio. Chris Ferris had managed to save his pistol, but had inexplicably lost one of his boots. Breanna Stockard had her knife. Stoner had his compass.

Injury-wise, they were in decent shape, considering what they'd been through. Ferris probably had broken a rib, but otherwise claimed he was fine. Breanna had torn muscles in her back and shoulder, and had possibly broken her left tibia. Stoner had sprained both wrists and could only partially close his numb fingers. All three of them had black eyes and various cuts and bruises on the heads. Their memories of what had happened since they ejected were mostly blank and in any event, irrelevant.

As were the fates of the rest of the crew, though Breanna insisted on scanning the water for them.

"Glare's going to kill your eyes," Stoner told her.

"Yeah," she said, then kept on looking. He admired that kind of stubbornness. He also admired her toughness—not a hint of a whimper.

Their water would be gone in twenty-four hours, maybe less. They'd agreed to rationing a sip apiece on the hour, but the sun was climbing and Stoner knew that the sips would become gulps within a few hours.

Making it through the day and into the night was a realistic goal. They'd shoot for that. Twelve, fourteen hours of search time—that was the best they could hope for anyway. What they needed was something to do, something to keep them sharp.

"I think we should paddle," he said.

Breanna turned toward him. Something happened with her eyes—she blinked as if reaching into his brain, then nodded.

She understood.

She was beautiful, wasn't she? Her raven hair and soft lips, her blue-white skin—if he squinted she could be a mermaid, singing to a drowning sailor.

"We don't have paddles," she said.

"We can use our hands."

"We can kick," said Chris Ferris, the copilot. "Like we're swimming."

"Tire us out," said Stoner.

"We'll take shifts. I'll take the first." He pulled up his legs and untied his boot.

"What do you think happened to your other boot, Chris?" Breanna asked.

"I think I ate it," said the copilot. He started to undo his vest to take off his flight suit.

"Want strip-tease music?" asked Breanna.

"How does that go?" Chris asked, then immediately began humming, or trying to hum, appropriate music. He kept it up as he got down to his underwear, which he kept on in the water. His right leg and arm were almost entirely black with bruises.

"That direction," said Stoner, pointing west. "We'll head toward the Chinese and Indians. More people to look for us."

Ferris eased himself into the water. He claimed it felt good, though it was obviously colder than he'd expected. He began doing a scissors kick. "I used to be on the swim team," he told them.

This was going to get old very quickly.

"I have a question," said Stoner after Ferris grew silent. "Why Rap?"

"Short for Rapture," said Breanna. "My mom was a hippie. It was either that or Acid Girl."

"Really?"

"No. Mom's pretty straight actually. She's a doctor. Long story."

"That's good," said Stoner. "Maybe they'll come looking for us."

"They'll definitely come looking for us," said Ferris from the water.

"A hotshot F-15 jock called me 'Rapture' a million years ago, right after I waxed his fanny in a Red Flag exercise. I was flying a B-52 at the time."

"That's a good thing, right?"

"Flying the B-52 or waxing his fanny?"

"Both."

"Both." She laughed. "He was trying to pick me up, I think. So I shot him down twice. How about you?"

"I'm not trying to pick you up."

"I mean, are you married?"

"No." Stoner laughed.

"What's so funny? Marriage is a good thing."

"Good how?"

"In all the ways you'd expect."

"I'm not sure I expect any ways," he told her, staring into her eyes. The raft was so small their faces were perhaps eight inches apart. If he wanted, he could lean forward and touch his mouth to her lips.

He did want to. He wanted to more than anything else.

She turned her head toward the sky. "We should see them soon. They'll be here soon."

"Yeah," said Stoner. He turned his head and looked toward the sky as well.

"Not a cloud in the sky," said Breanna.

"Great day for a picnic," said Stoner.

He would kiss her. He must. He felt the weight of her leg leaning against his.

"Hear something?" she asked.

"Just your heart. And mine."

"I think I heard a plane." She jerked upright, scanned the sky.

There was no sound except the water lapping against the sides of the raft and Ferris's breaths, now growing labored. Stoner wondered if she was hallucinating.

Or inventing an excuse not to be so close to him. He wanted to kiss her.

She leaned over the side toward Chris. "How you doing?" she asked.

"Good exercise. Come on. Water's warm."

"Later, I think." She lay back down, her head against the side of the raft. She'd oriented herself a little farther from him—but their legs still touched.

"So, Mr. Stoner, you want to tell us your life story?" Breanna asked.

"No."

"What will you tell us then?"

"Nothing," said Stoner.

"Private guy," said Chris from the water.

"I didn't know I was expected to perform," he told them.

"You must have some battle stories. You were in the SEALs, right?" She leaned over, balancing on her left arm. A twinge of pain flashed across her face—her shoulder and back were undoubtedly complaining—but she kept her voice light. "Tell me a story, and then I'll tell one. We've seen some shit," she added.

"I don't think I'm allowed to tell stories."

"Neither are we."

She wanted him. That's why she was flirting.

He'd kiss her. He had to kiss her.

Stoner began to lean forward. She watched, doing nothing.

Chris Ferris screamed. The sound was loud and so distorted that it took Stoner a second to realize it was a real scream.

The raft tugged backward, and down. A huge fin appeared on the side. The raft spun fiercely to the right.

Ferris screamed again. Breanna began to move—began to slide toward him.

Water furled.

"The belts, cut the belts!" yelled Stoner.

"Chris! Chris!"

Four, five fins appeared in the water and a sound like switchblades snapping open and shut filled the air. Stoner threw his upper body over her, grabbing Breanna as she slid toward the side. Teeth snapped in the air, and once more the raft spun right. From the corner of his eye, he saw a gun on the floor of the small rubber boat and, with one hand, lunged for it. A demon shrieked. Stoner emptied the magazine, but the scream continued. He pulled at Breanna and then saw a knife in her scabbard. He bent for it and felt her pulling away. Teeth and a gray snout leapt from the water. He sprang back, but managed with the knife to cut the line. They shot backward, the knife flying.

"Chris!" she screamed. "Chris! Chris!"

Stoner used all his strength to keep her at the bottom of the raft, and still she managed to squirm away. He grabbed her by the throat and pulled her so tight she began choking for air. Still he held on, certain she would jump out for her copilot if he didn't. Only when her body grew limp did he finally let go, collapsing himself over her.

Taj building, Dreamland
August 28, 1997, 2100 local (August 29, 1997, 1200
Philippines)

DOG TOOK A LARGE GULP OF THE EXTRA-STRONG COFfee and swallowed quickly, hoping the caffeine would rush to his brain cells.

As a fighter pilot, once or twice he had come close to resorting to greenies to stay awake at crucial points; he'd always hesitated, however, fearing they might become addictive—or worse, not work as advertised. If he had some now, he'd have swallowed them without hesitation. The few hours of sleep he'd managed had left him more groggy than refreshed, and as he walked down the hallway toward the elevator with his half-full coffee cup, he felt as if his head had been pushed down into his chest. He nodded at the security detail near the elevator, took another gulp of his coffee, then got into the car, waiting for it to trundle downward to the Command Center level.

Even though his quarters were just on the other side of the base, he'd slept on his office couch. He'd never done that before, anywhere.

Neither had he ever worried about losing Breanna.

Once, on the so-called "Nerve Center" mission, he'd had to authorize a plan to shoot her down. She was a passenger on a suicide mission to destroy an American city; the decision was a no-brainer.

This was different. She had been lost on a surveillance mission while technically under someone else's command—was that the part that made it so hard to accept? Did he feel the mission was unworthy of her sacrifice?

Colonel Bastian commanded a combat unit as well as a development facility. In either case, death was part of the portfolio. Who was to say what justified one instance and not the other? It was all the same to you, when you were gone.

He took another full gulp of the coffee, felt it burn his mouth. There was still a chance, slim but possible, that Bree and her people, *his* people, were alive.

They were alive.

Rubeo had just returned to the Command Center himself and was getting a briefing from Greg Meades when Dog entered. Meades started over for the colonel, ignoring Rubeo's frown.

The storm had passed out of the area a few hours before. Though they were mounting very aggressive patrols, the Chinese and Indians hadn't fired on each other; they seemed to be spending much of their energy recovering from the initial battle and the storm. The diplomats were busting their backs trying to get a cease-fire in place.

Pacific Command had launched searches for the F-14 and a helicopter that had gone down in the storm. They were also looking for Indian and Chinese survivors as a goodwill gesture—a move interpreted by both sides as interference, if not spying, though they had taken no action to prevent it.

Admiral Woods had allocated two frigates and helicopters to the Megafortress search, and was detailing a P-3 as well, but the Navy had its hands full. Besides the three aircraft that had apparently been lost, two civilian ships had floundered in the storm. The only good news was the Navy had, at last, found its unaccounted-for submarine, safe and unharmed.

"How's Zen?" Dog asked.

"We've expanded his search area," said Meades. "He thinks they were farther south when they ejected, that the plane arced back northwards before it crashed. It's possible."

Dog nodded. The scientist began detailing the UMB's performance—they were, after all, testing a new system, something that was easy to forget. The aircraft and sensor arrays were working fantastically.

"Fantastically," repeated Meades. He trimmed the enthusiasm in his voice. "Though, of course, that's small consolation."

"It's okay," said Dog, going over to the communications desk. "Let me talk to Zen."

The South China Sea
Date and time unknown

THE SURPRISE AND AGONY BURNED IN HER BRAIN.

Breanna had felt it before—Jeff in the hospital when he woke up.

Bright light filled her eyes. Her forehead and hair were crusted with salt. How long had she lain in the raft? How long had her arms, back, and legs soaked in the water?

To die like that.

God, why have you saved me and not my crew?

Water.

"Captain Stockard?"

Something blocked out the sun.

Jeffrey.

Stoner, it was Stoner.

"Are you okay? Captain Stockard? Breanna?"

His face was right next to hers as her eyes opened fully.

"I'm all right," she said. "God."

"We're all right."

She wanted to cry, but the tears wouldn't come. She'd held them back too long. She'd never let herself cry in Jeff's room after his accident. She couldn't cry now, even though she wanted to. She'd never be able to cry again.

"The sharks moved off. I shot a couple and they started eating each other. We're okay."

"Yeah," she managed. "Peachy."

Aboard Iowa
August 29, 1997, 1346 local (August 28, 1997, 2146
Dreamland)

WATCHING THE OPTICAL FEED FROM THE MINI-KH PACK-
age in the UMB's bay was like looking at a room through
a strobe light. Zen's head and upper body pitched slightly
with each image, responding to the pulse like a dancer
moving to a beat. He stared at the images so long and so
hard he found the radar, and even the video from the
plane, disorienting. The computer could take care of
everything else; he had to scan the images, examine each
one, dance with the darkness between them.

"Dreamland Command to B-5. Zen, how you doing?"
asked Colonel Bastian over the Dreamland circuit.

"We're on course."

"Good."

Bastian's voice betrayed no emotion; he could have
been asking if the garbage pickup had been made yet. Zen
wanted to curse at him. Didn't he feel anything for his
daughter?

No one did. She was already dead as far as everyone
else was concerned. He was just looking for bodies or
debris.

But Zen knew she was there. He was going to find her.

"Keep us apprised," said the colonel. "Dreamland Command out."

Yeah, out.

Something tapped him on the shoulder. "You okay?"
said Jennifer, leaning close and talking to him.

"Not a problem," said Zen.

"Want something to eat? I smuggled in some cookies."

Talking threw off his beat, and that made it harder to
concentrate.

"No," he said, willing his eyes back to the task. He
pushed forward harder, scanning the emptiness below
him.

This is what God sees, someone had told him once. It

was an orientation flight in the backseat of an SR-71. They were at eighty thousand feet, looking down at Dreamland on a clear day.

Picture, new picture.

Here was something in the right corner of his screen, the first thing he'd seen in fifteen minutes.

The rail of a ship.

The fantail of a ship.

A trawler, the radar was telling him, or rather the computer was interpreting the radar and telling him, in its synthesized voice.

He locked it out. He had to concentrate.

One of the Taiwanese spy ships.

"You're getting the ship?" Jennifer asked over the interphone, back at her station. Even though they were physically next to each other, she couldn't get the photo or radar feed until it was processed and recorded by C^3, which took a little over five seconds. At that point, it was available to Dreamland as well.

"One of the Taiwanese spy ships," said Zen. "Maybe they're on to something."

He was past them now, still pulsing over the empty sea. Picture, new picture. Picture, new picture.

"PacCom checking in," said Jennifer a few minutes later.

Picture, new picture.

"Anything you want to ask them? Or give them a lead or something?"

Picture, new picture.

"Zen?"

"No."

Picture, new picture. He glanced down at the lower portion of his screen, reading the instruments—the fuel consumption was nudging a little higher than anticipated, but otherwise everything was in the green. He selected the forward video—nothing there, of course, since he was coming through sixty thousand feet—then went back to the routine.

Picture, new picture. Picture, new picture.

"Jeff, one of the Navy planes thinks it picked up a radio signal. We're going to change our course and see if we can get over there," said Major Alou. "It's going to take us toward your search area. It's about two hundred miles from our present position, so it'll be a bit."

Yes. Finally.

"Give me coordinates," he said.

"I will when we have them. We're going very close to the Chinese fleet," added Alou.

"Okay." Zen reached to the console to pull up the mapping screen—he'd need to work out a new pattern with the team back at Dreamland, but he wanted a rough idea of it first. Just as his finger hit the key sequence, something flickered at the right side of the picture.

"Dreamland is wondering about the performance of the number-two engine," said Jennifer. "They're worried about power going asymmetric."

Asymmetric. Stinking scientists.

The map came up. Zen's fingers fumbled—he wasn't used to working these controls, couldn't find the right sequence.

Picture, new picture.

"What should I tell them?" said Jennifer.

"We have a good location on that signal," broke in Alou. "I'm going to turn you over—"

"Wait!" said Zen. He pushed up the visor and looked at the keyboard, finding the keys to bring the pictures back up. "Everybody just give me a minute."

South China Sea
Date and time unknown

AS HE LEANED DOWN TOWARD HER, SOMETHING caught his attention. Stoner looked toward the horizon. There was something there—or he thought there was.

"Water," she said.

He reached for the small metal bottle, gave it to her. She took half a gulp.

She was so beautiful.

"It's almost empty," she told him.

He nodded, took his own small sip, put it in his pants leg. "We have another," he said.

"Where?"

Where? He didn't see it.

She lifted up, looking.

It was gone. They must have lost it when the sharks attacked.

The radio was gone too. They had an empty water bottle and an empty gun.

"It's all right," he told her. "It's okay—look."

"What?"

He put his arms around her, then pointed toward the horizon.

"I don't see anything."

"Look," he said. Stoner put his head on her shoulder, pointing with his arm. His cheek brushed hers. "There," he said.

Aboard Iowa
1353

THE RESOLUTION OF THE OPTICS IN THE UMB'S BELLY were rated good enough to focus on a one-meter object at an altitude of 22,300 miles, roughly the height necessary for a geosynchronous orbit. A number of variables affected that focus, however, and the designers at Dreamland had found it more expedient and meaningful in presentations to say that, at any altitude above twenty thousand feet, the camera array could see what a person with 20/10 vision could see across a good-sized room. The metaphor was both memorable and accurate, and often illustrated with the added example that a person with that vision could read the letters on a bracelet as she reached to embrace and kiss her lover.

Zen saw it as clearly as that.

The edge of a raft. A foot. A leg.

Then bodies entwined.

Their cheeks were together—had they just kissed?

"I have them," he said, mouth dry. "Here are the co-ordinates."

South China Sea
Date and time unknown

"DON'T," SAID BREANNA, IN A SOFT, HOARSE VOICE.

"No?"

She could feel his heart beating next to hers. Desire began to well inside her, pushing her toward him. She needed him, needed to feel his arms wrapping around her, feel his skin on her skin. She needed to feel him push against her, wrap her legs around his.

"No," she said.

"It's there," Stoner told her. She couldn't tell whether he meant the ship he'd seen, or his feelings for her, or his lips. Suddenly she had an urge to throw herself into the water, just dive in. She started to move upward. Perhaps sensing her thoughts, he grabbed her; she slid into his arms and then said "no" again, then pointed.

Now she saw it too, a ship.

"The flare gun," she said.

"We don't have it," said Stoner. The words emptied his eyes.

She'd seen the same blankness in Zen's face when he told her what she'd known for weeks, that he couldn't feel his legs and would never feel them again.

Jeffrey. Her desire raged and she reached toward him. A wave pushed her to his chest, but then pulled the boat back; she struggled to push up, to throw herself around him, but Stoner was steadying himself in a crouch at the edge of the raft, trying to stand, or at least squat, waving.

"Balance me," he told her without looking, his voice a whisper. "On the other end."

She went to do so.

"No, they're not going to see us. Paddle, we'll have to paddle," he said.

"The sharks," she said, her words barely a whisper in her own ears. Before she could repeat them louder, he had slipped into the water.

"Wave," he said. "Shout."

"The sharks."

"Wave, jump, anything. Get their attention."

Airborne over the South China Sea
1355

"ROGER THAT, IOWA," SAID DANNY OVER THE DREAM-land line. "Hang tight a second." He slid the smart helmet back and yelled to the Osprey pilot. "I have a location! Survivors! People! Our people!"

He pounded on the support spar in front of him.

"We're hearing you, Captain," said the copilot. "You don't have to shout. Just give us a vector so we can get there."

Aboard Iowa
1359 (August 28, 1997, 2159 Dreamland)

THE IDEA CAME TO ZEN ONLY AFTER IT WAS TOO LATE: *Block the transmission, kill the feed. No one will know.*

It was absurd and murderous, and once it occurred to him he couldn't forget it: anger, jealousy, and shame surging together. But it was too late, fortunately too late—Dreamland had the feed, the radar had a good lock, the GPS data was now being fed not just to Iowa's flight deck but to the Whiplash Osprey.

Too late, thank God.

Zen took the UMB from the computer, altering the course and going over each move carefully with Dreamland. There was a minor problem in one of the engines.

The scientists wanted him to give back control, send the plane back to Dreamland.

Not yet. Not until the mission was complete.

He used the rocket, engine five, took the massive robot to 140,000 feet, setting up a ten-mile orbit. The computer cut the flight path into a perfect circle.

The Taiwanese trawler spotted earlier was headed in their general direction. Danny and his Osprey were about a half hour away. If it changed its course a little, the spy ship could reach them in fifteen minutes, maybe a little less.

"Dreamland Command, what do you think of giving the position to the trawler, see if they can pick them up?" said Zen.

"We're working on it," said the lieutenant at the com board. "There's another complication—hold on just a second, Major."

"Zen, this is Bastian."

"Colonel."

"Danny's en route. The Chinese are tracking the trawler. We're in contact with the *Kitty Hawk* on the eastern side of the Chinese fleet; one of their Hawkeyes is tracking the Chinese CAP. They think two planes from the carrier are vectoring toward that area. They're a bit far away at the moment—"

"Hold on." Zen went to the UMB's native radar, bringing up the search-and-scan panel. Look-down mode was limited; the unit had been optimized for flight requirements and, at this altitude and distance, the Chinese planes didn't show up.

"I'm going to have to take your word, because they're not on my screen," Zen told him. "Is it the CAP patrol?"

"Negative. They're going out to that spy ship at a good clip, and very low," said the colonel. "They may be armed with antiship missiles. Wait a second."

The line went dead a second.

"Jeff, at their present course and speed they're going to be on the Osprey as well. They should find her in about sixty seconds. *Kitty Hawk* is sending some Tomcats out there. They're a good distance off, though."

"Yeah, okay, thanks for the heads-up."

Why had she kissed him? Why?

The South China Sea
Date and time unknown

THE SHIP WAS BIGGER. BREANNA THOUGHT HER SHOUTS were bringing it closer, but it was impossible to tell.

Stoner was starting to tire. He punctuated his kicks with rests on the side of the raft that grew longer and longer.

The sharks must be nearby still. They'd hear the splashes, come for him.

She couldn't see that again.

"Help!" she shouted with her hoarse voice. "Hey! Hey!"

There was an airplane in the distance, a jet—two or three maybe.

A pair of gray hawks broke over the horizon, thundering between them and the ship.

F-14's? Or Sukhois?

The two planes rode up, then banked toward the south.

"Hey!" she shouted again, though her voice was so hoarse it was barely louder than a whisper. "Here! Hey! Hey!"

Aboard Dreamland Osprey
1505

"WE'RE BEING CHALLENGED," THE PILOT TOLD DANNY. "Pretty bad English."

"What are they saying?"

"That we're in protected airspace," said the pilot.

"We're being targeted," said the copilot. "Trying to spike us, the bastards."

"Shit," said Danny.

"They're just trying to scare us," said the pilot.

"They're doing a decent job," said the copilot.

"Tell them we're going to pick up our survivors and split," Danny said.

"I have twice," said the pilot. "Here they come. Everybody hold on, it's going to be close."

Aboard Iowa
1509

AS SOON AS ZEN HEARD DANNY TELL DOG WHAT WAS going on over the Dreamland circuit, he tucked his wing and plunged toward the sea. It was a mistake, a serious mistake—he wasn't flying a Flighthawk, and the B-5 flipped awkwardly through a roll and then headed straight downward, speed increasing quickly. An alert sounded and Fichera back at Dreamland said something in his ear about letting the computer's emergency protocol take over. Zen ignored the scientist and the computer; he held the stick gently, letting the plane's aerodynamics assert themselves. The nose began to lift, and now the trick was to control it, not by muscling it down, or shoving it around the way he would push the small Flighthawk, but gracefully, the way you rode an overemotional show horse.

The plane slid into a turn that recorded nine Gs against the fuselage. He took a slow breath, trying to hold his instinct back, trying to baby the hurtling, accelerating mass into a controlled flight path.

Flying the UMB was more thought and perseverance than muscle. Flying was always that for him now, without muscles in his legs, without his legs at all.

Without love either, it seemed.

The idea made him hesitate. He had the Sukhois now on the video; they'd turned south to intercept the Osprey. Zen tightened his hand around the joystick. He was at eighty thousand feet, still descending, coming through seventy-nine, seventy-eight, seventy-seven—the ladder rolled downward at a steady pace now, more controlled.

The video feed from B-5's nose showed the Osprey at his far right, moving so slowly by comparison it seemed to be standing still on the water.

The Sukhois were on his left, not standing still—530 knots, according to the information synthesized by the computer. They were positioned to flash by, turn, run up the back of the Osprey.

I thought these bastards were going after the ship, for cryin' out loud.

He wouldn't reach them in time—he was still a good sixty seconds away.

He had to move faster. Engine five, the rocket motor?

Too much, too hard to control.

He needed the scramjets now.

"Computer, Engines three and four. Accelerate."

"Engines are locked off until Flight Stage Three," responded the plane.

"Computer, initiate Flight Stage Three."

"Parameters are incorrect."

"Override, damn it."

"Authorization code required."

"Authorization Zed-Zed-Zed," said Zen.

The Sukhois had flown past the Osprey and were now turning.

"Activate engines three and four. Accelerate to marked intercept at fastest possible speed."

It was a bit too much. A half-second after the computer acknowledged, the jet whipped forward. He started a turn and managed to shoot between the Sukhois and their target at Mach 2.3, dipping up and then flying between the two planes. His separation from the first plane was less than fifty feet—hair-raisingly close, though it had no effect on the UMB.

Probably, the Sukhois hit their afterburners. Probably, they tried to pursue. Probably, the pilots would have to spend personal time with the dry cleaner.

By the time they got themselves sorted out, Zen had

rocketed up past twenty thousand feet and started back in the other direction.

"Engines three and four at specified parameters," reported the computer. It sounded as if it were chortling. "Phase Three test complete. Preparing for Phase Four."

"Computer, cancel Phase Four. Authorization Zed-Zed-Zed."

"Canceled."

"Hey," said Danny Freah over the Dreamland circuit. "We're clear. Thanks."

"Not a problem."

"Ten minutes to that raft—we don't quite see it yet."

"They're all yours," Zen told him.

South China Sea
1515

THE SHIP HAD STOPPED COMING TOWARD THEM. EVEN the Sukhois were gone. They were alone, as good as dead.

Bree sank to the bottom of the raft. Stoner had his arms draped over it, his head resting on the side.

Zen, she thought, I love you, baby. I love you. Why aren't you here?

The sun flickered in her face.

If she'd lived, they would have had a kid. They should have. It wouldn't be easy, would *not* have been easy, but they should have.

She felt bad for that. Jeffrey would have been good with a kid.

"Shit," said Stoner softly.

The sharks, she thought. Oh God.

She jumped up to help him, cringing.

But it wasn't sharks. There was another plane in the distance, to the south.

It moved too slowly to be a Sukhoi. It had propellers. It was loud.

It was an Osprey.

It was an Osprey!

Aboard Dreamland Osprey
1520

DANNY AND BISON HAD STRIPPED TO THEIR WET SUITS and waited by the door.

"You ready?" Danny asked the crew chief.

"Born ready, Cap." The sergeant put his hand to his earphone. They had to be careful about getting too close to the small raft. The downdraft from the big rotos could be fierce. Danny and Bison would jump out with life jackets and a Dreamland-designed inflatable collar to add to the raft's stability before the MV-22 moved in for a pickup.

"Here we go!" said the sergeant.

As they cruised parallel to the raft at low speed, Danny stepped off the aircraft, walking out as if walking off a board at the swimming pool. He felt his knees knock together as his feet impacted the water; his joints twinged a second, but then fell away. The water was cold—very, very cold. He pumped hard toward the raft, waiting for the surge of blood and adrenaline to warm him.

Bison got there a stroke ahead of him. The Whiplash trooper pushed Stoner into the raft, threw one of the preservers over his head.

"Here!" Danny yelled to Breanna as he reached the side. "Hey! Take the life preserver! Take it!"

Her face looked as if it had been pounded with a baseball bat. Her fingers were swollen and puffy. Danny pushed himself into the small boat, wrapped the preserver around her.

"We're going home. We're taking you back."

Aboard Iowa
1535

ZEN WATCHED THE OSPREY COME IN AS HE CLIMBED back—picture, next picture. It approached, it started to hover, someone was leaning from the door, a line was down, she was okay, she was okay.

He floated out over her, happy she was okay. He reached toward her but she was gone, the Osprey veering off.

"Jeff, we have that radio—it's a PRC beacon," said Major Alou.

"Roger that. I need the coordinates."

"Dreamland has them. They're plugged in. Thank God Bree's alive."

"Yeah."

"You okay?"

"Roger that," he said.

The South China Sea
1540

DANNY STUMBLED AS HE GOT INTO THE OSPREY, FALL-ing against Pretty Boy, who was helping one of the Marines wrap a blanket around Stoner. The other two Marines were stooped over Hernandez, who was kneeling over Breanna on the floor. The two rescuees had to be treated for shock and dehydration as well as wounds. Every member of Whiplash was trained in emergency medical care, and his two men were moving promptly and competently to treat the pair. Danny couldn't help thinking of Liu, whose nickname "Nurse" had been earned several times over.

"Captain, we think we got another one," said the crew chief.

"Where?" Danny asked.

"Pilot wants to talk to you." The chief pointed him toward the bulkhead separating the flight deck and the cabin area. Danny leaned between the two pilots, who were just completing a circle to make sure there were no other survivors in the area.

"Here's the deal," said the copilot. "Beacon off a survival radio about a hundred miles east of here. Top speed, we can make it in roughly twelve minutes. Means we'll have to tank on the way home, but we got a KC-10 en route with all the stops pulled out, so we think we can do it."

"Well, let's go," said Danny.

The copilot looked across at the pilot.

"It's right near the Chinese task group," said the pilot. "And I mean right near."

"Well, let's get the fuck over there," said Danny.

"That's what we say," said the copilot. "Navy has its own package en route with Tomcats and Hornets as escorts, but even with all the stops out, their helos are a good half hour off, if not more. Escorts'll have to stay with them, pretty much."

"Screw 'em."

The pilot answered by mashing the throttle to max.

Dreamland Command
August 28, 1997, 0050 local (August 29, 1997, 1550
Philippines)

THIRTY SECONDS AFTER THE DREAMLAND OSPREY TOLD Dog they were headed to the new beacon location, Admiral Woods's voice came over the line. The screen remained blank.

"Bastian, we understand you have another beacon."

"Yes, we do," Dog told him. "My Osprey is en route."

"It is? I thought they were on another rescue."

"They've completed that."

"I see. I'm told we have a package on its way already."

"It's likely we'll get there first," said Dog.

"We'll coordinate. Very clever using another aircraft," added the admiral.

It was impossible to know how he meant that—was he mad that Dog had sent another airplane into "his" territory? It could be interpreted as going against orders.

"The platform was scheduled to be tested," said Dog.

"Yes," said Woods. "Good recovery. Let's work together on this next pickup."

"We have been."

"Good."

The line snapped clear.

Aboard *Shiva* in the South China Sea
1612

THE TEMPTATION WAS OVERWHELMING. THE CHINESE destroyer was now just within his range; he could get his torpedoes off before they had time to spot him, but they had heard other contacts in the distance. Admiral Balin was determined to see what other targets the gods were presenting.

"Sonar Contact One is changing course," relayed the sonar room, referring to the destroyer. They gave a distance and a bearing. It was heading roughly across their path, but not quite on a direct course.

Attack now and destroy it? Or let it pass and hope for a juicier target?

"Other contacts?" asked Balin.

"Negative," came the reply. They were using only their passive sonar.

"Periscope."

If the destroyer attacked, they would lose their easy shot, and perhaps not get another one.

If a better target was nearby, though, he would not forgive himself.

Greed?

"Active sonar," decided Balin. "Prepare torpedoes to fire."

Twenty seconds later, the sonar room reported a large contact two miles beyond the destroyer.

"What is it?" asked Captain Varja.

"Unknown," was the answer. "Large, very large."

"Direct our course for it," Balin told Varja.

"The destroyer is changing course. They're heading for us."

"Target the largest contact," said Balin.

"It is a good day," said Varja.

"Yes," said Balin.

Aboard Dreamland Osprey
1616

"WE HAVE A DESTROYER BEARING DOWN ON THE marker," Iowa's copilot told Danny over the Dreamland circuit.

"Yeah, we got him on long-distance radar," Danny replied. "We're still a good five minutes away."

"I have the raft," said Zen. "Somebody's in it. One person."

"Understood," replied Danny. "How close is the destroyer?"

"Two hundred yards. Shit," yelled Zen. "They're firing at them!"

Aboard *Shiva* in the South China Sea 1620

THE FIRST DEPTH CHARGE EXPLODED WELL OFF THE port side. The second and third were even farther. As the sub shook ever so slightly from the fourth, the sonar room reported the large contact was slowing, probably to turn. It was now less than two and a half miles away.

"Is it the carrier?" asked Balin.

"We believe so," answered Varja.

"Prepare to fire."

The submarine rocked with a fresh explosion. The lights blinked off; it took a second for the systems and the crew to recover.

"We have severe damage—we've lost control of the diving planes," said Varja as the reports came in. "Ballast tanks blown—we're surfacing."

"Keep us down."

"We're trying, Admiral."

Varja said nothing else, but it was obvious what he meant to tell the admiral—they were no longer in position to fire. The ASW weapons had jammed the hydroplanes upward and mangled the controls on the ballast tanks, robbing them of their ability to maneuver below the water.

"Surface," said Balin, accepting the inevitable. "Then we will fire."

Aboard Dreamland Osprey
1622

"HEY, CAPTAIN! NAVY'S FOUND SOMETHING SOUTH OF us," reported the Osprey crew chief as Danny and Bison hunkered by the door. "The helo that was coming north for this raft, backing us up—they just spotted some wreckage. They think they may have a body."

"A body or a person?" asked Danny.

"They said body, sir. They're checking it out. They want to know if we need them, or if they can concentrate on that."

"Yeah, release 'em," shouted Danny. "What about the Hornets?"

"Inbound."

"Chinese answer the hails?"

"No. Don't worry. The F/A-18's'll nail the bastards."

Danny didn't answer. They were still a good two minutes off; he couldn't see the Chinese ships from where he was standing.

Bastards—he'd strangle each one of them personally.

Bison looked at him across the doorway. If the Chinese were shooting at unarmed men in a raft, they'd sure as hell fire at the Osprey. But there was no way he was stopping now.

Bastards!

Aboard Iowa
1624

IF THE HORNETS DIDN'T TAKE OUT THE DESTROYER, ZEN decided, he'd crash the stinking UMB into it. Let them court-martial him—shit, he'd willingly spend the rest of his life in Leavenworth or wherever the hell they sent him.

Might just as well now. Breanna didn't love him.

God, Bree.

Picture, new picture.

The gun on the side of the destroyer fired again. As it did, the sea exploded beyond it.

Bastards couldn't hit the side of a barn, thank God.

The fact that they were terrible shots wasn't going to get them off. Bastards. What the hell kind of people were they?

Picture, new picture.

A ridge erupted in the sea at the far end of his screen, behind the destroyer.

Picture, new picture.

Zen hit the resolution, backing off for a wider shot. There was another ship, a cruiser beyond the destroyer.

Picture, new picture.

It took the computer three more shots to get the focus right. By then, the ridge that had appeared was on the surface of the water.

A submarine.

The Chinese weren't attacking the raft at all—they were going after a sub.

Aboard *Shiva* in the South China Sea
1625

AS HE REACHED THE BRIDGE, ADMIRAL BALIN SAW HIS crew had been mistaken—the large contact was a cruiser, not the carrier.

It mattered little. The submarine sat cockeyed in the water, heeling over to the left. They were an easy target.

A shell splashed into the water a hundred yards away.

"The destroyer will hit us eventually," said Varja behind him.

Balin gripped the small rail before him and took a long, deep breath. The sun shone down strong upon him, the sea barely swelled, the air had a fine salty mist.

Would he remember this in his next life?

The cruiser was at 3,300 meters—not optimum, but acceptable, given the circumstances. His shot was dead-on.

"Fire torpedoes," he said, as the next shell from the destroyer's deck gun landed twenty yards away.

It took perhaps five seconds for the order to be carried out. In those seconds Balin felt every failure and mistake of his life rise in his chest, pounding like a thousand iron fists on his frail frame. But as the first torpodo left the boat, the regrets dissolved. He took a deep breath, felt the sea in his lungs. It was as sweet and heavy as the first breath he'd ever taken at sea. He turned his head upward, and in the last half-second of his life saw the approaching shell descending toward his vessel's hull.

Aboard Dreamland Osprey 1626

THEY DIDN'T HAVE TIME TO FINESSE THIS APPROACH. The Osprey banked low and slow. Danny jumped, so anxious he didn't tuck his legs right before hitting the water. He shook off the shock and, without bothering to check for Bison, began stroking toward the raft, which bobbed about thirty yards away.

There were explosions nearby. The Chinese were firing, but not in his direction. They weren't interested in the raft, or the Osprey.

When he was five yards from the raft, it ducked downward as if pulled toward the depths. Danny took a breath and prepared to dive after it, then saw it bob back up with Bison at its side. With one hard overhand stroke he reached it, grabbing the side with both hands and pulling his body over it.

"Dead," Bison told him.

"Shit," said Danny.

"Dolk," added Bison, turning the prostrate body over. "I don't see any wounds. Might've been internal injuries. Hey—" A plastic container slipped to the bottom of the raft; it was attached via a chain to Torbin's wrist.

"Those are discs from the mission," said Danny. "Security protocol is to take 'em out if you go. He did his job to the end."

He saw Dolk's radio near the dead man's foot.

The Osprey was approaching, its hoist line draping into the water.

"Sucks," said Bison, fitting a life preserver around the dead man's torso.

"Yeah," said Danny. "Big-time."

Aboard Iowa
1632

ZEN LISTENED TO THE OSPREY PILOT CALLING OFF THE Hornets, telling them the Chinese were not going after their people. Anger seized him, surging over his shoulders like a physical thing, a bear gripping its thick paws into his flesh and howling in his ear. The Chinese hadn't just shot down Breanna; they had made her unfaithful.

He hated them. He'd kill every one of them. He could order the Hornets in, claim he saw guns being trained on the Osprey or the people in the water. The F/A-18's would sink the Chinese ships.

Maybe, in the confusion, Breanna herself would die.

He didn't wish for that; he couldn't wish for that, but he could accept it, willingly. His anger that great. Uncontrollable, unending rage.

"Dreamland B-5 to Hornet Strike Leader," he said, punching the talk button and transmitting on the strike frequency. "Confirming what you've heard. Chinese are not firing on our people. Repeat, Chinese are *not* firing on our people. Do not attack. Do not attack."

The Hornet acknowledged. Zen took a deep breath.

"All right," he told Major Alou. "We still have one crew member MIA. I'm going to set up for a fresh search pattern."

VII
Into the future

CHEN LO FANN'S TEA HAD TURNED SLIGHTLY BITTER, but he savored it anyway. His mission, while not quite an unqualified success, had cost the Communists one of their prized possessions. At the same time, he had gathered considerable information about their other capabilities, and, incidentally, gained information about the Americans as well. A successful mission indeed.

More importantly, it appeared he had not been detected. The Americans and the Chinese knew the spy ships were ROC vessels, and it was probable the Americans suspected the atoll spy stations had belonged to him, not the Communists, but there was no evidence to show he had assisted the Indians.

While the diplomats had succeeded in imposing a cease-fire, the enmity between the two South Asia powers still simmered. His hope of drawing the Americans into a war had been too ambitious—but that element had not been a part of his original plan anyway. The Dragon had proven itself in flight and had, it seemed, gone undetected.

Objectively, a successful mission; but would his government see it that way?

Chen Lo Fann took a long sip of his tea. In some ways, he regretted he had not had the chance to use the robot plane to attack the Communists. Perhaps fate would provide an opportunity in the future.

Lao Tzu had written it was wise to retire when the task was done. But the way was a subtle way, a myriad winding of various wills. Chen Lo Fann recognized this; it was how he, a man of action, could accept the passivity implicit in the Tao. For now he would retire, deal with his government and its requirements. Fortune would once more present itself, if he were patient.

Surely, he could be.

Aboard Dreamland Transport Two, approaching Hawaii
August 31, 1997, 1636 local

DOG WAS ON THE STAIRS AGAIN IN THE METRO, BACK in his dream, looking for his daughter. Zen was there, and by some miracle, he could use his legs. But he acted oddly, sulking behind Dog as he trotted up the steps, angry about something he wouldn't share.

Breanna was just beyond the next turn, Dog thought. And yet she wasn't. He pushed up the steps faster, worried about her, fearing he'd never get to her.

She was safe now, his conscious mind blurted, trying to break into the imaginary world. There was no need for him to be haunted by this nightmare.

"I'm not going any further," said Zen behind him.

Somehow, in the dream Dog managed to keep jogging up the steps and yet turn around and yell to his son-in-law at the same time. "Don't give up," he heard himself say. "Let's go. Don't give up."

"Sir?"

Dog jerked awake and found himself staring into the face of the C-26's copilot. The lieutenant stood in the aisle of the transport with a quizzical look.

"Sir, Admiral Woods wants to speak with you," said

the copilot. "You said if there was anything important, to wake you up."

"Yes, of course."

Dog rubbed his eyes and forehead, shaking off the dream.

"So you hit a home run," said Woods as Dog plugged his headset into the panel next to his seat. The light, dual-engined utility aircraft had Dreamland-issue communications gear, allowing secure transmissions via satellite like any other member of the Dreamland fleet.

"Admiral?"

"The Pentagon and the White House are singing your praises, Tecumseh. Admiral Allen told me a little while ago he's convinced you averted a world war. Not to mention helped get the details on a top-secret Indian weapon and flush out a Chinese submarine no one had seen in the ocean before. Admiral Allen almost sounded like he wanted to have you come over to our side."

"I *am* on your side," said Dog.

"I meant, join the Navy."

Dog, who'd known very well what he meant, smiled to himself and leaned back in the seat. Colonel Bastian didn't like Woods, and thought more than ever that he was a jerk. But his animosity toward Woods had dissipated. Maybe that was because, as Woods put it, Dreamland had hit a home run.

Or more likely, losing several of his best men in the interests of preventing a world war had left him with other things to think about than an admiral's pettiness.

"You and your people did a good job as well," Dog told Woods. He was sincere—though the emphasis fell more heavily on the Navy personnel working for Woods rather than the admiral himself.

"I'm sorry about the people you lost."

"So am I," said Dog. Besides Chris Ferris and Torbin Dolk, one other member of Breanna's EB-52 was officially listed as killed in action—Lieutenant Freddy Collins. His body had been recovered by the Navy patrol that was backing Danny up when they recovered Dolk. Captain Kevin "Curly" Fentress was officially MIA, but he was almost certainly dead as well. A thorough search of the area, both by the UMB and the Navy, had failed to turn up any trace of the young Flighthawk pilot.

Woods cleared his throat. For a second—perhaps less than that—Dog thought the cocksure-of-himself admiral was actually going to apologize for kicking him out of the Philippines.

Then he realized the fleet would sink before that happened.

"Piranha and your robot planes obviously did well," said Woods, the edge back in his voice. "You must be feeling pretty good."

"Actually, the only thing I feel at the moment is tired," said Dog, killing the transmission.

He looked up. The copilot was just emerging from the cockpit. "Colonel, you have another call pending. Dr. Rubeo."

All of his favorite people were tormenting him today, thought Dog. All he needed next was a call from his ex-wife.

"Doc, talk to me," said Dog, clicking into the circuit.

"The disc that was recovered from the downed Mega-fortress contains an unidentified contact at long range that appears to be a U/MF," said the scientist.

"What?" said Dog. "Is it the search team?"

"Hardly," said Rubeo. "This occurred just prior to the shoot-down. We had no assets in the vicinity. The contact was a small, extremely robust aircraft, nothing on the order of the first- or second-generation UAVs available to the Chinese, or Russians for that matter. Nor was it large enough to be a MiG-29, which is another theory you'll hear. I'm quite sure, Colonel. I have one of the radar specialists and a member of the U/MF development team here to walk you through the data. I wanted to make sure you knew about this as soon as possible."

"Go ahead and plug them into the circuit," said Dog grimly.

JENNIFER MANAGED TO WAIT UNTIL THE CABIN DOOR OF the small aircraft cranked open. Then she launched herself at the steps, catching Dog about midway down.

"Hey," he said.

"Hey yourself," she said, hugging him tightly. She'd been waiting here for nearly six hours. Zen and Jennifer had arrived on the islands on a commercial flight out of Japan, while Iowa and the rest of her crew returned directly to Dreamland, their deployment over.

"I was worried about you," Dog told Jennifer.

"Me?" She took a step down to the Tarmac. "Why?"

"Because I was worried," said Dog.

"Oh, please. Why would you worry?"

Seeing he was going to explain, Jennifer did the only sensible thing—she leaned close and kissed him.

"People are watching," he said when they parted.

"You think we can do better?"

Without waiting for an answer, Jennifer kissed him again. When their lips parted, Jennifer leaned her head back slightly, then smiled.

"Third time's a charm," she said, kissing him again. It did do the trick; she felt him finally relax.

"What's the word on Breanna?" he asked when they finally started walking away from the plane.

"She's getting better," said Jennifer. "She's at Bright Memorial."

"I'm going to go over there right now," said Dog.

"I thought you would. I have a car waiting for you in front of the hangar."

"You coming?"

"I'm supposed to have a phone conference with the people on the Piranha team in about fifteen minutes," said Jennifer. "They've been asked to make a presentation to the White House first thing in the morning, so they're scrambling. Ray talked to you?"

Dog nodded.

"It's possible that the radar image is an echo of the Megafortress's own Flighthawks," she told him. "If the gear was malfunctioning because of the fire, it's possible. We'll have to carefully analyze the tape."

"Dr. Rubeo doesn't think that's likely," said Dog.

Jennifer nodded. She agreed with Ray.

"Where's Zen?" Dog asked.

"I think he's at the hospital. I haven't seem him since we landed in Honolulu."

Dog gave her one of his uh-grunts, the sort he used when he was processing several things at one. "We'll hook up later," he said.

"At the hotel," she said. "We'll have room service dinner and then R&R."

"Sounds good." He turned and kissed her again. "I love you," he whispered.

"Hold that thought," she said, barely managing to twist herself away.

AN HOUR LATER, COLONEL BASTIAN WAITED AT THE VISitors' desk of Bright Memorial Hospital in Honolulu as a volunteer fumbled through a stack of old-fashioned visitor cards, looking for Breanna's room number. "I'll find it, I'll find it," insisted the woman, talking more to herself than him.

Dog glanced down the hallway. His uniform would probably get him up to her room without a problem—except he wasn't sure where exactly it was. Not only was the private hospital immense, it had been cobbled together under several different administrations. Each wing seemed to be a maze unto itself. He didn't need a pass; he needed directions.

That or a GPS device.

"Here, oh, yes, here she is," said the woman, pulling

the card from her file. "Breanna Stockard. What sort of name is that?"

A name that her stubborn mother insisted on, thought Dog. He answered that it was Irish.

"Hmmm. She has a visitor," added the volunteer after giving him directions and a color-coded map.

Probably Zen, thought Dog. But it was Danny Freah he found standing at Breanna's bedside.

"Hey, you," he told Breanna.

"Hi, Daddy." She started to push up.

"It's okay, baby," he told her, putting his hand on her shoulder gently. He leaned down and kissed her forehead. She pulled her arms around him; he could feel her tears on his cheek.

His tears too, maybe.

"I'm damn glad you made it," he told her.

"Me too." She looked toward Danny.

"And you!" Dog turned and gave his captain a hug. "Thanks. Thanks."

Danny, looking embarrassed, shrugged when Dog let him go.

"Where's Jeff?" asked Breanna.

"I thought Zen was here already," said Dog.

"I haven't seen him since I woke up," said Breanna.

"Probably ducked out for dinner or lunch or something. I'm sure he'll be back," said Dog. He felt a flush of anger at his son-in-law for not sitting at Breanna's side, where he belonged.

"He flew the B-5," said Danny, obviously sticking up for Zen. "That's how we found you. They loaded a mini-KH package in the belly, rigged up a way for him to fly it from Iowa, and he found you. Thank God."

"So where is he?" she asked, her voice hoarse.

Dog looked at Danny, who shrugged.

"TV was on when I came in," said Danny. "You were just kind of drifting awake."

Breanna's face was puffy. Her eyes seemed to have trouble focusing, and Dog could tell that her head was fuzzy, either from her concussion or from the painkillers they'd given her. She had sprained her wrist and torn ligaments in her knee during the ejection; she also had deep bruising to her sternum and back. But mostly she was just suffering from dehydration and exposure. The doctors had told Dog she'd be up and around in a day or so.

"CNN was saying India and China have agreed to a cease-fire," said Danny, trying to change the subject. He laughed. "Of course, they also had unnamed sources claiming the Navy stopped a war. We did all the work, and they all get the credit."

"Piranha has to remain secret," said Dog. "And the Navy did do a lot."

"Didn't say they didn't," said Danny.

"I saw Chris die," said Breanna. Her voice was weak and hoarse, but still the words seemed to shake the room. "He was my copilot. I couldn't save him."

Dog looked at her, unable to think of anything to say.

"And Kevin. Did they find him?" she asked, referring to Fentress.

"We have to assume he's dead, Bree." Dog felt the words sticking in his throat, but he pushed them out, feeling it was his duty to tell her, not to sugarcoat anything, not to leave any doubt. "In that storm, with the rain and the wind, it probably took him under right away."

"We made it," she said.

Thank God, he thought, though all he could do was put his hand on hers.

Danny broke the awkward silence. "I have to get going. Bree, I'm really glad you're okay."

"Thanks."

"Colonel, if I could just have a brief word? If you don't mind, Bree."

"Just give him back when you're done," she said.

Dog followed Danny outside and down the hall, around a corner.

"Thanks, Danny. You and your men did an incredible job."

"Colonel, there's just no good way to say this," started Danny. His lower lip was trembling. "I want to resign my commission. I want to leave the Air Force."

"What?"

"It's a lot of things."

"Danny, you can't leave now. Losing Sergeant Talcom, and the others—I know it was an incredible blow. . . ."

"I'm not quitting because of that." His voice wasn't entirely convincing.

"I know it was—is—difficult," said Dog. "For all of us, but you especially."

Danny nodded. "It is. But I have an opportunity. It has nothing to do Powder."

"What kind of opportunity?"

"An election. Some people in New York want me to run for Congress. They think I can get the nomination. My wife's pretty involved."

"Congress? Really? Jesus—great," said Dog sincerely. "Great. That is great."

"You think so?"

"You'd be a hell of a Congressman—if you can deal with the bullshit."

Danny smiled. Still, it was a nervous smile.

"What's your timetable?" asked Dog.

"I'm not sure yet. I-I just decided this. Couple of months, I guess. The election isn't until next year, but I'd need time to get around and meet people, raise money."

The colonel nodded. "There is something I need you to do, or at least get a start on."

"What's that?"

Dog hesitated. "The disc you picked up from Captain Dolk—it's a record of all the radar contacts."

"Uh-huh?"

"There was a Flighthawk profile on the disk that we can't explain."

"I'm not following, Colonel."

"Well, the scientists are still analyzing it."

Dog heard footsteps coming down the hall. He took

Danny down another corridor, turning and finding an even more secluded corridor.

"It looks like, or it may be, that someone was flying another Flighthawk. Not one of ours," Dog told Danny.

"A Flighthawk?"

"Either a clone or something very, very similar. Some of the scientists think it's just a reflection or a problem in the equipment; it's at long range and the disc itself isn't in the best shape, but Dr. Rubeo is convinced. That's pretty convincing in and of itself. Given Dreamland's history," added Dog, "this will require a thorough investigation."

"If someone else has a Flighthawk," said Danny, "they stole the technology from us."

"Not necessarily," said Dog. "Several countries have unmanned vehicle programs in the works. But we have to rule that out. Absolutely."

"Agreed."

"Don't let this stand in your way," Dog told him. "If there was a security breach, it would've been earlier than your assignment here. It's no reflection on you. It wouldn't have been on your watch. You should run for Congress. Do it."

Danny nodded, then turned away. Dog watched him until he disappeared around the corner.

He'd make a damn fine Congressman. He'd have Dog's vote, no hesitation.

Maybe he shouldn't have told him at all. Let him start the paperwork, at least.

Dog was preoccupied second-guessing himself and missed Breanna's door. As he turned back, he heard her laugh, then heard another woman's voice as he entered.

A vaguely familiar, vaguely enticing voice.

"How are you, Tecumseh?" said his ex-wife, standing at their daughter's bedside.

"I'm fine, Karen," he said, letting the door close behind him.

"So what do you think of the news?" she added. She

fingered her stethoscope—she was a doctor on staff, and had arranged for Breanna to be admitted here.

"What news?"

"I just got an offer as chief of the medical staff at St. Simon's out in Las Vegas. We'll be seeing a lot more of each other." She curled her hand around his. "Maybe we can get Bree and her husband working on a new addition. What do you say?"

Dog shot a glance at Breanna. He thought he might actually have spotted fear in her eyes for the first time.

"Isn't that a great idea?" said Karen.

"Peachy," said Dog, glancing toward his daughter and trying to smile.

Medical Facility, Barbers Point NAS, Hawaii
August 31, 1997, 1836 local

"MAJOR STOCKARD?"

Zen spun his wheelchair around so quickly that he nearly knocked over the doctor.

"I'm Stockard."

"Hi. I'm Dr. Johnson. You wanted to see Mr. Stoner?"

"I've been waiting nearly two hours now."

"Relax, Major," said the Navy doctor. "He's just regaining consciousness. We have him on painkillers, but he really just needs rest. He has some deep bruises, the concussion, and he's very dehydrated, but he should be walking around tomorrow."

As the doctor said the word *walking*, he glanced at Zen's wheelchair and turned red, embarrassed. Zen was so used to that sort of reaction—and so intent on seeing Stoner—that he hardly noticed, instead pushing down the hall toward the room. He pivoted precisely as he reached the doorway and pushed in, leaning over to lift the kick-stop on the door and shut it behind him.

"Hello," said Stoner from the bed.

"She's mine, Stoner," he told him. "Don't fuck with me. You got that?"

"What?"

"I saw you kiss Breanna in the raft. I was watching through the UMB feed. I'm the one who got the Osprey there."

"Zen?" Stoner blinked his eyes.

"I'll fight for her. I will."

"I don't know what the hell you're talking about," said Stoner.

Zen wheeled backward a half stroke. His anger balanced on the edge of a knife blade. He knew what he had seen.

"Is Bree all right?" Stoner asked.

"Yeah."

"Where is she?"

"They moved her over to Bright Memorial. Her mother's a doctor there. She'll be fine. She was sleeping when I left."

Stoner nodded. "My head feels like shit."

Zen stared at him. If Stoner was looking for sympathy, he wasn't going to get it from him.

"Seriously, man, there's nothing between me and Breanna. I mean, she saved my life. And maybe I saved hers. We tied ourselves together so we'd stay in the raft. Ferris—we lost him."

Zen took a deep breath, letting his body lean forward slightly in the wheelchair. Why was it Stoner who had lived? Why couldn't it have been Ferris? Or Fentress? The poor kid, he was just getting the hang of the Flighthawks, just learning his damn job.

Why had anyone had to die? So the Indians and Chinese wouldn't blow themselves and half the world to kingdom come?

Yes, thought Zen. That's what it came down to. Their deaths meant millions of innocent people would live. It was their job, and their duty. The men would have said so themselves.

And yet, it didn't seem fair at all. If Bree had been one of the ones to die, he'd have been inconsolable.

"You got the helicopter there?" Stoner asked. "The one that picked us up?"

"It was an Osprey," said Zen.

"Thanks. We owe you a big one. You saved us."

Zen stared at him. He had seen what'd he'd seen. But what was it—their bodies tied together, their cheeks close?

Maybe they hadn't kissed. He trusted Bree more than that, didn't he?

"You're welcome," Zen said.

By THE TIME ZEN MADE HIS WAY BACK TO BREANNA'S hospital room, the others had left and she was sleeping again. He pulled his wheelchair up alongside her bed and leaned back, thinking at first that he would watch her TV, but then deciding that might wake her. He watched her sleep for a while, thinking of a similar vigil he'd kept some months back, after she'd managed to crash-land an EB-52 that had lost its tail.

Nothing harder than waiting in a hospital room, he'd thought then, but now he knew there were many harder things indeed. He thought of what she must have felt those long months after his accident, the one that had cost him his legs—the one that had cost her much of her hope for their lives. She'd stuck with him through that, even when he didn't want her to, even when he didn't know if he could stick with it himself.

How could he doubt her love after that?

It was his own insecurity he should fear, his doubts about himself, not her. He shouldn't doubt her at all. She was the one person in the world who'd had faith, who didn't treat him like a gimp, whose face didn't turn red when she caught sight of his wheelchair.

Ashamed, Zen reached his hand over and stroked her fingers.

"Hello," she mumbled, opening her left eye and then her right.

"Hey. About time you woke up. You been sleeping the whole day."

"I woke up and you weren't here."

"You did?"

"Yes, I did. Where were you?"

"I went over to see Stoner. He's at the Navy air base. I had a hell of a time bumming a ride."

"How is he?"

"Looks like you."

"Oh, thanks." She pushed up on her elbows; Zen reached over and slid her pillow, then realized he could adjust her bed by the control. He fiddled with it, getting her to about a thirty-degree angle.

"My dad was here, and Danny," said Breanna. "My mom. Did you meet her?"

Zen shook his head. "I talked to her on the phone twice. She didn't remember anything I told her. Pretty ditzy for a doctor."

Breanna smiled weakly. "That's my mom. Opposite of my dad."

"Yeah."

"I saw Chris die. I couldn't save him."

"You couldn't."

"Collins and Dolk. They're gone too."

Zen took her hand.

"And Curly's missing. Fentress." Her eyes welled up, but as she started to cry she laughed too. "Remember all your nicknames for him?"

"I was a bastard to the poor kid."

"You made him a good pilot. I couldn't save them, Jeff. I tried. I did."

"Sometimes you can't." Zen leaned over and kissed her. Breanna's lips were warm, but the exposure to the salt water made them feel like sandpaper, and he could see her wince even though he barely brushed against them.

"Sorry," he told her.

"It's okay, babe." She patted his hand.

"Listen, I saw you and Stoner in the raft," he said. "I

saw you two tangled together. I thought—look, I'm an asshole, but I thought you were in love with him or something. Last fling on earth. I went a little crazy."

Pain creased her face.

"I know you're not in love with him or anything," he said. "And that you didn't. I'm sorry. It was just the idea of losing you, you know? I'm sorry."

"That's good, baby," she said, drifting back toward sleep. "You know I love you."

"I do," he said.

Her eyes closed. Zen sat back in his wheelchair, his hand still gripping hers. Exhausted by the last few days, he slipped off to sleep as well.